The cover art was done with esteemed honor and passion by Michael Carr. Thank you for your fervor for artistry and how your integrity has given quite a blessing. A passion for a passion, as both collided and created prosperity to mind and life. Nothing else could possibly surpass such a notion which comprises the intangible, gratefulness and respect.

Conspiracy
Endeavor

Conspiracy Endeavor

Michael Jorgenson

Library of Congress Control Number: 2020922080
ISBN: Hardcover   978-1-6641-2856-9
              Softcover   978-1-6641-2855-2
              eBook   978-1-6641-2854-5

Print information available on the last page.

Rev. date: 11/17/2020

To order additional copies of this book, contact:
Xlibris
844-714-8691
www.Xlibris.com
Orders@Xlibris.com
819197

Precursor: a sign

LOADING . . .

Error!

Error!

Error!

File found . . .

Recorded Information

Error!

Recovered!

Date of recording not found.

Name of who recorded data . . . not found.

Info still intact . . .

Will provide unto you in a couple seconds.

Scanning . . .

Opening!

Date: Unknown

User: Unknown

Subject: Dwelling hopelessness / Regaining hope (logs pertaining to the incident.)

Title: Error!

Day 1: Kidnapped—many others . . . Error!

Day 13: Torturous methods—Error! Control of the entire mind . . . The soul-- Error! Enslaved for—Error! Where did we go wrong? Was it our own sins? This is crazy . . . Error!

Day 20: five of us died. Nobody knows . . .

Day 34: I escaped. My left arm hurts; it was dissected and implanted with mechanical- Error!

Day 40: Last message, I forgot to mention two others have also escaped with me, John and Karel. Error!

Day 69: John had turned on us- Error! His indoctrination had gotten the better of- Error!

Day 74: Had to kill—Error! Five days ago, crushed his neck. Karel was—Error!

Day 87: I've been in hiding for a while. No one's come for me. I don't know who to go to. Wait . . . there might be. Will anyone ever believe me? My assumption's going to bring me to believe I'm the only one of eleven to survive and escape. All others I assume are dead, unknowingly for sure, but . . . Error!

Day 99: I think hiding for a while longer will be the plan . . . This is my last log. Whoever finds this-- with fortune, a friend or ally? All Info will be encrypted. When deciphered, this'll allow you to find my location.

I'm placing this on the opposite side of the country. Address: Albany, New York. A friend, who lives there, will bring help. I'm bringing this to him personally. I'm leaving afterward and will never be heard of again till' found. Error! Error! Error! Info on the truth—Error!

> I was completely wrong about being unrecognized and was scuffled with a man that was experimented on just like me. My right leg was almost broken. Just a few bruises and cuts at least. Puzzled as to how he found me, but I shouldn't be. I'm OK for now, don't worry. The device was damaged a little during the altercation. It should work for you. The prime document on here is the overriding culprit that incurred some damage, of course. This will be easy for you. Well, my friend, it's going to be difficult time for me from here on out. Reckon I'd let you in on my life once more, a friend in dire need. Never would I forget the bond we once had . . . You're the only one I can reveal this to. Please, hurry.

The written letter was clasped in one hand, which was just read, and the device is grasped in the other. The just read note's set on a bookshelf. Now, both hands hold the instrument, gripping it tighter. The man strides over to a phone. Fingers dial a number quickly. The phone is stationed on the right of the person's head. The phone rings. "I found her! Thank goodness. Such a relief!" the male figure said with liberation. His left hand reaches for the appliance. He walks over to a nearby computer, and sets it down and turns the computer on. "I'll soon find out. We will have closure." A distorted voice on the other end of the line talks with no confrontational measures . . . The phone call ends seconds later. The PDA connects and integrates with his PC. He typed with precision, and the words and number are strewn across the screen. Looks like gibberish at first . . . A site is shown on a screenshot of her hideout. "That's where you are." the man says. An icon glows, specifying her spot in Washington DC.

Spark

Sundown comes soon, permitting dusk, and an hour remains before the prominent night. Kids start following their parents or back to their homes and some others are alone. Few cars pass through different roads, lights bright as day. A young man paces, with an indication he's in pain, on a sidewalk and both hands inside each pocket in the side of his pants. With abruptly quickening movement, he starts running; adrenaline spikes. He looks back and sees no one. His breath grows heavier with each step. Eventually he makes his way through an alley and runs through non-stop as if he has an agenda to complete. Out of a passage way, a school's in long distance and a field which gives much space before the school. His checks his lower abdomen: an apparent cut, blood slowly comes out, a gash in need of stitches. Pain doesn't slow progress down at all as he continues to run farther. Through the field, a car from behind speeds up; though noticing quickly from the revving of the engine, he grows increasingly frightened.

Anxiousness makes him turn into a panicked state. As the car catches up it flies past, drifting in front of the boy's path. Its tires tear up the grass and then it grinds to a halt . . . Suspense lingers in the moment. Two thuggish men quickly exit the car quickly. The boy attempts an escape again, going around them swiftly; they give chase as well. Not too long in time, one of the two thugs' reveals his gun and shoots at the ground near the running steps. The gunshots cause the boy to stumble to the ground. Looking back at the pursuing duo, he sees both characters approach him aiming their guns at him. He slowly crawls backward and eventually meets with the edge of a long ditch.

"I'll get your money back. A mishap with the others! Please. I'll get it all back!"

x

Bang! Bang!

Smoke escapes each barrel. Content with the results that ensure death; both thugs smile from their indecent conduct. They holster their weapons and they run back to their car and drive away. Blood flows from the chest wound that trickles to a small stream in the ditch, casually flowing from the body.

A batch of teenagers from afar witnessed the whole act; law enforcement's called. Frantic over what just happened; one strives to talk calmly on the phone. After informing the proper authorities, they all slowly move closer to the boy who lies lifeless on the ground. Witnesses stay at a range because the carnage is too unnerving. The police arrive in a respectable fashion. The lot of teenagers waves to catch attention; all law enforcement officers go direct to their location. Officers yield their vehicles and come out rushing. Securing the area, one officer obtains information from the group who were the witnesses to the crime. Exiting their vehicle with haste both medics dash down the road and onto the grassy field. A white sheet shrouds the boy after attempts to revive him failed; a CSI team joins them several minutes later. Upon checking, one of the crime scene investigators hands over a wallet found in the pocket of the victim. They go over its contents to find the boy's name . . .

Quietly among a dark room and relaxed, three figures: two reside on a couch, though, another, off to the side, stands comfortably. To commence: a male and a female, presently on a couch, both holding hands. One holds the right and the other grips the left, as they are both unperturbed on the sofa. Lastly, a taller silhouette stood, larger in size, arms crossed, off to the side and up against a doorway adjacent to the others.

(Choose one to initiate, and your fate will be set . . .)

David: Muscle bound/greater strength, low speed, moderate defense / headstrong / moderate stamina / iron horse / greater constitution / moderate in combat and weapons.

Emily: Middle weight/high speed, low defense, moderate strength / moderate stamina / moderate constitution / high cunning / inquisition proficient / logical tendencies / blade specialist.

William: Heavy weight/high defense, high strength, and moderate speed / high stamina / high constitution / emotional / moderate survivalist skills / inquisitive / combat specialist.

A phone sounds aloud. William opens his eyes from an engrossed trance . . . and picks up the cell phone to answer. "Hello?"

On the other side, the caller asks, "Is this a William Aletheo I'm speaking to?"

"Yes," William replies to the question.

"This is Sergeant Bingum. You're being requested down at the station. It's urgent. See you then." The initial caller said in conclusion. Unsure of why they need him, the only way to find out will be to go. He is sluggish at first but makes a good stretch from a long idle orientation and kisses the top of the hand he held.

"See you on the other side," David says.

"Be careful," Emily says.

(Choosing whether to just go to the bathroom, or shave as well?)

Walking to the bathroom . . . Now inside: Hot water is utilized in the sink. Steam rises and fogs the entirety of the mirror as the surface of his face is being washed. Slowly wipes the lower part of the mirror. Shaving cream is applied; a razor is next. Finishing: The remaining section of the looking glass is slowly wiped away and reveals his face. His head moves left and right, up and down, diagonally. An agreement with everything is met, and travels to the front door. Puts on a pair of shoes, departs from his darkened house, and enters his car. A key turns, conducting ignition . . . William now drives to his calling.

Each second is more suspenseful without knowing the exact reason for being summoned randomly. The streets are nearly empty; not many walk in the dark environment, either. Cars' windows are fully drawn; the wind blows persistently. The summer night's breeze feels marvelous on bare skin. The initial destination draws near . . . William pulls up to the relevant designation. He stops, turns off the car, exits from his vehicle, and closes the driver's door. He races up to the precinct's entrance . . . swings open the front door.

Bingum spots William entering. "William, follow me!" Both scurry to their captain's office.

Upon walking in, William is confronted by his captain (a.k.a. Ronald). "Please, sit down. I have news I wish to not ever speak of. I must though, lamentably. Chief isn't here to. So . . ." Ronald expels with fingers meshed, implementing some sort of worrisome implication. William waits in suspense. "Not too long ago, before you were called—um . . . we received word that two men were spotted chasing a young boy. They shot him, resulting in a recent killing that transpired simultaneously."

William wonders why he was told to come. "Who is he?"

Hesitancy overflows Ronald's mind. He reluctantly musters some badly needed courage and takes a deep breath. "It was your brother."

William's face drops and he sits back in disbelief; staring intensely at his captain's eyes, skepticism gradually increasing. (Optimistic choice +1) "You lie. This seems so random."

Silence assures him it's not. William clenches both hands and rises with a building temper. (Optimistic choice +1) "This is a fabrication. I don't believe this."

Ronald then stands. This means to expel the unrelenting supreme truth with a reason to William's summoned presence is inevitable, and he shifts to his right, walks around his desk to approach William.

"Could not be any more true, but we don't know anything as of this moment on why Dante was murdered."

William relaxes both hands then massages his face . . . Dropping his hands, he quickly speaks under a wrathful tone. "Don't you lie to me, and you clearly jest."

Utter silence . . .

(Descent action +3) William quickly lunges toward Ronald. Bingum apprehends William's irrational activity. "I speak truthfully!" Ronald says as the blinds on the window rattle from William's wrathful might as they make connection. Ronald continues to speak while the attending officer gains control, adjusting William's arms to a secure holding and bind him in cuffs.

"I acknowledge your feelings. We'll find who's responsible. I assure you with more than my words. I'm sorry." Ronald says as William sits down in a nearby chair. He glares directly at Ronald, but his eyes soon transition downward. Calming down, a part of William has become void. Happiness is stripped away; sorrow fills the emptiness, and tears fall for the dead.

06/17/2019, 9:30 a.m.

The sun shines to bring a new day, clouds float above quietly, and trees rustle in the soft wind. All represent a black lamentation before a grave. Silence covers all ground and, nevertheless, below. Many hide their faces to eclipse tears of woe; with the best attempts, they are more visible and stronger than ever. Death hides from no one; none can evade its inescapable grasp. William stands before the burial of his brother. A mother, a father and a sister watch as a young boy descends into the cold earth. A son, the brother—only the keeper endures. Failure: amid the worldly masses, a graveyard of past times. Many moments pass and become buried. To conceive the evolution of life, one must carry on, and after death. I've heard people say, "Dead eyes see no future." How do you know? You see it for them. The subsequent times are always changing, no set consequences, and no prearranged events. Just your choices decide the coming times, but ramifications derive from those decisions and remain with you. Of all pieces explain the premise. In the end, was it worth it? Make every second count; never falter, let your heart guide you; and grant your spirit the chance to create comfort. Every movement, word and deed transforms all surroundings consistently. Mold the definition of your existence to form a structure, and that entity is singular. Standing autonomously before the flood, all eyes observe. Which course of action would you elect?

Emily walks up to William and hugs him, while David gives rightful respects to William's parents. "I'm sorry. In no way do any of you deserve this. I'm always here for you. All too terrible what happened, but take as much time as you need. This is extremely hard on you as it is on your family. I'll call you later?" William nods his head, and Emily takes her leave to talk to his mom.

In all corridors of his mind, everything progresses at a slower rate. Leaves cascade creating echoes; God above radiates light upon this grave, glistening abroad the tombstone's face. Breathing turns gentler; the inner being calmly implies knowledge that one can rest in peace. Perpetuity of silence commences. Death's eternity, life's limited capacity. Words from divine affiliation spread among silence; the bell's tolls permeate the landscape, a sound to create awareness of death's increasing domain. The last of the words, William hears: "In death, don't fret. Adore the peace one's in, and don't forsake your life, for you will gain strength anew. Know your loved one has moved on, away from the worldly issues. Know your loved one will always be a part of you forever in heart and mind. God will see to it peace and love will be shared. Your tears will dry and you will move on. Upon memory, words of my ancestors: 'Live to see your longevity and your death will be shorter in comparison. Contingencies will emerge, but you are wise if cautious. Love thyself and others—for your deeds echo.' This young man has lived differently from you, but don't judge him just yet, because you have yet to see what you'll be before the twilight. This is the end of our service . . . and the end of his."

When they arrive at William's house, William, along with his family, exits from his car subsequently. The front door opens slowly. Lights turn on one by one from a flick of a switch but one. Under darkness, everyone enters the living room, but stops halfway in. Tears drop. All hands position on his shoulders and a sister to engender composure. No more heartache, no more anger, no more, nevermore. She arranges her hands upon his face and eyes open to look back at her.

Thinking to self: *Does death really bring people together this broadly? Must we all die to bring us in concert? No, wrongly questioning into disturbing territory.*

Sincerity and despair in her eyes, thoughts of oppression. "We're still a family. Don't fret or think you're alone, because we still love you. To our utmost dislike, an empty space is permanently set before us, but we'll unquestionably still stand strong. This will only give us strength. In the times of adversity, for the sorrow to take hold: let's not abandon who we are because we are all we have," Sarah tells me. I stand there in silence. My vulnerability is apparent. As a consolation, I'll always remember her words and my brother.

Nightfall . . .

William sits on his couch in a melancholy trance. His cell phone rings, vibrates, and shines concurrently. Upon looking at his phone, he sees Emily's name is exhibited. He accepts and answers, "Hey."

"Hey. You don't have to say anything. Just listen. I talked to Chief and he was informed what happened today by Ronald. He sends his condolences. I know me being there would pose more potential, but I needn't intrude. I was advised by Ronald that they captured the felon in question. But sadly, the man responsible, who we're assuming committed the murder, isn't responding to anything we say, and some of his goons aren't budging because of their lawyer. They couldn't hold them due to lack of concrete evidence. It's rare to find little to no evidence in a house that harbors drugs and weapons dealers, but you start somewhere. If anything could be done to reverse such a tragedy, it would be done in a heartbeat by the lot of us. Your space is needed. I won't keep you any longer. We're thinking of you, along with your brother in mind and in our hearts. I'll leave you be. We'll see you when the time comes. Take it slow, like I said earlier. Let me now if you need anything, I'll always be here for you," Emily speaks softly. She hangs up. The dial tone remains. William then turns his phone off.

"Tranquility in cruelty, cruelty's litany"

"Cradle me to sleep once more. It'll bring contrition to my eviscerated essence. Please allow my body your harsh embrace. Once I succumb under twilight, leave me be," William said and turns to his right side, now facing the sofa in a fetal position. A ghastly figure promptly hovers behind William and Dante emerges from behind her. The idea of his ghostly appearance: pale and cold. Both look upon William with eyes of malice. Spreading her wings of distress, wrapping them around William; he naturally submits under the unconscious spell as if the desolation and loneliness are aspects of internal solace.

"An interconnection broke in a family, a loss which refashions iridescent accents to a forced black setting. Saddened minds holding a stray soul grieve for a return, one last moment to be. Perpetual sentiments permitted in multiples—times change, but grief-stricken souls don't."

Chapter 1

Night Raid

An abrupt revisit

06/24/2028, 10:54 p.m.

One week later

It's a beautiful sixty-eight-degree spring night in California in 2028, quiet and tranquil. A SWAT vehicle pulls up to a two-story house, parking across the street to scope the area, and prepares to exact their positions, what'll allow them to apprehend all initial targets. Ten officers charge out. Captain Ronald then signals the rest into tactical positioning: three in the back, one on each side, and all else to the front. Ronald readies himself along with other remaining officials for entry. Ronald knocks multiple times on the door to receive an answer. First attempt was just a couple knocks on the door and vocal exertions. The second attempt was a couple more knocks and vocal exertions. No compliance after two attempts . . . Ronald makes a last call for them to surrender, but there was no reply. David and William converse among each other. "Are you ready? This is going to be a great rush of enjoyment!" David confidently says to William.

"Doth a choice be dust in the wind? Minds set astray, poisoned and lost, death's counterparts in progress," William says as he turns his attention to the door, averting eye contact with David. "Let's see how this turns out. With you and me, anything's possible," William then says.

(David raises his left hand midway. William notices David's action and decides whether to join hands in a brotherly bond or be too excited to care.)

(Ascent Action +2) They both join hands in a brotherly bond. David: William's best friend ever since middle school. Like William's parents, David's were in the military as well, moving every year or two, different environment, people . . .)

Some time passed; Ronald signals his team to break through the front door. A gang member jumps out of a side window, but Officer Ludren catches him with a complete grasp before he even hits the earth, slamming him and seizing any escaping opportunity. Ronald, William and David follow two others, Alan and Dalter, who break through the front door using a battering ram. As you know, there are additional separate personnel approaching other perimeters of this home. One team runs in from the front as the other men march inward through the back. The team in front spots two targets running up a flight of stairs, while other felons inside flee to the back. All officers commence a chase. William and Lieutenant Alan run upstairs in pursuit of the two suspects while David assists in securing the first floor. This house of dissipation becomes a vortex of chaos; police enforcement and criminals shout to one another amid the disruption.

Bang! The aiding officer, Alan, beside William is shot.

(William quickly decides between whether to extirpate or let live.)

The same suspect extends an arm out of a nearby room and shoots recklessly. As Alan remains on the floor beside William, clutching his right shin, William had dropped quickly as well and drags his comrade out of firing range. The enemy halts all actions. Alan moans from the pain. All ruckuses from downstairs continue. The shooter exits the room to flee to another and fires recklessly again. (Ascent Choice +3: William lets live.) William retains a locus behind decent protection of an exceptionally categorized cabinet, concurrently aiming at the oppressor between the cabinet's legs underneath. Seconds later . . . William then shoots several times, hitting the target's left foot, comes from behind cover, and launches one last attack against the offender before another round of bullets blaze, ensuring the wounding of the gun-holding hand, which halts any additional use of that same arm too.

"Don't worry, Alan, we'll get you out of here. William, you OK? I'll take this asshole off your hands." Officer Jenson, another comrade, appears from William's backside after she met with Alan, then apprehends their injured felon. "I'm continuing my search up here. Could you please send backup?" William says. Jenson nods her head. "It'll be done," She says. "Officer Alan has been injured, in need of medical attention on the second floor." Jenson proclaims over the radio to all others.

David discerns the call and commotion above from below, right before leaving through the back door, to now endeavor descrying the incident at hand. He also calls upon Officer Stevens to aid.

William arrives at a room, where he assumes the other convict invaded. Slowly peeking into the room, he discovers a man with tattoos, wearing a black T-shirt, jeans and sporting a buzz cut, frantically strutting back and forth. William slowly enters the room with his gun raised. This fear filled man turns, quickly grabbing the one woman who is within reach.

(William, deciding whether to shoot through the woman and physically approaches the individual or talk with reason?)

(Diplomatic stance +2) Responding quickly, William seeks to bring reason. "Keep your hands where I can see them! Neither does she need any harm! Just take it easy."

Pushing William's words aside, this challenger responds with agitation. "Don't tempt me! I'll do whatever it takes! I control their lives. They are nothing but whores—a body to fuck!" The firearm is pushed closer to her head, tilting it and the neck from the contact of the gun. Her subjection increasingly frightens her.

William acknowledges her subjection."OK, calm down. I'm sure you've taken many lives, but why relinquish hers? What's she done to affect yours? I don't doubt you the least—the power to kill someone lesser than you. This is all too simple for a man of your stature." A quick, calm rejoinder William applied. (Ascent Dialogue +5)

Observant of William, the overreacting man, who seems to be under the influence most likely, realizes William has consideration for this woman. Some other notions to add, and hearing his voice spawns a connection, or to a relative person. To go along with the scheme of things, and as he wipes his nose with his free hand, the enemy says, "No she isn't. Why does it matter to you anyways if I do or not? Wait . . . I know you!" Confounding twists of the mind, a revelation sparks. "You resemble him so much! Plus, he described who you are as a warning to us if we were to ever be in any area close to each other, just for security purposes. He didn't want any harm to come to you. I knew your brother. Nice kid—great transporter and a little naïve."

William became muddled, but he tries formatting the pieces to the reasons his brother would be a part of such an organization as this.

"I remember seeing you at the funeral, my grand masterpiece at hand: getting rid of the weak. You're probably wondering why I even went. Nothing like seeing the conclusion of one's own work," the convict said. William's perception focuses with intensity as anger rises while verbalization sustains from wickedness. "I remember his screams- 'I'll pay you back. I had a mishap with the others! Please! I'll get it all back!' So naturally, I shot him to shut his mouth and terminated his empty words from spewing out anymore." To increase the dramatics, he prolongs his speech. "Oh, my God! He was such a coward. A waste of my time! We could have been graced with such an awe-inspiring income, but you know . . . to cut a loose end that lost me that opportunity was a good move on my part."

(William, in idle: To finish this conversation or listen further?)

(Descent Action +3) An end comes to the conversation. William's fury has escalated, and he becomes fed up with each exerted utterance.

Through the vacated house, David and Stevens near the stairs leading to the second floor. Voices are heard from above. David upholsters his 9mm and carefully treads upward with Stevens, who's behind him. Before reaching the top, he notices Alan against the wall. David rushes over and checks his pulse . . . A slight heart beat resonates. "Officer Alan, who is injured and unconscious, is on the second floor still without any aid," David softly spoke over the radio.

"As I blew multiple holes—" William treads forward, placing the gun point-blank against the man's face, though, deep within his consciousness a shed of constraint withholds a sinful move. Rage builds along with unconditional aim to end this fiasco. Returning the favor, both their weapons are inches away from each other's faces. Seeing that the two aren't paying attention to her, the woman then flees from the room. Making her way out, she abruptly runs into David who's also with Stevens. Quickly acquiring a grasp, she squirms and screams, but David calms her down. "You're OK, we're here to help. Officer Stevens will take you safely out of here." She looks at him and trusts the said claim. "Could you also transport Alan down as well, please?" David then asked Stevens. As the woman calms down, Stevens escorts her downstairs.

David slowly approaches the room where this terrified woman came from. Trying not to make any commotion with each step, David arrives at the room where William currently is. Slowly looking inside, he observes them with weapons pointed at each other's faces, ready to pull the trigger at any moment. David then aims at the target.

(William decides to go down one of two paths: either to shoot, resulting in a quick end or approach the situation with another form of compromise during this confrontation.)

(Descent Action +5) William tries grasping what few straws of judiciousness remains but determines otherwise.

"How about this: let's settle this properly, hmm?! You're a tough, 'resilient' man. I bet you can take a punch. Then again, I also wager you're a cheap fighter." An agreement is made with William's proposal. Even with discontent, David keeps his massive body in front of the door.

"I came up here because of the activity I was hearing. Here I am amid a standoff, surprisingly. More violence isn't necessary. On another note: the woman that jolted out of here is safe. Is there anyone else up here?" David says.

"Not that I'm aware of. Is there?" William also contributes.

Their opponent shrugs his shoulders. "I could care less," the convict says. William stares unflinchingly with extreme sternness. Clenching a fist with the coming of violent intentions, their target's motive is also identical. David strives to avert William's choice. "William, are you sure? We could just end this, have him detained and transported to the station now. His worthiness of this attention is void. Don't do this again . . . You can do better than this. Don't make this personal."

(David verifies that William is making an illogical approach. He will remember this.)

"Don't purge this moment from me. This fucking—this man needs a lesson in brutality. Informing me of my brother's demise, the animal who stands before me. What are the odds of being in the same room for the justified reasons why we're here concurrently? This is beyond vengeance. It's not even business anymore, nothing of the nature . . . just a wound needing mending," William says angrily. (Descent Dialogue +2)

"This has turned personal. It's over. We have our guy and you can arrest him," David says forthright.

"You think he'll bend so easily? He's hasn't put his weapon down yet, and I'm damn sure he could care less. He seems pretty hell-bent himself," William says.

Sadism responds with cynical intent and with an attending crazed expression on his face. "This is going be an amazing experience:

eliminating the other half of my problem. I'm exactly who you're looking for. Call me Sadism." David continues to keep his posture, and with persistent vigilance, he closes the door for this standoff's duration and locks it.

Both drop their pieces . . . Sadism swings first.

Over the radio: "The situation almost expires. All suspects have been captured, excluding the leader. What's your 20, Bodun?"

David replies slowly and reluctantly to the call on his radio. "Let's just say . . . that William is confronting the main target of our operation as of now. Alan needs medical attention. I requested Stevens to move Alan, second floor."

A quick response is made from the other line. "What do you mean confronting?" Ronald asks with impatience and confusion.

Back to the fight between William and Sadism—blows are exchanged against multiple areas of the body, violently and relentlessly. David's request for backup never came, but some of the allies who remained inside hear a ruckus commencing above; they curiously journey upstairs to understand what it could be. Ronald takes notice of the loud noises over the com on his end. "I'm coming up. Prepare your selves," he says.

David is slightly distressed about the event, but he then tosses aside all concerns. David shouts at William, giving him the ultimatum. "Make this count! Our good old captain's coming up. He's not going to approve of this . . ." David dodges thrown items within this physical altercation. "This is intense!" he says with adrenaline increasing within as well. Sadism springs a snub nose revolver from his hip's left side. "Watch out! Weapon exposed!" David shouts out as caution to William. Sadism chooses to point the tool at David instead. Before David could get a clear maneuver, William needs to move first. (Special +2) William decides to rush the leader quickly, and grabs his right forearm, causing Sadism to misfire from David, hitting the ceiling. They plunge out of the second story window, plummeting downward to the grassy yard as glass falls around them. Affliction occurs from the immense impact, and it stuns them for a short time.

David hastens to the window and views the aftermath. "You OK? I'm coming down!" The window shattering has caught Ronald's attention, but sounds are also resonating from the backside; Ronald requests a couple others to accompany him to discern what happened. David retreats from the room and attends to Alan. A couple officers transition upstairs.

William and Sadism slowly move on the ground. Recovery is difficult. The aftermath resonates through their bodies consistently. Sadism returns to his feet first and trudges away with a limp in his right leg. William turns over on his abdomen and observes Sadism fleeing. William perceives Sadism's revolver—which is near him, in line of sight, with the streetlight reflecting off the chrome—and arises slowly but surely to begin the manhunt. David exits from inside with Alan's right arm around his shoulders, sets him on the porch, and travels down a path leading to where he last saw William. Now arriving at William's and Sadism's prior scene, after a couple seconds, despite the fact, William is seen moving quickly on the road farther ahead. Ronald shows up before David. "I assumed you were with William. Where is he?" Ronald says while also giving off an agitated vibe.

(Due to unequivocal actions, David attempts a supportive role.)

Reluctant to speak again, David directs the squad in the direction they went and says, "He's chasing our initial target on foot. You should have seen it! It was—" David retracts his excitement. "Call an ambulance. Alan needs to go to the hospital."

Ronald only cares for what's important. "Our priority is that criminal. I'll have someone else do it," Ronald says as he departs. David slowly retracts his thoughts with shame and attends behind as they catch up with William, who's still tracking their original mark.

A 9mm is uncovered, and shots are being fired by the opponent. Dropping behind a nearby truck to shield himself from all shots was a proper move. Primary persists to run. William peeks over the truck. Sadism moves farther in range. This hunt carries on.

(William runs through a different route to try and catch Sadism off guard. You could say it was a short cut.)

Down a different side street, William sprints faster and faster. An end approaches eventually. Greater distance ahead, he notices the man in pursuit nearby a playground. As assumed, Sadism enters that exact park and decided to stop next to a jungle gym. Sadism momentarily scans around for William. Presumptuous to any harm dealt and smiles at the pre-mature thought. Assuming all is safe, Sadism decides to move on. A moment later . . . fast pace footsteps are nearing from behind.

(Descent Action +4) Quickly running, William plows Sadism into a pole, forcing him straight to the ground in pain and dazed from the blow. William almost falls, but he regains his balance after their collision.

(Shall fear take place or restraint?)

(Descent Action +5) William picks Sadism up by the neck, breathing heavily . . . "Don't you just love a thrilling chase? The hunt is magnificent! All prey runs in terror and the fearless are bound to their doom. I smelt the boiling of your blood. The stench of fear drowns your very essence! You're in my claws now. I will personally make it that your pay for all crimes committed, not by my hand or the judges singly, but by the reality of your sins, too!" William says in a threatening manner.

(Either spare him or decimate?)

Much to his disdain, equilibrium sets, breathing slows to normal rates. With great intent, William decides the enemy's fate.

(Ascent Action +4) Letting go of Sadism's neck, he falls to the ground once again. William takes a couple steps away and takes a long breath. Divulging in another attempt to finish William, Sadism arises with a knife to cowardly attack from behind. His movements were detected on the wood chips . . . and William quickly reacts with a counter strike.

(Descent Action +5) Pain shall permit. Sadism's arm is snapped, both legs are taken out, and William grabs his head to then slam it on the ground, pinning him to the earth. By a strong hold, William then brings himself closer face-to-face. Fury has weakened William's resolve. (Descent dialogue +1) "You aren't even worth killing. I'll let the world be your ruin, for your sins to dig your grave!" William says frankly in ending a proclamation of wrath and assurance. Sadism laughs and produces a cynical smile. "For a man who upholds justice, you sure are a violent one. Reveal yourself in the reflection of my eyes as you beat me into oblivion. Your friend was right. You could have just taken me in." Mockery hides behind Sadism's smile. Silence is generated between them, although a continuance to instigate takes place ever so quickly.

(William has a couple of choices: react to a demanding will or leave the target be.)

Sadism, wanting to get an arousal out of William, shouts, "I'm glad I fucking killed him."

Tensions rise to extreme levels . . .

(Descent Action +5) William stands Sadism on his feet and straightens up his ensemble. William places his hands behind his lower back. Sadism wonders what he's doing. Slipping brass knuckles on each hand, he closes his eyes and nods his head to a song he plays in his head, metal on metal tapping with the beat.

"What are you doing?" Sadism asks.

William raises his right hand to his mouth to shush Sadism. Sadism becomes concerned when he sees one of the brass knuckles.

William soon opens his eyes and stares at Sadism with increasing rage . . . A barrage of punches come forth reflecting the chorus's message. Each hit makes Sadism take a step or two back, disharmonic in all accounts. A few more hits makes Sadism step back once more and now on to one knee by the power of its musical genre. Williams picks Sadism up to his feet, takes a few steps back, runs towards Sadism, and kicks with all his might to the crescendo causing Sadism to soar over the lower half portion of the slide. William angrily leers at Sadism through flames which fill his own eyes. Some people stand on their porches from the expelled noises outside, all down the streets William and the drug agent had trekked on—and in addition to all who live around the park as well. William looks around: numerous bystanders in confusion, many look out their windows, and some stay hidden inside their homes from the gunshots minutes previously. Officers in the squad vehicle notice the citizens' appearance, making them assume the two are near. Additional emergency lights are perceivable from a distance and off of other surfaces.

Gaining ground farther ahead, David then averts to his left and quickly says to Ronald, "There! That may be them."

Ronald abruptly stops the vehicle. They quickly exit and run toward the two. David reaches William, but checks their prime objective first and is content that life still lingers. A couple of officers detain the criminal, sitting him up against the slide. Injuries were observed. An ambulance was called after their analysis of the drug agent's wounded state. David places his hand on William's shoulder. "Are you all right? I brought the whole gang. At least he isn't dead. We can question him and get results now. It's good to know you didn't let him escape, but did your violent actions need to happen again?" David lowers his arms.

William, with slight sadness along with added justification, says (Concerned dialogue: +2), "I know. But when push comes to shove, he put drugs on the street, let innocent people parish. The ones who are relevant to the trade aren't worth the satisfaction of killing. No one is. I'll let eternity decide his destiny. He made certain choices, and so, this man was dealt his rightful due. Unfortunate to the end, any other path could have been chosen for both parties, I guess."

Remainders of their squad meets up with all else, shortly after a perimeter check. Ronald gravely looks at William. Disappointed with the former clash, William can only look down in shame. An ambulance a couple miles away comes towards their location. David regretting his inability to persuade yet somewhat accepts William's actions back at the house . . . and only for this reason: their main target isn't dead.

"That was one hell of a fight. But I should say it was extreme, especially when you two flew out of the window. Not saying you should do that again. Importantly, you shouldn't let it come to that scenario, logically." David says.

William looks up at David with sadness and says, "Before you came in, a revelation was spoken. He mentioned a ghost from the past." (David takes notice of such downheartedness.) During William's walk of desolation to the SWAT vehicle, David fixates upon him with a feeling of empathy.

Reaching the van, William enters and sits down: eyes move to David, but momentarily after their eyes met, shuts one of two doors slowly to block the view of him from all others. Their notified ambulance arrives, sounding its alarming resonance. Medics rush out of the vehicle, in addition to asking where the injured man is. Ronald points both medics in a specific direction and then walks back to the van. More law enforcement officers show up soon after. David stands in the middle of it all, contemplating the obvious, but knowing William's undertakings permitted in the night were against protocol. Lamentation fills his consciousness and he accepts it. David moves on. All else get in and ride back to the station. Most are loud except David, Ronald and William; the entire ride back is uncomfortable for them. Ronald attempts to break the silence between the three. (He will remember this.) "It's going to be interesting trying to explain your performance to the chief. Quite the story it'll be. Better hope Alan stays alive."

David decides to speak for Alan. "You can't blame him for that. Two radio transmissions were conducted, and no one came to his aid but me, even though my support wasn't the quickest."

Ronald keeps his focus ahead of him. "After Jenson and company came down, she then told me, and I said to not worry about him. She opposed it, like you. You and everyone else were told not to burden themselves about anything but the mission. At least some can keep that notion consistent." David turns to Stevens . . . Stevens looks at David. David turns back around. "You're a cold son of a bitch," David says toward Ronald. A quick response comes forth from Ronald. "We knew our target was extremely dangerous. Our goal was to acquire him, and we did in the end. Not the way I intended, but we did. Take in consideration you can't make the tough calls. Abscond from the idea as you must. I know where I stand." Detestation comes forth in David, and he glares forward through the windshield with disgust for such a trait. William sits in the back, already knowing what the obviously known consequences are. He's not excited, in a way satisfied, with what was done. Their transition continues their movement to the station.

"Each being, no matter who you are, had made rational or irrational choices. Within those choices prepare many others. Don't mix or misconstrue good or bad. Rely on better judgment alone, because that single decision could expel the worst repercussion as a beneficial outcome or as a life changer, and especially for others around you."

Chapter 2

"Practice, Admiration, and Fame"

06/25/2028, 8:00 a.m.

We arrive at the precinct a day later and find out a little more of what had happened previously.

Ronald commands two officers to move to appropriate areas to ram the front door, before consecutively signaling three other officers to check different rooms when inside. William performs a signal, allowing the front door to be rammed; then he quickly tosses a smoke grenade for defense after the door's forcefully opened. Each personnel runs inside to inspect each room. The first room has a simple layout consisting of one couch, one simple table and a chair. Empty. The second room—different from the first: one bed, a dresser, and a bathroom. Walking in further, an officer checks the bathroom, slowly and quietly. The next step could be absolute. Next to the bathroom's doorway is the subsequent objective. Steadily entering . . . Nearing the shower . . . Right hand reaches out to grab the shower curtain from the left side; curtain rings rattle. Gun ready to fire . . . Empty. The third room—living room: one large couch, two side tables, one television and miscellaneous objects strewn everywhere. Empty.

The fourth room—the garage. William enters quickly. An attached flashlight on his rifle illuminates the darkened area. Looking around, but then . . . Everyone else gestures to give validation for the cleared zones. Only one room remains to be cleared; the main objective will almost be complete. Soon the other three officers meet in the garage and find the unthinkable. Through the doorway one sees William in an offensive stance. All rush in and get into position. "Drop the weapon! Put your hands up! No one needs to get harmed! I've already said it twice." William shouts to propose peace prior to any chaotic, violent initiatives. After several warnings without compliance, William fires with deadly accuracy three times. "Threat secured. Our hostage is alive," William says with much assurance.

Ronald congratulates them on another successful simulation of a raid. "What a wonderful job. I strongly believe they'll be unsure how to confront our tactics. Yes, this is a simulation that had no animation. Just keep up the confidence. Your teamwork is greatly improving with informing and tactical recognition of each other. We're good for the day. There will be a meeting in an hour, though. Dismissed."

(William's whole stature increases by +3.)

William and the others walk back to the locker room feeling pleased, beyond content with their current progress. William goes to sit on a bench between two rows of lockers. A longtime friend of William's, Chief, stands in the doorway and proudly says, "Everyone is showing much promise out there on the field. What an honor to have you select few to prove in possessing instinctual capabilities, comprehending any situation and your surroundings." Every person in the locker room acknowledges Chief's appreciation.

(Emily is another long-time friend of William's since they met in kindergarten. Their friendship has expanded with such a wide berth, even though middle school was when they met David for the first time; when their whole friendship triangle started. All three are inseparable by any means.)

Emily appears next to Chief in the same doorway, but faces opposite of the men's locker room for respectful reasons. Chief begins a conversation with a statement. "Good thing we have someone like you to put these testosterone-filled specimens in their place at times," Chief says glibly, resulting in Emily laughing at the notion.

"Me? You're too kind, but I'd say their mothers may have raised them respectable, honorable and educated. Then again, I'll show them how to truly respect each other while keeping them in check. Don't congratulate them so soon. Their integrity should show during real events," Emily says in a dominantly and astute fashion, but also in a joking manner.

"Well, I'm glad one still knows the limits and can place rank well within its boundaries. But seriously, they're doing quite well. Morale needs to be kept up too. How are the recruits doing with you anyways?" Chief says.

Emily approves of his question and humbly responds, "They're learning quickly—totally amazing that they have the aptitude for handling and fostering calmness under high-pressure situations. The one, you should see. I swear she could talk a miser out of their last coin. Quick learners are always a plus. You indisputably and intelligently pick them." Chief snickers with humbleness as a concordance with her response. Emily smiles over the reaction.

William turns around and realizes Emily and Chief are conversing with each other. He forces himself to communicate and approaches them.

(He chooses to approach slowly and humorously while stating a smooth, sophisticated yet simplistic promulgation.) "Her gracious presence at the men's locker room excites many; all stand at attention. I, to see a beautiful face was more than enough to calm by fiery spirit." (Jester +1)

Smiling as he ends his assertion, Emily responds with a grin and says, "Nice to see you as well, friend. I heard what happened yesterday, Justice Bringer. Your engagement must've been worthwhile, but you should be more careful though. It's no surprise, really." Giving off an interest with his daring moment, William's face slightly drops from the fondness between them. A sensation of awkwardness overcomes Chief. To break its hold, a command is given to William. "In other news: I need to see you in my office in five minutes. Confidential." Chief winks afterward and acts with a subtly suspicious facility.

Chief decamps to his office. Emily questions William's frequent visitations, speaking with insinuation. "Well, latterly, Chief's been calling for you personally. You better be careful or you'll become his bitch. It's coming to be a personal bond between you two as of, as I've meant, lately it's been noticeable."

"I'm nothing special; only the norm with him and I," William modestly replies. (Ascent +1) (Emily will remember that.)

She smiles a little sensing his reserved response. "Whatever it is, you and I should have a "talk". All those times you insisted on neglecting . . . Oh well." She then withdraws. A short distance in front, continuing to be flippant by choice, but considers concluding their exchange with another statement. "Or maybe you're his pet. You might not know. Enthralled and indoctrinated. Shrugging her shoulders and vaguely turning her view to William with a smirk. Reacting, William grins somewhat. He knows what she meant.

Emily disappears around the far end corner. Then, David, out of nowhere, places his hand on William's right shoulder, making him turn his head. "Hey. Would have joined you three, but I had to take a phone call. Was there anything tantalizing?" William answers with a shoulder shrug and a slight grunt. Concerned for him, he studies more of William's unenthusiastic demeanor.

"Lately you've been indifferent. I'm worried about you. You've transitioned into a taciturn and reclusive state at most times. What's troubling you?"

Softly and a little restrained, William says, "Just thinking, reminiscing. I'm not ignoring you—closure is preferable." William's returns his attention to the locker room from hearing the other guys laughing among discussions. His back is facing David, and he takes in a deep breath and then exhales. David soon understands why William chooses to seclude himself and withdraw all feelings quietly or avoid expressing himself vocally.

"I can take it is hard for you, but sometimes the past shouldn't be placed in the now, or allowed to control your life. Talking to someone about these inhibitions is imperative. Bottling things up only affects you adversely."

David's insight is correct, and William turns to face him and expresses what he thinks of all concerns stated. (Ascent dialogue +1) "True. Losing a brother . . . comprehending his affiliation with the wrong crowd makes it even harder. He's gone. Trust is absent in a ceased life. Peculiar of me to say, but incongruously, I forgave him, though it's not my place to judge exclusively."

(David took notice to that.)

David nods his head in acknowledgement, places each hand on William's shoulders and gives an asserted reciprocation. "Do what you must. Make sure they're for the right reasons from the right choices. Don't let your sorrows blind you and become a detriment against your existence. Make order where due, and you will be free. PS: he is your brother—your family. It means you do have a reserved seat to judge. To presume, I can say you discerned the cause of your brother's death from last night?" William shifts his eyes downward and nods his head in agreement. Walking past David, William puts his left hand on David's right shoulder as a similar gesture. David remains stationary while watching William walk away, but takes a deep breath to attain serenity. He stands still, and great concern for his best friend dwells within him to full capacity.

William reaches Chiefs' office. He knocks, enters, and then sits down.

Beginning the conversation quickly, Chief says, "You heard about the kidnappings lately, right?"

The random question baffles William. "Yes. They're high these days, and we, hitherto have no leads or evidence to even assume the frequency."

Chief enlightens the conversation by shedding some light on the current kidnappings. "Speaking of assuming—how unbelievable this has been recently. Only a couple of eye witnesses claiming strongly that they've seen suspicious activity—sketchy vehicles entering and leaving an old abandoned asylum about ten miles down 'Recluse Avenue'. More Information would be better. So I decided to make a squad under surreptitious means, but you're also a part of it. Additional help is provided with the group you're already going to accompany."

(Special +1) William replies to Chief's notion by saying, "What's going on here? How many have you told about this operation? Who else knows? So I'm just forced into this? Is this a part of my punishment? Is this going to show me my wrongs and deliberately prove that I can be an obedient servant to my uppers, and therefore: my weakness controls my very movements and words, that it creates such a design to have me redeem my own self every time I get personal in my encounters, hmm?!"

His eyes are wide open while he moves closer into Chief's face. Chief begins to awkwardly titter with a small amount of fear and replies with a trembling voice, "No, I trust you, David, and Emily out of anyone else here, candidly. I've told others about this, but in a different fashion."

William questions this intent of confidence by crossing his arms and intrepidly asking, "How so?"

As Chief is ready with intent to explain specific consent, he says, "I told Kyle that he and others are going on another raid, that they'd be possibly promoted. One of them is new. He was hired three days ago, and I'd figure this would be an opportunity to increase one's understanding and experience firsthand. It shouldn't be too hard. Your additional company will already be waiting at the site. When you arrive, they'll move in on another route."

"You picked Kyle and his little lackeys . . . as they will soon have, but as he already does, an ego the size of a planet. He's going to revel in victory. The glory will fill his egotistical mind with substantial joy, plus an increase in arrogance. Too bad our initiate joined them," William replies with an obvious thought to add.

In agreement, a conclusion comes to Chief's intentions. "Yes, it'll keep him quiet. Whilst he's performing his latest rants in the building about how he should be a higher rank than everyone, most oppose his personality."

William looks down and shakes his head then lifts it back up. Also, an unsettling thought arises about this undercover mission at hand; he exerts a worried statement. "I believe that is unwise. Look, if anything were to happen, I don't want you to get blamed for all this. Having to worry and/or deal with issues daily is stressful enough." (Ascent +1)

Replying in opposing relevance, Chief heavily states his reason. "That's the exact reason why I need you for this job. I believe you could accomplish this feat with ease."

William is unmoved and remains unconvinced. "Kind of doesn't make sense. I'm flattered, but not convinced in the least," he says before being cut off.

Chief abruptly stops William's claim by saying, "You're one of the best. No. You're the best on this force that I and everyone else has ever had and seen in years. Years! There's no one else I trust as much as I do you. Remember when you busted one of the largest terrorist groups in their own hideout three years prior? They weren't a significant crew, but we were able—you aided your captain and commander under some pressure from that assignment solely—successfully, nonetheless. Everyone was grateful, and you should revel in it! Everyone acknowledges your feats. Even I'm still wondering how to remain sane after all these years. *Sigh* I shouldn't have to doubt your integrity." Doubt swirls in William's mind about being called "still sane." Chief and William now reminisces on the whole scenario . . .

Interlude 1

Wrongful Action

03/11/2025

In remote lands, a single vehicle passes through a desolate area outside of Los Angeles. William, with the whole squad, drives up a hill beyond their initial position and unloads a small unit of snipers. Driving back down to start their first part of the planned operation, William and the remainder of the crew park behind another hill opposite of their snipers location. Reconnaissance (sniper elite team) relays from their point to the 'ground group' after finishing preparations. "There are twenty-five that we see so far. The figurehead, we suspect, is in the— there he is. You'll be able to spot him quickly. The only one that isn't dressed cliché-like: wearing a red shirt, jeans, and beige bucket hat—a high chance that's him," Clarence (from the SET) says.

The first group (SET) sees him pointing men in different directions, relaying orders to move certain objects, and writing on papers given to him by messengers. Pointing out the watch towers too, both squad mates above inform William to move him along with his company when and where to move. "That man we described seems to be getting most of their attention. That has to be him." Clarence says to reassure him. Through their paranoid trek and close eye on the enemy, they finally reach their destination which is a depot of small buildings. Guards in all four spires are called to switch turns. Clarence, a.k.a Mist, tells William and all others of the ground team to continue quickly. An easy approach between patrols switching turns. Ground team soon stops on the backside of one mobile house that stands outside one of two gates, before the sentinels in the watch tower finish their rotations. William peers slightly around the corner and notices three people standing outside, in front. He then looks up and observes a couple of men taking watch in the towers exterminated one at a time by the snipers from afar.

William interrupts Chief's story. "Whoa, that's not what I told you in my report. Well, it wasn't a large encampment, and it was only a few mobile residences. They were big in scale, but only eight of them to be exact. It was a 137 mile drive. Give or take a little farther from this building. I hate driving long distances."

Chief continues his point. "Fine, I'll be honest then. Ronald made you drive the entire way? What a prick." William shakes his head and chuckles aggravatingly.

As William peers around one of the mobile homes to get a better look, he then signals his men to move in. Both Clarence and Reave get into position at the vantage point and begin to radio in with more news of the layout. "We already know the inner and outer areas, and we'll try not surprise you guys from far off, or within. No promises." Providing assurance to ground company, they continue their plan. A moment later, before ground team advances, Clarence informs William with confirmation that the only targets are focused in the epicenter now, not outside of the proposed claim before, and moved. Clarence and Reave ready themselves to blitz again. A small group William commands infiltrates one of the mobile houses up ahead. Nothing inside was note-worthy, so afterward, William and his squad go around another way to find the headman of the operations at hand. William suddenly makes a decisive move to go into one house ahead of his past position, but a couple of lookouts spot them. Before anyone could be harmed, each sniper above shoots all defenders that spotted William and his men. Falling quickly from quickened blasts, the ground team continues into the house they were intending to enter before the lookouts intervened. "Reave had moved to a different location out here. Sorry about the surprise," Clarence says.

William designates a command to apprehend all persons in the household. They accomplish their breach inside, and a couple of the officers start saying, "Drop what's in your hands and raise them. Put your hands up now!" Officials quickly handle all selected persons then place them on the ground in cuffs. William moves to the entrance of the house, peers beyond the doorway to see if any opposition is presently nearby. Quickly retreating back inside, the leader and a band of his men are waiting patiently for a short time now. Starting to worry, he tries to maintain serenity—not just for him, but also for his allies. There's no other choice, but to walk out. By doing so, William steps out, lays down his firearm and any other weapons and conforms to the situation at hand. An observation: the third group have been detained and tied up in front of the leader's guards who are ready for the execution, including the commander. Men are ordered to move in on the house to detain the rest of William's band.

Walking up to William, the leader says, "So, may I ask why you're disrupting the peace we have here? You invade to then kill my people." The leader gestures to eradicate all detained personnel; William is overcome with anxiety for his comrades, and hastily defends them against their coming doom.

(Ascent action +2) "No. You're right! You're right. Please. I was the one who brought them here. It was my call. If anyone's to be hurt, it's me."

Clarence and Reave are about to fire, but they see more friendly collaborators disperse from a house, while viewing through their scopes as well. A small, break-off squad of three go around executing a flank maneuver. Reave contacts William. "You have a backup of three ready to flank. When they commence fire, we'll strike as well." William pursues his façade to benefit the present issue. Each of the three travels in different directions. By picking a target, they point their guns to the back of the guard's heads from a distance. William's wallet is taken from his pocket. The contents are under inspection, and an identification card is acknowledged. "William Aletheo. To introduce: I am Oman Shero." Oman respectfully returns the wallet in William's pocket. Oman continues to speak "It's honorable for someone to admit one's actions; you seem like a reasonable, decent person. Perhaps, we could talk for a moment? Seeing that it's only twenty against eight, no more bloodshed is needed." William agrees either way.

More of Oman's guards emerge behind the team that was supposedly to flank, but are caught and apprehended anyways. "What are they going to do, insist on shooting my people too? You're in my grasp now. It's my turn," Oman said with an intense stare while maintaining a relaxed stance. William counters from observing a said contradiction (+1). "Your men were just as ready as we were." Oman shakes his head a couple times, closes in, and then whispers something into William's ear. Oman shows William a photo of his family within the spoken context. The expression on William's face changes from what is being whispered. From afar, both snipers have William and Oman in their sites. Although, Reave and Clarence wonder what is being whispering to William. Oman smiles and then takes leave.

There's an incoming message from Clarence: "We're going to terminate."

Oman and his men retreat all together. William ponders an idea.

(Don't let them shoot or let them finish this mission . . .)

(Ascent action +2) "Don't commit. Stand down," William says. Nine hundred yards away... Bang! Oman hits the ground instantly. Briefly frozen by the terrible scene, William watches Oman murdered. Other stray, non-detained allies come from another path and start shooting. William runs for cover. Bullets whiz by, screams of pain, flesh pierced, blood flies. Stragglers rush out of a couple of the mobile homes, firing relentlessly. Some of the officers are pegged from the bullets, but their bullet proof vests saved them from being killed. Some heads nearly explode from being blasted by the snipers. All Oman's men fall, even on the watch towers, lying still and dead . . . William is appalled by what happened. Captain Ronald calls for William to come over and help untie their fellow officers. Standing in shock, William is hailed. Responding to his Captain's command, emotions are tricky to withhold as William goes to Ronald. Bending over to untie the remaining companions, Ronald then says, "You did a real fine job. Nice stall tactic. We won't forget this." Ronald sets off shortly after. Shock is still fresh from the violent event.

(William ponders whether to lash out or speak in defense for their "supposed enemies".)

William turns toward Ronald, and great ache pierces his heart. (Optimistic choice: +1) "They were going to defer from further conflict." Staring directly at his Captain, Ronald turns and heads back to William.

Getting in William's face, Ronald exerts "righteous words." "They were exactly who they were to be. We stopped another attack on humanity. Commence our reprieve."

Staring at each other with intense concentration, William insists on replying with a firm offense against these killings (Ascent +3). "No, they were an anti-terrorism faction working with others of the same pressure group. We were wrong; you were wrong—heavily misled to begin this turmoil."

Ronald grabs William by the collar, pulling him closer. "There was much ignorance on your part as well until recently. Now you know what's best? You would've gone against my orders, committed treason, and embarrassed our law force because of what he said?! You truly believe his words?" William looks down in shame. With saddened words, he explains his reasoning.

(Ascent dialogue: +3) "He has a family . . . besides them, they've stopped multiple attacks from happening a few years back. They assumed to have a lead on another foe, but they were still looking in on it before initiating—that's what they were doing here. Also, his family was part of an attack not too long ago . . . He was tired of his own people committing genocide for ludicrous reasons. Because of that, he started his own organization. He meant no harm toward us. What are you going to say to them now that he's dead?"

Surprisingly, Ronald finds justification in his words (Ronald takes notice to his compassion/relationship changes). Though, he is still committing to not sympathizing with these supposed terrorists. "Maybe or not, but they also took the course of killing. A few less enemies, the better, and you know that. Trust is hard. Who says I'm going to say anything to his family? I knew you weren't ready for this," he says in regard to his opinion. Ronald turns away and resumes exiting the war zone with a victorious thought. It's really all in vain because of the murders—victims of war. Only a feeling of autonomy surrounds William. Void of all detection for his compassion for these losses, he exists alone. Through his distress, and to himself, heartfelt words are expressed internally. "Our world is a painful place with each passing. We breed misery and death. Woe to us harbingers of the sowed seeds of chaos, to then reap all the benefits selfishly and its ignorance that guides us."

Chapter 2

Opposing Chief's admiration, William still denies his own impressive caliber of self-potential (Ascent + 1). "It's still wrong that they had to die. If only— I wish I never saw any of it, by no means wished to be a part of it since it came to that conclusion, either."

William's dejection over the events is understandable; Chief gives him some advice to turn around such disconsolate thoughts. "True, but you're such a downer half the time. You can't manage everything or its outcome, only how you deal with it. Don't let if define you as a bad person, or consent to emotional distraught. Knowing how much sympathy you had for them shows a lot, and consenting to a ceasefire is even greater. You can't always think like a hero. Idealism can only go so far as one believes. At times, you'll have to act quickly even if it goes against what you believe. The only way to end most quarrels is generating chaos, sadly. It's gotten no one anywhere, but, well, you know . . ."

With a benevolent response, William says, "Going beyond protocol had always placed me into compromised stages plenty of times. There's no pride in this field of work I possess, nor is there any glory in taking a life. There's always another way to settle disputes. I have contradicted myself, but . . . You may not believe that. I do. Contrary to my job, that choice was made." He shakes his head in a woebegone fashion . . . "I'm sorry if I've or had been ungrateful or negative at times. Most reasons are unprecedented to me. Guessing . . . someday it'll be obvious." (Chief takes notice of that.)

William moves to the office's door. Before he opens it, Chief stands up, approaches William, then kindly responds "You know I'm always here if you need to talk. We do have an open-door policy as well. A stronger exception will be made for you. Favorites aren't applied. Don't let it go to your head. I like speaking with anyone, specifically mending their personal issues. I respect you, and with immense praise about how self-glorification doesn't come as a priority in your life, from what's been seen or known about you. I shouldn't be judging others anyways."

In a sad and melancholy tone, William replies modestly. "Thank you. Enough of your time's been wasted, sir. Much appreciated for the confidence in me, even if it was exaggerated. One more question . . . How come the armed forces didn't intervene in that operation? I felt as if that was out of our jurisdiction."

"The threat level wasn't high enough. We gave Intel about it to specific persons. Paradoxically we were told to perform the action instead. Apparently, we were in proximity and posed with higher mortality from proposed claims, as told by the mayor. He was informed by the governor, from the president. I guess tax-payers' money versus threat level was 'too much' and 'too far between'. If that makes sense, I too thought it was weak," Chief says.

William acknowledges the parameters of the orders given but doesn't allow any acceptance for its reasoning. Outside of that question, Chief responds without hesitation and/or reluctant conviction for William to talk amongst each other at any time by saying, "Anyways, not at all, my boy. At least I get to find out a little at a time about you with our talks."

(Jester +1) Ready to exert a somewhat witty comeback, William says, "I'm sorry to keep you waiting, sir. I'll make sure to speed dial when the time comes."

They both share a mutual moment.

"There's that smile we all love to see," Chief happily says.

"I can guess why you avoided telling me about our 'friend' we captured yesterday," William claims.

"You wouldn't have been at your best if we did. Everyone's needed at full integrity. Don't take it personal. We care for our men and women. Pettiness and trivialities aren't our protocol—our job is to only achieve, uphold the law, and safeguard even the weak," Chief says logically.

(Thinking . . . to embrace or to deny Chief's words?)

(Supportive dialogue +1) "You're right. That's exactly who we are. I acclaim the purpose. 'Protect every soul.' I'll see you at the meeting." William walks out so he can head to the conference proposed by Ronald from earlier. Down various halls, there is a great deal occurring. People are hard at work filing papers, tapping at keyboards, transporting files on a metal cart, while random criminals are brought in by other police officers.

The room where this meeting's being held, William finds a seat in the back to patiently wait for the assembly's launch. Over time, half the rooms filled, but he doesn't see David or Emily. Moments later, a few more S.W.A.T members walk in. After thirty minutes, Ronald emerges, holding a tan folder filled with papers. (Thinking: it could be profiles, reports, or anything, really.)

After finishing organizing all scripts, Ronald starts the assembly. "Thank you all for coming. As you know we are here to catch up on our progress. We're making a real difference out there; you all should be proud of what's been accomplished. Drug commerce has decreased on most streets by 23 percent. That's a change for the better. Void of any positive change: increased kidnappings and murder. We need to find out why it's increasing at an extremely high rate; I emphasize need because we need to know why they're happening more often than they have been on average. In general, they shouldn't be taking place at all. We can't ask everyone, hence it being a difficult task to begin with. No leads have come around, or anyone that can share any evidence to these vile acts. We'll eventually, I hope. I hate to give numbers . . . Well, this month alone forty-five people have gone missing, either from home invasions at night, off the streets, pulled out of their cars . . . They're quick with their methods through any of these scenarios. These bold performances are growing rather higher. Having the ability to escape quickly is greatly alarming."

Chief enters inaudibly with David. They sit a row behind William in the back too. Happy to have them in the room, William notices Chief whispering to David. Curious as to the conversation, he gets up then moves back a row. Approaching them from the side, William asks curiously, "What's the word?"

Chief gives them the recent info. "Another kidnapping occurred just twenty minutes ago, it said on the news just recently. Whoever's indulging in this callus strategy is making a big statement."

David, ready as always, says, "So when do we depart on this grand quest?"

William waits for an answer as well. Emily enters the room finally, scurrying quickly and quietly to the back. Ronald acknowledges her late arrival, but says nothing against it. She sits next to William and joins their conversation; William informs her on what was already said.

David continues his questioning of this secret plan's initiative. "When do we start?"

"Please continue," Emily says.

To ease their anxious minds, Chief offers them a conclusion. "All right, I'm going to have you three with another trio: Mark, Ron, and Rookie. There will be others to accompany you lot, as well. You three already have the knowledge of what's at stake, how to execute."

Emily, who does not fancy much the three mentioned, responds annoyed and upset. "Oh boy . . . here comes a profusion of sexist jokes along with mass deprivation of the decent atmosphere."

David reassures her. "They're all talk anyways. You think what they say has any meaning? No."

Emily, who's still not convinced by David's words, says, "Yeah, right."

To keep this topics' relevance, Chief extends his speech. "You'll only have to work with them this once. And for a while I won't have them with you after this, OK? This mission is just a "get in, get out" deal, simple. I know it's supposed to be the 'you know who's' call with these, but I'll distract them." Emily grunts in dissatisfaction. To see if they comply with the assignment, Chief asks for their reply. "After here you'll go. Ready?"

Excited, David says, "Yeah, you know it. The gang's back in action."

Emily's content to a degree. "I'll restrain my disgust for now, but I'm always ready with you two."

Ronald notices their ongoing talks. "May I ask what's with the interruption?!"

Chief gets up with a fake, nervous, disrespectful reaction to Ronald's question. "Sorry. Just explaining some details I was allegedly to give them— my interruption?! You intervened with my conversation." Slight tension is building from Chief's remark. "You know what?! You see, with Ronald being at your side, me and him years ago, Mr. Attention loved being in the center of it all. When we were at his house for Thanksgiving—"

Ronald interrupts his derisive speech with a clearing of the throat. Chief stops, looks at Ronald, but proceeds. "What? It was an interesting night. I, you and the whole family getting drunk off cheap spirits—people's clothes were disappearing!"

Again, Ronald clears his throat from embarrassment; everyone in the room laughs or chuckles.

Officer Quinby's interested in hearing the rest of the story. "Damn, Captain. I thought you were only work and no play. I wonder what else you did that night! I'm curious. We all are!"

Ronald shouts abruptly to end the fiasco. "We'll conclude this convention till later today . . . Thank you all again for coming; let's hope next time we won't get diverted and humiliated again."

Ronald walks by Chief and asks to talk in private. Amused within the Captain's presence, Chief says his farewells for now to William, David, and Emily in a low tone. "This'll be fun. I'll see you three later. Let fortune be with your objective." Whispering to William, Chief says, "William, I took the liberty of persuading them to not lay any strikes against you for what happened yesterday. When you have certain influence, it helps. See you around, son." Chief puts his right arm around Ronald's shoulders, but he isn't enjoying it.

They both exit. Speculating on the fun time Chief mentioned David is overwhelmed with enjoyment. "It must've been a fun time if it came to those factors. It would have been an entertaining story as a whole."

"If it wasn't for him, this place would be monotonous. How wearisome all would be," Emily says in response to Chief's cheerful personality. David laughs, Emily then too; and William produces a grin from the comments as well.

"Control isn't always available when needed at certain times, but foremost, it's how you take authority of your outlook which exists continually. Give compassion where it's needed; give attitude where the perspectives needed. Honestly, what you say will cause an effect after its moment of impact with another."

Chapter 3

Discovery

After Chief's wonderful, exhilarating past-time story, Ronald, William, Emily, David, and the others (mentioned in Chief's idea) walk to the locker room to change for the upcoming mission. Thrilled as always to be allowed to participate, David explains his mood by how exceptionally ready he is for the assignment at hand. "It's about time I finally get to do something new. It's not like I can't handle myself, or had I ever been incompetent. At least Chief understands me."

"Amen," William sarcastically replies.

As David looks at William after he spoke, sarcasm is apparent, but continues to speak for himself. "It's not like I've done anything wrong. Does the captain think it's too much? Have I done something to piss him off? Maybe some instances can be recalled. Most of my work's from Chief. Eh, it doesn't matter. I feel exhilarated. Like a renegade with a secret which we're hiding right under their noses."

Going off on a tangent, David says, "Also, why don't I be the boss? I can still abide by the rules. I have no problem with that."

"You should! You know what? Write a petition stating what your intentions will offer this new position, what it would offer our great establishment, and even its men and women in law enforcement. I bet they'll go for it directly." William replies with sarcasm and "assurance" (Jester +3). David understands mockery. William continues. "I'm being serious. You'd be amazing! Hey, it's not—"

"What did you say?! It sounds like someone needs special attention someplace else so he can calm down. Turned irrational when your pride is hindered, and compensation seems to overflow every time." As Emily interrupts the two men's tantalizing conversation, whose appearance is in the doorway, she "acts surprised" by the conversation between them.

Other companions start chuckling at the observation she made. David readies his defensive stance to counter her uncertainty; William notices his insecurity and finds an opening. David turns to see William is enjoying the moment as well. "What are you laughing at? What makes you think I can't? When has anything uplifted you lately?" David verbally scolds William in an indomitable tone.

In reply to such a question, William rebuts with a frank statement. (Critical dialogue +1) "That's none of your damned business, little boy. My fair share was given to me not too long ago from a wonderful woman." Others become immersed in their confabulation. Emily feels a little saddened by William's assertion and bows her head downward.

Such a blunt remark by William, David gets up to speak in his own defense. "Little boy? I see . . . With you being so down lately, you might need to get laid as often as possible so you can be happy for once, yourself, or do something."

William controls himself within the moment; soon states a well-placed defense. He rises and walks over to David. A foot of space is the only thing that separates them now. They stare at each other with great intensity. One of the officers says in a subtle tone, "Uh-oh . . . this might escalate. What do you think?" The spectators wage bets against each other if a fight happens and who wins. Emily sits down against the wall with enjoyment by the performance of William and David. After sometime, William begins to speak again.

"Sex doesn't make me happy. I prefer life's wonderful gifts and my breath. Anyways, I heard from a bird that not even the renowned David Bia Vodun can stand at attention, or for that long to be exact." (Jester +1/Ascent +1) David's in slight awe from that response, also fracturing an ego nearly with embarrassment, looks at the audience before him then moves closer to William. David, ever so taller than William, casts a disgusted glance down at him. William gives a facial gesture that represents his vocal trump card. David lowers his head and laughs. "Let's get going smartass." The other officers who waged a bet are disappointed, and they all turn back to what they were doing before. The trio and the others then walk to the garage. Their teammates stray ahead elatedly.

During their saunter, Emily looks at William. "I didn't know you were courted."

"It's not a topic I really talk about," William speaks quickly.

"Oh . . ." she says unhappily.

(William figures whether to go along with the lie or tell her the truth to initiate a process of romance.)

(Ascent increases slightly +1/Romance option used) "I don't have a relationship. Never was one. You are the only woman I like being around. There are times when a person needs more than just the aura of another. You understand that feeling yourself, right? The answer has been known for years." (Emily will remember that.)

She looks at him quickly and blissfully says, "Y— really?! I . . . I mean— I see. Since we're being honest, I have been in a relationship for some time."

"Oh, really, with whom?" William fearfully says.

A quiet moment arises from exultant feelings between them, but they also realize what's really wanted. "I've known him quite a long time, the only friend closest and loyal. Not a day goes by that it seemed any different," Emily exerts with conspicuous referencing. Her mind fills with happiness, and she chuckles subtly. William looks down at her and ponders the truth; she keeps her concentration straight ahead. William too turns his attention forward as they walk on to the car depot.

(Innocence perishes / Revenge- A short informative chronicle regarding David)

"Cold-blooded or justified means doesn't matter in the end, during the conclusion, as well as after, death or unrest only remains."

06/02/2028

A few weeks before capturing Sadism

Following leaving work at 5pm: upon a house, deep in the concrete jungle, far back in a cul-de-sac: a reprise from utter woe of past times. *Click* The hallway lights are turned on, shoes placed by the front door, feet scurry to find rest . . . a couch is in site that David will sit on. Mind's all flustered from tiring work; daytime slowly fades to nights' glory.

A couple hours before nightfall, but a call's made to his mother before all hours. "Hello?" David's mom responds.

"Hey, Mom, how's everything?" David speaks.

"I'm all right. How are you? You always call me at the same time. I can always count on that," She relays in a happy manner.

"I just wanted to see how you were doing?" David wonders.

Knock knock subtle sounds coming from the front door. "Hold on. Someone's at the door." Setting his phone on a nearby table, David then advances to the front door.

Unlocking the first lock . . . Now the second . . . Opening . . . A man dressed suspiciously greets David. "It's been a while, but I believe its past due."

"Excuse me?" David questions with confusion.

Two larger men come from the side, outside the doorway, and forcefully grab David's arms to keep him still.

"What's going on? Who are you?!" David questions.

"Take a good guess, David," the man replies.

Both lackeys are commanded to transport David back inside and plant him on his couch; they stand guard in proximity if anything were to happen.

"I . . . I don't know. I have no recollection of who you are or any of your friends," David defensively states.

As his phone sits on the nearby table, his mom makes a slight cough. David glances at the phone. The suspicious man sees his reaction and goes over to it. Slowly picks it up and sees the name above the number reading "Mom." Seconds after, he hangs up and places it in his pocket.

"Don't worry, she isn't our target. You are, though. Since I didn't get my full income from your father, I guess you're the next in line for that miracle. We should go back to where I reside." Signaling both men makes them pick David up and move him to their car. Leaving out the front door . . . down the steps . . . David decides to act boldly and breaks free. He clobbers the man to his left, and then the one to his right. One's dazed on the ground (not knocked out), and the other stumbles back, right hand holding his face. David holds his right hand due to the pain he caused himself from those punches he threw.

The leader pulls out a gun. "Hey now, be careful."

Walking closer . . . The gun is point blank in David's face. A neighbor peers out their window to now witness the scene at hand . . . alarmed and ready to call the police. One henchman aids the other.

"Look down the barrel. It's what your father viewed through before I stole his life. Not the same gun. You get the point." Lowering it . . . then quickly smacks David with the blunt end knocking him unconscious.

The two men grab David and haul him into the vehicle. Doors shut in a haste, car revs up and they drive away. Voices are unheard to David's unconscious state; they converse with each other, but who knows what's going to happen. Fifteen minutes in, and the car comes to a halt. Three doors open, David's moved again. All three doors are shut afterward. David's still motionless and unaware. A fourth door opens, but this time they enter a house. It's the head quarters. David's set on a chair, head hanging low. Tied up . . . Both henchmen depart to a different area of the household. Cold water is poured on his head, abruptly awakening him. "Ugh!" The cold water catches him by surprise. Tapping quickly on the holstered gun, the captor moves to him.

"I know there's a hidden cache your father possesses."

David (a little discombobulated still) says, "I wouldn't know. What do you mean my father?"

"I don't know if he affiliated you with everything we have done, but I'm getting a hunch about it. Just tell me and you're free."

David scrunches up his face. "I can't. I'm not familiar with the situation. Try and try you will, it'll never come to light, mostly due to my ignorance."

Still displeased, head faces the right, and aggravation fully composes his captor's body language. A quick punch comes across David's face. His head turns from the blow . . . then he looks at the despicable man in anger.

The henchmen come back with a mobile medical table. Parked on the left side of David, The cloth is then ripped off, revealing rusty surgical tools.

"We can do this violently or you can tell me where he hid it. I implore you, please pick the second choice."

David examines the grotesque tools, but turns his full attention back to his captor.

"The men your company follows, one of my best employers, I found out a day ago and figured revenge was plausible, to stall. He's my top supplier. If he loses his job, I lose a great majority. You couldn't let go of the past? You should have moved away from that house. Good thing it was easy to find your location. Let's try something new. I'm going to free you, OK? But, my men here are going to hold each arm of yours out, stretched, palms up. Each second you waste, this scalpel will be cutting down your arms very slowly. I'll try not to nick any tendons, or an artery. Though, as much as it would please me, I won't. Every man has his breaking point no matter the condition. Let's commence." Humming a Christmas carol, he brings the rusty scalpel close to David's left arm. He tries to break loose, but their grasp is too strong. Struggling, trembling in fear . . .

During the scene from earlier, David's neighbor had called the police. Two policemen approach Sally's house. Up the front yard, they then reach the front door and knock twice. Sally opens it. Relief overcomes her stature.

"You made a call about a kidnapping? Your neighbor, you said?" Officer Thomas questions

"Please, come in," Sally quickly says.

All three sit in the living room.

"There were three men that took him captive. A conversation was happening before, while pointing a gun in his face. The one pointing a gun at David knocked him out and then had two other men transport him in their vehicle and drove away. I thought he had them before, as he fought two of the three . . ." Sally proclaims undoubtedly.

"We'll call our station and make sure we can find him. Is there anything else? Can you describe what they look like?" Officer Yong asks.

"They were wearing dark clothes. The two larger men were scruffy looking, facial hair, um . . . The main guy had a trench coat, black. I was at a distance, many facial features I couldn't really convey. I got a better look at the larger man, I guess," Sally answers.

"We'll have dispatch call for someone to sit outside his house just in case. We'll also let others know so they can patrol." Officer Yong says to bring reassurance to Sally's worried state.

"Come with us. We'll show you some composites and see if you can spot the accomplice," Officer Thomas insists.

Sally is escorted to the police station.

Back to David's situation: "Another thought: before cutting further into you, I presume it's hiding in an unmistakable spot. Nah . . ."

David's torture is excruciating, but the blade's use is stopped again. A better idea comes to mind. "Maybe this is a waste of time. You know what . . . let's go back to where it began. Both of you go back to his house. Be careful! Watch out for any police or bystanders. You two hear me? Do it within boundaries to find it. Be discreet. I emphasize the word. And David, for introductions: my name is Jonathan. It might ring a bell."

Both men leave the two to return to David's house.

"While they search, you shall remain my prisoner. What's the point of continuing to torture you if they find anything? I'll return with harsher methods if they don't," Jonathan says.

Upon exiting, the lights are turned off. Complete blackness surrounds David; and no noise either. The door slams shut and locked. Blood trickles from his wounds, pain amid the everlasting blackness.

Back to the house, parking farther away is the plan's beginning. Night revels infinitely. Wary of all else, both men trek forward. At the end of Vicious Avenue, two streets from Circle Boulevard, they turn a corner. A cop's stationed inconspicuously there, adjacent to David's house in an undercover car. Not aware of the unobtrusive watchman sitting just yonder, a quick trip into the back yards for concealment. The officer in the vehicle stationed not far from David's house has night vision capabilities equipped in a screen inside the middle console, and has cameras positioned on all four sides of the car too.

"This is Sergeant Peter. I'm stationed at David Vodun's house; two men just lurked behind his house then proceed inside it seems; dubious in all nature. Back up would be appreciated. Over."

"Two units will be arriving in one minute. Dispatch out."

At the station, Sally is given a composite book; she is flipping through each page, but still no match.

"He's part of our SWAT team, right?" Officer Yong asks Thomas.

A revelation comes to Thomas: "Yeah. Hold on." Looking through the system for the specific field, David appears. "I've never talked to him, and we do work different hours and departments." he says.

"He might have his phone on him. You think we could track him, just a guess? Give me a minute with Samson. He'll be able to pinpoint the location." Yong astutely claims.

At David's house, the two promised units come to his aid. Each enforcer exits their car and heads closer to the house.

"Both went through the back," Peter says to the others.

Near the back yard, quietly, tiny noises can be heard outside from the inner walls. The back door is still unlocked. Small lights move around inside. All five officers make their way indoors discreetly.

Each henchman travels into another room. Using a tactical approach is appropriate. Creeping shadows, a quick initiative.

"Put your hands where we can see them!" Pat exclaims.

A deceitful look comes abroad one henchmen's face to his fellow other. All five stand parallel to each other, horizontally, guns raised and ready. Turning quickly, trench coats whip through the air, shotguns blaze. Two officers are gunned down, but the other three fires away repeatedly: penetration, blood and death. Barrels slowly allow smoke to escape; both bodies drop. The two officers who were shot have bullet proof vests on and are on the ground in pain.

"Defensive procedures occurred and we have fatalities," Peter advises over his radio to head quarters.

People close by in the cul-de-sac heard the gun shots. Lights are turned on, doors open, and windows are ajar for people to see what's happening. From outside, no one can see anything nor hear a sound after the shooting stopped. Ambulances will soon be appearing, and so will more police enforcement.

"What the hell is taking them so long?" John wonders.

Walking back down to check on David, he opens the door to the garage and flips a single light on. A smile forms on John's face. "My, my . . . Where could he be? Just like your dad: so sneaky and strategic. This'll be fun." David has disappeared. Above the doorway, David falls on top of John from above. Scuffling on the ground, David smashes John's head repeatedly on the floor. John soon counters with both hands; a hard shove with both legs tosses David off. Each rising, blood comes from the back of John's head, but he decides to place his weapon on the table. "Fight to the death. Who'll reach it first?" John proposes as he pushes the table to the opposite side of the room. CRASH! Rusty tools jingle or fall off the table down below.

Back at David's house- "Make sure they're not fatally wounded and take off their vests," Peter worriedly says.

Lonny helps unbutton their shirts, then the vests; no penetration, but they will have some bruises.

"I'm going to need medics and two bodies to be picked up as well. You know my location," Peter relays over the radio.

John charges! David dodges and ripostes with a choke hold, picks him up and slams him harshly on the ground. David goes to stomp on John's head, but misses as John rolls away. John taunts David by gesturing with his left hand to step forward as he stands up. On the offense again, he handles David by the waist and lifts him, slamming him ruthlessly into a shelf. Breaking it shatters the entirety and pieces fall. Readying again, David throws the first punch. John dodges and moves to the side then hits David in the abdomen twice. David pushes him away. Two steps back, John goes to superman punch. David ducks under it. Another attempt with a hard strike, David blocks, and clobbers his opponent several times in the face before singly striking the mid section. In ending the combo, clutch's John's arm and twists it, and strikes downward with his elbow on top of John's elbow—Crack!—snapping it in the process. "Ah!" John yells in pain.

"There he is!" Thomas shouts in relief.

"Location is at the Walters' former residence, which is still on the market. I was there not too long ago because some kids were on the property," Yong proclaims.

Leaning against a far wall, John and David meet eyes . . . Focusing full attention straight at the gun, they rush for it. Near it, John tries to push David, but the attempt was in vain. David wraps his arm around John's throat from behind, clasps one of the surgical tools and stabs ruthlessly at his throat. Blood squirts from the wound. David picks up the hand-gun. He pushes John a few feet back, and then fires several times. Ten shots blast forth: some hit the abdomen, chest, and one final one to the head. The body drops to the floor . . . Retribution: yet so cold, not so rewarding. Releasing it, the desert eagle rattles below, and he fiercely glares at the man who murdered his father over greed. Moving next to the corpse, thoughts of incomplete retribution swarm a discontented mind. A couple minutes later, police rush to David's position. Cops surround it and people wait among its borders, curious with confusion about this chaos. Bolting out of their vehicles, reinforcements surround the building. After breaking down the front and back doors, a thorough search for David is carried out throughout the house. Nowhere to be found yet . . . One last place: the garage . . . Upon entering, they see David vigorously washing his hands.

"David. You OK?" Officer Gild asks. ———

No response for being traumatized from his aberrant confrontation, Gild slowly approaches him. While moving, Gild looks at the grotesque scene: Jonathan lies dead in an ocean of blood . . . and the entirety of his face is caved in.

Interlude 2

Mental state

Relinquished ethic/Gradual conviction

David

06/22/2028

Two days before the group's capture of Sadism, and three days before 1st incursion (asylum project): David enters a psychiatrist's office; patiently waits on a couch. A woman enters a minute later. "Sorry about that. Wish I could've spoken to you sooner. I had to take personal days for myself. Glad you've come. How have you been since our last meeting? I overlooked the report beforehand."

David shrugs both shoulders and says, "Ok, I guess . . ."

Grabbing a notepad, she looks at David with a concerned and an unappeased look. "That's it? Something new must have come around for you nowadays due from our meetings prior. I'm sure of it."

David sits there uncomfortably, unenthusiastic to speak at first.

"Take your time," Laura says while waiting patiently for him to respond. She then quickly scans the long scar among the smaller ones on his left arm.

He speaks up at last. "Laura, I met a ghost a couple of nights ago . . . Well, symbolically, assumingly? Uh, he—it—spoke to me." Interested, Laura sits silently to hear him out. "I know my father is dead and he isn't coming back. But it's like I was meant to hear him out one last time, in a sense. It was vague at first—surrounded by darkness, a meeting solely between him and me. He just stared at me for a short while. Then suddenly began to talk. Most of his words were muffled.

After a bit, his voice became louder and comprehensible. I remember: 'complicity, acts, sorry.' It was unnerving, but I'm managing."

Laura begins to examine the thought of it in her own mind. A needed resolve to add up an answer, she reacts intelligibly. "The mind itself can be very reassuring, abundantly full of doubt, or during dreams by the messages they serve. Many aspects can appear throughout dreams with everyone: fear, happiness, sorrow, death . . . It's a collaboration of recent events or long past and its complex institution of images, scenes. Not to forget its exuberant output also. Maybe your mind was allowing you to think what you needed to hear and see? Letting it fester deep inside could've conjured this vision. It could have been something past anyone's comprehension but of your own. Trying to cope with and/or accept can be hard for many. This dream of yours could've been your easiest route to finally achieve peace, or to push you towards an answer."

David's very mind swells with uncertainty. "I don't know. getting back to sleep was difficult after that. All I could do was gaze at my ceiling, turn to my walls—nearly complete darkness; only a streetlight to shine in with minimal integrity."

She acknowledges his feelings. Laura now asks how another personal experience is going. "How's therapy been? I assume positive results, hopefully?"

David looks up at her then back down. Laura produces only a feeling of misconception of her own faith but waits for an answer. David then confesses his issue. "I had a moment of weakness again . . . Telling myself I didn't need its support, I caved." David sits in shame with gradual breakdown of strength for his act. He confesses further. "It made my problems disappear for a time. Knowing I went against the trusts beheld for me, betrayal of my promise. They could've sent me to jail for possession—thrown away my only chance. I didn't know what else to do. I know there is plethora of other means to uplift me, to divert from such erroneous actions."

Her facial expression turns to a sad gesture. "I hear you. I know not completely of your physical or mental stress myself. I know you can muster your strength against it. Don't let weakness reside in you. You have more confidence in everything you do; more than everyone combined that comes through here, beyond the people that came through here—the whole world itself. No one's perfect. Nobody's life has a straight line, and it always branches out into many paths. Some are blocked, some forced into, some are forbidden, and some are meant to be."

David understands her wisdom, and collects himself quickly before he speaks again. "Thanks for listening to me. It's nice to get some insight and encouragement," he says with gratitude. Her utmost compassion for his personal experiences is always welcomed. Laura gets up and approaches David. He also arises.

Placing her right hand on his shoulder also gives him a vote of confidence. "You can always come to me anytime, call whenever. OK? Just do one favor for me, personally. I need you to remember who you are, where you come from. Don't let your weaknesses define you. Always will there be a choice as to what path lies in front. Don't think for one second this sums up your existence. There's a plethora of hope for you. Each of those incidents are petite to the David I really know." Joy gradually flows through him like never before, waxing evermore. Her words have nearly revitalized David in such a way that he can exit with credence from her advisability. "You come in here quite often. We both know a lot about each other. Keep it up and you might have to take me out."

He could suggest a date, but David has too much respect for her. "I would graciously take you up on that offer. He wouldn't be happy to know his wife was with another beyond certain standards."

Smiling at the thought, they share a laugh over it. "Maybe, but I'll never know that for sure."

All noise quiets down soon after. "Sorry," David says.

"Its fine," Laura replies.

"It'll take time, I know. At least I have someone who cares. Thanks again," David says before departing.

Maybe her words have changed him for the better in the long run. There might actually be some light in it all. Confidence moves David somewhat gracefully; all thoughts equalize.

"Faith can be restored in a person. When a person dwells in incertitude and/or hopelessness, that's when true despair comes forth. Ironically, doubt can be a form of confidence building. No matter what formulation of revival's made, it's how and when you decide its' restoration . . . also, it's capacity."

Chapter 3

Throughout their drive: some words were exchanged, and not all was well either. Only a couple miles to their destination, the recruit (Rookie), speaks to Emily in a condescending fashion. "You sure it's safe for you to come? I mean, you're so delicate. What were to happen if the only woman were to get hurt?"

Some enjoy what was said. Emily gestures her finger at Rookie to come nearer; in doing so, Rookie moves to her and wonders what she's going to say. Quick reflexes allow her to grab his left arm and force him down to the ground quite rapidly. Rookie grins while expressing pain in the position he put himself into.

With much fortitude, Emily exerts her response by saying, "Delicate you say? You're a strong, capable young man, but I don't see your point. You don't even know me. So to assume I'm weak holds much arrogance. You're so clichéd." Rookie intently glares at while being assisted back up into his seat. Everybody somewhat calms down. William locks eyes with Emily and expresses how impressed he is. She blushes.

Another officer who's still amused is Mark: as dumbfound and inconsiderate, he opens his big mouth at anything for any unknown or known reason. Mark looks at Rookie then Emily with a vile grin. "You better watch it now, boy! Little Miss Menstrual is quite feisty when it comes to her insecurities."

Emily stares back at him with disgust.

(In this moment, William decides either to defend Emily or remain in silence, letting Mark continue his insulting remarks.)

(Special +1) To resolve the tension, he comes up with a riposte to defend Emily. "Insecurities . . . Does your mother know how you talk about or to women? She'd be so disappointed." (Emily will remember this.) (David respects William's action.) Mark glares at William as he continues to speak and stating an insightful, yet also a disdainful comment (Ascent +2/Jester +2). "I wonder . . . Through your whole life, I bet you're the "one guy" who assumes at any given moment you could get with anyone so easily without ramifications, right? Everyone already knows that you possess such an ego of immense caliber, vastly grandiose in scale. It's amazing you find people who carry the same perspective in life just like you."

Anger overcomes Mark; a readied choice to start a fight with William occurs, but instead, he tries to threaten William. "I'm going to kick your ass, you fucking faggot."

(Jester dialogue +1) William returns with a witty come-back, causing abrupt interruption. "Whoa! First, I don't fuck faggots. Second, you should be careful throwing those words around, mister. On the other hand, you can, but I'm sitting and quite comfortably. I mean, what are we . . . five miles in? When we get there, my ass is all yours. OK? Can you wait that long? Or is the calling too strong? You smell that? It's the smell of shitty victory."

As Mark chooses to go over and start a fight, thinking again, he decides to get personal. "Coming from a guy who separates himself from the crowds, who is so melancholy, and believing every feat he performs gives the meaning of 'hero'. We all know what you've done. That doesn't make you any better."

William defends himself, but with slight provocation. "I don't, actually. You wouldn't understand, given your mental capacity."

"What about your brother?" William's face drops, and he stares into the void with guilt as sorrow climbs. Mark is still firing shots to prove a point. "What did you do to help him? He lay there, dead in a ditch. I saw you praying over his casket at the funeral. What's that going do? You got your vengeance afterward, did you not? Some brother you—"

Emily quickly ends the confliction. "Alright, that's enough!" she says while looking at Mark. "That's neither necessary nor fair in any way!"

Mark gestures a middle finger at them and ignores everyone for the remainder of the ride. Being that their venture is quiet, awkward enough as it is, but the tension between most is even worse. The heated argument only left hurt souls.

The site mentioned by Chief is near, and every one readies a stance against whatever could possibly be inside this "abandoned" building. The SWAT vehicle comes to a stop. Everyone then prepares to exit. Everyone conveys an acceptable analysis of the outer foundation and complex from where they're positioned, wondering what or who could be operating in such a rundown building.

"How old is this place?" Rookie asks with curiosity.

"It was an insane asylum built in 1932, which obviously held our worlds, at the time, most violent and delusional people. It even held Monaco "the Masochist" Telluci. Many others have had their share, but this one is very unique. There's quite a history here, actually. Not important as of the moment, but we'll still be cautious. You never know... Watch out for any strays," William responds. (Jester dialogue +3)

Although, abundantly obvious and unnerving about it William is slightly scares Rookie, making him feel frightened. "Yeah, careful . . . Sure . . ." Rookie says. Mark pushes through Rookie with his shoulder, telling him to man up and not worry about anything else than completing the mission.

"What's the directive?" Emily questions.

William informs them all. "To approach this properly: first team can start at the top and second team can head through the bottom. If a basement is present, start from there instead. Chief also said that there was another team to aid us here. We could check the other side when someone can get a clear view of them to see if they're in attendance. It's blocked from both sides, and knowing the other entrance connects with the thruways' opposite side, down a wooded path connecting to it, we don't really have any knowledge of its inner concept. Strange, we should've heard from the others by now. I, David, and Emily will take the roof—"

Mark rudely interrupts William's commands with a displeased tone. "If present, send us through the spider infested darkened area. That's how it's going to be?" David smiles at Mark, and Mark returns it with an angry expression.

"Since we recognize our positions, we have our radios; we'll venture through, and then meet at a point. Say, at mid or whenever necessary?" William says to conclude. Everyone agrees in their own way with Chief's plan told by William, and they soon head to their conceived routes. William, Emily and David quickly move to a stairway leading and leveling high above. The three ascend. A couple of officers stay back near the vehicle with their driver and an extra tagalong, standing watch outside. Mark, Ron, and Rookie head toward the lower setting.

Upon approaching a low placed window, before turning the corner to see if a doorway exists, Mark bends over to see what's inside. He breaks through the window to get inside. "I've worked from the bottom up too many times to be thrown into the dirt like this."

Rookie shares some confidence to convince Mark of the rewards at hand. "Think about it: when we come out, we'll be in a better spot at the precinct. Remember?"

Rookie's claimed statement gives a revelation to Mark. "That will be our grand reward, so let's get to this issue at hand quickly and show them we're competent. Still, keep an eye out for any dangers. Kill anything in our way that's a threat. There's no room for errors."

As they venture inside of the basement, darkness upholds much fear. A shred of light can be seen farther in; the only source of light they see is from an open door that lies farther in. Mark uses his flashlight to achieve better visibility. Looking around . . . Only to be perceivable are old shock therapy devices, washing machines, dryers, and medical tables. Ron makes a statement about the cobwebs and spiders as the only hosts in these parts. Curiosity comes to mind about how many people were used on these shock therapy appliances. Each undertakes confidence.

Rookie moves closer to one of the therapy machines, but notices it's been used recently. Boldly choosing to touch it, a sound somewhere around them clatters as if somebody dropped something. All three of them are alert and concentrate on the area, assuming where it occurred. Shining their lights everywhere, not fully able to find what caused it, they separate from each other to cover more ground. Ron turns from hearing another sound and shines his flashlight in the distance . . . soon to see a figure in the back right corner. Closer toward this shape, he comes to realize it's a person. Who though? In respectable distance, he leans down on both knees and places his gun to the side. To see if the person is responsive, he asks, "Hey, you OK? Sir or ma'am, what's—" Attention concentrates at Ron's eyes. Barely having a complete face causes concern. No nose, no ears, traces of rot, and a deathly stench exude from the mouth.

Ron is paralyzed with terror. This figure grabs him tightly on the arms; both fly to the other side of the room. Mark and Rookie turn to see what's going on. Both start calling out each other's names. Ron does not answer. Searching and searching, yet to be found . . . Rookie unexpectedly steps on a wet surface. A pool of blood was the cause. The trail is slowly followed as he lifts his flashlight up and up, to suddenly be abruptly confronted by a horrific sight. Ron is hanging by his intestines! Exceptionally petrified, and turns to run—Bam!!! Something hits him harshly, and he falls to the ground.

Mark hears another noise and calls out, but no one reacts. Turning around again, he sees a flashlight on the ground and walks to it. Looking over, he sees Rookie lying on the ground. He helps him up, but removes himself from Marks aid. Rookie moves himself against a support beam that's close by and sits against it, while unaware of anything else around him from the gruesome scene he just witnessed. Mark starts to question Rookie. No answers . . . just a point of a finger focused toward the scene that bestowed Rookie this consuming discomposure.

"What happened?" Mark wonders.

Rookie continues to point his finger where Ron dangles lifelessly by his own intestines. Mark turns his head, points the light in the commanded direction. "Nothing's there." He puts the flashlight in hand, pointing all light upward on his face as if he was about to tell a ghost story, only to continually mock at no expense.

Rookie looks up and sees a figure rising behind Mark. Becoming frightened further, he starts mumbling louder and louder to try warning Mark, void of an ability to make any comprehensible words by how heightened one's trepidation is. A looming, ominous humanoid stands over Mark with dominant purpose.

Rookie mutters a couple of words. "Turn around."

Still skeptical, Mark turns and looks up. Face to face with an unknown being with bloodlust covering its face—intent to kill at will. Fear increases every second. Backing up, this demon tracks Mark with every step. Speaking in an unknown tongue, it looks down at Rookie, and then returns its concentration on Mark. Reaching out—terror rising—it pulls Mark's head completely off, then quickly reaches down his torso and rips out his whole spine. The body drops and the creature slowly turns back to Rookie.

A sound can be heard past the doorway. The beast turns its head towards the direction where it came from. Rookie reaches for a flashlight next to his left hand, picks up a hand gun, too, which is next to his right hand. Shining what light resides in his hand, every light inside the room suddenly turns on automatically. Nothing and no one is to be found. Horror and dread still floods Rookie's mind, controlling his very thoughts. Searching and searching . . . Oblivion . . .

The first team arrives at the top of the building. William peers over its high peak to see if their aiding support has arrived. No trace . . . He begins to wonder if there ever was another squad.

"Maybe they're not here yet," William quietly says to himself. David walks over, curious to see William's composure. William replies by telling him there's no sign of the other company who's supposedly to be their aid. David attempts to reassure William by saying they're probably momentarily held up which explains their late arrival. William becomes more reassured by the thought, even though he knows the other entrance's purpose. They begin their venture inside. Emily opens a hatch door on the roof. One by one, they proceed. As William is last in, he shuts the door.

Descending, its integrity is outstanding from the inside (even though they just came in, but still.) Questions come around. Making their way to the bottom of the spiral staircase, all three soon walk into the main room of the top floor. Their surroundings are determined; what else could possibly be in all its 'glory'?

"The inside is quite deceptive compared to the outer facets," William proclaims strongly.

Emily quickly assumes another reason for it. "Maybe this is to purposely fool others into thinking abandonment, though in turn it isn't. This has to be on purpose."

Many halls connect to this one room, but which direction to make headway. Inside has a marble interior, pillars made of ivory along with black candles strewn throughout, and statues of unknown figures stand erect on either side. A church like concept, promisingly. Pews consistently placed next to each other, and a long red carpet leading to a podium on the stage. As confused as obvious to them they seem to be, everything is strange in itself. William comments about the layout looking like a church, albeit it's in near perfect condition by speculating on its placement and purpose.

Emily mumbles something, but David and William didn't hear what she had said. "Black candle mass," Emily says again in a louder tone. William and David look at each other with concern and slight dread. "This is making the atmosphere feel more unnerving. It has to be some kind of cult." Emily additionally asserted. Not exactly sure of the cult's true value, they began moving into their first hallway.

Soon to approach multiple rooms . . . all three look in room number 1. David opens the door, and after reading the room's layout, he says, "What are those machines? Why are they hooked up to these?" David gazes with great curiosity. Emily takes a closer look: tubes coming from the machines go to the back of the person's head. They have an intricately built metal helmet that covers only the top half of their head, leaving their mouths down to their toes exposed. All persons are bound to a chair and naked.

William intervenes with quickness. "Don't touch those. Anything could occur if we were to detach those tubes, seeing that it's attached to this machine, and it's inserting some kind liquid into their cranial region."

Upon further inspection, David stops what he's doing. Soon leaving this wretched room (more questions than answers so far). "This is becoming more bizarre. What cult does this? Whoever is doing this isn't sane," David says in disgust from the view of people who are tested on. They advance down the hall. Each room has a consistency of emulated testing like the first room they encountered.

"We'll not know for sure until we find which person or person(s) is behind this monstrous technique," William says.

William travels by the last room residing in this horrific hall and examines the inside. An imagination runs wild; what William perceives exaggerates his cerebral images. A massive mechanism sits empty, abandoned . . . Through the door's window, only sadness, torture, pain and pride. Channels hang freely, and a cage to hold something or someone; dust coincides with metallic surfaces and bullet holes . . . many bullet holes. A serious moment that took place, but its nightmare was ended with a life saved from prideful experiments and an arrogant exploitation. Placing a hand on the door, a thought of relief comes into existence, creating an uplifting moment for William. Hope comes to arise shortly within his mind. A smile forms knowing this particular person is safe, with knowledge of its happening to be nullified forevermore.

The dilapidated room contains only an erect flatbed connected to a tall machine with some wiring and straps.

David and Emily see William gazing into the room he's in front of. Both walk up and look inside.

"You see anything?" David asks.

"Everything is well," William happily says. (Ascent greatly increases +5).

David, Emily, and William continue their expedition.

A few feet ahead of them, another opened room. One huge console is stationed in the epicenter. Many screens cover its front, possessing different views through other cameras inside many other rooms, levels and stairways. It reveals people in similar positions of being tested on as well. As William scans every screen, taking much time, he gains a feeling of paranoia from a familiar figure—too familiar to be exact . . . Increasing zoom capabilities on this specific person, he recognizes a specific feature on one of the females. Thinking to himself: suspicion is only taking place. William's worried state increases, zooming in more . . . He identifies a tattoo immediately, and distress overcomes his mind. The picture is fuzzy when zooming in to a certain degree. Still, it raises concern. William quickly scans the other individuals. Nothing else catches his eye. Turning left then right, he sees that Emily and David are occupied by other means. Looking at the screen once more, at the topmost right corner of that same monitor, it shows "4th level". Inquisitiveness prominently takes over, and William quietly slips away.

A few moments later, David goes to talk to William, but there's no trace of him anywhere. "You know where William went?" David inquires worriedly.

"I have no clue either," Emily claims.

"Fuck," David says as he leans on the console William was at earlier. Taking a deep breath, he gazes up at the monitors, and scans them to then see William in one of them. "Emily!" David quickly exclaims. Emily rushes over. "You see him?" David poses rhetorically. Emily shakes her head as she focuses complete attention to one of the cameras. The camera he was spotted in was located on the eleventh floor's stairwell, four floors down.

Before William uses an elevator after going down a couple levels, he says to himself that it might warn others. So each floor he descends to is through the stairways only. Rushing faster and faster and finally reaching the fourth floor. Each level, along with their corridors, seems simple enough with what's been seen so far. Before turning a corner, two guards walk across the hallway. He watches them until they disappear past the intersection farther down. William now continues to the room, which holds a person of importance. Upon reaching it, he scans to see if this is the correct room he remembers on the camera. Opens the door . . . and feels dismayed. The immense room reveals a gigantic mechanism with twenty-five people and a separate mechanism in the back with five others connected to it, consisting of the same scenario in a sitting position, pipelines running to the back of their heads, bound and naked.

Frantically walking around this behemoth of a machine . . . William eventually comes to a stop. Standing anxiously . . . moves a little again. Getting down on one knee, he notices these cranial devices are different from those on the upper floors. A flap can be seen. Taking a risk by slowly lifting it up . . . Frozen and shocked, he sees the unknown woman's eyes are missing. Only holes are present. William turns away from the gruesome scene and close the flap. He looks to the right and discovers the tattoo which was seen over the monitor from earlier. The tattoo represents a black phoenix. Panic rises to immeasurable capacity. He elevates the compartment's covering and reveals his sister is subjected as well. William wonders if his mother and his father are possibly here too. Tears are vaporized by rage. William places his head on his sister's legs. Nothing can redeem what was witnessed.

David and Emily scanned each screen so they can see where he'll end up. David and Emily make their way down, but with a probability to be confronted by guards who could cease their movements at any turn.

"What is he doing? It must've been important if he ran off. Why alone, though?" Emily vocally exerts in a profound tone.

"We'll find out when we meet up," David replies.

The stairway is chosen. Descending two floors already, they see that no guards exist here. Coincidentally, Emily and David go down the same way William did, but their course has shifted. Now on the thirteenth floor, the stair case seems to end abruptly.

A singular door's before them. Opening . . . Another passage stretches far ahead; it twists continuously—mind contorting and bizarre, with windows stretched down it every twenty feet. Walking by each one slowly, seeing that horrible figures reside inside, but no door leads to their prisons from inside. Creatures walk from place to place, sit in corners, and you can hear their cries. Deformed animals rage or cower, malformed people lured into madness. Dying souls yearn for life. Half way down this wretched corridor, one of the imprisoned creatures (a wolf, on all fours, extremely large, is nearly the same height as David and mind you, David is six feet and six inches) waits at a window staring at both David and Emily with firm focus. Both then stop. Emily looks through her peripheral vision. "It's staring at us."

David, just as Emily is seeing, says, "Yeah, kind of freaking me out." Full agreement between the two is evident. They wholly turn to look at the creature. A feeling of terror forms around them. Their minds fill with discomfort; its white eyes pierce through their souls like a blade through flesh.

Images flow esoterically inside their psyche, expeditiously and vaguely. Both unexpectedly transition to an opposite side of the hall's width by a mysterious force. Dropping to the ground, visions stop. They lay on the floor in agony from their minds having been forcefully penetrated. No memory of the visions; just as they came, they went as quickly to be lost from all existence. David arises slowly and helps Emily. He looks around to see the giant beasts absent from the window and the room. Looking at each other with a perplexed fix, the only thing to do now is move on. They're nearly recovered, but a small amount of aftermath remains.

"What was that?" Emily says while shivering.

"That was beyond anything I've ever experienced. I don't want that to happen again," David says while panting.

Nodding her head in agreement, she then austerely says, "We really need to get to him and leave."

Sinking deeper, each floor contains lunacy and vile experiments tormenting these innocent people (not like the thirteenth floor experience, everything has gone back to what it originally was when they first entered). Each turn of the head, the opening of another door just creates more despondency. All the injustice this place perpetuates can never be justified; to see it end is a number one priority for these three.

"Turn away from delving too deep into any secrets. Secrets that should be left alone, deprived of any acknowledgment, or see any aspect of days' lights: functioned with animus, played by the puppet, fortunately fortuitous or abject and ill-content."

Chapter 4

Uncontainable Lividus

Upon the fifth floor, three more guards stand watch up ahead. Before they can reach William, a plan must be devised to move around them and/or strike if possible. The circular hall's concept gives him opportunity to move stealthily around the enemy as they too walk around it during their patrol.

Emily and David finally make it past the necessary levels. Only a small stretch remains before they attain their objective.

By one room that has a bigger window layout, and fortuitously, Emily and David see William on his knees. His head lies on Sarah's lap. Entering, Emily moves slowly toward him. "What are you doing?! This place isn't—" She quickly realizes he's distraught and moves even closer to sit beside him. William mumbles incomprehensible words. "What'd you say?" she asks. William explains to her that his sister is a part of these sadistic experiments. Surprised, she gets up, and notices the movable parts on the cranial devices he mentioned. Lifting the single flap: nothing but absolute truth which spoken of reveals what was said exactly word for word. William steps aside to reveal it to David, with a face projecting sadness and a stance of discontent.

"You sure that's her?" David asks.

William puts them back on just for safety measures after he removed them beforehand; anything could happen if the head compartment is off or off too long, and he says to put them back on again for safety purposes.

"My sister is here and she's a lab rat for whoever condones this horrific concept," William softly speaks.

William glares with concentration at David to reassure him. An uncomfortable feeling swells. David begins walking around the room to reassert his composure. Both hands massage his face while he swears a couple times. Emily tries to comfort William, but it's not helping him.

William mumbles to himself. Emily starts hugging William.

(Descent Action +2) He forcefully shoves her aside. Surprised by his action, William rises and heads toward the door. "I'm not going to idly standby and allow this house of utter torture to continue!"

"This place isn't what it seems. I don't know if you saw what we did, but you mustn't wander off alone. We have to call ahead. This facility's 'other' containment isn't natural," Emily says as a forewarning, even though William didn't care to listen.

By the door, where all three have entered, David defensively blocks William's action. "Don't do anything rash, friend." William tries to go through, but David places a hand on William's chest and speaks again. "I wouldn't do that. Just recollect your thoughts logically, and we'll solve this. Leave your requital behind. This is no place to provide your enemy with blindness. Don't play with your life again like last time." Stern silence hangs between them for a moment.

"Goddammit, William! Will you stop and listen for once! This facility is harboring unnatural means. These experiments are the foundation it seems. Just stop and think. We don't know the true purpose, but what we can do is call Adam at least. This is out of our reach," Emily shouts.

(William thinks on whether to oppose David and Emily or listen to their logic.)

(Descent Action +3) William grabs David's hand . . . David grabs Williams hand as a counter. "Last chance," David said so acutely. With every ounce of inner might, William counters hastily, twisting David's hand and arm, taking out the left leg and causing a loss of balance, and pushes him over. (David will remember this.) While rushing out the door, William closes it, locks it by lowering a lever connected to the door so they're denied an exit. William looks through the window—regrets nothing—averts his eyes from Emily's. (She will remember this.) An obvious notion about his wrathful plight against this whole ordeal at hand, Emily glares disappointingly. William sets off to finish an objective conjured in his mind: complete and utter annihilation of the wicked, retribution at its finest.

Emily walks up to David to see if he's all right. "We need to stop him before this gets worse." she says in concern for everyone's well-being. In pain, David is assisted up and says, "That's an understatement. It already has. You know him, just follow the carnage."

Quivering and full of fear, Rookie makes his slow, shuddering walk through the complex's abhorrent halls and is too scared to realize he could leave through the same window he entered through earlier with Ron and Mark. Instead, he travels through other floors while walking past the guards. They don't even take notice of him. Wondering who these people are, clear thinking's disabled due to the horrific scene which was bestowed upon him in the basement. Excessively aghast to even find a way out, a continuation to only ascend is likely as a disembodied, bellowing voice speaks to him.

Yet to cross paths with William, Emily or David, some time passes during the slow venture. On the fifth floor where Emily and David are, Rookie mutters with critical fear—hands quivering, lost within. David is trying with much effort to open the locked door—with difficulty anyways, due to its latch posing strong integrity to break or weaken from the inside. The windows are next in his attempt for freedom. David bashes it with great intensity, but no luck there either. "What can we do?!" David asks as gradual aggravation sets in from their predicament. Out of frustration, he sits down on the floor and takes a deep breath.

"Help should come soon. There's no way we're forgotten," Emily optimistically and calmly says. Rookie soon walks by. Emily notices his presence. Running to the window, she shouts at Rookie to get his attention. "Hey! Hey!" Rookie turns toward the calling, but Emily's suddenly frightened from the look on Rookie's face. Muttering to himself constantly, his words cannot be heard clearly enough. "Can you unlock the door?" She asks. Rookie returns to the door, and unlocks it by swinging the three latches upwards. Emily tries talking to Rookie, who has so strongly succumb to absolute shock that the ability to even respond properly is hard.

"He seems exceptionally traumatized. We can't take him along," David claims. Emily agrees. She tells Rookie to sit behind cover within the room and remain quiet. (Knowing Rookie's state, she knows not much can be done for him, nor can he receive any proper use currently).

Bent on a vindictive quest for retribution, and then abruptly comes across two lookouts. Peering around the corner, eyes swell with imminent death. As they near, William forcefully grabs the guard's shotgun from both hands, and nearly blows off both the guard's legs. Quickly pointing the gun in the other's face makes any more movement cease. Screams from the wounded is only attracting attention, William strikes hard with the blunt end of the shotgun, creating a knock out. Guard number 2 takes out a pistol. Before any harm arises, William quickly drops his shotgun, grabs the man's arm, breaks it, and slams the guy's head against the wall. (Descent increases +7)

William moves to another stairway. Halfway down, he perceives another set of defenders (three to be exact) walking downward as well. William shoots at the middle positioned guard with his shotgun, killing one of the three. He jumps down and ends up slamming the two outer positioned men and himself, into a wall. All three fall to the ground after. In pain from trauma, the left positioned guard pulls out a hand gun. William grasps the guard's hand, and rolls over him. Before the right positioned watchman fires, William squeezes the gun in the left guard's right hand, making it fire and killing the guard on the right. William then forcefully brings the weapon down on the man's head. The enemy tries resisting, but is shot in the process with no compunction. (Descent increases +5)

William transitions into another hallway, which is a medical wing. Three patrolmen protect a couple of rooms. They have their backs to him. William quickly devises a plan to surpass all odds in this coming moment. He quickly moves to a room near the stairwell. With quick perception, he takes a light, which he can mobilize and utilize to fit his idea. Under construction, but just his luck, a circuit breaker is present; the electricity seem to be up and running. William also notices a pile of wood stacked next to a wall near the doorway and looks above it, to the ceiling. Next, after applying the previous notion, before throwing specific light switches off, he plugs in the lamp that was acquired just seconds earlier . . . He slowly peeks around the corner to see if their positions had changed. Reading each breaker's initial point, he shuts off any to this sole hallway. The hallway, stairway corridor, but the room he's in presently is dark. Carefully moving through darkness, William places the lamp past his position. He turns it on and all three guards become blinded by it . . . perplexed. "I'll inspect it," one of the guard's says.

The guard who appointed himself walks with caution. A hand over his face is enough, to block most of the prominent brightness. Every step gives William more of a chance to completing his task. Close enough to the lamp . . . Unexpectedly to the others; the guard is pulled forward into prevailing darkness. Confused, both other sentries are motionless and silent momentarily. One shouts out, but no answer. The lamp dies out . . . their guns blaze chaotically. Lighting up the hall, flashes produced, nothing gained. The lamp's been demolished and is on the floor. Visibility returns in the wing, still no trace of their fellow guard. At any time they could've shot him from a blinded view. Checking each room—no trace of this strange happening. As they are exiting from the last checked room, subtle sounds come from a near wall. While they are occupied by their own ignorance of the whole situation, William drops down on them from above.

Guard number 2 hastily arises. Before rising fully and firing, William kicks swiftly to the gut, handles him with control, and throws him aside. Guard number 3 rises completely; William takes guard number 3's hand gun that is bolstered to the hip's right side, and punches him several times in the gut then twice to the face. Guard number

2, who's on the ground, initiates an offensive stance. An attempt to tackle William greatly misses by a large margin; as an alternative, he hits a wall and knocking himself out. Guard number 3, who's still dazed and hurt from the physical blows, attempts to grab the other hand gun that's on the floor near him. William steps on the guard's hand, glaring at him in all seriousness.

(William thinks whether to continue to kill or be remorseful.)

William swings the shotgun towards the defenseless man and aims. Any movement of sorts is concluded. Bang! The shotgun blasts the man's head into pieces. He then shoots the other unconscious guard. (Descent increases +5) William persists with his quest. On the ground, blood starts traveling outside of the wall close by, and the puddle travels slowly along the floor.

William transitions through yet another stairway. Entering the third floor, he sees three guards are present; William runs to oppose his targets. Within appropriate distance, he jumps in the air kicking at the far-right positioned guard, causing the man to plummet. William hits another in the head with the butt of the shotgun he's carrying. The third guard goes to fire, but William ducks and then runs into him, slamming him harshly over a railing that's in proximity, and tumbles down the stairs. The man William kicked readies himself and pulls out a knife. William throws his empty shotgun down, and both of them prepare to fight. Jab after slice—missing with each hit, William just flows around each attack. Soon he grabs the guard's right arm, twists it, takes the knife, beats the man with the blunt end multiple times to the face, and then shoves him to the ground.

(Before William changes to another stairway again, will taking extra ammunition be the logical choice, or will irrationality take over?)

(Special +2; whole stature changes- Ascent -1/Jester 0/Descent +3) He decides to arm his self with some ammunition, and the injured/ dead guards weapons and explosives were acquired. Vengeance will be done!

Upon opening the door and entering the stairwell, those two guards he neglected to kill appear, pointing a machine gun at William's head. The guard he did kill in the stairwell possessed it, but William had paid no attention. "Our given directions were correct. Well, quite a warrior you are. He won't be happy." Blood randomly trails from their mouths and other facial areas. William's curiosity heightens as to who their leader is; he becomes defensive by showing compassion for every person subjected to the despicable examinations. (Ascent dialogue + 1) "This is nothing but an atrocity against humanity," William says with no hesitation, masked with a strong fervor.

"No. It's going to stabilize humanity. It being limitless will cause a purpose of secured thoughts. No fears, no death, and no misery . . . only peace," the lackey says.

William remains to be convinced in any way. (Righteous dialogue +1) "I highly doubt such a ridiculous claim proposed by people condoning a despoiled concept."

"On the contrary, your irony serves you no justice," the guard exerts, insisting on defending their master's ideal. William only laughs at such a comment in return.

(Back to the wall: William thinks whether to continue talking or rid himself of these fools.)

(Descent action +5) William subtly gives partial attention to a grenade on the man's vest. "I didn't notice that before. Was that there last time?" William said to himself silently.

"Killing our brothers in arms and ceasing this grand operation to pacify the world . . . too much for one to even comprehend." The oppressor's righteous speech lingers . . . Quickly thinking, William moves the guard's gun from being pointed at. In succession, he punches to his right against the second guard, hitting him in the throat, and then pulls the pin from the grenade. William rushes the initial verbal provocateur that stands in front of him, forcing him to topple over. William quickly rolls to recover and then lunges into a nearby room. BOOM!!! The grenade explodes, flesh scatters; smoke covers with great measure. Yet to clear, William moves on anyways.

Reaching the second floor, he enters another hall way, which leads to a room farther ahead. "What madness built this vicarious labyrinth of nightmares?" A quick look behind to secure his thoughts of being followed, and then he stops to take a breather. A moment later, he raises his head to eventually see a mob of patrolmen further past him, gathering in numbers. Calming himself down, heavy breathing discontinues quickly, only to be startled by greater numbers awaiting him. (Also, this area he's presently in is also under construction. Planks, metal beams, wood beams, and tools are against both sides of the passage.) Two largely proportioned men slightly move away from each other to reveal another person behind them. Unable to make out what this person's layout is so clearly William can only wait for what's coming next.

"It's like a magnificent fable. Retaliation for his family—the ones who captured or killed get the pointed end of the sword, as the tale goes. So this is who wreaks havoc in my palace?" Staying strong in this growing moment, William's stands autonomously while opposing the foe, and seconds later, he says, "You invent these experiments? They give purpose to . . . what? I wouldn't call this proper or sane!"

This mysterious figure is amused by William's words. "To understand is to know, but to presume guarantees ignorance with repercussions."

(Ascent dialogue +2) William opposes these words of wisdom. "You assume responsibility and with a cause to 'better' humanity when this clearly defines manipulation! I don't assume . . . More like a gut feeling! Unable to comprehend complete knowledge to know what is erroneous doesn't make me any less keen to your own methods."

The mysterious man dwells in thought for a short time before responding. "Oh? Eyes only limit the person. A man to stand his ground even when all odds are against him, foolishly done over many millennia, but still admirable, and I guess I could say respectful at most. Answers you seek to only be returned with emptiness."

William grins, and defensively says (Ascent +1), "I sometimes let faith guide me in hoping I find those answers. I've come pretty damn close! And FYI, don't ever prefer the odds are against me. I'm just as much an anomaly as you are."

Benevolent words are hard to agree with, and acceptance is unable to happen. "What has that done for you? A trail of death, loved ones lost, growing misery of yours, everyone's everlasting wake." A moment of tension comes around. "Well, meet Gadreel and Arakiel the corrupted. Don't worry; they're within your limitations as a human. For now . . ." This mysterious man backs away, disappearing behind the group. A circle forms around William, implying some sort of physical altercation. Both outlandishly larger men walk to the epicenter, readying themselves to initiate a fight. While meeting his opponents simultaneously, each giant charges. Close enough, they concurrently grab and throw William many feet away. He hits the ground hard afterward . . . William speedily recovers and prepares himself again.

One gestures to the other to offer more afflictions, and William walks forward too. A massive swing let's forth, but William dodges and savagely kicks Gadreel in the back of his left knee and forces him to collapse on it. William pats him on the head while saying, "Be a good boy and stay down." Arakiel moves forward to perform a tackle, but William side steps to the right. "Be more tactical." he says with confidence.

One guard lobs in two, two-by-fours into the ring. Each behemoth obtains one each. They walk up to William and begin another offensive. One high and one low, William dodges both attacks. One goes to vertically strike. William hops backward and the hit misses, but runs up the three-by-four to hit Gadreel's face with a powerful right knee. Stumbling from the blow, Arakiel approaches from behind, swinging at William, and knocking him out of the air. As he plummets to the ground, Gadreel, who was kneed in the face, just shakes off the pain, and continues the physical onslaught. Arakiel picks up William by the left arm. Gadreel begins pummeling him like a piñata, repeatedly.

After several contacted strikes, adrenaline kicks in further. "Harder! Beat me senseless! Leave trivial remnants behind to rejoice in!" William vehemently says. Grabbing the three-by-four, William whacks Arakiel in the crotch with his foot. Released . . . As Arakiel is bent over, Gadreel goes to bash William again, but William attempts to forcefully acquire the piece of wood. Gadreel releases his grip and tries apprehending William, but he fails. William dodges and counters . . . Whack! As Gadreel's legs are smashed with great incandescence, each shin bone is shattered, and it is heard loudly. The two-by-four is in pieces, fragments scattered on the floor. This hulk of a man drops, concurrently yelling from the physical affliction.

Arakiel rushes forward, jabbing the end of the three-by-four into Williams back, stunning him as he plunges to the floor and slides a couple of feet. William tries getting up, slowly ascending back to a standing posture. "You can do better than an easy shot. Come on." William runs . . . prepares to attack . . . The grasped three-by-four is dropped instead. They almost make contact: Arakiel goes to grab William, but William ducks, spins, and moves to the hind side of the enemy. William tackles him, incapacitating both legs from behind, and making Arakiel collapse from a swift impact. Arakiel turns to grab William, but William grabs the left arm, positioning in an arm bar, and making Arakiel fall on his back. Pulling with all strength one can muster . . . Snap! An unpleasant sound is heard by all when Arakiel's arm is bent the opposite way. Trying to gain a hold again, William moves dexterously, heading to the other arm. Arakiel moves to his left side, but William utilizes his right foot to transition Arakiel facedown, steps on his right elbow, pulling and pulling . . . Snap! William remains silent through a grandiose victory. Gadreel lies below quiet and silently filled with rage.

Grand confidence is expressed from battling. In a 360 radius, William is surrounded still. (Menacing dialogue +3) "Are we finished? Two against one with a largely sized differentiation and fifteen more to go won't make any difference to me!" Silence still lingers. William continues to angrily scrutinize every guard. "You're fortified around me. These giants have fallen. This was supposed to intimidate me?! Show me your strength!" Two guards open up the circle. William turns to see an opening, and they gesture his departure by letting him go. William is consciously aware of this test and progresses past the group.

David and Emily aren't sure how they're going through so easily. Among their movements, both notice trails of blood and death strewn throughout. Easily figuring that William has been here, both think the worst. "What has he done?" Emily says in sheer distress.

"I hope he's satisfied," David says unhappily.

William closes in on the first floor. Running through his mind screams justification. Chaos is developing, swelling as a vindictive motivation. The final door to his freedom from this war zone is at hand. Sedation closes in after every confrontation, but an end to the notion arrives as William is halted by a clothed being in a black, red and white outfit. It looks to be a light fitting. This new opponent seems to be nimble, quick and deceptive. William decides to make a sharp comment about this new foe. (Jester +1) "Ah, an assassin I am to meet, how clichéd. A battle's to occur with absolute prowess to display. Are you to fulfill the whim of death?" The shadowy individual turns around, and then slides a sheathed samurai sword on the floor to William. Confused and unsure, William picks it up anyway.

Before William's erects his body upward fully, this random challenger closes in quickly and begins to strike. The sheath flies off William's sword. Blades clash, sparks flying, loud clings from swift impacts; every intention from this foe is ever so clear. William tries to keep up with this sword base style of fighting. Some movements are too fast, elusive. High hits, low hits, mid strikes. It's all complex. After a while, his adversary backs up and bows to William for his reactions, especially to his resilience for survival. Heavy breathing from the action at hand, William is cautious over the whole polite gesture. The battle commences, and it's fantastic!

Emily and David reach the second floor. David slowly creeps to the door's window to convey visually beyond it. "There has to be two dozen of them. This is grim." Emily also sees the horde of guards standing along the walls. "You think he got past them?" Before an idea was construed, the figure William met appears out of a black mist. As the figure stands near Arakiel and Gadreel, he places his hand out, and something bizarre happens. A strange white energy comes from the two men as they yell in pain. The unknown figure and the guards start to evaporate into dust. Much to their amazement and curiosity, they have no words. David slowly opens the door. The room is silent. "You have any tantalizing ideas? What in the fuck just happened?" David asks Emily. She shakes her head no, which expresses her ignorance and bewilderment. The previous scene ceases their grasp of reality.

Moving to the first floor, they enter the hallway and pass by the room where William's currently. Noises are heard coming from inside. "Hold on," Emily says as she hurriedly moves toward it with suspicion. Two knives blow through the door, passing by Emily's and David's face, ricocheting off the wall behind them. "Shit! Too damn close there," David says. Opening the door, Emily and David watch helplessly from the doorway. Deciding to find some way to help, they try to come up with a plan. Obviously, they can help battle with William against this unknown fighter. This new situation is nearly unknown in every aspect why William's fighting another with swords. Sairentoookami (Silent Wolf) takes notice of Emily and David's presence. William's too blinded by his quest and doesn't notice them himself just yet.

Change of mind: both enter and engage in battle. David takes the right and Emily takes the left. Opposition takes notice and readies for a three-versus-one confrontation. William still ignores the fact that his best friends are here to help. Silent Wolf looks left to right, back and forth with both eyes, ready to react at any moment. David tries to wrap his arms around the enemy but is kicked in the abdomen, knocking the wind out of him. Emily kicks at the left leg, but is countered and tripped. David suddenly wraps his arms around the foe from behind and bends backward to slam harshly. Rolling away after David's attack, the enemy rises quickly and is rushed into by William from the side. Before William and Sairentoookami fall over, a grenade is thrown on the ground, and a cloud of smoke arises.

Perception is diminished . . . Emily is punched in the face twice. David's hit four times in the abdomen, then tripped. William's hit three times to the face, twice to the left side of his torso, and then to the left side of his jaw. Silence covers the area as the smoke slowly drifts away. "Enough of your tricks fight me properly!" William shouted. The enemy appears behind William, but then swiftly pierces the blade through his back's left side and through the left pectoral.

(Descent action +5) Turning quickly causes his foe to lose grasp of the sword's hilt; William's face is covered with rage. Sairentoookami becomes disarrayed from the reaction. William drops his own weapon and confronts the assassin immediately. "To trounce me that easily, a weak attempt at best." William forcefully places both hands around his opponent's throat. Many attempts for a release by hitting or rendering William's grasp multiple times incur no damage or fazed reactions. William pulls him closer to the blade, penetrating from his body. A sadistic method produces. "Let's begin," A gesture for mercy, none is given to nor any remorse against ceasing the intentional suffocation. Forced to his knees, William squeezes tighter and pulls him closer to the blade. Rage overflows the single aggressive intention. Centimeters away from puncturing an eye . . . "My family kidnapped, tested on like rats. You leave a man with no choice. What am I to do but fight back? Yes. Feel my everlasting wrath!"

Emily shouts from afar, trying to reason with William by saying, "You've done enough! More bloodshed will not—it'll never solve any of your problems!"

(In this moment, William could listen to Emily and accept what she says, or he can continue with his vengeance.)

Weakness slowly approaches from blood loss.

(Bitter dialogue +3) William is still as enraged. "To be a part of such an evil, to know what somebody can really do. You bring force to an opposing side, and it will bring back much pain tenfold! My vengeance will never be complete while I breathe life into this body!

William thinks to himself, *"One life to save many. I'd rather save them all. He didn't have to die."*

Bang! Bang! Bang! Crash!

The supposed aid barges in through the doors from the left, aware and with guns ready. Upon their revelation: "We've spotted them Chief. They're OK. William is in rough shape though. There's also a casualty," one of the officer's says. Swat teams venture inside to each floor. Inspector Cohan enters, gun raised. A couple officers help William outside to an ambulance already at hand, and he is taken to it. Seventeen minutes later, the trio spot Rookie exiting with another officer. Observations clearly prove an abundance of fear is written over his face completely. He is still mumbling to himself incoherently.

David asks Cohan, who is walking Rookie over to the ambulance, if he's going to be fine. "He's going to. Just rattled it seems. That's all. We'll make sure he makes a full recovery. Good thing we were contacted. You know, it took us twenty minutes to open that door. Nearly rusted, it should have only been done with one swing. If you were in there, how come you didn't hear us?" Cohan replies.

"Good question. We didn't," David says as he pats Rookie on the back when walking by. "How'd he manage to reach you?" David asks.

"Very little to none was said in detail, just 'Help' was said. He reached us through his phone. We located his coordinates and followed. The other two were unconscious when we arrived—Don and Bobby, who were in the van out front. They're all right at least," Cohan says.

(Expectations for William's actions, Emily and David's feedback are clear-cut. In doing so, William's Descent increases +10, but for that moment with Sairentoookami, Ascent increases +5.)

"I don't know how an explanation is going to be possible. Disbelief courses through me because of such a commitment. An impetuous act was made," Emily says worriedly.

"He won't. He can't. This goes against so many morals and ethics. What only resides next to him that's worse than his decision is the implication that will be applied as well," David says with certain doubt for any coming amnesty. A medic team exits, carrying William on a stretcher, and then they load him through the rear of the ambulance. David and Emily walk over, get in the back, and are driven to the hospital. (Emily and David will remember this.) "We have two bodies down here. You're not going to like this. It's a mess. Oh, God . . ." an officer says over the radio to Cohan.

SWAT members still travel in and out of the complex. All floors above the basement are thoroughly checked; no other bodies or any personnel are found yet. A continuation with finding any evidence besides the dead bodies and innocence is consistent, except for every single machine that had numbers of people connected to them. As this mysterious man proposed to William, that promise was kept: every person that was experimented on was freed from the tests alive, but also with one warning untold. They're unconscious. A couple SWAT members walk along the hall possessing that monitor console that William last used to inaugurate his faulty gambit. All screens are off. One checks every room; the other makes headway. Small whispers occur. The officer hears the shadowy murmurs and concentrates on the large console; one screen turns on, and to his surprise . . . grotesque scenes appear. The screen turns off after several seconds, and a USB stick pops out. In possession, he heads back to his partner.

"Willing to open strange doors for answers long sought. Comes to finding an answer but not of what you wanted. A choice made—sacrifice is needed, commitment obliged. Is it worth the absolute risk? You make the decision."

Interlude 3

(Mortal Interest)

Surreptitious Reparation

Appearing in surrounding nothingness, a flame portal opens and quickly dissipates. In a kneeling position, then stands and remains quiet. Humming is progressively increasing. Silence then takes abrupt significance . . . An explosion ensues. Fiery walls appear all around, heat that burns hotter than the sun. Whispers are strewn throughout its inferno. Demonic roaring occurs; decibels rise uncomfortably. Fright sets in. "You already know?" Grunting in response to the mysterious man's words, a calm, disembodied voice says, "Now we know, consciously, who our threat is in this whole feud. Inevitability will not take place. I assume you have improved procedures to make up for what's lost?" Nodding yes, and says, "I do. We shouldn't approach this in a typical style. It should be predictable yet not predictable but possible." No response, he continues to elaborate . . . "I'll just show you. It'll make more sense." A random, extraordinary pressure pushes on the mysterious man, forcing him on both knees. Resistance is futile. "If you must . . . I warn you: years with our reasons, years of our existence has become lessening. No one listens but to whom resides above. Revel in sin and never betray given power. With vicious incomparability, I'll see to it myself, if need be."

Total nothingness surrounds one entity. A notion developed for William: perceived design—two faced and wicked, heartache with despondency.

A fiery vortex swirls, and the mystery man disappears.

Chapter 5

Repent

Thou Shall Not Kill

> My vengeance: a performance of revenge caused by another, bringing one to a level of insanity and blindness; or rage by one's ignorance or knowledge of the current or past circumstance(s) promising a lead to (a) worse or (a) better scenario(s).

Anything can push a man to certain extremes. Only the bearer can be compelled to go beyond the boundaries of sanity. Is it because leaving a man void of choice? Or is it not? Only the person behind the mask of wrath can convey such a question. Therefore, leaves others in question for his/her motive(s) and the execution of such (an) act(s).

Sirens blare, warning others to step aside; wheels spin rapidly to accomplish a mission, prioritizing its goal to higher medical needs. Everyone in back remains quiet during the venture. David stares out of the back doors' windows, and Emily stares at William with a rightful reason for frustration. William gazes upward, even though she can be seen staring continuously by viewing through peripheral vision. A blank look covers William's face. No remorse, no care, only vengeance. What he thinks absolutely pure and justified is not what everyone else agrees with or believes. Their ride takes fourteen minutes, but Emily's glare starts to make William reflect on his actions. Knowing she's not taking it lightly, principally for reasons well known. They now arrive at the hospital. Coming to a stop in front, a couple doctors and nurses wait outside; doors open fast, and medics take William out then into the hospital. Emily and David follow. Arriving quickly, a handful of medical personnel speedily join inside. William is escorted to an OR.

David and Emily momentarily arrive inside the main lobby and search for a seat. Their silence dwells with many thoughts. A long waiting period of two hours goes by. Dr. Blaine appears casually through two doors. "Is there any who are waiting for a William Aletheo?" Indicating a reaction from the two, Blaine approaches Emily and David. "He's fortunate that the blade didn't penetrate a major artery as in the left pulmonary. We had to give him a blood transfusion because of the severe blood loss. Quite fortunate we had some in store with a matching type; his is rare, AB-. We also checked to see if he suffered any blunt force trauma, any other internal bleeding, also in addition with any other abnormalities, but nothing more than minor mostly. Your line of work—whatever you do seems immensely dangerous. Just be careful now. You never know . . . You may go see him if you like, but he's asleep from the anesthesia. He'll need his rest for a while." Emily and David both agree to see him.

Upon entering, their eyes want to perceive his wrongdoing, actions, and injuries which have placed him in a regrettable circumstance. David approaches William to comfort him with kind words. "Just glad you're OK. Knowing we all made it— well . . . most of us, I mean. We have yet to hear anything about Mark or Ron. Don't take your fortune for granted." David looks over at Emily; her face expresses anger. "We'll leave you to get your rest," David concludes, and then departs from William's presence; both he and Emily leave in unison. William lies alone and stationary with his injuries, a costly action that circumvented death.

06/30/2028

Five days later

The doctor leaves with William to the waiting room. "Please stay safe, young man. Be well. You'll be seeing me a few more times this year just for checkups; I'll receive updates from your therapy sessions as well," Blaine kindly says before leaving. David moves in front of William. "You're looking no worse for wear. Bet you're thrilled to return." Emily stands up quickly and approaches the duo. Unable to uphold anymore patience, she punches William in his face, and starts pushing him while exerting built up irritation with excessively grown pain inside. Other visitors watch in shock. David then grabs her and is restrained from furthering her physical contact against William. "Let me get this straight: you have this untouchable, desirable mental state which comforts you?! Running off on a quest to brutally redeem your family's lives, nearly getting yourself killed! Every second we're thinking with a high probability that you're dead. Come to find out you almost had achieved that!" William holds his face where her fist impacted. Emily's eyes tear up. "Seriously, what formulates in your head? Acts of so-called heroism, grotesque executions, and, foremost, acting blindly. Don't you ever think?! Answer me, you bastard!" Emily shakes David off and then gets in William's face. Tears run down, a beautiful face constrained to growing sorrow. In conclusion to her personally verbal application, she pushes her way through William, hitting his injury.

He leans slightly forward from the impact of her harmful action. "She's right, though. You had us both in distress. Huh . . . The whole time—" Cutting this speech short, David places his hand on William's back. They both leave from the hospital subsequently. Mixed emotions stir during the car ride. (Ascent action: +2) William turns around to say something, but Emily turns her head, implying having no interest in talking. William is observant of her posture.

Back at the precinct, Emily stays in the car while David and William walk inside. Strolling through the lobby, then the corridor of offices, total quietness spreads wholly; everyone awkwardly averts all eyes from them. The atmosphere brings certain notification of their acknowledged initiative from earlier days. "Don't mind them," David says to William. Ronald exits his office, stops, looks at William, and walks on by. William and David enter into their actual Chief of Police's office. Before they sit, Adam sits on a black comfy chair in such a manner of disbelief and undeniable vexation. "Don't sit down. Stand . . ." David wonders how serious the implications will be. William doesn't really take consideration of this whole situation, nonetheless intimidating at all and rolls his eyes. They all know what's coming... "Reckless abandon is your game?" Adam spoke seriously in combination with a stern look at William. Persistent with assertion, Adam continues . . . "This should be the ultimate strike against you. E pluribus unum! An absolute reason to sever ties permanently. This sure as hell isn't the first time. Nevertheless, the last it will be. For some reason, we keep you . . . *sigh* our real point being here is you initiated a mission without my acknowledgment— assuming you could play the protagonist, huh? You put my people through danger; some are deceased because of it."

William becomes astonished from the word deceased. "Assuming I wouldn't find out—thinking you'd get away with this misconduct and arrogance of yours. Such defiance against upholding the law is immensely frowned upon. What were you hoping to accomplish?" (William's actions were obviously noticed.)

William's attitude changes and he averts his eyes down in shame from the truthful words. "What were to happen if everyone had died because of your haughtiness? Leading everyone to certain doom, an act of ignorance. Was this your idea alone, or did other accomplices abide with your proposal? Another could be in this . . . very room . . . right next to you." Purposely averts all attention to David. Surprised in return, David looks at Adam with astonishment. (Roger: a.k.a Chief) who's standing next to the real Chief of Police (Adam) looks down, but thus train his attention on William.

Still, William is conscience-stricken; soon speaks up in one's own defense after taking time to mentally reconcile logically. "I'm . . . I . . ." William takes another breath.

(William ponders whether to proceed defiantly or act reasonable to Adam's reaction.)

Cloud coverage thickens the sky and the office becomes mostly dim, as if the light on William's face puts him in the spotlight. All others slightly fade in the background and witness. "I have no legitimate excuse for my acts of defiance against the law and order of your precinct, or extramural. I've realized all efforts were implausible in every fashion possible, possessing absolutely no excuse as to why I started a quest of vengeance. But trying to maintain my sanity through it was absent. I have performed irrationally as much as foolishly; with admittance of my fault with other misconducts that were performed before you along with the whole agency. I am eternally apologizing to embarrass, create negligence, spark complicity, defy order, show disloyalty, and for everyone here to witness treachery. Their deaths—and there's nothing that can be said nor is there anything to redeem myself for those undertakings. Ultimately and alone, nothing will come to be so easily rectifiable. Might never at all . . . Atonement for any sins would be an insult to everyone." (Ascent dialogue +5)

The clouds slowly part and light resumes shining in again. David feels awful; he doesn't know what to say. Roger looks at William with guilt as every ounce of blame is absorbed, and not informing Adam that Roger himself had this whole idea made up to begin with. As William finishes his mitigation, Adam nods in agreement to what was said. "I believe you." William reveals an incredulous reaction from Adam's remark. "I respect that you accept your own faults and acknowledge our good men and women unselfishly. Honestly, I expected a different story from you. At least you still have your honor intact, I'll give you that. Your words come indistinct from many. That has worth, intangible value. Knowing what you're capable of, I am proud to say we are exceptionally grateful to have you." William is thunderstruck further from these words of compassion but expected more of a beat down by verbal abuse. Instead, in a way, praised. Roger smiles at William. David's relieved it came to a more peaceful conclusion. "May I have a moment with just us two, please?" Adam asks David and Roger to leave. David passes by William and puts his hand on William's shoulder; Roger does as well. (David and Roger will remember this.)

The door shuts. "I have here a piece of evidence that could totally destroy your reputation as an officer, and your life." Adam turns his computer's monitor on . . . He moves the mouse cursor to a file that resides in another. A video emerges and plays. Adam skips to the important parts to make a point with this chilling proof. Through different intervals of its records, no ounce of proof is acceptable to William. "This is what I wanted to show you." Seconds after the scene was shown, Adam stops it suddenly. The paused screen shows William standing over Rookie with blood spattered all over himself: rage, terror and gore. William looks up at Adam and leans back in his chair slowly. "You know I would never. This can't be real. Emily and David can vouch for me with much conviction of our method, and as our teams separated to cover more ground, we went separate ways. Our group—I never made it to the basement. No . . ." Both hands position on his head from disturbance and own confusion. He rubs his face slowly to relieve some tension then drops both hands back down.

(William has a couple ideas to this "evidence" against him, but decides quickly.)

"It's unfortunate to have been found with full sanction," Adam states.

William hurriedly stands to his feet. "The only blood on my hands was of those sickening associates. Your discovery is nothing but a fabrication to mend what was lost. All else who convoyed with me would say the same. What about my sister? She was forced with those preposterous methods as well. My parents could have been exposed too." (Adam takes notice of this)

"I have yet to receive any information on her whereabouts. It's been some time, and I know you're concerned. When I do, I'll transfer all acknowledgments to you personally. Fortuitously, hopefully not, you'll have to go before a judge at some time, assuming if it fell into someone else's hands . . . And I do wish you luck if it comes to exist. We'll all be present. But luckily, no one will see this except who had sent it to me and my own self too. I'll go over it in the meantime, personally," Adam proclaims. William is quietly aggravated but shows an understanding as well. "I know there isn't going to be room to slide so easily if this comes to be true. Justice must be served, in some way, no matter by whom. There's a contradiction to what I said, but I hope you understand as well? Who knows when they'll summon you? It could be a day or weeks from that time. I might change my mind. To add one final part: you're going to be taking a break for a while. I'll call you when you're able to return. What I'd be worried about is them incriminating you thoroughly with what they'll find. That's about it. Then again, all will point against you. Otherwise, you did do your job. It wasn't correct, but it got done. The maneuver wasn't needed, albeit a lot of lives were saved. Reports came in saying nearly every person that was found connected to those machines for experimentation are well enough . . . unconscious still, but alive," Adam says.

William finds comfort knowing most who were constrained to the experiments are alive.

"I'm glad, relieved. At least the bargain was made," he says.

Adam, confused, focuses his attention on William and says, "Excuse me?"

"I'm just exhausted," William quickly exerts.

"Yes. The fact is your feat precedes all repercussions, and they will have an encounter with equal measures. Not to kill you, mind you," Adam concludes.

"I understand," William says, and makes an exodus.

"Before you go, could I get some actual insight?" Adam inquires. William turns his head to the right, which indicates minimal fears, expelling great verity. Turning fully, William locks eyes with Adam, a still fixation, but emotionless. "By your reaction, it seems you're apprehensive. Is there something that's direr than what had happened?" Adam questions William.

(Aggressive assertion +3) "No. Watching that fallacy you call evidence really debases my mind. A specific mental capacity seeks what's justified, and what I fought were humans: humans that committed to unfathomable measures. With no doubts, all intentions were condemnable to most, but to me it was justification through retribution. To validate your first question: yes, you can. Have you ever had a time in your life or just a moment you thought complicit and made amends, even if it went against what you believe? That was my moment."

"I can't say I have, because my timeline never lavished an exultant event for me. To an extent, your words have covered a majority of my questions, though not entirely. Why the recklessness? Adam says.

William's eyes avert to the left, away from Adam. (Descent +1) "I don't know if I have an exact solution. Maybe one will conjure itself at a later time, or I have already answered your queries, but with great ignorance, you find it difficult to understand." William exerts forthrightly and then looks back at Adam.

Adam nods his head slightly up and down a few times. Grabbing the USB stick from the computer, he keeps his elbow on the desks' surface, and then lifts his forearm and hand, up a couple inches from the desk. "Somewhere in your vocal exertions, I guess I do. Sensing no intentions of randomness or blatancy, I've come to deduce your logic to gain 'justification through retribution' weren't from evil motivations. However, of some form of righteousness instead. The human race—what I've studied or seen over the years, no one has seen anything of this nature. Personally, not all blame would be placed on your exertions by me. You saved those people, and they gain a second chance at living. Note has been taken for your bravery. Don't get cocky over what I've said, or over your sheer luck." Adam returns the USB stick to his desk and relaxes. "You think this incriminating evidence is a fallacy? You believe someone tampered with it? Almost makes you think we have a rat in our own ranks."

"You never know. I wouldn't be surprised. Then again, look at what were up against. Now it happens. Of all people . . . me, the one who came as a blessed hero to save the innocents," William replies glibly and jokingly.

William accepts what Adam has spoken; it may have caused an impact upon William and changed his perspective. Truthfully, that's up to him to endeavor upon the logic of options and consequences. "I hear you loud and clear. Thank you," William says. He turns back around to face the door, and bewilderment runs across his face. He opens the door, exits the office, and closes the door shortly after. Adam gazes at the USB stick, contemplates, and integrates it with the computer to review its contents.

Through the precinct's main hall, William exits to his car soon after. Before fully exiting, David stands up from a chair and approaches William. "What's the word?" William takes a moment before he replies. "I'm being forced to take some time off," he says contently.

"Trust me. You need it," David speaks, offering reassurance.

"Apparently, there was a video found showing myself murdering our fellow officers. It was showing my location in the basement. I never made it there. Plus, you two found me on the first floor fighting an assassin." (David becomes worried.)

Upset from hearing this news, David then replies with a worried tone. "They never made it out of the basement? That's interesting. That is true, but there was nothing left by our unknown foe! Dammit. We were separated for a while. What am I saying? They'll be forceful. I know what you did won't be taken lightly, but at least you'll be honest about it, in hoping. I don't believe you did because you couldn't have. You're not that crazy, right? Even though you did go rampant, I wouldn't believe that visual farce of corroboration if I saw it. I bet it's just a bold move on our unknown enemy's part. I know you didn't care for that arrogant son of a bitch, but kill him? No. Anyways, what're you going to do in the meantime? How long will you be off duty?"

William responds quickly. "Adam said he'll call me. To really know the exact concepts' integrity, I'm not sure. My objective: I'm going to try escaping reality. I'll see you later," William vaguely concludes to depart from David's presence.

William departs from his duties. As he walks down a flight of stairs leading from the precinct's entrance, Emily is positioned parallel to William farther down, viewing the horizon afar. He stops up next to her. She remains silent—arms wrapped around her sides, projecting a stance of discontent. William realizes she remains irritated from earlier; among the discernment, he remembers being hit and yelled at plentifully.

(William ponders whether to be thankful or to be upset as well.)

Choosing to be thankful, he creates an admission of guilt. "I don't deserve your apology. You're upset, which is obvious, made me think how much you foster for my well-being. I admire your fervor. Forgiveness isn't going to be enough for me to resurrect my welfare... my status as well. I am willing to pay for obvious wrongs, which I'll then wait for fairness to take a foot-hold on my life. On another note: a strong demand to go on a mandatory leave of absence was declared by our Chief. So you know." (Ascent +2) (She'll remember this.) Still no response though. Emily watches him leave her presence and head toward his car, but turns her head, trying to consolidate her feelings and convictions about William through her frustrations. Emily takes her leave, ascends the staircase with arms crossed, and soon enters the facility; William observes unflinchingly as a good friend disappears into the precinct. He shamefully drives off after a moment of contemplation.

"Anyone can be forgiven. Forgiveness is shrouded with mercy. Any performance will have a side effect: either against you, another, or both. Would you accept it? Would you need it? Shame is a beautiful process. You can always prove your better person's existence at anytime. Self-integrity is always note worthy and respectable."

First Fragment: an Ode to (In)justice and Fear

This isn't the first time William has attained retribution on his own. Let's go back eleventh years, twelfth grade: when high school was a relevant time. A Thursday afternoon, all kids travel to their next class. Emily passes alone amid a large crowd of people. Books concealed in a backpack, but too full. She wears a regular clothing style: jeans, white T-shirt, and her blonde hair hangs freely. From the crowd pops out a kid named Tyler. He gently constrains her up against the lockers, inconspicuous to others of initial plans that revel in deceit. Uncomfortable, annoyed, vulnerable . . . Emily keeps her gaze on him. "So what is your problem? Why do you ignore me? I hate doing this."

    "Then why do it?" Emily interjects.
Shall we recollect our meetings on June 23rd last year? I wonder who you told . . . because if you did, I'd have to . . ." Tyler said. Emily's face expresses disgust but with a hint of courage. "You're so cliché. It's sad, really. You know it would be easier if you could just take a hint and walk away. We could just live our lives. Though, you prefer to bother one person out of 100's here. There are others you can pester, you know," Emily spoke forthright.

"How long must I wait for your answer?" Tyler says with impatience. Silence still lingers. She transitions her eyes to the right, then back at his.

Tyler smashes his fist against the locker, inches away from her face, and Emily quickly nudges her head away from it. Tyler grins from assuming nervousness and uses it to his advantage. Multiple students look over at the scene. Seeing that attention is acquired, a rowdier route is taken. Some start to stop and surround them. "It's been almost a year. Yet you still ignore me!" Some laugh, and some try to stop this nonsense. William is in a class room, a couple rooms down. Hearing the commotion, loud enough to be honest, he goes out to see what's happening. The view past other people is agitating enough. Moving through the crowd slowly, he shifts some aside to get through; and it becomes apparent, slowly but surely, increasing total comprehension.

"Always hiding . . . What the fuck is your problem?!" William stops behind Tyler now. Ready to end this mess, William is presented by Tyler's friend. Turning around, face to face now, Tyler says, "Can I assist your nosy achievement?" William responds defensively: "What is the problem? And why cause so much fright?" Tyler scoffs at both questions, and throws his fist hastily at William. Unflinching . . . unmovable by a useless tactic to be graced with a fake punch, a fist lies a couple centimeters from William's face. Tyler laughs at him, but no effect was met with satisfaction for the opposing persons'. Looking to the left, he sees a couple teachers come forth with the principal. Tyler moves backward a couple steps. William remains unmoved. Emily looks at William and smiles. "What's going on here gentlemen? I heard about you Tyler—that you were engaging in a threatening manner against Emily here." Aggravation exudes from Principal Stather's intervention. Tyler keeps quiet. "William. Emily. You both may go. Mr. Aluunci and I are going to have a nice chat. Everyone, please return to your normal schedules! This is over now!"

William turns to Emily and says, "How are you doing?"

She nods her head, to then reply, "I'll be all right. No worse for wear from a Neanderthal like him. About time he gets a lesson in humiliation."

William chuckles at the retort. "And next is punishment," William says. Both watch as Tyler is escorted with a shameful posture to the principal's office together with Stathers. "If you're wondering why I was down this way, it was for reasons to speak with you. Guess not, now. I better get going. Thanks again. I'll talk to you later today?"

"Yes," William replies. Emily makes her leave to get to class; William does the same.

3:00 p.m.

School lets out. After retrieving what he needs from his locker, William walks to the front of the school and waits. Five minutes later, Tyler and his two friends walk out while laughing about God knows what. Within a safe distance, a pursuit is initiated. Both friends part ways down another road; Tyler goes down another. A couple blocks from the school, a scarce amount of people. William waits for Tyler to turn the corner. Pursuit continues. No sight is apparent from other eyes while this stalking method commences. Premeditated motives come about inwardly as every second comes and goes. Standing at another corner, complete observation is imminent as Tyler enters his own house. William remembers the house and the street.

'Ring ring' "Hey." On the other end is Emily. "So what's up?"

Scoping out the area, he then turns around and begins to walk home. "Oh . . . just obtaining a better idea of my down time for tonight."

A sunny day with a slight breeze; the wind blows through the trees making the leaves sing. "What would that be?" Emily asks with interest.

"To clarify my true feelings of free time on how it's justified by a hard days' work." Cars pass by. Winds forced from their high speeds. Birds fly in different directions, chirping sounds from lively existence.

"Sounds tantalizing . . . Go hang out with some friends. There are others you know, distinct people. Ahem. Hi!" Emily states the obvious.
William smiles at the thought. "How about we get together this weekend?"

Emily sighs quietly, and then says, "All right, all right. I see how it is, friend I knew since kindergarten. I'll just do my homework alone."

William bows his head, and then lifts it back up with a smile. "Acknowledged. I get the idea. There's too much inner conflict now, and I've been flustered for the past couple days. Nothing personal against you, I'm mostly just troubled by something."

"I'm sure I can help?" Emily claims.

"I know you could," William says. (Emily takes notice of that.) "An aspiration for myself, I feel. I'm so close, though. I know it, a revelation in time."

Emily really wishes William would relax; she understands his plea. "Well, you know where I am. I hope the best on your journey. Tomorrow's another day."

William is now four blocks away from his own house. "Yes, until then." Emily hangs up. William puts down his phone and looks at it. Call ended. "That's a stapled moment that'll stay in her mind. I'll make it up to her. Somehow . . ." William finishes his trek back home.

Four steps up, a chair sits at the right end of the porch. An unending gaze into all the beauty of life's offer: deep concentration, thoughts reflecting sinister entrapments. To escape certain pain... No good. Deep breaths relieve some tension. William's sister, Sarah, walks out the front door. She stands nearby. "I'm glad that mess at school was over. Hopefully, he'll leave your girlfriend alone."

"We're friends. It was time for him to understand his indecent ways. He always had a 'thing' for her, but it was mostly to trifle against others because he's too insecure. Could have wanted someone to be with or to talk to? I don't know. Seems there's more to it. He falls under the trap of good looks, and true value isn't seen for whom people really are." William says.

(Sarah takes notice of that) Impressed by his words, she somewhat agrees. "That might actually be true. Then again, he seems hopeless to me."

Appalled by her second sentence, William makes a riposte. "How could you say that? No one is hopeless. There's always some amount existing, but at times people just need guidance or some just require it." (She will remember that.)

Sarah questions William by saying, "You're so confident—why don't you, then?"

William has had enough of her negativity for now. "Why did you really come out here?" he asks.

She grabs another chair and places it next to him; she rests upon it and answers his question. "A reason, supposedly—an excellent reason to push me to the reality of no communication between you and me for almost a year now. A boy comes home in silence, no acknowledgment of his family, quiet through the day and night like shadows on a surface." A truth well said, but he has too many issues to come out with broad confessions, just yet.

"Possibly it's more complicated than I or you think. Too excruciating to the point where it exists in dormancy. Slumbering till what might awaken my ability to speak." (She takes notice of that.)

A little spooked by his dark tone, Sarah shows compassion for his misery. "That's enough for me to know my own brother is suffering not from others but from himself. There's no one else on this planet, excluding Mom and Dad, who knows you best. You know that. Come here." William grunts at her. Sarah leans over and tries pulling him up. Assisting her with her action, he also arises. She hugs him tightly and he hugs her back. A moment to realize she's right: finding stability where no order would be present in.

"Let's go inside. It was nice to talk to you again," Sarah says. Both walk in, and Sarah fastens the door. Later, at 5:30 PM: Dante, William, Sarah, Rathekel, and Celestine sit in an orderly fashion at the table. Food is passed around respectfully. "I came upon some info that you got promoted to the leadership position in your "News for You" group in school," Celestine says happily.

"I was going to say that," Sarah says in disappointment.
"Sorry. I saw the letter. I couldn't resist," Celestine says in excitement.

After Dante finishes devouring his food, he readily expresses his thoughts that evince his excitement. "Well, seeing that I'm going to be moving to the ninth grade, I'll be of age also. You think I might finally get my permit?"

As a reply, Rathekel says, "You're going to have to train first. No sense in going out on the field without being prepared."

Celestine looks at Rathekel in a condemning fashion. "He's not going into battle, even though I do miss being at our last base. Anyways, we can teach him on the weekends for a while."

Dante's excited as ever and flashes a smile that could last a lifetime. "How's school going for you, William?" his father asks.

"The year is nearly done. I'm glad I started picking up my grades two years ago, but other than that, nothing really. The same: homework, tests, etc."

Rathekel stares at William but won't intrude on his dilemmas as a teenager obviously goes through. Fiddling with a butter knife, Sarah sees more frustration coming from him. Dante just enjoys the food he's eating. Celestine and Rathekel continue eating. "William has been telling me about what his future after school will be. It's pretty interesting," Sarah proclaims. William raises his head in an astonished fashion at Sarah, and both parents look in return with curiosity.

Tapping a knife continuously on the table, and then abruptly stopping, William finally spills all information. "SWAT . . . I want to join law enforcement. It's enjoyable and I believe I'll end up liking it. I've studied their regimes, methods, and laws. The movements behind them are interesting (as in how they work together on the field), and they serve a purpose not too many would commit to. You push your mortal existence out there, stop the chaos, and it makes a great statement. Something I should do more often . . . put myself out there. There are definitely better professions out there to express myself. Oh well." With everyone a little surprised and interested, William looks back down at the table. "Can I be excused?" He asks.

"Sure," Celestine says.

As William exits, Rathekel says, "It's great this was planned out. I'm proud of him for choosing a life goal." Celestine, Sarah, and Dante agree.

Twelve steps to climb: hand on rail, calm breathing. A black void fills the upstairs area. A light switch rests on the wall. *Flick!* Light illuminates through what it could pierce. William's room is far, down the hall, straight ahead. Dante's room is to the right, Sarah's and their parent's rooms are to the left. All doors are closed. He reaches for the handle; the door opens wide. Evening light barely shines inside. *Click!* A lamp's light brings better luminous coverage. William plops on his bed and lies down. Eyes stare upward and dreary images permit foggy interpretations of his life shrouded by doubt. Twilight event: dark scenes compliant with a restful state. Bound and contained rage, a sensation held for now . . . A couple hours passes by. William awakes . . . Preparations for his self are made to go for a walk. The lamp is left on. A trek downstairs, his mother and his father sit on the living room couch, talking. Dante and Sarah are in the computer room. "I'll be back. I'm just going for a walk. I won't be long." A pleasant Thursday night: 67 degrees and somewhat breezy. Covered in a complete black ensemble, his motive is clear. Immersed in thought- "Night takes its apex form which gives me solace for the duration of its subsistence. Your very surroundings covered like a blanket. Silhouettes tail closely, but only when light is present. To live in darkness, I shall be; embraced by the void. Of all, you have given me a strange kind of love. You cradled me to sleep when no other has. Sad and weary: the pain lets me sleep. Shall we coincide once again for this event?"

Two blocks away from reaching his destined target. Moving through empty space, nothing stops these aggressive movements. On the initial street, William autonomously views from the tree's umbra, waiting patiently for a specific moment to occur. The visage of innocence is succumbed by darkness—substantial and encapsulated. Patience still thick, trepidation transmutes into an undeniable reality . . . not of who thinks it, only the one who will succumb under a methodical reason. Thirty minute's pass: no sign of Tyler yet. –"Linger among the darkness as it hides a multitude of sins along with an upheld immense capacity, desire that holds a grand magnitude of intentions, a need to be expected. Where—" William's awareness is precise: Tyler makes his way down his porch's staircase to his mother's car. White and glowing the eyes are—perceiving the first strike. It seems Tyler is on a mission, but William makes his final movement: walking faster and faster, unaware of the other person. Closer . . . William then kicks Tyler in the back of his right leg. It then smashes Tyler's head against the side of the car door. The auras of death rises from William's body—the cloak of many sins. A quick look around to see if anyone hears them. Tyler falls over in pain, but the dark figure swiftly covers his mouth.

Tyler is pulled into utter blackness, and tossed down like a weakened dog. Perspiration from distress: one hand grips an injured leg and the other hand holds a wounded head. A dark, frightening figure looms over the boy. The dark figure kneels and gazes into frightful eyes, with eyes turned crimson now. Slowly letting a hand off Tyler's mouth, who says, "Who the fuck—" But quickly places a hand back on his mouth. Struggling to get loose, the dark figure speaks in a demonic tone, "You revel in shit, striking fear into others from your own insecurities. This is a pleasant moment for me to correct your ill-willed life. What motivates your actions: a consciousness to live only to harm? Pleasing to see how many strive for placement only to be rejected. How pathetic. I'd rather leash you and walk around in humiliation with you." Fighting back . . . hands of violence seek vengeance—swiftness in all regards, the dark figure grabs Tyler's left arm and forces it down. It punches him in the face, and blood quickly disperses. "You have too much weakness. I'll be your harbinger of reality—the monster that stalks your continuation of existence, followed by everlasting perception of your motives, ploys, and degradation for mankind. Life is a commendable teacher, brutal and honest." Tyler frees himself briefly and clobbers the dark figure's face with the back of his hand. The dark figure regains control and slams Tyler's head on the ground multiple times. "Ah!" Stunned from the blows, the dark figure closes in: inches away from each other's faces, a shape, which causes despair to seep deeply into Tyler. Crimson eyes pierce through body and soul. Nor a smile or sadness covers any on the surface; the darkened face upholds its tenebrous features.

"I've watched, I've witnessed. Be careful where you tread. Evil tends to feed off sins and emotions. To sin begets implicating the seeds of venom." Terrified, yet finding some courage to speak up, Tyler whimpers, "What do you mean?! I don't understand." The dark figure continues to "spit fire" at the lad once more: "Today, at 1:05! I would have approached you . . . could've caused endless torment, but I'd rather sit back and watch. I'm stricken with an interest for all petty beings." Enough is enough, remorse will be given. The dark figure rises slowly and quietly backs away, sauntering off into the night. Black wings spread from the doomed aura, misty and frightening, speed increasing. The departure leaves Tyler perplexed, scared and shocked. Considering what he was told, Tyler formulates an idea of what exactly this "figure" meant. Hard to upsurge, he eventually does; but when finally walking back, he enters his house moments later.

"My god, what happened?" his mother says as Tyler walks inside in a distraught and broken manner, in addition to the bloody mess from the inevitable vicissitude.

William's abnormal features slowly change and his pace has picked up: rushing and sweating, not even a smile occurs. House bound and near. Standing before the front deck, William takes his hood off. Normal facial features are visible. First step, second, third, and at last, the fourth. The front door opens. A dark and quiet atmosphere saturates the household. Moon light barely shines on the stairway upward. Mother and Father are in their own room; Sarah and Dante are in their own as well. Each step is as quiet as a vampire's. William opens his room's door; the lamp is still lit. He sits and takes a moment to clarify the previous deed. Staring blankly through the doorway, a thought comes to mind: "*Lie waste to those who have become abominations. Wrathful you are, observant none the less. Inner demons cloud your mind, lessening your ability to keep faith. But what keeps you alive? The doubt turned hope? Or is the undeniable faith which is your ascent? Maybe both . . . I mustn't change into what I detest, challenge, contradict. Release me. The grip of degradation will not slow me nor seize any of my actuality. I choose poorly and it deems me a scum. Lord—help me in my time of need."*

Friday morning: arriving at school, William rummages through his locker, preparing for the day. Emily sneaks up behind him to attempt a good scare. Unfazed, William turns and looks at her. "You're no fun. You ready for this weekend? Oh, yeah. I was talking with David this morning. He said he won't be in today. Said something happened last night. Vague as he was, I'm concerned," Emily says. Tyler trudges by the two and looks at Emily. "Sorry about yesterday." He then glances at William, but it spooks him. William has his hood up, but bad memories from last night occur in Tyler's mind. William turns to look at Tyler. Suddenly he is terrified and leaves. No sign that Tyler knows it was William though. "That was quite the talk the principal and he had. A wonderful turn of events . . ." Emily says in amazement. William continues to stare at Tyler as the frightened boy flees, and Tyler looks back only to see a set of ominous eyes penetrating his very soul again. "Hey," Emily says.

Snapping out of it . . . "I hear you. I'll call him at lunch." As their day rolls along its typical schedule, Tyler still doesn't know it was William who forced him into submission. Just know: even in the present day, Tyler is more agitated and paranoid since the happening, but it hasn't completely changed his "moral" integrity. There are times where immoral acts are performed. As few as they are, but well... Yeah. Other times they can be decent, for the most part at least. I guess among the discomposure, repercussions were to be amended and justified. However, in the dark, a useful tactic being unkind, there was power behind it. Maybe inside all the chaos, light can perforate, shine through . . . or maybe . . . it was injustice.

Interlude 4

Responding to the Signal

William arrives home. The car comes to a halt: turns it's off, but remains inside for a couple minutes. (William tries deciding whether to reflect or let his emotions fester.)

(Ascent action +5- Reconciles all thoughts and postulates with the chaotic realm that dwells in unfathomable depths of the consciousness.)

Cloud formations begin to take place; symbolism states the battle is coming to a loss from within, which is then expelled out skyward.

"Eyes avert to heights where Gods reside, and for all mortals to witness godly wrath or beauty thereof. Coincide with your enemy— become the nemesis or align with goodness—become an exact embodiment of your enemies' fears. Both choices can be that sort of aspect, an aspect to become an example to many, yourself. Lights flicker to represent hope, or darkness overpowers from fears. Depths of depravity drag souls to everlasting nothingness, but hope can pull a man from his own hell. Bring faith where none exists; and bring light which guides the spiritual essence. To let the infinite nihility swallow the lands begets the mighty and life stealing desolation to overflow your surroundings to encumber, permitting your fall. Can one live without the other? Can one allow others to coincide? Will it be an eternal battle? No! Let both flow! A wondrous peace offering to celebrate years of renounced conflict evermore; nevermore will both be separate by category. They must be one—a unity to bind all that is conscious and alive. Its embrace will be inviting, so phenomenal. Survival of existence—all life down to the smallest organisms must grip this notion and prosper through this unity whilst promoting longevity. Extend your reach to the sky and rejoice! Rejoice!"

(In addition, Ascent increases by 15 and Descent decreases by 15.)

Although, the storm persistently commotions above, certain chaos inside had been pacified. Equilibrium has been restored. His eyes open: hope reaches through darkened clouds, shining abundantly. The aquatic barrage from above slows, and tempests part, leaving only the heavens to control its skies once again with ceaseless light. A breath is exerted, and despair has vanished. The car door opens; an exit from former internal war leaves men speechless. Each step toward the house reassures a consciousness with confidence and peace achieved. The door is inevitably nearer . . . you reach for its lock, which you possess its key to. Unlocking the door is to move forward from conflict, allowing you to start anew. Closing of it represents the shield against coming and/or former chaos. But of the sanctum's interior, new doors house other mysterious as well . . .

A Friend in Need

Three knocks at the door: it couldn't be ignored. Feet gallop, indefinite thrilling wonderment. Who comes hither to my doorstep, of all hours to be bothered? Bestowed upon by another being: a mysterious figure that thou are? Thrice I heard before . . . Three knocks at the door, it couldn't be ignored.

—Visitor

06/30/2028, 10:34 p.m.

Click Door opens . . . David stands tall. "Hey. Thought I'd come by. I thought you might need someone after everything that's ensued . . . and for me." William shifts to the side and gestures his granted entry. After walking in, William shuts the door.

"Make yourself at home," William says with hospitality.

Plopping a rump on a soft, cushiony foundation, David sits down.

"Need anything?" William asks.

"Water will be fine," David answers.

Multiple footsteps make way to the kitchen; one glass grabbed from a cupboard's bowels. The faucet runs, and cold water fills the cup. Returning to David, William hands him the cup of water.

"Thank you," David says politely.

"You're welcome," William says in return.

A couple sips are taken. The glass is then set down on the coffee table. "How are you feeling? No adverse affects from that transfusion?" David asks.

William nods left to right, indicating nothing has negatively happened. "Besides being whaled in the face, I'm feeling better," William says.

David chuckles from the claim. "She can hit quite hard, can't she?" he asks.

William sits back and says, "Don't worry about me. How have you been since . . . you know? It's none of my business, I know. You don't have to say anything. I shouldn't have asked."

David tilts his head downwards. "Recovering . . . I felt better talking to our renowned therapist. Her words really helped me, but I still feel regrettably impartial." David sits back and lays his head against the back side of the couch from a dejected attitude. William acknowledges the sensation.

(William decides whether to communicate a reprieve or encumber a distressed friend further with immense candor.)

"Dreams can entail an answer one might actually be seeking consciously, or obliviously. Elaborating: I guess it would be considered blasphemy by religious associates, or be claimed a liar by others. I was sitting on the ground along a familiar street. Depressed looking, lonely . . . A figure in a white robe, sandals, but neither a face nor skin I could comprehend. The voice was distorted and bellowed. Our meeting was comforting, I felt warmth. It, or whatever the figure was, told me everything will be all right and to keep my head up and continue. I couldn't comprehend some of it. Then I was pushed into the street, I think? But it was a cloudy atmosphere. Upon returning from the vision, my body felt as if needles were prodding me, my heartbeat was hastening, but my breathing was calm. Maybe I was stressed? Maybe something moreover was bothering me? Could my subconscious be helping me? Or was it real? I read up on how your mind can literally go full survival mode or any relevance to that and bring you a reprieve from an overload of such things. I don't know . . . It felt too real to be a subconscious curing. This is not a subject matter that was told to anyone. It's profoundly special to me. I'd bet it would be controversial, wouldn't you think so? To my knowledge, this isn't something you give interest to, typically." (Ascent increases: +10) (David will remember this.)

David lifts his head and looks at William stern like. "I concede, only because you're my friend. Sounding sincere persuades me enough, honestly. This dream has suspicions arising nonstop, likewise with the thought." Both share a mutual silence, personal moments colliding not without inquisitiveness. "Maybe in the same sense, my dream had just the same integrity," David says in supporting William's claim. Could it be a mere coincidence?

"An interesting topic to contemplate: dreaming. Could there possibly exist a deeper meaning? I believe so," William says.
David crosses his arms in pondering what to speak about. "You know what? Want to go for a walk instead?"

William nods yes.

William and David arise; walk to the door, exits, William closes the door, locking it from the outside. Down each step to the walkway, a beautiful day is ahead. Tranquility, rest among the chaos. After the storm, rapture reveling. David casts a gaze at William and says, "What do you do on your down time?"

"Besides my mind consistently ever so fleeting, I usually go on these small expeditions, listen to music, play video games, or ride my bike," William confesses.

Switching back to a frontal view, David openly says, "Sounds lonely . . . I or Emily is always here to do something. Solitude isn't my forte. No offense."

William's head slightly turns to the right, eyes concentrating in the present direction. "I don't mind at all. The living causes conflicts. A predilection to self-indulge in my preferences and revel in the fact I don't marvel about my seclusion. Thorough enjoyment comes from the choice, on the contrary." William answers David's frank statement, and concentration returns to normal. (David takes notice of that.)

"You have stayed well within it a little too long. You start doing crazy things," David says critically.

William smirks and looks at David. "Or its' because I've adapted to it . . . Maybe a decision was made from humanity's horrors. You should be careful what you expel to someone. That person might remember such claims of judgments." He turns his back to its normal position.

Looking at William in a protective fashion, David says, "What? I'm just being honest. Not for cruel reasons, just concerned."

(William contemplates whether to reply with an angry retort or a quick-witted remark or acceptance.)

(Quick-witted dialogue: +1) "It's a promise, excluding malicious intent. Not for cruel reasons, just concerned for my own health, that's all," William says. (David takes notice of that.) David smiles and laughs over the smartass remark.

"Where are we going, anyways?" David asks.

"A simple path I made. We're going five blocks, turning left at each corner," William replies.

"Emily sure is in complete disagreement with you back there. Why act unjustly?" David says.
"Spontaneity, irrationality, anger," William apprehensively says.

"Anger . . . you seem real down to earth mostly," David asserts.

William feels crushed. An explanation isn't too easy. William stops his pace, drops his head, and rolls his eyes upward and says, "Bottling up so many feelings, no release. I believe that moment was the tipping point. A toll was taken, and I feel mortified, totally unsound," William says in confessing true feelings. He turns to face David.

"Remember how I told you to not let your past define you, or let your feelings get the better of you? That would've been the exact time to reflect," David says truthfully. William stands in silence, but he also agrees. "Come on, I'll take you somewhere. It's appropriate for the moment."

Time in, William asks, "Are we going to our spot?"

"You know it!" David happily says.

Through bountiful woodlands, twigs snap from heavy steps, and branches are moved aside to allow further passage in. Moving the last bit of branches aside, an immaculate sight appears. "Over there is our spot. See the two rocks we sat on, about a hundred yards over there?" Walking along the side of its cliff side, caution must exist. "So beautiful, as I remember," William says with nostalgia as he looks below. An immaculate deep trench: water rushes down below as multiple mini waterfalls are strewn on the wall, causing the effect; floral and other vegetation endlessly extend across the walls. Reaching the two rocks, both take a seat on each. Leaning against a well placed tree, they relax and contemplate peacefully. Sounds of water cascading to the lower foundation, birds chirping while flying to and fro or in trees, trees rustle in calm winds; sun shines through crevices of space between all foliage and branches. Both inhale deeply, and then exhale. A single sparrow lands on William's rock and relaxes upon it as well. "Thanks for sharing your thought about the dream of yours, even your feelings," David says. William looks over at David, who reassumes his relaxed position and rests his eyes. At ease inside, William is relaxed too.

The Other Side

Many compromises devoid a body of a soul, but misery is the foundation that helps find a casket. Delightful comfort to rest, the ivory lid fastens gradually. Hands lay rested on each side, legs lie straight, and a heavy head squanders not. A breath's reprieve not gifted, unrest eternal. Another's dark destruction dealt, another's mirrored end result . . . Conclusion: disregarded decency, faltering love to woe unto whom created the wound.

—The empty shell

06/28/2028

A couple days before David visits William

Emily loosens her emotions; all scenery slows to a crawl. Affliction sets reprisal looming forever tall. Overloading forces implode with all emotions swirling farther away from redemptions grasp. Shades cover casually, hovering to cast deathly shadows, lively forms, lies to envelope innocent souls. Emily stops within Roger's office's doorway . . . "I'm troubled inside. Help me," Emily says. Roger looks up at Emily and gestures her to enter. Fully stepping inside, her hand grasps the side of the door and closes it. David watches her the entire time as she makes her desolate walk through the precinct's main hall. Adopted reflection gives similar feelings.

Following day: Rezden Allegiance: (GNC) Global Negotiation Center.

A group has seized the entire building for reasons we'll find out soon. "The hostages have no relevance to your ploy!" Hanson, the police negotiator, says.

Up above, on the second floor, sitting at the window, a masked man shouts back, "They are the reason why my family wasn't allowed to come into your precious country! There's much relevance!"

"What can we do so you release them? We can allow their presence here, if that's your only wish," Hanson says aloud.

Disappearing for a moment . . . A woman's scream becomes louder. Forced out the window to prove he'll do whatever it takes, but held to prevent falling out completely. "Don't toy with me! My intentions are serious!" Civilians watching gasp, hoping she doesn't come to any harm.

"Hold on! Why would we if we can find some kind of resolve here. What else is it you need?" Hanson speaks aloud.
The woman is shoved back in. No sound . . .

Emily and David stand ready with eight others farther past the barricade. Positioned on either side of the vestibule, a signal is needed for action to be permitted. Ronald and Adam reside in a van that's behind the barricade. "Among the group, we only know of the man who's apparently the leader, were assuming. His name is Projenack Diervsevly. No criminal record until now. Age twenty-nine, born and raised in Moscow, Russia. Profession is unknown. Entire family is from the same country, no siblings, and has been a citizen here for 5 years. Nothing else important, really, to this situation . . . Obviously trying to get them inside the States, this isn't going to get him anything, sadly. He's just another fighter for civil rights." He then sighs. "Besides from that, send them in soon on my mark. Any longer and it'll just result adversely," Adam says in detail.

"There's nothing on the others inside he's with? Well, my team is ready whenever. Seeing our target isn't budging, it's been forty-three minutes," Ronald responds.

A blank stare: emotionless to the present. David sees her adjacently and whispers as an attempt to get her attention. "Hey. Emily." When she doesn't budge, David subtly whistles. Emily looks around then notices David averting his eyes at her. "Just focus on the now, we can talk later. Come on . . . It's affecting me too, but don't let this cloud your conscience. These hostages are important to retrieve," David says.

"I can't promise anything, but you're right about this moment," Emily says in a bothered tone. David prolongs his stare but soon decides to look back into the entrance's windows.

"Ok! A little cooperation and we can end this." The leader of the criminals speaks aloud. Adam's top negotiator goes along with the plan.

"We have the papers to verify their existence in this country, the whole process in a quicker form. Right here states their rights and privileges. We need a signature for them from you and from them as well. Or just you, that'll be fine. I'll throw it up to you!"

Agreeing, Projenack suddenly shouts, "No! I want you to bring it to me. I'd have to bring them here or send this to them so they can sign it. But we'll at least get somewhere."

Hanson turns to look at Adam. Adam nods yes, and Hanson turns back to face the captor to say, "OK. You get what you want. No one gets hurt. End of story."

A subtle silence; then the leader speaks up, saying, "That could be the new concept if demands are satisfied. Hold your bargain, and I'll hold mine! Leave your guns and other items behind. You will be checked." Complying with the orders, he takes off his jacket, relieves his firearm with holster, pepper spray, cuffs, wallet, and keys. Hands are raised. "No need for your hands to be up. Your men stay at bay! No tricks." Lowering both arms, Hanson continues to the entrance. One of the accomplices meets the negotiator at the entrance from inside.

The revolving doors are now unlocked. Some fear, but courage must be a staple. Patted down for extra security but too quickly; both men now start walking up the stair-case that resides in the lobby. Gun in hand; ready to use. Reading the accomplice's posture, an illogical action takes place. From behind, Hanson grabs around the man's neck with his right arm and tries to pry the weapon away with his left hand. Unnerving combat . . . The accomplice breaks free and pushes Hanson. Hanson uncontrollably falls down the flight of stairs; the criminal watched as Hanson plummeted downward and stopped below. No movement . . . the closer he walked down to him... Quickly, a snub-nosed revolver is pulled from negotiator's sock.

Bang! Bang! Bang!

"Charge in!" Adam says. Hearing all three shots from outside, all officers are commanded to move in. Crash! Blasting through the glass, David and Emily, along with company, charge in.

David rushes in first, turns the corner inside the lobby and sees their fellow officer on the ground. David runs over to help Hanson. Guns loosely fire from above. All squad members move while David pulls Hanson to the side, away from incoming fire. A couple hide behind the front desk, some go around a wall, and the rest hide under the staircase. Adam and Ronald wait for an answer.

"James is all right. The man he encountered with, however, has been killed. The rest are above and ready to execute. We were fired upon. Without a doubt, I bet you heard it from out there," David reports.

"Do as you will. They clearly are hostile no matter what. You understand?" Adam says.

"Yes sir," David answers. Lance sneakily moves his head out fairly to see if anyone is waiting above. Back against the wall, he pulls out a flash-bang. Taking a step out from underneath the staircase, he throws it above to the second floor. The flash-bang grenade rattles on the floor above, creating a distracting sound, it then flashes brightly and imposes temporary blindness. Everyone rushes upstairs: David and another rush at two of three culprits and decide to tackle them. The third gets taken down by Allie. Their approach has been a success so far, and all three are escorted below then out. "A few of ours are bringing some out," Lance conveys.

"Acknowledged," Adam replies.

Four officers from the external area grab the three convicts; the accompanying S.W.A.T trio reports back upstairs. "The two rooms—" Before finishing her notification, Emily hears a sound from the closest room. The emanations draw attention . . . nearer, now in the doorway... "Rise slowly with your hands up! I implore you to." Emily said. Complying, a man comes out from under a table in the far reaches of the room and both hands are raised. "Don't turn around. Who are you?"

The man trembles. "I'm Paul, assistant manager."

Emily lowers her gun. "Is it safe?" Paul anxiously asks.

"Not really, but for the moment, yes. You can relax. Come towards me. I'll guide you. Walk to the left until I say stop. OK, stop," Emily says with suspicion.

Paul advances from compliance. "I'm glad you're here. Don't know what they would've done if I was found."

Oddly said, Emily questions Paul's luck. "Walk backwards now. You were in a conspicuous spot. Lucky for you, I guess. You may turn to face me."

An awkward moment arises. "Yeah . . ." Paul says. Tension . . . Another officer comes up behind Emily.

"Strangely quiet now . . . Who's this?" Allie says. Emily averts her attention to Allie to give an answer; suddenly, Paul abruptly tries pulling Emily's rifle away. Allie raises hers quickly.
"Release the weapon!" Allie exclaims.
Emily reverses the attempt and pushes Paul to the ground. "What were you to gain from that?" She says as she and Allie point their guns at Paul.

"I don't need to explain anything." Paul says menacingly as he rose to his feet.
Emily quickly says, "Stay where y—"

Bam! Blood spatters everywhere, covering Emily and Allie, but the bullet barely misses Emily's face and hits the doorway by her. Projenack shoots from the second doorway that's parallel down the room to the left where Emily and Allie are.

"You will follow me. Rules were broken and now a life is taken," Projenack says. Cold steel's placed against Allie's back. His lackeys have taken control of the raid team in addition. As everyone is transferred to Projenack's initial room, the accomplices sit everyone near him, who is standing by the window he's been communicating from.

"Your attempts cost someone's life! I have your people in my grasp! All deals are off!" Projenack shouts in a serious tone.

Adam utilizes another strategy. "They give us no choice. Unleash plan Ru1n4t10n," Adam says.

"Not the best course," Ronald says in absolute disagreement.

"What else do we have? They have our officers, and all we're doing is standing here," Adam says in defense.

Ronald isn't in agreement still. "I can't do that. Plus, it was a premature action to force them in," He says.

"The people come first, just like our men and women of the law. If you compromise my orders, if this option completely transitions negatively to this mission, I will see to it myself that you'll be escorted to my office and your job will be laid to rest. Don't make me into a typical authority," Adam says in an indomitable tone.

Ronald's shocked from the ultimatum. "That's my fate if I object . . . You're ruthless," Ronald says. With no other way, Ronald makes the call.

"Do you want to make the calls and live with the consequences?! Wait . . . You're no different anyways," Adam replies.

Bound and tied, sitting on the floor. Projenack paces back and forth with intentions known. Emily whispers to David, "How'd this happen?"

"We moved down to another section and were flanked with heavy weaponry. We tried to make another entrance for reinforcements beforehand," David says. He speaks again, but does so because of impatience with Projenack. "Is this really worth it? All this risk when all you could have done was use logic."

Infuriated by David' words, Projenak hastily approaches him and whacks David with the blunt end of a rifle. "Ah!" David grunts; his head hangs low from the excruciating pain.

   "My business is not to be treaded upon. They need this. My hand was forced," Projenack says.
"Need what? Hold people prisoner against your irrational plan?" Lance says to oppose.

Snipers take their stance around the building; all scopes point at every opposing personnel. Extra hands take route climbing up near the group from outside, but inconspicuously with smoke grenades and flash-bangs. The last cluster head in from the back. Luckily nobody is stationed there. With them, heavy machine guns are equipped. Remaining lackeys stand watch with the hostages, stupidly not looking in any other direction . . . mostly due in part to their leader's attitude and ignorance of a hostage setup.

"Paul was uncanny, predictable . . . Oh well, a loose end to be no more," Projenak says.

Emily figures out the bleak attempt by understanding everything that has happened. "I've noticed a lot about you. Reading your body language, how you speak. Your idea is flawed. Every move you've made, even with us, has foiled this completely. Every second since we've entered this building, your life has become lesser. No elaborate backup? No extensive or second thought to what could've allowed your victory?" Emily says with observation of the situation.

Anger rises, his mind all a rage . . . Flashes arise; blinded nearly, vision blurred, but stumbles towards Emily . . . Closer . . . Smoke grenades unleashed. Closer . . . Gun flails about as he's trying to aim at her. It's difficult with the tense situation Projenack has been dealt. Unable to see him, gunshots are fired wildly, and Emily fears for the worst. Snipers shoot through the haze . . .

Bang! Bang! Bang! Bang!

Bullets pierce his chest, lower torso, and head. Upon opening her eyes after the sniper's shot four times, Emily sees that blood has spattered all around and some on the team and her too. His deceased body had landed on her lap. She looks down and stares into the dead eyes that stare at her. Her increasingly fretful moment and haze creates an illusion, making Projenack's face look like William's. Shocked from this happening, locking eyes with the dead constrains fraught. She closes her eyes again, and then shakes her head. Opening them . . . Projenack's face had returned to his own.

The reinforcements come in, blazing their machine guns as the unit uses special goggles that can see infrared as well as through smoke, just like the snipers. The remaining enemies fall, a fate aligned with death. All sounds become muffled, staring into an empty shell, focused on reality. Something inside has changed her attitude. She takes a deep breath . . . and "wakes up." The final moments within the conclusion of their mission has revitalized her in a foreboding way, transitioning her from a sorrowful mood and the utmost deep, dark despair.

After their incursion at Rezden Allegiance, a private session with the precinct's counselor inaugurates a day later (06/29/2028). Emily contemplates organizing her thoughts for the session. Walking in, the counselor takes a seat across from her. Examination of body language indefinitely describes Emily's current mood. "Can I start by saying—" Emily uttered then abruptly halts her words. Emily looks to her left, controlling her emotions, but then turns back to face Laura. "I never realized, in a severe style, how any second could be your last, even when under duress from a chaotic faction. That's obvious.

What really swayed my mood was staring into blank eyes, a body where vacancy is at maximum, an empty shell to squander six feet under all life, but wonderment has me curious about whom that person really was, or could've been."

Laura considers an appropriate response. "You leave a person with no choice; irrationality can come in full force. Family is forever to most, but it can mean so little next to none to some. Trying to figure out this person's purpose in life or character has no relevance to you. However, it has caused an impact upon your nature as proof of your current state."

Emily looks down at her hands, clenches them then releases: a reaction posing as a truth. "Death literally had lay down on my lap so casually and gazed at me eye to eye. To cease does not bother me, but it was the moral of it all."

Laura acknowledges her disconcerting attitude toward the events outcome.

To bring light to their conversation, she carries curiosity to the conversation. "Do you doubt yourself with the line of work that you've chosen?" Laura asks.

Emily ponders this momentarily. Both eyes scroll southeast, her right leg begins to nervously move. Then the movement ceases, and Emily looks back into Laura's eyes. "I succumbed to the harshest depths of truth." Laura presumes to understand her syntax. Emily places her left hand on her mouth . . . Laura leans forward. Emily begins to cry. Dropping her left hand, she clenches both hands together. Laura decides to sit next to her and embrace her to bring comfort. Laura rocks back and forth, and Emily releases her true feeling. "Why does the sinister domain have to create specific profound revelations?" Laura comforts Emily constantly, assuring that she is heard loud and clear.

Chapter 6

Visitation (Intro)

07/01/2028

Into the future, time to heal has been amended.

Lights rise leisurely, piercing through the window on the left side of William's room. Warmth comes from above to seize the day: a moment to wake, reasons given to start anew. He opens his eyes to view the current day, witness new comings. What to ponder and choices to make? Breathe in air that fills your lungs and also travels to the brain. Flow with oxygen to live, passing to and fro. What can be created to move through the time of day? What amount of time will you use to accomplish your tasks or your dreams? Relaxation is quite pleasurable, but refers to the lazy soul whose day was wasted. Action can be tiring, but it will prove time worthy and rewarding.

William lies in bed with a blanket that covers only his lower body. Sunrays slowly establish light through every window. Calm breathing accompanied with a heavy sigh to verify complacency. Sluggish movements to rise, views for times to come are displeasing. To an upward position, tired and bored . . . There's a knock on the door. He slowly directs all perception to the doorway's direction and manages to arise. A couple steps come with a slight sigh. Knocking comes again. Reaching for the door handle . . . he opens it. Emily stands before him. William stands there nearly naked and quite surprised by this visit. Scratching one eye from sleepiness, Emily walks up to him and hugs him softly. She embraces tightly; William commits as well. Even though he's standing in his front doorway in only his underwear, it's comforting to hold her and have no worries of anyone else seeing a man standing roughly nude in near public. They release, and she steps back. "How are you?" Emily asks.

(William decides whether to let her in or not.)

(Special +1) "Before we talk, you want to come in? It's a little breezy out here." Emily walks in as William steps aside. The door is softly shut. He turns around to see her looking back as the light above shines on her. William divulges in another response, but nervousness arises. "I'm well. I'm healing up—recollecting in the process." Guiding her to his living room, William shows her a place to sit. She chooses to sit in a recliner. William walks back into his room to put on the rest of his clothes. Looking around as she waits, an observation of a picture on a table near a corner gains interest to mind. William appears before the living room. Emily focuses on the picture she found compelling. "Everyone is happy," she says.

"Moments I cherish every day: an infinite thought. It was a family photo during Dante's fourteenth birthday. He even got his learner's permit that day," William explains to her (Ascent +1). Emily deduces an uplifting, calming sensation from William's delightful words. A cheesy thought comes to mind and he says, "Quite an endowment." Emily's eyes follow William as he goes to sit on his couch's middle section. She walks over and sits at the left end. William stares downward in part due to nervousness. "Thanks for coming," William says.

"You're my best friend," Emily replies.

Looking to his left toward her, William returns with a kind sentiment. "And you're mine . . ." A mutual silence befalls them for a couple seconds.

"How's everything else been?" William asks. Emily scrolls her eyes downward with apprehension to answer truthfully. Her eyes focus back to William's. "Nothing one can't handle: typical days, typical people. You didn't hear about our encounter at the GNC."

William quickly says, "I had caught glimpses of it on the news coverage. I usually don't watch the news due to the grief and doom that's displayed."

Emily adjusts herself on the couch in a defensive position by crossing her legs and folding her arms together. "Not much to divulge in. Everyone's doing all right."

William can sense her downheartedness and asks, "You don't sound upbeat about it."

Emily smiles from awkwardness and snickers.

"I've been thinking lately about what's happened: a moment where you could've lost a piece of your life," she says poignantly. William continues to keep eye contact with imminent realization. "To never escape the thought, it's so palpable," Emily concludes. William looks slowly to the right, the reality of the moment.

(William chooses whether or not to give Emily some consideration or dodge the fact that his own actions and the repercussions are real.)

"My thoughts are an archetype. Choosing poorly in my regime against whatever we're facing, it weighs heavy on my conscience. Where my logic and consciousness exist, I was simultaneously misplaced while complacent. Anger is a powerful aspect." (Ascent +3) (She'll remember that / the relationship has changed to valued.) Emily considers his words and says, "There are other methods. I don't know about what's recently happened, or is happening wholly, but I'm glad a friend hasn't left us. What was the reason, besides being a recluse? William thinks quickly, massages both hands, and then looks at her. "Conceptions echo, enigmatic proposals, paradoxical paradigms, alleviated depression, and strange mirth from pain." Emily moves closer . . . "You can't possibly think of yourself that way? Don't hide. Solitude should never be a constraint."

"People caused me to acclimate to seclusion," William confesses.

"You did by choice," Emily straightforwardly speaks in return.

"Penetrate my mind, travel through my hallowed halls, and ponder on the portraits that explain my life. Ghastly figures follow your every step, watching for a mistake. Every event, sin, death, crime, inhuman occurrence, debased personification has created these demons . . . the haunting."

Emily places her hand on his mouth and says, "Take a break. My visitation's reason is because I care about you. Don't take this time for granted." Abstractions run through a mind like a cascading river. Immense collaborations come together, forming a sensation like no other, reflecting feelings like a mirror to hearts of love. Heart-beats quicken, William shakes within the moment. "It's been too long," Emily says.

William's curiosity arises. "What has?" he asks. Emily attempts to entice him. "You and I both know that answer. You hide and deny. What are you cerebrating? Am I the only one you see? Or am I just another face you'll place so far away, letting it wither away in time?"

(Unsure what to say, William tries to speak, but his mind still wonders. To assume an answer, but he doesn't know if it's worth putting her through more suffering. He contemplates whether to take a step farther in their relationship or continue as friends to avoid further damage.)

A breaths' distance away, she places her hands upon his shoulders, ready to . . . Her eyes look up; his eyes avert down—connecting with symmetry with an exactly replicated heart beat with pulses that quicken at a consistent rate. "If I were to hurt you again—we've been dealt a copious amount of my nonsense. Would you really need that furthered? I couldn't bear seeing you in pain again from my mistakes . . . or worse."

(*Chuckles *) "Even so, but it doesn't wholly change my view on you. You've done more for me, especially in the past. It was nice to have someone protect me during high school. A selfless choice, though you didn't have to. It was appreciated, honestly. We've always worked as a team: I, you, and David. Behold, we're still here, strong as ever. Otherwise, you don't think I notice your eyes wandering in my direction more than half the time? Well . . . I do have little birds who tell me, too." Emily responds with a heartfelt and compassionate statement. William blushes a little. "Nothing could tear our relationship apart. Not even what you've attempted before will change my mind." She pushes William backward; he now lies on his back . . . Left hand on the left shoulder, right hand on face; Emily hovers ever so slightly from touching lips.

(A decision to crave more than a friendship blooms into a beautiful outcome.)

(Romance option chosen) "You have me there. I could never let such beauty perish alone. A flower amongst the chaos symbolizes hope. You know: I do need this, more than ever—"

"I'll give you . . . every . . . thing," Emily softly says before making connection. Eyes close and skin merge into one. A union none other can despoil. An embrace between two people, a unique bond only two minds can connect to. Her soft lips release and she slowly opens her eyes and smiles. William grins in conclusion.

Live in the moment like it's your last; feel the rush when two souls are guided. Ascend high above heaven itself and witness a singular force that vanquishes all others. Emily soon rests her head upon his chest. A smile forms on William's face again as he knows someone cares, even though possessing a defiant, reckless, heroic personality, and making careless, irrational, blind choices, but she still needs him most. Forever memorable, William will do anything to keep what was created between them for an eternity.

Chapter 7

Visitation

Pt. 2

07/07/2028

Just under a week has passed since William was confronted with votes of disapproval concerning specific illicit acts. Heading back to the precinct, we come across a scientist/logistics employee for the SWAT enforcement named Roy, who is in Roger's office as of this moment. Roger appears soon after. "You know," Roger says abruptly. Startling Roy, Roger's sudden appearance and vocal exertions make Roy jump somewhat. "It's been a while since we had any major kidnappings, but they still do come here and there. Any kidnapping is major. I meant to imply larger ones," Roger says to conclude. "I didn't hear you come in. Here's a quick revelation in knowing they've been appearing through the percentage of kidnappings within a month's time. Within the statistics, I mean. It appears they perform under the rates to be unknown, or to be overlooked, if that makes any sense. On the contrary, numbers slightly change every month, increasing by a couple all over the country. Here in California, there aren't many, but it has increased moderately, though nothing spectacular ever since your team had their special incursion," Roy quickly says.

Roger understands what Roy is stating. Roger begins to wonder if peace will ever happen, even with his own plan intervening between those sadistic experiments were halted because of . . . But something's amiss.

"I haven't heard from our illustrious chap in a while. He should be all right by now. I've never seen or ever worked with anyone of his caliber. His accomplishments exceed most here," Roger speaks aloud. While praising William for such feats, Roy tries to tell him that William's not the only figure who's had great achievements within their time here. Such pride for self-work, acknowledging much action through his time, Roger still view's William's work with a greater capacity, in addition to admiration.

"I'm just glad we didn't lose him, as he is one to run against any enemy nevertheless. At times, he surpasses standard human capabilities. Pride should have a limit, but I don't believe that is his issue. Yeah, I'll try to give him a call later. If not, I'll try to get a hold of David or Emily to see what's going on. They'd know more than I would," Roger says.

Roy has obtained an understanding from an observation of Roger's regards and upmost respect for William. "You really think highly of him, don't you? I still don't understand how they let you and them continue with your shenanigans," Roy replies. Before leaving the room totally, Roger stops. "It's probably because we do accomplish our duties . . . mostly. Of course, I think highly of him. Why not? He's . . ." Unknown to Roy, Roger turns sad. "Before I go, how was your trip to Albany?" Roger asks Roy. "Well enough. Attempts to introduce new armaments and defensive procedures went both directions. The best part was a revelation about an old friend, but she's in D.C. and doing OK for herself."

"You two go back a while? Or there's something beyond it?" Roger curiously asks.

"At one time, there was. Life sure has a way to separate a beautiful union," Roy despondently says.

Roger acknowledges Roy's feelings. "Sorry. Forgive my intrusion. I should go make that call." Roger leaves, walks back to his own office to see if he can get in touch with William. Roy watches Roger exit and then slowly turns to face the window in a melancholy fashion.

Roger enters his office and moves straight to his phone to dial William's number. A couple of rings until the voice mail's activation; a second attempt gets the same result.

His other options are to call David or Emily. Roger calls Emily first and asks if she knows William's whereabouts. Unfortunately, neither she has heard from him since last visiting a week ago. Emily hangs up the phone after notifying Roger and then sits back for a couple seconds. She looks over at a photo of them three together: David and William pose in it with her. Recollecting certain events, only to begin feeling sorry for what she did at the hospital. However, while visiting William at his house, an apology never happened. Presuming it wouldn't vex her . . . It did. So in needing to comprise an apology for her performance at the hospital, a level of emotions rises, but a decision to call David came first. During the call with David, equally unaware, he too doesn't know where William's been over the course of time since his visit a while back. Puzzled, they plan to assemble at William's house.

Emily has a hard time settling with talking to William on the subject of the hospital, but calling too many times and leaving messages might make it awkward. For some time, William's presence has been void, and knowing communication between each other has been apparent with David and Emily. Explaining what's been going on in the meantime during a prolonged leave will be uncomfortable enough. Day by day, it's been lessening, turning increasingly suspicious. David and Emily go through with their pre-meditated objective to see, if ever, William's "absence" becomes ever so clearer every second they'll divulge.

David halts his car and parks in front of William's house. "He and I had talked around late in the day at my house a little more than a week ago. As told by him, a letter was sent from an anonymous person stating the whereabouts of other operations pertaining to our previous expedition. He even sent it to forensics, but the only discovery was his finger prints. Otherwise, we can't really substantiate its message clearly," David truthfully says.

Annoyance covers her face as she turns her head toward David. "Wait . . . you could have told me earlier?! We could've done something, but it's too late now. It's blatant, coincidental, and odd to me. Of all people, he gets a notification verifying 'other operations'.

Where, is the question? Did anyone else question this evidence?" Emily says with suspicion. She soon gets out of the car and begins to approach the house.

David follows. "He probably lied to them. Not sure. I'm sorry for not relaying the event. He wanted it kept under a low-profile. I really shouldn't promote his ideas. *sighs* Figures this would happen again. We're on a path already. No turning back . . . Anyways, feels strange that we're going inside his house without him here. We'd pretty much be breaking in," David regrettably says.

"I hear you, but it's still odd with his side of the story. All we can do is move forward." Emily finds it "uncanny" as well, but nonetheless any different from such an unusual nature that William possesses.

David knocks on the door. No answer. He knocks several times again; waits a few seconds. No answer. They go around back. As the approach the back door, which is a sliding door, David goes to open it. "Huh . . ." David says in sarcastic amazement. Entering the vacated house, both make a quick scan from where they are initially standing. A quick walk around to every room to scrutinize to know if he's home... Behold, they're amid an empty house after all. Full of questions, answers yet to be known. Conversation establishes among each other about William's possible presence and Rookie's situation. David mentions that Rookie (his real name is Jin Fei Koya) went back home to Japan, where a good portion of family is, mentioning how everyone feels exceptionally terrible for what has happened to him. With much time to recover from such trauma, Jin retained his sanity by doing simple work (or simple chores) in and outside the house. He helps with his family's business (which makes clothes for the less fortunate). Second, wondering where William could be, since no clues are found still; they'll need to produce something to prove his disappearance.

Sometime passes during their excursion. Emily enters William's room and notices it's a mess compared to all other areas inside. Some clothes lie on different spots of the floor, and some other materials are strewn all over or atop other counters. An observation constitutes for her curiosity. She travels to another side of the bed. Papers lie about on the floor in a neat fashion. Discerning them, she sees that they're pictures that were drawn personally by him. With much interest, one catches her eye. It's of his room, and it shows Emily in it just as the drawing does, but she's standing by the window, peering outward instead . . . and has a small star on the edge of the bed she's closest to. She makes nothing of the thought on the star yet. As the crudely drawn pictures are sifted through, in the corner of her left eye, something sticks out of the box spring. Referencing the picture that caught her interest and directs back to the exact spot it's located at. A small opening occurs when she pulls it. As it opens, a letter is revealed from inside. David must see this. Walking up to him, the found paper was presented to him. "I found this in his room, inside the box spring," she states. Emily reveals its contents. One side has a small written paragraph and the opposite side has an edited map on it. "See what else there is and I'll keep looking on this side," David says.

She scans it thoroughly, and then flips it to read the message silently to herself. "Before the Lord I bow, for all my problems are washed away. Cleanse me o' Lord, I know I've sinned. Hear my words: I shall be renewed through your wisdom and ways; enlightenment is what I seek. Shall you ever find it in your heart; heal this forsaken world and its inhabitants, not for me but for their sake."

Emily recites every line again, one at a time, though (assuming it's supposed to have a meaning). Before continuing, she speaks surreptitiously. "A random excerpt to be placed on this doesn't match anything on here. Maybe it's just a thought he jotted down." Slow steps around the house, constant vigilance. "Hmm, before the Lord I bow . . ." Moving her head upward to see a cross above on a wall several feet ahead; she moves to it. Movement stops a couple feet away. A revelation! Takes another wild guess to see if this excerpt has any correlation to what else lies inside. "For all my problems are washed away..." A sink is perceived to her left. Another guess for this riddle . . . "I shall be renewed through your wisdom and ways . . ." She looks around from her initial position but takes notice of a Bible on an end table to her right. Another assumption: "Heal this forsaken world, not for me, but for everyone's sake." She looks down at the map. Trying to make it comprehensible to her imagination on its meaning, and looks up straight ahead, wondering where this is leading her. Both eyes catch the attention of four small black risen dots that reside on the wall beneath the cross. Perplexed at first, she starts to recognize the familiarity.

Many attempts pushing the buttons, David notices her occupied attention toward the wall she's near and approaches her. "Find something else?" Emily performs a Catholic gesture with one hand by pressing them on the wall, and then lowers her hand back down.

A moment later: a section of the floor in the living room open's. A subtle sound releases, averting David and Emily's attention. They move their eyes up at each other, raising their eyebrows with a surprised gesture. A darkened descent awaits them. What could be down there? What mysteries await them? Will their everlasting curiosity be quenched? A multitude of concepts flow through their minds as they guess what's below, Who knows? He could be a secret murderer . . . Dastardly plans, a maniacal twist of character, depths of depravity sinking ever so farther into a never-ending abyss as his victims pile up... kidding. So funny, laughter all around! Anyways, continuing!

> "Secret secrets are no fun, they could really hurt someone."

Chapter 8

Conspiring with the Conspirator

Let's check on William. We'll start at on 07/03/2028

Two days after Emily's visitation.

Ever since I've received the anonymous letter, it's put me through numerous tests: exceptional physically and mentally. Certain doom is well prepared for, my supplies were replenished, and assured preparedness to initiate this calling was validated. First: I followed a few cars around town that were used in the kidnappings (as told in the letter). While doing so, infiltration took place at a local building while following those supposed cars, after. Small tests were being performed inside the complex that I noticed when walking through, but no altercations with anyone, to my discovery. I ended up shutting it down permanently and additionally finding more information as well during that excavation . . . the precursor to the profound escapade. Little to nothing I couldn't handle. Covering my tracks before notifying the authorities was obvious. In succession, upon scanning the found information, there were three other, bigger operations inside our own country. But to my amazement, they were close by as in a state away . . . each . . . except for one. It was a manmade island off the coast of California. That's where I met my great hindrance, my search for absolute truth nullified, but only in the short term . . .

07/05/2028

Here's from the beginning. My first location was in Washington: a sole, one story complex stood before me, located off the shores between Washington and the Pacific Ocean. Observing its area with precision, assuming there'd be immense security, but not a hint was outside; so, getting inside was no issue—primarily a plus. Next set of doors reveal two men standing not too far inside another room, facing away from the doors behind them. I inconspicuously looked inside that room and viewed another subject currently tested on. You know . . . the usual. I eavesdropped during their conversation being permitted amid the pair. As deceiving as they were, intervention must happen. They were soon called by another person inside. Continuing to peek through the door's windows, I saw a scientist was receiving help from both men; they were lifting something large in a container, though its weight was trivial to them.

"Alex, what exactly is our boss trying to accomplish?" a guard asked. The scientist replies with no hesitation and pride by saying, "Well, it seems all astute observations he's made were quite remarkable. Besides him hating the faithful people, reasons are due to what was found destroyed every sense of reality. Vague, but first it has to do with this planet and humanity's current state. Besides from your limited understanding, if I told you everything it'd ruin the surprise." Their talks discontinue after such a frank remark made by Alex.

William quietly enters and hides behind a table, watching their every move continuously. Both guards stand by a different doorway. The scientist begins moving near William's direction, but William tries to hide in another spot to avoid detection. Success! Strangely, an awkward silence overcomes every inch inside.

William peeks around the corner from his hiding spot; the scientist— in khaki pants, white shirt and a lab coat—confronts William and has him in full sights.

(William thinks quickly on the newfound situation: either be quick and inconspicuous or take down the poor sap.)

(Ascent action +1) A choice to converse instead of killing is made. Before a full shout can be presented, he grabs Alex's legs. Falling down, some tools are knocked off a table while trying to get a hold of a secured footing, which Alex also fails to do. The duo turns the corner, look around, and then start to call out the scientist's name . . . but no answer. William has his hand around the man's mouth to negate further noises, or to alert anyone. William's hand gets bitten.

Releasing his hold, William attempts to grab again. Success! Nobody can be alerted still. Each is unaware of the whole debacle.

William aims to get some answers. "What purpose do these tests prove!? These people aren't gaining anything. I wouldn't call these ethical standards. Witnessing these innocents, it's for certain you're inconsiderate of their well-being. I'm going to let go of your mouth . . . If you scream, that's my final warning." (Persuasion passed/Ascent +3) Giving this man another chance to live, William lets go. In doing so, an exchange has been made.)

"I'm already informed. You'll never value what's being done. This discovery will change life itself along with all its aspects we view as is," Alex says.

Obviously against Alex's treacherous words, William tries to reason, and says (Ascent +1), "No one has to suffer this sadistic method. It needs to be stopped! All I see is anguish and a blind regime."

Alex cares not for William's words of compassion. Instead, he says he needs to continue this assignment, or the guards will get suspicious of his own absence. Allowed to leave, Alex gets up and walks in the direction of the subjected person.

Both guards come back in, and one says, "What's with all the noise back here?"

(William ponders on what to do: remain hidden or confront?)

William rises slowly to confront them boldly because he knows he won't be kept secret for long. Quickly recognizing William, guard number 1 says, "Look who it is—our fabled hero!" William stands there with a gun raised and pointed with precedent means, but theirs are also raised and aimed.

"Oh, like you knew it was me." William says sardonically. "The image was implanted," Guard number 2 says while pointing to his head. Guard number 1 recites a message from orders given earlier. "If you were to ever encounter William, which I know you will, you are to confront with absolute force upon arrival. I'm sure he'll have something to say . . . just let him say his last words." Both smile cynically at each other.

[William's mindset is focused on saving these people.]

(Ascent dialogue +3 - He chooses to speak up for the innocence's affliction.)

William's face drops, but he decides to speak out his sorrows for every soul being tested on. "All these people: families, children . . . all hooked up to these machines! They're basically dead. Their lives taken away! What logic is this?! How despicable. This was meant to save the people from all harm, 'revitalize' their 'souls', and bring peaceful prosperity? That's hard to believe. Eventually, an operation like this would be refuted."

Laughing with impertinence, void of care, guard number 2 says, "That's some kind of gall you have risking your own life, except it means nothing—empty words placed at our feet."

(A certain emotion gets the better of William.)

(Descent action: +3 - William's hand is ready and able to grab his other side arm.)

The guards are distracted by William's moving speech, and with precision, he quickly shoots left positioned guard in the chest, and then rapidly shoves a nearby table at all three, knocking them over. Guard number 2 rises quickly and begins to shoot, but William has vanished. Appearing behind him, William grabs guard number 2 in a choke hold. Breaking hold, guard number 2 punches William in the face again and again. William blocks him finally, countering one of the strikes, and hits him in the abdomen. He pulls a gun out quickly, and two shots go off as William gets tackled concurrently by guard number 1, to then be rammed into a standing device, which breaks from impact. It's unprecedented if guard number 2 was ever killed, but he's nowhere to be seen, oddly. Guard number 1 goes to shoot William from behind. Perceiving this, he turns, quickly grabs the gun, and jumps to the side, then back to the ground. Guard number 1 hastily walks over to William. Pointing the gun at his opponent, William on one knee, subsequently stands up and forces it in the opponent's face to shoot point blank. Alex, out of nowhere, tries rushing William with a random hard object. Seeing from a peripheral angle, William dodges and kicks Alex forward, knocking him into a group of chairs farther ahead. The struggle continues . . . Guard number 1 grabs William's gun in hand before it could be fired. The gun is forced in William's face. Resisting, William forces it back . . . And the other gun... BANG!!! BANG!!! Two shots to the head . . . Guard number 1 body falls as blood flies everywhere—even on William's face and body as well from the blow back.

William looks around for Guard number 2. Not too far ahead, at the front door lies the other defender. William followed the blood trail. Upon closing in, and perceiving the damage: only one bullet penetrated the lower abdomen, but too much blood was lost. Another bullet created a bad shoulder wound as well. William ties the man's hands and feet with some chain and rope that was probably meant for other inhuman experiments. William has a handy medical pack and works his best to wrap the wounds. Luckily, the bullets escaped the guard's body when he was shot.

(As the man moans from his infliction, William chooses whether to cover his mouth to shut him up or to just continue helping.)

Tolerance takes place (Ascent +2). The injured foe is attended to first before William approaches Alex again. By finishing proper aid, the hardest part seems to be over. William soon walks away to conclude this quest's part. When entering the main room, Alex obviously shows fear. "OK! OK! You win." Alex says pleading for his life.

(Merciful action +1 - remorse is given.) Placing each hand on Alex's shoulders, William says, "Those guards would kill just about anybody. You have any idea what they were going to do to you once your task was completed? I overheard them before I came into the room. Now,

I need you to take that man you're working on and unhook him safely. Most importantly: make sure he is alive. Okay?"

(Alex took notice of the idea.) An agreement is arranged: the subject is released, also to remain alive. "What would they have done?" Alex asks.

"Something that would have been gruesome. I don't think you want to know," William says. (Ascent +1)

Alex becomes greatly disturbed by the disclosure.

Observing William's body language, a question is asked. "You seem bothered. What is your aim in all this?

William moves his eyes toward Alex with visible anger. (Critical dialogue +1) "I have my objective. My target is somewhat known—not in full sight, lamentably. You wouldn't understand. I did notice those strange aspects on both guards... Something was indifferent about them. Their eyes and skin were a little odd. They also seemed . . . somewhat competent. You're the closest to understanding these methods. You tell me."

Alex replies with approval to his claim and says, "I realized that, too. Ever since his intended plan was foiled a while back. I assume that was you? Able to acquire significant help to protect his subjects was needed. Our leader doesn't inform us of much but to tell us to do our jobs, or else. I've seen things that would twist your reality, something that would envelope complete distortion around you. He's creating an army and they're called Legionnaire de' diabolic."

Interest rises with each word spoken. William can only envision what's known for the moment at hand. William implores Alex to call the police and to refrain from expelling any information to anyone about his (William's) own plan or position in this procedure . . . "What is this legion and plan?" William asks himself.

Guard number 2 slowly burns off the bindings and walks over to where William is. Swiftness, unsuspectingly, William is thrown across the room, and he smashes into other devices and equipment. "Seeing that our initial dependent wasn't fully transformed like me. Oh well... potential was high." (Tattooed black lines cover the sentinel's body, and small horns protrude from his head, eyes glowing red with black pupils; he has voice only the damned would possess.) William grunts from his minor wounds and rises to his feet in shock to what was perceived. Intensely questioning his own integrity, to self, "How am I supposed to fight him?" The abomination draws nearer to William.

"Unfortunately, my powers have to recharge. You should be able to manage yourself in the meantime," the demon speaks.

William quickly shouts, "Get that man out of here. Make haste!"

Infernal Fiend 1 (title/Tier I) ignores Alex and the experimented as they move outside. It continues to attack.

The battle between opposites rages on; only destruction is allowed. Having to deal with unfair abilities—trying to understand the means behind this—William soon gains an "adaption instinct" against this demon's patterns of attacks and recharge times. Luckily, every power exerted isn't too fatal, but it's possible to withstand. The only power this demon wields is strength, save for only a limited time or exertion . . . and a projecting fire blast—only once every cool down. William grows keener and comes closer and closer to defeating this Infernal Fiend. To add: William patiently waits for a fatal strike to approach.

Alex has safely transported himself and the subject out and alive due to careful detachment, even though William's battle is intense. Alex watches over the unconscious man outside from all mayhem inside. William's soon thrown outside through two doors from within. He is launched forcefully and hits the ground, then slides across it. Infernal Fiend walks quickly forward, applying deathly intent.

(Descent action: +4- Subtracting all fears, learning to harden his heart for the enemy, to never allow weakness to be evident.)

Picking William up by the neck, however, before performing any more damage, William says, "You shall be eradicated!" and quickly breaks it's intended grab. He takes a small plastic cross out from his pocket and slams it against the demon's forehead, resulting in burning and loud screams from punishing agony. As the cross burns its way inside farther, William travels behind, unsheathes his giant fucking knife, chops menacingly with the straight edge, and then places its serrated side throat bound again, pushing and pulling slowly with great force to inflict maximum agony. Harder and harder, black blood sprays outward. Infernal Fiend's head gradually becomes severed from its body . . . and falls to the ground with the body concomitantly. To finalize, a massive pulse emits before the demon's body reaches the ground. William is pushed back several feet by the pulse as well; hurriedly lifting his head, he sees the body disintegrating to ash. Lying on his back from the pulse, there's much relief with the battle's conclusion. It takes some time getting up . . . However, he is able to stand; mobility is existent. William locates his knife eventually. Blood vaporizes from the cold steel before he retrieves it and scrutinizes the blade with curiosity. William walks over to Alex to see that the patient is well and alive, fortunately. Relief and happiness overcomes William nearly completely.

(During the duel, William gained a passive ability: Intuitive instinct—he has gained the ability to understand his opponent early in battle or a slight chance (15 percent) to obtain any additional info before any altercation happens. Read body language, words expel more detail; understand your surroundings quicker, and prolonging a fight can bring further bonuses giving you certain permanent advantages against them, no matter who your enemy is (or similar enemies). Bonus- Ascent, Jester and Descent attribute increases by 10 each. Also, more 'Dialogue and Action' options for them become available!)

(William informs Alex to call the police again, and to not tell them any bit of information on what happened here, except the fact that another innocent person was found. The only way to get a legit answer will be to go further into incomparable chaos. This adventure will not be easy by any means. It will only pose more of a threat to come. Alex points William into another direction, which he marked on the map. William immediately sets off to finish what was started by him personally. Violence will only continue; it's only persisting with exceeding struggles.)

"Void of reality—indirectly part of a larger scheme—aware of any participation and blinded by heroism. Stay wary of your motives; be attentive of your actions."

Chapter 9

Visitation Pt. 3

David ventures into far-reaching darkness first. One light turns on by itself as he curiously succumbs below. Emily descends a few seconds later. "This should be educational, though unconventional to the normal house. Then again . . ." Emily says. Strangely to her, a small device descends with a laser and scans both of them thoroughly then retracts; she glances to the left side, finding a clue, even though David already passed the entrance and is at the bottom of the staircase. As Emily is at the top, black lights turn on rapidly in the tunnel, revealing a know-how-to description on the wall to allow a proper venture through. "Well, that's convenient," Emily says as she reads some of the texts' explanation about the map's true purpose. Although, she notices some of the clues glowing from the light and lifts it eye level, front side facing her.

"It says there are questions/riddles you must get right to proceed. Once completed, an answer will be revealed to you. If answered correctly, a number will be given to you for input as well. In receipt of those answers, you must add every number to create a whole. I trust few souls—reasons only known to a trio that we can comprehend—a question each for you two and me. Once you pass through all three stages, you may enter. You will gain the locations of my quest and the last destination I have reached. (PS: specifics and order does not matter. I know I could just tell you my whereabouts, but trust is hard to come by these days, ironically said.)"

David finds this quite easy to conquer. Emily proceeds. First question is for David. "For many days we've known each other, and within that time we've explored every corner of Earth; many years have been seen, but only certain ones were paramount among us." (Ascent increases: +5 for William.)

With no hesitation, David answers with, "Space Academy and its rooftop. I remember going there for a week with him. We used to sneak out at night and go on the roof with a telescope we stole from one of the labs, so we could see what constellations were out. Camp counselors soon caught on to our little rebellious act.

"Arcane Jump Pond was another. It was quite the spot. A 150-foot oak tree stood sturdily. A long ten-foot rope was attached to its last branch, which hovered many feet above. It had to be at least one hundred years old or so at the time, still strong to this day. Anyways, we would step back as far as possible then let physics do its job."

"Another is: Val's Tree House. I remember that kid. He got all the ladies. Not really . . . I gave him credit for trying, though. His tree house was amazing. It consisted of a DJ table, TV, game consoles, and many other fun materials. Good times."

"Next is Nostalgia Grove. I swear every time you'd go and relax you'd be overcome with nostalgia—hence its name. I and William would always go there if we were upset or down about anything else. I can't be more obvious on that."

"Last one is Eleven Street. Its name preceded all who walked among it. One day, I and William found a blocked off dead-end street that led to a drop into the town's neighboring lake. The street had a sixty-degree slant. Kids would ride their bikes, skateboards, or whatever down it that had wheels attached. But it was closed off for good reasons. We always said the eleventh hour was among us . . . A kid didn't go far enough and hit the rocks below. We didn't know him. Anyways, that's about it for my part, I believe. David adds up each number. Only two of them meant more than the others. So two, then add it all together as one. That makes seven." (David finds comfort from this.)

This next question is from and is for William. "By now, you three recognize me as a man of faith with a high degree, but how much faith you two have is the real question. Here's something you both would know . . . If I look north bound, I see one horizon; if I look south-bound, I see a flock of ten geese. The amazing part of this view is when you look eastward or westward, but at different times, most people miss its magnificent show.

(William's entire stature changes indifferently, and due to David and Emily already assuming the answer correctly: Descent -2, Jester 0, and Ascent 2.)

Emily responds with "Dawn." David responds with "Dusk." "1, 10 and 2 equals 13," Emily adds up.

"I saved the best for last. I know you've cared about me more than usual, more than a brotherly figure. The whole time, it shouldn't have been avoided. Nearly everything you do is truly amazing. Acknowledging how much a person cares for another promotes much hope for humanity . . . or for a man himself. I wouldn't understand such fervor if it wasn't for your constant vigilance. And tell David to mind his own business. I know how much he hates being showed up in front of everyone. You know what I'm talking about." David laughs at the comment.

"Your question is this: The day we met was as if everything stood still. All the times we spent together were eternal. That look in your eyes when we connected was ageless. No one else would have shown me such passion and grace. This greater mutual bond we now have for each other—our love is undying. Do you remember the exact date when we first kissed?

Emily begins to blush and answers softly, "05/18/16 . . . That makes 39." Emily becomes quiet for a moment after answering. (Emily finds comfort in this) (Romance increases: +5)

David abruptly says, "Wait, you guys actually . . . I mean . . . you OK? Need a moment?"

Emily replies by saying she doesn't and clenches her right fist, then says to just move on. They reach the final door. David adds up all numbers: 7+13+39. "Fifty-nine is the answer." Feelings greater than content come forth. The door opens suspenseful like; what awaits them is unknown . . .

Interlude 4

Conspirator's endeavor

Process of Derivation (The Induction)

As William makes an exit, an intended call for aid was completed. Alex patiently waits, sitting in silence as trivial wildlife creates noise, bugs crawl around, and other vibrant life scurries around. Ten minutes in, reinforcements from law enforcement and the military comes from all directions, and even from the skies. Randomly, a figure appears behind Alex, grabs him and they vanish. Reappearing deep within a lab setting: sounds of machinery at work, other researchers travel from station to station and experiments with bodily limbs examined thoroughly on steel tables. A woman is seen in another room. Her face's lower portion is covered, the ankles, neck and wrists are immured by metal bands; monitors keep symmetrically balanced with the rhythm of her heart. Two tubes leading from both arms to and fro with a machine extract small portions of blood. Other researchers examine her entire body as she watches them.

A man in the room says, "That's exactly what I needed." Looking at the scientist (Alex), he acquired from the site William intervened at, makes him uncomfortable.

Alex asks, "Why? How . . . how were those men even alive, even with those augmentations? This I don't understand. You never told me. What about the others?"

Soulless eyes stare at Alex, then "MoS" replies, "Why? A likely chance to distinguish anything important from your enemy . . . the more you'll be aware when time comes." Understanding perception one can equip places fright within Alex while listening. "Here's what we know: this William is compassionate about saving people, has prowess when fighting, but likes to remain anonymous. You see, were not going to expose him at all. We'll give him that secretive position.

Let's have our next post increase in difficulty to recognize how strong these capabilities truly are." The woman mentioned earlier, opposite of them, looks at "MoS"; both make an unnerving gaze toward each other. She ensures what's construed in her mind . . . and closes her eyes seconds later.

"After a while, or shortly, therefore, under certain circumstances or happenings, wouldn't you question yours or one's line of work?"

Chapter 10

The Conspirator: Chaos rising

07/06/2028

The next day after William's first encounter, he takes some personal time from an outstanding scene that had happened, knowing completely it won't be an easy accomplishment to continue. On another note: a stay at a hotel for now is a good idea, but getting rest before launching a new quest is logical. For his sake, which would be idiotic if he forgot, to realize what he's up against has great integrity; unbeknownst to his knowledge, unfortunately, about the tougher opponents coming next, who will provide a challenge.

07/08/2028, 10:14 a.m.

Two days later, I arrive at the borderland of Nevada, adjoining California, from a quick flight to Reno. A rental car is used and I make way to the second location mentioned from uplifted-anew scientist Alex, who he encountered yesterday. Arriving . . . Scanning the area . . . surrounded by a mountainous concept. After searching the perimeter, I noticed that there were two guards in front and two in back. When every external personnel made their rounds (by an understanding of their routine), that is the time for me to enter. Making way down a hill, a couple of hired hands are coming in my direction, though having to avoid detection by dropping down a couple feet off the edge from my earlier position. They fly over me on weird machines I never saw before. Nearly quiet at least, but still noticeable. They almost resemble small cars, but they hover.

However, trying not to contemplate about, I head a little farther downhill. Halfway down, to observe one of the peons making its rounds was closing in; contact is quickly avoided by jumping into a nearby bush. I turn to see another coming my way, next. With hoping they didn't detect my presence, I maintained a silent stationary arrangement till they've passed. Closer and closer they come—abrupt gun shots are heard, but only to wonder if they know of my presence. They are firing chaotically, so it's a possibility they don't. Not too far along the paralleled path of firing, someone's naked and running near my vicinity. To postulate, it's one of the subjects most likely. He is trying an escape!

(Ascent action: +4 - I decide to help him to accumulate an intervention along with their chase.)

To start, by shooting in the air makes one guard's attention shift to me. He begins to come my way. Currently in front of me now, he view's all directions. I arise slowly, but instead . . . my leg is snared by a branch, and its leaves rattle as the branch is whipped back. He turns quickly. Rapidly slashing the tendons near the wrists, his gun drops; viciously slashing upward, sever the neck, and blood sprays on my face. After apprehending this guard, the corpse is placed in the bush, but I insist to instigate the other one who is still chasing the escapee.

Now one hundred yards ahead . . . I spot one of those machines they are riding around. Ignorant at first, observing all switches, every button . . . assuming the best fortune. Not so hard after all. My target is in proximity; I'm going to ram into the bastard. Before I could land a killing blow upon him, I jump off my vehicle, albeit it misses my target, though. As it breaks into a thousand pieces, my enemy turns around and hunts me down quickly. (It was a cool idea until it didn't work). My fall wasn't as soft as intended, either. An uncompromising recovery, a scheme is made to capture the fleeing person. I then quickly spot a naturally formed rock formation shaped like a ramp (it stands 20 feet tall) and run up it. Its peak approaches, and I jump off . . . landing right on top of the pursuer. We both then fall right to the ground. His mobile machine disappeared past us. Hurt from the action ensues, and we begin fighting. Not lasting long, a quick maneuver made by ruthlessly punching his head with brass knuckles.

Catching up to the escaped man and thinking to call him out, but the notion changes. I decide to just catch him myself. Frightened beyond belief, he falls over because of his current state. Meeting up . . . before gaining enough ground, the man cowers when he sees me. "Please. Please. No more! No more . . . My family is in there. They don't deserve any of this."

(A vicarious reminiscence of a past event occurs in me, how my family was a part of these experiments, knowing that I wasn't the only person with so much to lose either.)

Staring compassionately with empathy over personal troubles, an attempt to calm such fears, informing him of my insight of the situation; slowly a calm sensation takes form. Bret, he said his name is. We talk for a couple of minutes before departing and finishing what was started originally. He gives me some info on the whereabouts of this unknown man over a conversation that was eavesdropped, while tests were being commenced almost a week back. I ask him how it was possible, but Bret is unsure himself if luck played in or given chance to elude was allowed. Hence, being the only one to release himself from those diabolical machines without harming his own self or others, too. I tell him to stay put while I deal with our remaining threat. Agreeing completely—and I obviously make sure he is equipped to handle himself just in case anything will happen while I'm absent, so he is given a gun.

Logically, an endeavor to call for backup would be wise, even for Bret's rescue to occur. Their infiltration of the building won't be so soon; they'd be void of any guidance, in addition to withstanding, or understanding anything about these abominations, if now. They wouldn't know what to do with them. I could be caught with my arrogance, as I don't even know what I'm doing. Highly hoping this meeting won't be as violent, also excluding the supernatural like the last . . . Approaching the building with extreme caution still, so many questions on how they managed such a feat to transform people into demons, literally. How? Maybe they weren't. Who knows—it could be all a fallacy to put fear into the masses? Maybe just make us realize our own? Oh, what am I saying? Of course they are. How else could they perform such applications with their own bodies? Could it just be modifications? Anyways, Bret, whom I helped, did say that there were ten inside; there could be more, possibly. Myself, trying to devise a plan on how to approach the odds, but to divulge properly with my performance against them all is going to be an interesting interaction. Thoughts are recollected, a time for calming—praying for the best . . .

The venture to my destination makes me nervous. Amid this large building, I soon peek inside a window through its front doors to see if any are in sight as mentioned before. Surprisingly, no cameras are outside. Already spotting those two other guards that are patrolling from outside, besides the two I took out already. I'm surprised they didn't hear my gunshot from earlier. Worked out for the best, I guess. Carefully moving onward as a silent shadow . . . Well, not the shadows exactly, though *stealthily* would be the choice word. Upon entering, it would be rational to move behind a small obstruction and check my surroundings first. Both men walk into a room further in, greeting others as they enter. Perusing my arsenal, I see that I have one flash-bang grenade, one smoke grenade. Not much, but it'll do.

Upon revealing my perception of the inner area, it's a simple construct. A flash-bang will be utilized first, while covering my eyes, and also while moving on. Both targets are blinded from it and stumble. I put on thermal goggles to prepare myself; I close in quickly, subduing them by swiftly cutting their throats firstly. I use the smoke grenade in a larger room, which I roll it toward just before the doorway adjacent from me, so the smoke would reach all rooms. "All eyes towards there and take cover. Be alert!" one of the guards profoundly yells out. I make haste inside and try to take as many out as quickly as possible before the smokescreen dissipates.

Killing three at least, three more come in from some other part inside, spraying their guns all over. Fortuitously, they kill some scientists and guards in succession. Or is it on purpose? A dumb move on their part, though it is odd. After killing their comrades, the smokescreens' strength diminishes. I am hiding for the moment. Removing my eye-wear . . . What just happened? Obviously they were shooting, but to just kill them unbeknownst is just strange, like I said.

"Hey," a subtle voice speaks out. Looking around in the room I was literally by, I see nothing inside. I veer my interest back the other way, and those three continue surveying the room. "Open my prison." That same voice speaks again. I look in a second time. Yellow glowing eyes glimmer. Again, a decent perimeter check to see if the enemy is growing near, but instead, all movement go to another direction; all three split up on different paths. As I slink across the floor, crawling to the being who beckons me, soon a sizable, robotic cat-like paw gently places itself on my right hand. I stop with trembling fear and ready my gun. This being speaks again. "I can help you. You're not the only one that witnessed immoral acts performed here." I look to my right, and up. The glowing eyes appear again.

"A talking lion? Impossible." I say.

"Now that's not important. I'll help you at any cost if you're here to put an end to this nightmare," the unknown being says.

(Open the cage or not?)

(Special +5) New teammate unlocked. A shocking revelation and reassurance for me to make it seem everything will be OK. Hopefully this creature was being honest with every word that was spoken. He seems to oppose the current event. I can't ignore it now. Right now, an ally is beneficial.

Cautiously unlocking the cage, I suddenly hear someone approaching my location, saying, "Something doesn't belong here." Adrenaline courses through the entirety of my body, and sweat drips down my face. I get ready to act. Unlocking the cage is easy. When leaving the present room, a better arrangement away from all opposition would be wise. Assuming to be spotted, each enemy takes different paths through the main room again. I can feel every bit of tension rising with exceptional magnitude. Three, two, one . . . I get up and rush the closest to me, smashing both of us into a window that leads to an inner room of the larger one we were formerly in. Guard number 1 stands up and tries to grab me, but I hastily move by rolling away. Up and readying myself again, another foe assists, and four separate hands grapple and throw me airborne to a differing side. They are relentless. "Our master was right in his foretelling of your visitation. Let's see how much of a perk these powers are," Guard number 1 says.

On both feet, two of three guards are already in front of me. Picked up by the neck, I'm punched by guard number 2 in the face, and then I kick guard number #1 in the abdomen. Fazed somewhat from the blows, and continuing to punch the living shit out of who was choking me, which felt appropriate. Aggressively moving Guard number 2, he then falls over from a multitude of strikes, while guard number 3 jumps above to strike me. I dodge the impact. Guard number 1 and number 2 come forth again. I run at them. On my way, I pick up a heavy device. No idea what it could be? I use the device to smash guard number 1 in the face exceptionally hard, an instant knockout. I then turn right and swing it at guard number 2. Grabbing it like the badass he is and takes it from my hands and throws it away. Guard number 2 smiles with such evil determination. My self-knowledge of being too engrossed certainly is opposing. This fight lasts for some time, greater strength of any human's capability; possesses the same attributes as my last battle. Still bearable and able to fight against them, their blows do hit harder than usual.

The battle goes on for almost half an hour. I'm growing tired and trying to stay alive concurrently. Unexpectedly, a shot is fired. One of the two scientists in the room randomly shoots guard number 2 in the chest; he looks down at the bullet wound and shouts in pain as he begins burning alive. A pile of ash remains in the aftermath. The remaining demons apprehend the scientist and rip him in half. My eyes open wide from a gruesome sight before me. No remorse, no sympathy—only death. I step backward slowly and try to create an appropriate intention to reach that gun. Both enemies walk quicker and lunge, but a successful evasion from the incoming attacks accumulates. I fall to my knees, rolling frontward, retrieving the gun, and rush along with a proper scenario. Instead of simply striking, I grip guard number 3's extended arm, which was reaching for me, and shoot it and each leg. Before completely falling, the tool of death follows to the cranial region of guard number 3's, one last shot directed as head bound.

The final enemy awaits me. No hesitation, no guilt. How many shots are left in reserve . . . matters little to none. To resume an assault is a must. Sharp claws try making contact with my face a couple of times, but I dodge, uppercut its chin, and provide a couple punches to the abdomen and then to the face again. Kicking the demon back a couple of feet, intent to walk over and annihilate its face with my foot is imminent. Lastly, I repeatedly shoot until all ammunition is rendered. No mercy given; a blackened heart for these abominations was there only reward.

The last of the abominations turns into a pile of ash . . . Only that remains. What have I started, what will be the future for us? Surround ourselves in ruin?

One more comes in ready to kill. It's as if this one was amped up, bulging with unnatural power, as its heavy wheezing increases. Spotting me, but before it could charge, a horrifying roar is unleashed. That creature I encountered moments prior jumps over me. No apprehension's shown with a strong clenched bite to its neck, ramming it through the wall simultaneously. Rubble lies in waste from complete destruction. Astonished and speechless, I have to see the aftermath . . . only to look past the cavity and see the altercation. The beast rips and tears with no remorse; blood rapidly empties. Lastly, it opens its maw wide then crushes the foe's head, a crunching noise so loud, it was horrid.

My consciousness turns me around to check on those people who are experimented on. If any have life existing inside . . . to my trepidation, no rhythm, absent life—nothing exists. Sorrow and anger rapidly grows inside of me, rising with intensity. The machine's thoroughly examined. It's destroyed. Yelling loudly in anger, and I bash both my hands against the metal corrupter. No way of fixing it; all I can do is stand in silence for their hastened wake. Upon wishful thinking to save everyone and to help all, this singular task is for an idealist. Being one myself, but I've failed in doing so. Have I botched this hope, or their hope? Have I a war with myself to blind me evermore, to only stretch down a road of never-ending destruction whilst performing with such wrathful intentions? Is this preternatural or abnormal? To redeem myself and the people is a grand task for a hero, not me! Stationed among the dead with a faltered soul— silent pain for the fallen. Life is wept for, though revitalization is in vain. Their deaths disconcert me deeply.

The lion approaches me, scrutinizing for anything. He stops in front of me and looks up. "You did your best. I have no doubts. These specific subjects—"

"People," I say to interrupt.

The beast continues. "People . . . have been extensively subjected to major afflictions internally. I watched for three days what these monsters— it can do. Such horrors inflicted on innocents. None of these atrocities can go unpunished. You halt these advocates of the being who's strayed from grace?"

I look at him, giving a direct stare of certainty. "This thing has already acquired my family and others. Guessing I'm too far past my reach. Am I going insane? I'm talking to a cyber lion. I'm losing my mind, aren't I?"

Laughing not out of disrespect but in response, the lion answers me. "Domination for this world isn't just over all humanity. Even the animal kingdom has threats. I'm not the first to be tested on. You say your family was taken from you? I just hope this isn't plain vengeance, and you're just heading into pandemonium with a clenched fist. I'd be careful. You have any idea what's happening, honestly? To answer the second part: this thing had a specific agenda. I can't entirely explain it."

I look up and say, "No. Maybe it is. I don't know. Something inside me is compelling me."

"Just know: a planetary divide will commence. I believe we are witnessing the coming of our judgment," the beast truthfully says. William's eyes show conviction. To no end, it'll only push him farther; such an experience will only bring greater pain.

I notice my acquaintance leaving. "Wait. Where'd you come from?"

He stops moving, and tells me, "I was to be a figure of terror: the Nemean lion, derived from mythology about being sent to Peloponnese to terrorize the city. Seemingly more like the world, now. My robotics is irrelevant. I feel like a badass ever since this repurposing ploy. I prefer to be called Cithaeron. More fitting, I believe," Cithaeron says. My reaction is in full support of his claim. "Just leave this place, for there's not much you can do here any longer."

(William thinks on whether to leave the victims in an unnatural, tortuous position or give them an honorable funeral.)

"No one should be left like this; they need a proper funeral. You can join me, or go." (Thoughtful deed +3)

Cithaeron decides to agree with helping fulfill my wish. I pile a couple bodies on the back of Cithaeron to carry. Though, I take each body out one at a time. Any shovels or tools relevant to dig a hole aren't around anywhere.

I return inside to see if there's something else that could be close enough to be used as one. He uses a piece of damaged metal that was from the previous altercation. A pole is attached to it, and he ties whatever he can use to combine the two pieces to replicate a shovel's head. Back out, William witnesses something from the exit's doorway. Cithaeron circles around an area, implying a good spot to dig. He stomps the ground with his front legs, making an oval shape appear. The lot of earth rises above, hovering. William watches in amazement as Cithaeron continues.

Cithaeron calls me over to help place them in the hole; calling me again breaks my trance, and I walk over. The first body's laid respectfully, but I focus on the hovering earth. "It'll stay. Just focus on bringing them below." Expelling an obvious notion, I say, "If you can levitate earth, can you focus that energy on the bodies?"

Cithaeron awkwardly replies, "It would look weird."

I agree, and continue to bring each body into the earth. "But the floating dirt isn't strange to see? That's normal," I say. When finished, Cithaeron slowly shakes the hunk of earth back as it piles on the corpses. In addition, each second becomes gloomier. Shaken dirt lies comfortably as the sacrifices rest underneath. The earth meets bottom, as well as the people who died for a fallacy.

"Anything you'd like to say?" Cithaeron asks.

(William decides whether to give honor to the dead or just leave without any spoken words.)

Silent momentarily . . . "Respecting life is to give love. Nothing is stronger than that ideal. What have we stumbled upon? How can we give love when we promote death endlessly? I've walked with ghosts, and eyes stared back with sorrow. Their eyes clout me with hopelessness and despair, cutting my heart with unintentional tribulation. Images spread through my mind—witnessing tyranny for self-gain. Blood flows below your feet consistently. A stolen life, a stolen heart: a person who's nevermore. Never will I let them die in vain. I'll be their hero and bring the light back to their eyes." (Ascent dialogue: +3)

Cithaeron walks over to William, sits down, and turns his gaze upward at him. "I can see to some extent why interest comes to mind from our foe about you. Not solely by your words, but because of the fervor. Sometimes the guards mentioned a said person of interest. Are you him?" William just stares at the freshly shifted earth; to no end do the feelings of righteousness and confidence slowly slip from his mind and circle the abyss below, forever swirling around his failures.

"Your eyes are a portal to the soul. What really hides from that which no one else can grasp? What images are flowing? What notions are processed? What is truth? What is false? Certain views can blind one-self or bring around that exact truth which you seek. I've witnessed madness, cruelty and monsters that reside deep inside the consciousness. Well aware of their own actions . . . or do they not? Exposed to such people and/or you allow your surroundings to drag you down. There's is light in it somewhere, if you believe it. Go as far as you can and reach for the sky. Be careful to not let the darkness tread on you, swallow your soul, or become one of its everlasting slaves."

Chapter 11

Visitation

Pt.4 / Finale

Emily and David will momentarily walk into the room William had sealed off, seeking to comprehend his very purpose, hoping to figure out every intention. Great suspense before them; interest becomes increasingly abundant. A door opens completely . . . Slowly walking inside—a mystery revealed. They notice through their perusal: pictures of his child hood, drawings and trophies from his achievements during sport events as a child. A large pedestal sits among the epicenter, surrounded by anonymity. Interest surmounts indefinitely from scattered materials as they search for clues. Some words are exchanged during their ploy. "He sure is a crude artist. I give him credit for trying at least. Is this what he really conjures in his head?" David says.

"Maybe, but why do you think they were drawn? Perhaps they do have a story to tell, or it's just part of his personality that's expressed through these drawings," Emily professes in William's defense.

"You really think this is not a state of insanity? Ponder these wild pictures of devils, angels, and the afterlife. He's really this much of a believer? You ever wonder the reason he secludes himself from the crowd? He always acts weirdly around everyone. The main concern is this lair, and the fact that he can be eccentric at times," David frankly says as his remarks are birthed from a worried state for his friend, increasing unceasingly.

Emily turns to him and understands every single ounce of frustration; she walks over to David and tries to comfort his mind. "We're both at a loss . . . Don't let your anger cloud your thoughts. We've made it into this room which has this solution to finding him. Who knows what's happened. All we can do is hope for the best until we reach him. You know, hopelessness is not an aspect of his. We both know that quite well. Yes, going beyond one's own boundaries, his firm grasp is in territory unknown. And I just think nothing has happened to him yet . . ." Emily pleads while trying to stay positive and not ponder adversity. Deep down inside: fear's greater form is evident; faith's trivial compared to the initial state she's currently in. Both can only manage as much as they can, while trying to stabilize their thoughts and maintain equilibrium concurrently. Searching wall to wall, David approaches the pedestal. Confused for a minute, but then he begins to see if anything pertains to its purpose.

While Emily continues sifting through William's belongings, one picture catches her interest: it supposedly shows the state of heaven and hell. Curious of its meaning, she conducts a full scan of its entirety. Angels happily flying around, a kingdom in the background, braziers lit all around a palace, and gates to everlasting life. Down below: people falter in the depths of hell—screams of who suffer from afflicted humanity; ever-lasting entropy. She sees two different distinct characters: an angel looks down from above with a sad expression; a devil like creature that seems to be holding entrails and upholds a blank stare directly at you. Also among the pictures: that of a third figure that in relation could possibly be the Grim Reaper, but she's unsure, really. David finds a groove on the pedestal and follows it down a couple feet. Its extension stretches across the floor. David arrives at the adjacent wall and follows the groove upward with his hand. He feels a place on the wall that's been disturbed. Upon pushing it, a sound emits from the pedestal. A screen reveals dramatically up front: eight feet by eight feet, to be exact.

They turn and see a huge map displayed from the projection. David moves near her; Emily focuses down on William's picture again for a moment before placing it back where she found it prior. Attention is now averted to David's discovery. Mesmerized and in awe, trying to understand, his eyes scroll at every possible place William's been. "He's traveled this far. What are you doing?" David softly says. Emily remains quiet. As a final point, they have a precise destination where William is presently located.

Happiness overcomes them indefinitely; confidence is restored slowly every second they come to reaching their friend. "Wait . . . He's been traveling around this much and didn't take us along?!" David comically mentions.

"We're going now, aren't we?" Emily says as she looks at David to then produce a smile from this revelation they've uncovered. An idea is devised between each other. They know, otherwise assuming, he's at the last location mentioned (as it was circled with a different color, and he specified a time next to it as well). Every second counts toward William's safe return or demise. Through William's radical placement in his own reasons, each come to a conclusion on how to approach this conflict, which holds a continuity of multiplying questions abound. No remorse will be given once completed and returned from this adventure. They, too, know all consequences at hand quite well. William's prospect of being rescued diminishes each wasted second, but a strategy has sparked quickly.

Soon leaving William's house, a straight path to the precinct is made certain. "I guess we can breathe a little, huh?" David says in slight relief.

"Sooner we get there . . ." Emily softly utters. David's perplexed about William's motives and ideals that seem bleak.

"I'm actually quite mystified with its theme. What would you call this: ambition?" David says.

Emily expresses her thoughts, clinging with frank assumptions. "More like a subjugation. Subversive nature accompanied with deceptive methods? Sure."

Sometime in their socializing through the car ride, David notices in the rear-view mirror that they've been followed by a car for seven blocks now. "Speaking of ill-intent, that blue car's been following us for a while," he says.

"You're just being paranoid," Emily bluntly accuses David. David assumes to "not know" and acts casual during their drive. David soon changes logic by acting irrationally instead, and accelerates. The car in pursuit emulates the quickening action. "What are you doing?" Emily despondently asks. David then presses the brakes down hard, and their pursuer impacts their car from behind. Affected from the impact, intervention stops for now. David and Emily are rattled as well and drive on. "You OK?" David asks, concerned for Emily.

"I am," she says after taking a deep breath. Warily through a large parking lot, David and Emily scope their directions. No one is coming. Exiting the lot a couple seconds later, two different cars appear. "I knew this wouldn't come easy!" David loudly declares. Entering a new street: hastily driving . . . Next to the exit of the parking lot, the enemy closes in on both sides. Intentions are clear. Tires screech, and David speeds forward through a construction site. The gate protecting that site becomes trampled over as they flee continuously. Under the unfinished building, transitioning between pillars, each car persistently follows. "Never mind, you were right. They're on either side of us!" Emily exclaims. Their speed increases, but both cars divert to another arrangement. "Where are they going?" David questions.

Out of the construction site now, but to now move down a lone street, all is quiet. David and Emily near an intersection. Upon crossing, both drivers from earlier, on either side of them, intercept quickly. David picks up speed and approaches a stoplight. The light turns red, but David rushes through it. Other cars begin moving. Closing in, almost near . . . Several feet away . . . More speed. Barely squeezing between the vehicles, David breaks hard again and looks behind them. The pursuers hit each other along with a couple other drivers within the intersection of the stoplight. Continuing . . . recovering. The chase continues—gaining quickly from behind. Surprised they've survived such a disaster, and moments later, other pursuers approach. "These guys are persistent!" David says as he tries to drive while conscious of the others on the streets and sidewalks. David soon cuts through a nearby neighborhood. The thruway is next . . . Their chasers behind them have no care for pedestrians or others in parallel lanes, plowing through any who get in the way with reckless abandon. Shifting through lanes quickly and in between other vehicles is quite successful with every attempt so far. An on-ramp looms; David drives up quickly, drifting through the curvature. He makes it and races through the city streets as another short-cut comes to mind.

The carnage behind them increases; the police soon interfere between them. With assurance at hand, David assumes the outcome. "Good thing, they'll definitely help with this chase. I know they'll be confused at first. No worries—we'll get through this." Dodging bystanders and all else nearly every second, they progress down other streets until they eventually approach their destination. Another four-way intersection comes near. Before entering it, a car from the left speedily comes forth with violent intentions. David reacts with a quick reflex of his left eye's perception. Contact is almost imminent; regrettably, the one driver from the left ends up hitting a group of other vehicles. Glass, metal and other fragments fly air bound. A couple of cars flip, and some catch fire instantly. Adrenaline pulses as this chase continues. Only a couple more miles left. Two more vehicles come around separate corners from the left and from the right, right at Emily and David, aiming headlong. David boldly acts . . . and grins confidently at the thought of winning this hunt. Out of nowhere, poles rise from below, resulting in both smashing brutally against each other, tilting forward, and flipping over and back down.

Traffic causes them to slow to a stop. To presume an end, David expresses his thought of the situation. "How fortunate that was. I forgot we had those around here. Hmm. Quick of whoever activated them. Hopefully that was the lot of them? Probably not, but this traffic is not helping us."

After the intensity, Emily informs David of her feelings. "Nice driving. I think I'm going walk from now on." Widespread destruction before them is an unpleasant site to be. Smoke, broken windows . . . the front ends are completely smashed in. Slow movements from other vehicles pass by their pursuers, and wayfarers curious of the event check inside to see if anyone's still alive. The police catch up, even at the other crash sites. The police surround David and Emily by seizing further progress permanently. Coming to a complete halt, the police surround every angle, shout to vacate from inside, with their hands up and comply with orders given. A team advances to detain them, but David tells them they are a part of the Sacramento SWAT force. One cop digs through David's pants to find a badge in his wallet. Another goes to obtain Emily's, but she gives the officer a foreboding stare; it doesn't stop the man from doing his job. Freed after questioning, law enforcement converse about their current status. After a short while, David and Emily leave.

1:21 p.m.

Arriving at the precinct after their unrelenting chase between random individuals, a formidable position allows a confession for the newfound recipe with Roger. Walking in, no one seems to notice them or acknowledge their presence. "No one here has heard yet? I highly doubt it." David whispers to Emily.

"Just keep moving," Emily whispers to David. Continuing to Roger's office, Roy appears from one of the offices and stops suddenly in matching paths and comes to an abrupt stop and pardons himself for intruding, and then moves on.

David wonders who the passerby was. "Who was that?" he asks. Emily shrugs her shoulders. Entering Roger's office seconds later . . . Stepping in and ready to talk, but it's empty.

Too quiet . . . no indication of Roger's presence, David peers outside the office; small clatters arose. Averting attention back inside, but having trouble finding where the subtle noises come from in the dark, reasons being there's no point analyzing due to the confined space of the office. Lastly, David looks up... "Thought you could come finish me off, huh?!" Roger said before he plunges down on top of David. Bam!

Squirming on the ground, Emily starts chuckling and helps them get up. David's confused, Emily laughs.

"What were you hoping to accomplish?" David asks with a smirk. Roger tries to inform them it's just a joke. "What were you doing up there?" David asks.

"I saw you guys coming in, but I thought maybe I'd play a little friendly joke," Roger says.

After everyone has calmed down, David gives an uncomplicated explanation. "Our personal paladin has become a recluse again. We may have solid evidence—otherwise, no other known reason or reasons for the incident."

Although, confusion is clear, and with slight annoyance on knowing of why William disappeared, Roger says, "I see. Listen up." Near the office's door, Emily is told to close the door. "David, you stand on the left side of the door. Emily, you stand on the right." Roger walks to his desk to push it aside, with any other objects in or near the middle. Moving back to the middle, Roger stands and stares at the two.

"What now?" Emily asks.

"Just stay against the window. Close the blinds, will you?"

David and Emily do as he commands. All blinds are closed. Raising his right arm, hand spread open, he points a laser points to his palm and scans it. The floor nearly opens quietly. Formerly ignorant, knowledge is gained now, and intrigued eyes explain astonishment and flustered minds. This activity is inconspicuous and quiet to others outside Roger's office. As Roger stands in the middle, his area doesn't change. Attempting to not fall in, they stay against the windows, as told before. "Well, not being a bad idea: why not be prepared. Roy helped with this idea . . . mostly him, honestly. A staircase is in front of you," Roger positively says. A vast array of weapons hangs neatly along all sides of the shallow pits' walls, six feet deep and along two ten foot wide walls.

"Let's get started, then," Emily says.

Everyone comes to an agreement. One's best course of action is to check all surroundings first, level of threat, rationing ammunition . . . Going in blindly is basically the "only way" for them to ensure this happens, unfortunately.

"Wrapping up our conversation, it's all yours. I'd wait until night to acquire these; it's too suspicious in the daytime. You have no idea how hard it was to get this project done. I had to ward the big cheese so many times to even accomplish . . . And a bunch of fibs were attached . . ." Both look up at him. Roger smiles. "I had all the finishing touches inducted after your excursion through that asylum, if you're wondering why I wasn't in my office at all during those times before," Roger says.

"You're a sneaky son of a bitch," David replies.

Roger shrugs his shoulders happily and says, "I thought it was cool. I just wanted it for 'aesthetics' even though you didn't see it."

"Should we be worrying about you too?" Emily jokingly asks.

Twilight: 07/08/2028, 2:00 a.m.

During their preparations for the upcoming mission, a worthy try in giving each other encouragement and/or anything of value through words alone.

"This is going to be interesting. Here we go on our own against the tides of evil, to save our best friend from unquestionable doom. Can we condone his altruistic motives and destroy his tyrannical methods? Is there a possibility to save him? I believe so," Emily says with credence.

"Ha-ha, I'll believe you with that attitude. We're the ones to constantly save his ass every time no matter the reason. I know he's grateful, but he should learn not to run off, especially into the unknown," David says with truthful instruction.

"At least he— I assume he'll have something as protection for this spontaneous expedition. Unlike someone I know," Emily states the glib remark at David.

"Hey, at least I don't get myself in trouble—better yet, almost fired. I'm just bemused with this wholly, just going nonchalantly. Don't you think we should get extra help first?" David states his defense and certainty.

"We are going off trivial guidance. All we have are our instincts, weaponry, and expectations. That map is our key. If you have any more help to give, I'll be open to listen to you, but no one else can learn of this, including the Chief," Emily states seriously.

"I'm still feeling impartial. Anything could happen, but we should be going, even if that's the definite truth," David says insecurely.

"He said that no one else should know of this, as I said before. The more people involved with this mess will only lead to further problems. Lesser, the better . . . I agree with you wholly. It's only logical that we bring in help, but we can't. Who knows if we're even going to survive? I have faith in our abilities and faith in our potential as a team. With much hate in saying this, most of the work is done already, thanks to the contribution from our friend," Emily says to finish her logic with confidence and slight doubt.

Emily places the map in a tan folder; it lists instructions of William's plans and locality. She doesn't want to depart from David's company too soon. It would invite surmise. Upon leaving, she inconspicuously sets the folder on the receptionist's desk, in the 'Send' bin. Outside of David's car, doubt rises; but their mindsets must be amended. "Are we ready for this? Not true, nobody would ever be ready for the magnitude of our dilemma," David says.

Emily nods her head.

David looks at Emily, and she looks back. "What is it?" she asks. David hangs his head down with concern. Looking back up, fixated eye to eye symbolizes their mutual understanding between them. "We'll find him," Emily says to reassure him, and she puts her left hand to his left cheek.

David raises his head slightly, and says with reassurance, "And he'll be safe."

This will be the biggest sacrifice for another—their friend. Setting off to conclude William's mission, and with realization that every second means absolution to an inevitable fate. It all seems too unreal, but they've started on a path that has no return. Only consequences will arise, and only disorder will stir. Will William's hunger for justice be humanity's tremendous downfall? Will it give aspiration to the masses? Is anyone meant to be trifled with, or do we need to understand our thoughts collectively? What if we're being linked together without technology or telepathic abilities to know our every action, but turn them against the evil intentions before they happen? Would that make peace or just cause further conflicts? Idealism is a pleasant notion, but many only seek a singular path. Everyone has their opinion(s) and/or own predilection(s). One man can't solve everything alone; sometimes we need help. From time to time, help is needed.

Not one person has ever accomplished anything on their own. There's always someone or something guiding them on their path to help them to the end. Hero and villain: nouns used excessively; but does one need to be labeled this to acquire a legendary status, or be known at all? Even one feat they enact before the people creates such a declaration as some higher personnel of humankind or otherwise spiral in to a dawdling descent that becomes an icon of fear. Life is a test. Well, to me it has been. Due explanation as people you meet, locations you've been to and through, friends, adored ones, family, rivals, enemies, peace, disorder. You can either choose to contain the chaos with control and maintain the order, or create an imbalance to tilt you in to the abyss for an eternity. I've lived in that abyss for many years, standing and peering to the upper edge (not all from choice, mind you). Life was barely a view, and no one cared to look down. Learning to cope with such despair, seclusion from the world, I've witnessed the light reaching for me multiple times, giving me assurance. As I would strive for peace, it was found, but hard times can postulate. A firm grasp is excessive, but trying to understand is easy. Though, attaining its beauty, its grace flowing, is an immense blessing to anyone. Your demons surround you, trying to place their claws within your soul, but the light is excessively strong for most. For some, the darkness is consuming.

Interlude 5

I Conclude My Strategy.

"Acknowledging that our prominent soul has made it past two out of three levels, let's put together a welcome mat to our humble abode," "MoS" says contently. "MoS" grabs Alex, who's still present, by placing his hands upon both shoulders and pulling him. "You see, my friend, I like to be civil about this confrontation. This will be a continuance for the future. We're not going to approach this crudely. I'd like to be more respectful in terms for my adversary. Adversary . . . Hmm. Being evident and oddly polite with our preparation, there's much assurance our design will succeed either way. I know, arrogant of me. Throughout history, much death, spilt blood, and awfully placed ideas occurred. It's come to mind that it'd be healthier to know it isn't to be just irregular or sloppy, but to be revitalized by a decent motive that expresses every race's survival."

"MoS" changes direction and walks to a gigantic mirror which stands in the back of the office. Positioned in front of, facing it . . . "You're most likely wondering what I mean." He turns his head slightly to the left. "What's most precious to a person?" "MoS" asks. Alex stands their silently, waiting for an answer. "What's truly loved?" The two-way mirror changes, climbs the wall while slowly moving upward then sideways . . . and lastly, reveals a row of children bound to chairs among the other side.

Sadness rushes through Alex's mind.

"You have truly destroyed the soul," Alex says.

"MoS" smiles from such a thought and pivots to face the subjects where residing. Children sit crying, their faces covered and machines hooked up to their bodies. Some cry out loudly, but no hope is given. Alex walks to the window... stops. It is obvious how scared each one is. Devilish hands situate on Alex's shoulders. "Tell me what you see."

"Just fear, hopelessness, utter doom," Alex replies with sheer sorrow.

"MoS" agrees with Alex's answer. "Yes! Revel in your darkest moments. Rise with it." Machines activate, tiny voices yell in terror. Loud roars unleash within, steam shoots from arbitrary points, gears turn, and lights flash. Alex's anxiety surges with every second. One by one, each kid turns lifeless, and each light that shines above is turned off to represent their death. "Life is all so frail. Love brings inevitable desolation. Friendship, disloyalty is amongst any. Betrayal is the ultimate injustice. Beauty's but only to be skin deep. Healing only exists because of pain. Guidance: to all who is lost, but to lead them with lies. Hope: an illusion for the abandoned. Mankind: a never-ending cycle of death. Order, given an unbounded reprise due to the fact chaos is infinite." A moment's pause for the silence of death . . . "I will not be fucked with! His attention was averted, and I acquired what was needed. Sacrifices were made, tests completed. Our friend has open wounds—and my claws will reach into his soul with crushing force. Arrival will be soon. I conclude my strategy."

Chapter 12

Island 404

07/10/2019, 12:43 p.m.

Two days later

Treacherous events were bestowed upon me, every step turning into a paranoid reaction. Gaining knowledge on certain interests was not a likely fortune on my part, although remaining nearly successful this far. Tired and restless I've become, witnessing my fate coming closer evermore is unnerving as intimidating. The unknown is before me—an absolute must to face, heeding its eternal legacy. Is this to be destiny, or is this just a nightmare?

"I took the last flight to my final destination. Taking a cab to the beach of Malibu, there was a shop that allows you to rent a jet ski on sight. A final voyage: my third destination, as I hope. On quest . . . Top speed 110. Not a long trip, five minutes max. An island off the coast nears. A few miles past Malibu, as mentioned before, is covered mostly in woodlands. Upon arriving, assuming intervention by opposing forces, but nothing so far. High expectations with matched treatment as before, you know: bad guys, heavy resistance, and people turning into devil-like creatures. Fortunate as I have been this whole time to continue trespassing on blind luck with no hesitation isn't increasing my chances of living. So I'd say it's been a great run. Not really. On second thought, with much to my wonderment how David and Emily are doing. Oh, yeah . . . They're going to be pissed, a level of anger beyond my own comprehension. Maybe, but I'm going to have to answer to someone eventually. Or everyone," William says internally. Farther in the trees' abundance, inner space begins to shift wider. "A building comes abroad my sights far off; surprised there's no resistance yet. Getting in was easy, oddly enough; still sketchy, however. Too quiet—paranoia rises within me while looking around for any guards or "demons . . ." No sight of them in any direction.

Further venturing in, more it seems like a trap. Fortune favors the brave for a time being, unexpectedly," William says to himself. Within looks to be recently built: a nice white interior with black, red, and grey stripes flowing along whitened halls amid other inner aesthetics. Catching a well-hidden camera above me in a corner before a turn in the hallway comes, but not hidden anymore since I found it. Obvious of this notion, many must be among this building outside and inside. With a prolific count just like those other buildings that had their own security cameras, apparently. "Could I have been watched this whole time, tested, played with, or, worse; led here through my own will, allowing my actions to be permitted through this adventure? Who knows? I don't. In due time, presumably." William questions to himself. Before going through another door, a couple guards stand watch in front of another down afar, past my position, though, their backs are facing me. Distinct setups for these buildings—you could say: an archetype. No difference, but this is the largest to come across, giving the impression.

"I see more guards approach the others who are presently guarding their stations up ahead. They may come my way. Doors open . . . Thinking quickly, there are pipes along the wall that are accessible to climb, and then position myself higher above and within its structure; luckily, it has many bars strewn across the ceiling allowing me to get a grip and attain concealment. Closer they came towards me increasingly pulsated my adrenaline through my body ever so, growing intense. Stopping right underneath me, but to look up, and in my face is a camera. Saying 'Fuck it,' I then move slowly through the pipes and release my grip to purposely fall on them."

Everyone quickly stands up afterward. Their guns were released from their grasp from William's action upon them. Reversing their strikes, kicking guard number 1 in the head, guard number 2 is flipped over William's body, and throws a couple punches to knock him out to conclude. Guard number 1 holds his face for the pain that was inflicted, but William sweeps both legs from under him and smashes his head against the floor, knocking him out as well.

The guards farther ahead didn't take notice, but back
to the camera I spotted while trying to hide earlier.

(Deciding whether to shoot it or leave be.)

(Forgetting the camera, as it didn't matter anymore, I lower my gun and proceed toward a near stairwell.)

"Up a floor, to now come across a bigger section. Constantly scanning over my shoulder, consistently browsing everywhere to make sure being spotted is negated. Too quiet, suspicion grows. Eight minutes have passed, this section seems almost endless. Before turning around another corner, I notice seven guards, and I stop quickly before continuing to deduce my options. To my observation of them, they stand as a fortified group in front of a gigantic room with black tinted windows. My curiosity is hungry, a must to know what's in there. It's the only significant part of this place so far; something important must be safeguarded inside. How to get pass this dilemma? How does one surpass seven in this situation? Looking behind me to find another way around, remembering it's a one-way area, it will only lead me back to where I was originally. Turning my head back toward the seven guards—they're gone." Confusion arises but . . .

Bam! He is knocked out from behind. Unbeknownst about the individual who performed the maneuver, then again, it could have been another guard or those two guards which were apprehended earlier? Maybe one or a couple of the seven he was going to intervene with? William's dragged down the hall by his feet by two guards. His vision has blurred from the blow; slightly opened eyes can't visually comprehend fully. Trying to wake up, but he falls unconscious again. Markedly, unknown to him, he's been followed for some time. It's been continuously planned for William and his friends who have been going through each point to be given leniency. (Remember: All the pawns could act in any way, shape and form. Rules were set, but not his slaves' actions absolutely. Said prior, its meaning was towards William's fighting prowess and what "MoS" originally set in motion.) Seeing how far one would go for their own ideals can reveal much character. To know would be its personal tale. In anyone's position, would you go this far? Would you sit back and just think until it's too late to act? To understand one's motives could be complex or simple. Would you really blame his or her motives categorically . . . wholly? Not in all cases, though; theoretically, if not for that motivation but for other reasons, would you have had committed such an act, righteously or malevolently?

07/12/2019, 8 a.m. present time

Forsaken steps make profound ripples toward William's rescue. Only thoughts of his assumed situation roam through Emily and David's minds. Trying to wrap all ideas behind his subversive, surreptitious purpose and form an answer, but only producing questions— questions that only pile up, creating a mountain of mystery. Suspense is prevalent, growing every second. Every movement is closer to supposed rescue as shadows follow closely behind. Infernal eyes keep close watch, continuing the pursuit. Everlasting doom grows nearer, an abyss to hold remnants of a past: doubt, pain, despair, loath, fear, sorrow, and a haunting presence—a precursor for the doomed, an integral continuum for the damned. But to journey through the tides is left, short and unnerving. Unfathomable depths hold many horrors, many nightmares—every drifting movement across water brings trembling thoughts, becoming weary. Drunk from wavy motions . . . "I think I'm going to puke," Emily says quickly while holding her mouth.

David chuckles at her condition. "Ay! Among its vastness, many deceitful points may be a-foot. The beauty of its mass is worth any risk." David emulates a pirate's accent to calm Emily, but much to its failure, a worthy attempt at best. "Not if you have issues with motion sickness," Emily replies with a trembling voice.

"Doomed who follow the sirens call. Foul beasts, deceptive beings. To who waits whilst during the long journey, reward is near. A vast! Our destination approaches!" He continues to amuse and distract Emily from her motion sickness, and she becomes relieved at the site of land drawing near, and somewhat enjoying David's rendition. David slows their vessel down at a distance to get a view of any danger that exists by looking through a pair of binoculars. "It looks tranquil so far. This was his final stop which was mentioned on his map. Good thing I wrote down the important parts," David says from his scrutiny. Looking with the best his view allows, they move onward, after. Closer to Island 404, anxious with fear, void of any idea what's in store. Any movement could be their last; one wrong idea could cause an unfortunate turn. Taking their first steps on land: cushioning, warm, and relaxing. Emily rids of what few reserves of puke from inside then gets off the boat, relieved and grateful. David peers into a tree covered valley that covers most of its surface. A small part of them inside their minds assumes it'll be quite the walk, but they could find their initial point sooner than they think. Emily collects herself then moves next to David. "You feel better?" David asks, putting a smile on. Emily replies by just walking ahead quickly. "I'll take that as a yes," David says as he too moves onward.

With conception to the forest, it has an ominous feel. Not to forget mentioning: unclear as well— too quiet by any normal means. Cautiousness with every step is logical. Resuming . . . Deeper in, thicker settings accumulate heavier than its outer view. They have no intentions of turning back. Nearly absolute darkness surrounds them; light dimly shines through all natural thickness of wholesome copiousness. Eerie feelings they succumb to juxtapose everything about this forest—closeness, darkness, fear driven mentality. Staying close, ever so alert, keeping on their feet, and leaving no stone unturned. Their path is scathed with utmost suspicion. Foremost: an initiative to save their friend and to consent to total eradication of this chaos. Increased proximity to the assumed area of William's position, but all too easy with the approach they've made in accordance to their plan. Festering in Emily's mind: wonders why it hasn't been too harsh knowing what has happened over the course of time, but additionally, why it's been so easily manageable ever since. Only assuming, everything could have been worse. Her ambition with this quest has only given her a greater motive to be more confident.

Understanding William's every move, every intention; every motive to seek his fulfillment of vengeance has truly blinded conscious judgment, allowing it to decay his better character. As David's uncompromised state holds, he walks ahead with little to absent distress in sight. Tossing aside fear and anxiety, David marches onward like a legion unceasingly. Behold! They've arrived. Its darkened green outer walls stare into the forest's depths with no hindrance to its foreboding presence. No windows are seen from outside, yet only one door in and assuming it's the only way out. David looks around with the fullest extension to make sure they don't trip any wires or activate anything to alert whoever's inside this wretched building. A final breath for courage, but potentially relinquishing their lives to enter is a reality. They can begin their plan to save their friend from his own certainty of demise. Both open the single door concurrently, and they enter willingly into the profound nexus of pain.

Interlude 6

Mental state

Internal war

William

06/09/2019, 3:00 p.m.

The day before Dante's death: a session with William and his psychiatrist are present before certain inner demons, so she can fathom an idea of what actually molded him into who he is. William sits on a couch waiting to start. Laura moves a single seat chair ten feet from in front of him then begins talking. To start, she asks him what brings one here finally. Knowing every session has been skipped; all the other officers have made every appearance but him. William responds by explaining his own will to answer self-problems. "As time passes, I can formulate a logical answer to vanquish issues on my own; throughout my day another person's actions or words could create that answer in combination with mine, also. Doesn't always work . . . Maybe it was time to exert them unto someone else to guide me away from personal strife."

Some time in, Laura tries to understand William's feelings and personality as a combination to sum up a complete meaning about every problem he faces in explanation—how he expels a darkly poetic with a slight adventurous movement into his world of irregularity. A dark, devilish output flowing through a troubled mind brings fear into the room. Laura tries to grasp her pen to write down notes, but there's a greater interest with the mesmerizing vocalization as his pain flows through his body and mind as if she was living through it as well. While in the moment, every spoken assertion is surreal. Laura begins to see that his suffering is from doubt and a deeper unknown conflict within. How can someone think such immoral thoughts of one self, inner confliction becoming realities slave; maintaining a sane posture or spirit? Very few can. Laura abruptly stops him mid way and asks how he hasn't ever explained to anyone about these specific evocative upbringings. How could he have not have been affected mentally beyond repair?

He explains his thought process further by saying one word: "Sanguinity." Laura finalizes through her questions and ends with one more. "What is their initial point?"

William replies with an example. "I'll look in darkened or lit rooms—cracks of doors or slightly opened ones anywhere and see a black figure or sometimes multiple figures. Its hands grasping the doors side—only half its body is visible—glaring red eyes peer into your soul, and their claws scintillate from light, if there is any. And even darkness, as their prominent position, shows their modus operandi. You can't touch them; they can harm you beyond any known infliction, though . . . Those things patiently wait for the perfect moment to strike. Witnessing despair is to descend your soul farther into the depths; inflicting pain unto yourself will only make you an easier target. To know every weakness is to destroy your very fiber of existence. I always tell myself not to give up and move forward, become stronger, and let adversity be the teacher. That's when it disappears, or the lot of them, when you've risen from such a state. Fallen from grace . . . they may seem somewhat innocent due to their curiosity, but they'll tear anyone down in an instant."

William stands up . . . Walks to a mirror . . . Stops . . . Stares into his eyes and confronts himself. "Is it just a hallucination? Am I really losing my grasp on reality? Am I even here? Am I just an afterthought free falling? But I'm not falling. I'm floating through the wind unseen, unheard . . . desolation." Averting his eyes toward Laura, he says, "How can I conjure up a being that seems so real, so vivid, but only in my eyes? Is any of it really existing, or am I just unconscious?" He averts his eyes toward the mirror, but returns to his seat moments later. Staring at him with only heartfelt sympathy for maintaining a tortured mind, Laura explains that everyone has some sort of issue haunting them, save for as he says: "You overcome your troubles and rise, become better than your former self and shed the skin of your past." She starts examining his body language and facial movements.

William arises. "I hope we're both right, because that new skin could be the definition of evolving madness, a façade to cover the truth." A slow dance commences. "The calliope plays, revolving around my conscience. An eloquent dance for my amusement, commands to play the role of expression for the show, to express the story. We dance like fools for the kings, and we do it willingly. Stuck in the middle of logic and madness, I feel so willing to dance to forget my pain so the falsity of my life can be reveled in. I came to you to perform." William pauses and looks at Laura then bows. "Have I amused?" William waits a few seconds in his bowing pose before returning to his seat for dramatic effect.

Assuming he's exhausted every thought, she sees through his soft exterior. Keen to the ruse, he surely has more to explain if given the opportunity to. Mercifully, not to barge in on his personal life any further, Laura cuts their session to an end. She tells him that he has a potent spirit, nonetheless an indistinct personality. "For one visit, being your first as well, it was poetic and dark. Sharing such deep, personal quarrels is impressive & brave of one. It's not easy for everyone to explain what bothers someone, let alone bring courage as well. Nothing else can explain how you feel—only you can decide your path. On the other hand, it's not every day that someone exerts intricately of their true feelings," Laura says compassionately. William smiles inside from the generous compliment and graciously thanks her for listening too. "I shall return to entertain not only you but myself as well. The crowd is inviting and lovely." He then leaves. Laura goes over her notes, realizing there were none; she closes her journal and places it in her desk.

Chapter 12

(Pt.2/Continued)

Multiple massive machine-based constructions run softly: lights flashing ubiquitously, pipes stretched from and through, and subtle sounds heard from every direction as every room's filled with atrocities. A depressing site to witness . . . Extremely aware and cautious, plausibly, David and Emily decide to stay together, particularly adding up what has happened over the course of time.

Slowly venturing in, a giant door slams down in front of them. Surprised by this occurrence, they back up from the barricade, looking for another way around . . . if it's even possible. A voice over an intercom takes notice to them. "To have such determined company visit my palace is grand. An indication I sense you're to thwart my principled plan? Such audacity! My actions thought complicit. You just don't understand humanities need for a change—a needed revitalization. I'd rather keep you two alive. However, your untimely deaths would be of great amusement. You have two options: either you die where you stand, or do you have the will to continue? This won't be easy at any expense, truthfully. And for your friend: tick tock, tick tock."

The intercom goes silent. Standing in quietness . . . David then begins to search while Emily stays in deep thought about William. David yells at Emily to start helping. A moment later, the wall begins to draw spikes. They hastily search for an escape and become frantic. David tries breaking down any door with whatever is usable as a battering ram, even his own body. No success so far. Emily travels around inside to find another way, but have no luck either. The spiked wall closes in with every passing second, doom comes closer. There's only a few more tries to find an escape before being crushed. David uses all his strength. "I am not going to die in this manner! It's going to take more to bring me down!" David exclaims his comportment of survival and self-assured mind. Their entrance is blocked. The other wall is coming closer, closer to crushing them.

Backing up toward the entrance, just a couple feet away from them, the floor opens unexpectedly; a quick descent into total blackness initiates. Each wall meets, stops, and then the floor closes. Sliding quickly through nothingness, they soon drop into a pool of water. An underground spring it seems. Splash! Splash! Swimming to the top in complete darkness, David calls out Emily's name. She answers repeatedly. Something around them is making an abundance of noise. Trying to follow his voice, both swimming around . . . Finally meeting up, they grab each other's hands when they meet. They continue to keep their heads above water. A giant screen flashes above and blinds them for a couple seconds. The screen reveals William's position, a consequence made from wrongful choices. It depicts him chained up, wrists and ankles bound. His arms are stretched, forced on his knees, head hanging down, and sweat drips from his skin. He seems unconscious, and tubes lead to his arms, torso, and the back of his head.

An identical voice from earlier comes abroad again. "Welcome to the pit. It's worse than it sounds. Albeit, what's shown to you at this moment is your dear friend. I hope I didn't scare you too much earlier. No harm in a little fun. He-he-he . . . This is where it all started for me: born in nothingness, but striving for purpose," "MoS" says.

David shouts in response to his cruel humor. "Fuck you! I can't wait to wrap my hands around your fucking neck!"

Spoken words from David haven't affected this mysterious man's one bit. "He's doing quite fine, taking all tests well, responding to each experiment with no ramifications, or any physical rejections. An amazing specimen this one is. The mind is amazing—sifting through fears, hope, sorrow, happiness, anger. Oh, the memories we each hold. Extravagant whilst mesmerizing, how your brain waves work: a beautiful and divergent art. Well, getting to the point—I want you to come; I need you to understand my reasons. This was on purpose.

Your fate is in my hands. For now, enjoy your view from the abyss," "MoS" confidently says in conclusion.

The screen remains on. Locusts consistently fly, surrounding them in swarms. All they can do is observe William's suffering state in progression. Not giving up, both try to find a way out of this abysmal trap. A larger sized figure is seen moving across the screen at a quick pace. A breeze follows shortly after . . . Something heavy hits the water. Halting . . . David is soon picked up, then airborne. Emily turns in his direction quickly, yelling for him. Wings flapping up above, eyes that glow white. Moving from the light the screen emits, whatever it was takes David to a different side. Emily continues to call out for him. David shouts out stating he's OK and doesn't know what's happening. Emily is soon lifted from the water and taken to where David is. Frightened from the random occurrence, flying through dimness . . . Landed . . . She crawls quickly toward David as soon as she is released. Light barely shines from the T.V screen toward their current direction.

The creature appears in front of them. Before acquiring a chance to stand, Emily and David look up, but notice the creature isn't even looking at them. David rises . . . Walking towards it slowly. This creature still doesn't make any remarks. David nears the monster, for some reason having this odd confidence to face this unknown being. Upon further scrutiny, to David's knowledge, what appears to be half man and half demon combined, assumingly, it seems to have absent oculus ability, and also entails aging as if of an old man, the stresses of many millennia passing. "Are you here to torture us? Kill us?" David asks the creature.

The creature decides to walk around Emily and David, trying to identify them by other sensory capabilities and assumptions. Movement stops . . . "This man . . . You know him? A fallacy maintained through ages, heresy strewn across all lands. He never dies, only comes back tenfold and intensified."

Emily and David become disturbed from this odd exchange, looking at each other to see if they can answer this upheaval of a revelation.

"I've been asking myself what has happened for years. No one has answered. Surprised? So am I. You wish to save this William? Yes? You can gain access to his freedom quite easily. This place can be foreboding, but it's all a ruse. All his guards are up where your friend is by now. His research is extended due to the significance William poses. The ultimate prize has been acquired."

David tells him they are here for William, but only he would know who this enemy is. David then asks why this creature's down here. He receives a straightforward answer. "Then the fifth angel sounded, and I saw a star from heaven which had fallen to the earth; and the key of the bottomless pit was given to him. Revelation 9:1. My only purpose was to open the abyss, but I was deceived as someone made a false calling and was entrapped for a couple thousand years. Over time, when the age of technology and human advancement came, I ended up down here where I'm supposed to be initially when landed, to start the plan, but more likely experimented on instead, beforehand. The outcome: a deformity not of any normal means. I was initially meant to kill whoever was sent down here—originally above, really, but I could never since the revelation. There was confusion. I thought my purpose was excessive. I thought wrong when I saw his torturous methods and lived it. I gained a conscience where one never existed. I didn't think we had the very idea of morality or logic. Otherwise, yes, the TV is contradicting. No need to ask that, I can't watch it anyways—only listen. It was merely to make a final confrontation by him that allowed a last moment between any victim and their sins before they were supposed to die. Many have died by my hands. I am a monster. He hasn't found out about some of whom I released during prior times during my founding of morals and dilemmas. And those he did find were killed instantly. I gave them some of my power, just in case any confrontations arose; thus, also leading to my weakened state. Unknown to me if any still live . . . your means are perceptibly heroic. I'll lead you to the door out of here. That's as far as I go. Over the years, even though it took a while, understanding humans further, and continue to. The more encounters the more that was learned. Their cries didn't go unheard. My mind was only meant for destruction, and it left me no place to question. Eventually, emotions crawled from the depths as my kill count increased. The first question I asked myself, 'Why are they here? The bodies are endless, a mountain of death.' Each day thereon was more difficult than the last. It became harder to do its will. Tears fell as I witnessed each person, and I fell to my knees with humility. From taking myself from up here to down where life dwells in the moment of my spiritual demise."

David and Emily listen and convey the troubles this being exerted. Even upon hearing of such troublesome events, they don't know how to return with such grace to heal a troubled heart. Confusion and ignorance negates such tendencies to occur. Their focus remains on William, but that doesn't mean they can't try.

Chapter 12

(Pt. 3/Final)

Unexpected Redemption

Their exit is shown by their new acquaintance, which opens it for them. Emily turns and asks, "What now . . . for you? You can't leave. So you'll just remain in the dark? Will you ever be unshackled? How torturous this is."

Consecutively, David asks, "You're saying you're a god pretty much, but how were you so afflicted? I acknowledge you as a test subject, but . . ."

David is ignored momentarily, and turns to Emily as artificial light shines on the left half of his visage. "Are we ever? Opening this door has been a relief, so much beyond my prison—a hopeful experience I'm soon to revel in. Maybe one day. For now, it's only a pipe dream. What's the saying—'A man can dream' He-he, or for this fallen angel I am. There is no other purpose for me except what I am meant for, much to my lamentation."

Emily smiles at the connotation. David now receives his answer. "When you reside in the living world for a time being, your barriers can break. Its properties are damaging me. It applies with physics, reality, pain—it hurts. I can't perform as elegantly as I used to, hence me being in this dark, forsaken chasm for over four thousand years. The neglect of light caused this blindness, but this frailty mostly, not all, developed from those experimental procedures."

"Life can be forbearing. It can also be beautiful," David optimistically replies.

Before closing the door, a name is given. "My name is Abaddon, if you wished to know." Emily and David turn back around. Before they can give their names respectfully in return, Abaddon says, "I already know yours. Let them be heard loudly." Abaddon closes the door. Emily and David try to attain a sight on the large screen before the door closes and blocks their last view of William, for it displays their reasoning to be here. Abaddon then walks back through his prison. Blind eyes stare in the direction, not directly, of the huge screen. William is still bound against his willpower, but that determination has led him here. "Wrath unto them will come. Uphold the sin you value, and vengeance will be yours." Abaddon softly speaks. Abbadon stomps his foot and poses in an aggravated stance. "Deceiving God . . . How? The command can only be made in the great domain. It wasn't time to execute yet. Was this the outcome we were supposedly to be given?"

William is kept under high security, knowing anything could possibly occur. "MoS" asks each assistant about the diagnostics, trials and stress tests performance. They reply one by one with, "Uncompromised integrity, devoid of change, and complete stability." "MoS" analyzed William's outstanding bodily endurance, in addition to how William's control is steady and organized. Confound and greatly intrigued, "MoS" still searches for William's continued robust state's focal point. An invigorating feeling overflows, and he asks one of the assistants to add a single stronger dose to William's brain: a small experiment to see how resilience plays out. "It'll likely kill him. If he lives, a phenomenon this'll be." A light blue liquid substance courses through a single tube with no hesitation, and reaches William's brain uncompromisingly.

Moments later, not even the slightest shred of evidence is apparent of a reaction with convulsions, spastic vocals, or unconsciousness. Of the worse, death neither . . . Suspense rises with every second . . . William confronts himself at the two-way mirror. His face expresses lassitude along with hardship: a torment not wished upon anyone of this caliber. "Positioned like an animal, readied to be slaughtered. The wretched human mirror portrays me bound and manipulated. Are my actions not worthy of your graceful love? Have I forsaken myself because of my actions, or am I being punished for my sins?" William says loudly to himself as he gazes at himself.

William questions the validity of this assay for why it's been prolonged and with extra attachments. He expresses his everlasting struggle connected with the chains and tubes. Only silence only accompanies him, knowing others are watching closely. Why else would there need to be a two-way mirror present?

William continues to speak under growing wrath. (Descent dialogue: +4) "You chain me like an animal, inserting your poison in me! Your tests are merely misguided! Feeble attempts to change me are absent. I am not your slave! You convene me to define and answer for your 'work'? All you've shown for it was a fallacious result! This empty process is a diversion, a joke. You mean to take humanities hopes and fears to destroy their minds. For what?! To let you reign over us all—'to show us the way'? The only possibility of stopping us would be if you extirpate our spirits, what we truly love. As a mighty unity: we, the grand legion, will step up against you. You will witness true condemnation!"

(William's captor will remember that.) A response comes shortly after . . . Slow claps as a glib stance against William's bravado along with fearful words, but is unmarked by such tenacity. "Perhaps . . . You have provided me with enough empowerment to allow my objective's completion. There's no denying that. Allow me to hear you cry in agony one more time." A button is pushed, releasing a whole container of gas that seeps into the room. "You are my slave. You have been from the beginning."

Slowly encumbering, William starts to cough and choke. Another button is pushed. Each tube fills with a different substance that flows into William's body. One of the assistant's shouts to describe that death is imminent for William. "MoS" could care not for what's occurring, is increasingly delirious from one's own power. William shouts through his torture; shackles are frivolously yanked. Pupils increase in size, then turns white as snow and extreme convulsions arise as life is stripped away artificially by force.

All personnel are concerned about this enactment. They decide to vent the room. As the gas clears, venting for safe measure, no tubes inject anymore liquids, and everything is quiet. An order is given to any one scientist to personally check on William. All are frightened by this whole scene. No one wants to take responsibility for the request. "MoS" grabs a researcher randomly and manhandles the chosen person. The assistant stumbles from being pushed, then looks back as the door closes and locks. Making every step as hesitant as possible, fear grows quickly by the second. Approaching closer . . . William's body convulses. It scares the assistant, but still moves forward in terror. One monitor reads dead, but blood still flows through William's body. A hand reaches for William's head and pushes it up slowly. No sign of life is detected. They check his pulse—none to be found either. The assistant faces the window and shakes his head.

"MoS" immediately utilizes a microphone he is near. "It shows he has vitals. Check again!" The assistant returns to William as told. Before inspecting again, other monitors power up abruptly. All results show an increased heartbeat, pulsating faster than any human capability; an oddity is present too. Heat is produced from William's skin. The assistant is unable to stand closely from the rising heat.

The other assisting scientists are baffled by the readings. "What . . . what is happening?" Unsure of an answer, they look upon William in awe from the sight. "We injected him with everything we had. This was not supposed to happen!" another says. "We had inserted everything, which in the process killed him."

"MoS" diverts from logic and stabs the medical analysis upholder in the head with a pen from his jacket. William starts to convulse again—involuntarily yelling, eyes beginning to glow red. The forced individual inside becomes extremely terrified and backs away. Then total silence again . . . A few moments pass . . . William clenches both fists, breaks the chains connected to his legs and consecutively stand erect. He hangs his head and moves both eyes to look at each bound arm. William lifts his head. Everyone can only watch while in a petrified state. A logistic worker points out that his vitality level readings are going beyond any normal means for a human, or for any living being. "It surpasses the gravitational power, sun bursts of a hundred suns, and the extreme integrity of a hundred black holes. These are not standard statistics. This is unreal," A scientific researcher candidly states.

William's eyes glow red; heat steadily emits from his very body with intensity, and a red aura surrounds him. "I've had enough of this trickery. This whole debacle was weak! I have tasted the blood of my enemies and continuing to be void of amusement. Claiming domination through simple intentions, you make me laugh at your notion. War is what you want? War is the beginning, never the end. It defines who the strongest will be. Never forget the sensation of victory. Oh, it is magnificent . . . Enough cowardice was witnessed in prior times to know that more than enough of my soldiers had died in vain from spears of lies, swords of deceit, axes of disgrace, and the fires that burn all dreams to nothingness!"

Any remaining intact shackles are destroyed, and he walks to the two-way window. The subjected associate cowers fearfully into a corner. "Oblivion will be your only reward. You are what I walk upon. You are what sow the webs of chaos, a definition of the broken crown. I will dethrone the abomination. You need to die."

William receives a cynical leer. "*THE INFERNAL ONE'S REIGN WILL BE INFINITE*! Not what I expected. You're out of place. Or did you come out of your own accord? Even to summon you is odd, if so. Born from the blood-soaked earth, cold steel implanted to shape your frame, and the mortal ashes of flesh and bone that formed your skin and frame. The horsemen of destructive gallops, fire and ruin left in the masses' wake: apostle of war." The possessor evilly grins, and it strikes panic into the soul of the abomination . . . if it has one.

Chapter 13 (Pt. 1)

Scorched Path

Claws slowly scrape the wall that stands and stalls a great battle between two dominant entities. All lights inside dim quickly. War's aura is mostly visible, and a silhouette can be seen also.

David and Emily are subjected to the darkness as well. Inside lightly shakes. Lights turn back on. Silence . . . shrouds of misty black overcomes the appearance of "MoS". Vanishing . . . Quickly, War reacts to retrieve this evil that escapes to the outer world before completely escaping. A tremendous energy burst nearly destroys anything that exists as it surrounds War. Scientists fly in every direction, doors blown away. Walls crumble, the ceiling collapses, and glass shatters. Fire burns ferociously in war-sought eyes of rage that can only be quenched through victory. War creates his destructive path throughout the building to give pursuit. Through the first hall, two guards confront quickly: skin dark, wearing armor of some kind and wielding swords. No fear—only death is in mind.

A unity of strikes . . . War grabs their blades, grasping cold steel, but melts them in an instance. They try to grab War, but he dodges the bustle. War picks them up by their throats and crushes them instantly in succession, throws them through the ceiling, making them disappear above. War's journey isn't even about to begin; vengeance will only be the outlet for everlasting peace. Turning the corner, five men stand aggressively, pointing their guns. The firing squad unleashes, and one lets loose an RPG storm. "My wrath shall envelope you like an inferno," War exerts with certainty before bringing assured doom to any who dare resists. Dodging bullets: spinning around them, ducking under, shifting side to side. Adrenaline increases higher, time slows down before his eyes; he literally watches an RPG slowly come. His mind is thrilled by it, and he lets his hand run across the whole propelled grenade.

Time speed back up to its normal flow, then jumps forward, kneeing two in the face. War grabs the gun pointed at him, forces it at another and shoots while killing two others. Another gets up. War punches the guard in the face. Significant pain courses through faces of agony. War takes out the right leg with immense force, shattering it throughout. War stomps on the man's face crushing it into pieces after he fell. One goes to swipes with two knives. Turning quickly, War handles them and arcs the guard's arms, forcing both knives up in the enemy's chin and deeper into the head. Tossing each defender aside with ease consistently, War takes another out. Lastly, he finishes the remainder, who is lying down, with a vicious stomp to the spine, making him bend in a V-shape.

Nothing can stop his movements; nothing can discontinue his absolute wrath. Ten more enemies rush forth. "Like an eclipse, the light will vanish from your eyes," War spouts with undeniable anger, a hardened confidence never stricken below maximum capacity— numb from complete madness, blind rage opposing anyone. One of the lights above is targeted with a telekinetic blast; shattered glass falls. As it causes a distraction, War plunges into the crowded territory. Grabs one's arm and breaks it, sweeps both legs and utilizes a gun he snatched, shooting the first man dead. Two personnel are pushed into a couple others, and then he jumps up, elbowing one to his left, straight on the top of the head, and forcing a knife through the skull. Guns start firing. A body is used for protection; none of the projected lead constitutes contact with William's body; it lifts the body upward, spins and throws it at the remaining foes. Knocking everyone over, War jumps up . . . and massively slams on top of them. Everyone crashes through the floor, 3 floors down, breaking through with ease. The hazy debris eventually clears; and War rises with no pause to his vengeful intentions.

No one's capable of stopping his destructive impetus . . . Yet forces in droves line up to test his arduous might. War heads forward and blasts open a door leading into a courtyard. Trees line the border, a fountain is in the center, and the floor is entirely covered with gray marble. Suspiciously quiet for pleasant scenery . . . Assuming nothing is what it seems, a plethora of assassins gracefully descend and surround War in a unified circle. War is struck in unison, and the blades shattering event permeates fortissimo. Surprised by the occurrence, the enemy backs up and tries to access a better front. "A painful death is preferable, I make no assumptions." Every assassin pulls out another sword, but this time they're different—a black blade with a dark aura emanating. A colossal strike in unison commences. War jumps up high, and the opposing presence does the same. As everybody ascends, a dark energy stretches from their upward swings, malice in greatness. Darkness surrounds War, cutting him multiple times. All strikes are shaken off; he raises his arms then pushes down forcefully, pulling the surrounding opposition downward, forcing them to crash with extreme pressure below. None was entirely fazed by the attack. They get up just as fast as they can attack. "Finally, I can challenge someone worthy!" War says while running to his first target. But two more come to his target's aid.

War sweeps their legs out from underneath but grasps one and slams him harshly to the ground. He then kicks another one up into the air a couple feet. The third throws small knives at War. Impaled in the arm with no reactions and removes all weaponry from his flesh, to then throw back. All throw daggers are dodged. War persists with every motive versus the assassin; all others rush to aid each other. A thrust to the throat . . . War clenches the man's hand, rips it off, and uses the large dagger in defense and slices the head off hastily.

A low blow by the assassin in an attempt to cripple War, but he blocks and counters with a deadly stab to the foe's heart. Another strikes for the midsection; War counters by severing both arms and slicing vertically to split the assailant in half. A third makes a higher swing, and War steps back from it, deflecting away from himself instantaneously. One-on-one battles commence. "Are you even aware what war comprises of?! The trembling sounds of the horses, cries of every victim. Blood spilt in vain! As my sword pierces your very soul, the Valkyrie ride among post-battle to claim what's rightfully theirs! Your lives will mean only comfort for the Reaper!" War says to intimidate (Descent +5). Strikes continue to exchange during this battle; the rest joins against him with no reluctance. Three jump and spin above-ground, releasing dark, swirling projectiles.

War jumps between them with enough space to squeeze through. War slashes through one horizontally through the waist, splitting him in half.

War moves to another and continues his onslaught. Each one expels strings of black whips from their tragedy blades, but all is failing as War gains nearness quickly. Surely you'd think this would have at least affected his momentum . . . Fortunately, it's hardly doing any effect. He rips through their offense and slices each one down. Blood flies, body parts drop... All who oppose War are dead. He breathes heavily with great satisfaction from a violent demeanor, a witness to abject carnage by his hands. No remorse given, no care for anyone. Making way to another area, only deeper travels are acceptable. Crashing through the next door, three stand ready: two on their knees, one stands holding a rocket launcher to fire and decimate War with. "I'll sweep my hand across this nation. You will know true power by my decree!" says War as he runs forward. They fire, one by one. War flips over the first and runs on the wall; another fires, but War barrel-rolls over it. The third fires a rocket propelled grenade. Adrenaline increases, time slows again. Coming near . . . War snatches it and points it in the appropriate path . . . releases. All desired are susceptible. Quickly blasting a gigantic hole, mangled bodies flop air- bound.

Past the destruction, War comes to a dual route, splitting into a V-shape. Coincidentally, he notices Emily and David in another hallway. Droves move toward where War is. "Your allies, I assume?" War says.

"We must get to them," William says with difficulty in his own consciousness as he tries to regain control. But the possessor doesn't reply.

Heavy is the thought, unrestrained war must continue (Descent +5). David and Emily still search throughout. Having to deal with all the chaos amid the place, they find themselves on the other side of it all, unfortunately, but have to deal with some altercations at times, though. David notices William before he strides the other way.

Shouting out; no response is given. They try to find an opening by blasting through a window, to then go the same way William went. Turning the corner, seeing his very state, both call out his name. Still no response . . . Drastically blinded by his rage to notice his friend's intentions to rescue him, and chooses to fight inwardly. Suddenly he feels light-headed and confused as to where he is. Bullets zip from a room in the distance at William, piercing easily. War returns in a rage and lusts for revenge. "The tribulation is almost over, but yours will be eternal." Spoken words emitted while running into the frenzy. A couple of guards emerge. Picking a target, he punches one with an earth-shattering impact, creating a nova blast that sends the lot flying. The hallway rips and disintegrates while a massive pulse travels through it. "I'm keeping you alive!" War says. William shakes his head frivolously, thinking it'll get rid of whatever's happening.

Williams contemplates how completely reality was lost from those extensive experiments—void of believing what he's seeing. "You need me to end this!" War candidly says. William returns to the real world again and says, "No, what's going on?!" He flails around recklessly with confusion from what's palpable; his skin is burnt worse than other sections. Possession occurs again.

"Don't be a fool! You're the only hope for the masses' survival," War highly proclaims. Emily calls out for William, making him turn, and notices her and David standing several feet behind. William's eyes open wide from their presence, but he runs opposite of the two. Upon entering another section, Emily and David's frustrating state increases from his repetitive activities. Coming to a door, he enters, closes, and locks it. William's former position is reached, and David aims to open the locked door. An attempt to knock it down has failed as well. "What is happening? What are you doing?! How did you even do that?" David asks frantically.

William has his back turned against them, standing silently with his head hanging. "Answer us! What is happening?" Emily exerts with anger and impatience.

War turns around—eyes glowing red, and bright red colored veins stretching through his skin—and walks to the window. Stops . . . and stares sternly. William fights the immortal occupant; some time is gained before it happens again. Sounds emit from the distance from coming evil. "Let your grip go!" Relentless while equipped with formidable mental strength to stop the possessor. On both knees, he falls to, in agony from resistance. Heavily breathing, William looks up at the two. "Help me." Desperate for mercy, much can't be done. Emily utilizes reason with William, but he won't let them through. Three guards come from another direction. David sees them coming, and he hits the window to warn William and says, "Behind you!" One aims at him and fires. Only three shots go off, hitting William's back directly. Agony is exerted from the shots. "Ah, you seek death? You will unearth it!" War rises to his feet and heads for the new targets. Persistent unloading; projectiles ricochet off William's body in every direction. War grabs one of the guard's guns and causes the man to fire in his own face, then kicks the guard next to him into another with impetuosity.

After killing off the first, he strives to pick up a nearby foe by the head and smash it continuously against a wall until only a bloody pulp remains. William successfully mentally and physically fends off War again, but at a mistaken time. The last remaining man hits William with the blunt end of a rifle. William falls to the ground, on his knees. Hands and arms hold him up from fully collapsing. David and Emily try to stop him from killing William with a distraction. Their shouting is ignored . . .

Bang! Bang! Bang! Bang!

Flesh is perforated; William's absolution is made. Weakness overcomes him, and he buckles to the ground. A pool of blood forms seconds after. Emily cries out for William, but David seeks to render thick glass. It doesn't even crack. In sights, the last remaining opponent walks to the door. Possession takes over William for another time.

In the background, they can see William moving. Before the door could be opened, movement ceases. Involuntary movements betide . . . William's right hand penetrates the torso; a bloody hand smears the glass. War lifts with one arm, raising the enemy above his head and turns him sideways. "The hands of the dead will embrace you." War inserts the other hand, splits him in half. Blood sprays and entrails splatter on the nearest windows and walls, covering other nearest surroundings in blood and William too. The site's only appalling. Emily and David are horrified, but are relieved that William still lives; yet they grow ever so impatient at the same time. "You think legends die? We are who mark history," War spouts with stoic words.

Emily's enraged state heightens from the self-satisfaction that William poses and with the abundant bloodshed he's caused. "I've had enough of your antics. Your reckless, relentless attitude is drawing your end quite closer! You fucking bastard. I swear . . . There is no honor. You're only a monster!"

Her and David's only reason to save him merges into more of a hollowed welcome: an invitation to hell. "Innocence destroyed by lesser beings—the leader of the rats who controls them has made an exodus. Presumably to hide from a real threat: I. His illegitimate nature is grander compared to your own worries. This proverbial action, to dominate all mankind—it's all so embarrassing." Emily bangs on the window, a fury widely known between the three. "You're always punctual with pissing people off. Your actions misconstrued your very thoughts of rationalizing—always getting in harm's way. Does death not frighten you at the least!? What about us?! What are we to you?!"

William's possessor delves deep into his mind, causing a revelation to be understood who he really is, but it has complications at first.

(Fighting whether to calm his mind or continue being furious.)

"This William . . . whom I control? I can see why he means so much to you: quite courageous, admirable and foolish. A grand warrior he'd be, but he has too much doubt in himself. Aside from that, let me ask you two a question none have answered yet. Let's see if any of you can.

Why do you live?"

Confused by this notion, a response to the question isn't important to them at the moment, but they would rather hear what the possessor will say. "Life has a section in its definition that none can comprehend. Contrary, however, to how you etch the scribe which defines your life and others around you, life, yet not simple, but can hold many treasures and many monsters. Dying is easy. Living is the experience we're all given. It can be a deciding factor in the end, whether to be content or dislike it with your very own existence. You can throw yourself into despair . . . A better idea: rise above your calling. Every moment, experience, love, disaster, happiness, sorrow, trauma, healing, place, and person that comes across your line. No one but you can make those orders. Yes, many are guided. Yes, many follow their own instincts. You alone are a formidable presence among anyone—indifferent by your cause, distinct by your efforts; prevalent where most falter. You will fail, you will fall. But it only matters how one chooses to act, how one gets back up. Show resilience, express good character; most importantly, be you—everyone is unique. This is William's calling. He is answering on one's own terms. He dragged no one into this and is aware of his workings. Not by what I've done, but he will learn the consequences." (Ascent increases: +10)

Intrigued by this figure's words, they can only hope what happens next is nothing unfortunate. "This isn't showing good character; nor did he not drag us into this," Emily says.

William's possessor replies, "As I said, 'contrary.' With an obvious notion, you both had the integral diligence. Each of you made a choice to follow. Never did he say, 'Follow me.' You were motivated, it proved your true desire to help, and hence your choice to commit. It was the love you three have for each other."

Emily turns her head away from frustration.

"Will he die if you release yourself from him?" David wonders with strong concern. David receives silence. "Will he survive his wounds?!" David becomes increasingly impatient and upset from the absence of assurance for William's life.

William's possessor releases instantly. William's eyes return to normal, glowing red, the veins diminish, and the aura of heat vaporizes . . . William collapses. Extremely worried, they speak his name a couple of times. Acknowledgment finally happens after a couple of seconds. William uses what strength is left to sit up against the door. "What's happened to me?" he says in a traumatized state from forced mortal renouncement, wondering why tragedy resonates consistently upon his body. William scrutinizes his body: evidence points at burned areas and three bullet wounds in his back, accompanied by four front placed holes in the torso. Coming to terms about dying, he shares some final words. "How do I know it's you?"

David and Emily sit next to each other with their backs to the door, to then look through small windows to see William. "Look at us," Emily & David say.

William does exactly that. Muscles are less tense, little relaxation occurs. "Am I going to die here? That's what I get for doing this. How do I know you're not both emulations?"

"We found your map and the little tests we conquered under your house," David says.

Emily cries over the thought and says, "No, you're not. You'll be OK. Why'd you even come here?"

David thinks and exerts a fond memory to evade all which caused woe. "Hey, remember when we used to hang out on top of that jungle gym above the slide in Babylon Park? We talked about what our futures alone would be like? Who knew we would've been all together in the same job. We do now, but you know . . . being subservient on every mission, working as a team, creating bonds between each other, staying loyal . . . but I believe this does go against everything."

As David continues talking, William slowly and arduously stands, and stumbles toward a nearby door like he's in a trance. They don't notice it till he opens that door that he moved toward. The door clicks loudly when opened. David and Emily react quickly. Through blood spattered windows, they attempt to perceive what he's doing. "Where are you going? We need to get you out of here! You won't be able to sustain yourself for much longer. You've done enough damage here. Don't expend what little grasp of life you harbor for a selfish cause. We're here, and we can help you. Just open the door. We can go home. Is it worth confronting what you seek so badly to compromise your life further?" Emily says in an attempt to persuade William from proceeding.

William turns to face her without reservation, and says (Optimistic dialogue: +2), "To save this world, yes."

Emily lowers her head and then looks back up at him. She watches him as he disappears into the doorway he opened. The blinding white light is making it hard to tell what's inside. Suddenly, a foot in, William topples again . . . The door slides closed. During that moment, sorrow fills their hearts as they can only assume their friend died.

Roger's Upshot

Caught Within The shadows

07/11/2028, 11:00 a.m.

Roger's paranoia swells, save for holds total composure for a time being, while William and other counterparts progress through their secret itinerary. Roger ascends from his chair and conducts a quick thorough scope outside of his office from the doorway with an assumption there'd be some other person, or people, to adhere to his plans with confrontation about William's shared deception. Roger sits back down in his chair and continues the tedious paper work from present days. Nervously bouncing a pencil off the desk multiple times, flicking between his pointer and middle finger. A calming sensation is difficult to create, but his mind still wanders through this rebellious motive allied with commitment. Paranoid by the assumption of being watched, he turns toward the windows behind him, only to see people walking about, cars strolling down the street, trees blowing in the wind, birds flying and chirping.

Roger is greeted with the presence of two men in formal attire after he turned around. Quick processed thoughts with efforts that'll allow an escape and says, "I see . . . And who might you lot be?" Also, it increases his ordeal by giving a stern stare while he squints his eyes too, which gives a dramatic effect. "If you think you can stop me, then you'll have to catch me first!" An abrupt decision to rush through them; both men hold their ground. With all his might, Roger struggles, but breaks through them at last. Both men fall over. Roger bolts down the main corridor to reach an exit. Presumable tactics cause laughter. He reaches the back door, opens it . . . Adam, Chief of Police, and Commissioner Prat hastily draw a gun each in Roger's face to turn down a fleeing endeavor. "It seems my return was well needed. You have quite the explanation to give. Don't think you can get away so easily. Our department has an insurmountable quarrel with you and your counterpart. Or shall I say counterparts?" Commissioner Prat says.

Roger swallows some saliva from the reaction and laughs awkwardly. Other officers come around the corner to give aid. "Long time no see. How'd you know I'd be coming this way? Too bad I can't just transport someplace else." Adam shakes his head and responds with a rejection to Roger's call. "I wouldn't be surprised even if you did, but it wouldn't happen. Not this time," Adam says. Roger becomes worried from the spoken conviction and surrenders. As he's escorted to be interrogated, Roger stays calm for the most part . . . although he has a hard time remaining quiet. "So, Dad, where are we off to now? Going to throw me in jail for trying to save this city, treachery against all morality of this state, or will it be for the better of humanity?" Adam loses patience quickly and returns with a statement of great assurance to shut Roger's mouth. "You and your cohort's treason and insubordination are plentiful. Sound familiar?" Adam says.

"You're acting like were committing these offenses in the military. Come on," Roger says.

"You're missing the very important point," Adam claims.

Roger: "No—"

"Yes, you are!" Adam says to interrupt Roger. The lot enters an interrogation room. Roger is sat down forcefully, and one light shines above him. A grim, cold room is uncomfortable enough. "A cliché setting that creates the mood for being interrogated—finding a weak point; ridding my composure to find every answer. I bet: good cop bad cop, right? Give me a good smack to the face. Then close in as we might kiss. Oh, wouldn't that be a surprise?! You'll be completely quaint and patient . . . but you would hit me to conclude the moment! Not so much on formalities, are we? This will make for an interesting date, then." One of the CIA agents slams his hands on the metal table. Jumping a little from the gesture, Roger silences his tongue. "Shut your fucking mouth! I'm tired of hearing about your exploits and adventures. We need to know what is going on with three of your officers. The giant stunt with Emily and David a couple days ago and

William's outlandish results at the asylum was proof enough. I don't know where you get the authority to do these acts."

A knock comes from behind. The second agent opens it. A womanly figure enters with Commissioner Prat. "Before everything becomes too heated in this testosterone-filled room, I was the one that informed them, and was conveniently clued up by one of ours earlier about this grand attempt. I thought no way was this going to happen. Appears I'm too late. It put me against my disposition. I couldn't keep it a secret much longer. How could I? It jeopardizes their lives because of your man," Laura says as she glares at Roger. "We all know who that is."

Complete blame is arranged toward Roger. Her words are truthful, but could be no more authentic. Can you really blame her? Some would, some wouldn't. "He's making a difference. What came out of everything he's accomplished essentially in succession? He's the most formidable, direct, elite . . . officer we have. I know we have stepped out of bounds multiple times, went against your regulations and upholding the law by taking our own motives against the unlawful," Roger expels with verbal context about the integrity of the rebellious souls they became.

Adam and all others try to wrap their head around why someone would commit to such a technique. "You're supposed to uphold it, not go rogue. Among my company of people, we all share a similar goal: 'We maintain the order. We contain the chaos.' Can you say the same, or follow? Apparently not . . . right under our noses, literally. How do you think this will sit with others knowing of William's and your exasperations? What about the committee?! Or worse . . ." Prat openly says. Roger sits in silence, trying to think of a good enough excuse for them to understand his reasons as well. (Resulting from William, Emily, and David, it seems throughout the time he's come to enjoy them. He decides to be supportive.) "Your silence answers for much," says Adam.

Roger replies after Adam's remark, with a logical and personal standing of his own thoughts that he ensures they'll understand by his exertions to explain. "You have to admit, though: we had some pretty amazing feats."

"Heroics don't excuse you," Adam retorts.

Everyone looks at Roger with a change in expressions, but sustain their current mood. Roger takes notice and changes the thought. "OK, you're right. Listen, please. Sometimes we need to go beyond boundaries, beyond the control, flow with chaos. A man with great morals can be measured with that integrity alone. It's in his exposition I find that hope and the significance for life itself. Rebellious as us two are, it can be mesmerizing to the mind—to go out on a limb, to take chances, and to understand through a different perspective. That rush you feel from the action at hand, the subterfuge and illicit acts. We didn't stray that far to become nomads, but we had our limits . . . until now. Haven't you ever gone against orders, your parents trust, or your own intuition? I may not know—I have no clue to his whereabouts or any other supplemental arrangements at hand. Emily, David, and William are alone in their quest for all I know. I knew of only early news. To be honest, they're probably coming home right as we speak. Otherwise, I'm sorry I can't help you with any other questions."

Adam takes a breath and tries to deal with what's been said; he laughs from an uneasy, awkward feeling. Both CIA agents in the room are silent as ever, still. "That's great, theoretically. But these are lives we're talking about," Laura says, while throwing a folded paper on the table. They stare at it with slight confusion and curiosity. Laura leaves abruptly, slamming the door. Arms crossed, fearing for the worse. A sigh expels from her mouth as she slides her back down the wall and sits with frustration and worry.

Back inside, CIA agent Wallace tries grabbing the folder, but Adam denies Wallace, allowing Roger to pick it up instead. "Do you know how absurd that sounded? Commitment is apparent. You condone this adventure—how about finishing it? Any incurred issues; those are your consequences to amend. This is on your shoulders; I'm not here to be trifled with, so deal with it now!" Adam sternly says.

Roger looks at Adam with no fear and all confidence. "Locate where they are. I haven't thoroughly updated myself from these papers, and neither have our special guests. I trust you, and we've been working together for over twenty years. Though you've never failed me . . . I'll give you this one chance to prove me wrong on your deliberate handiwork, that they are justifiable by what you're saying. This is your issue now. There is no knowledge of this until an assured development appears. Understood?" Adam says.

"This operation belongs to the government now. You can't just hand a folder with sensitive documentation around so casually," Wallace exclaims.

"He just did," Roger says with a grin.

"Nice job stopping my casual hand off," Adam says to the livid Wallace.

Roger rises from his seat and decides to leave the room, but Wallace challenges his progress. One of the Commissioner's officers seizes the attempt and allows Roger's departure. "Both of you will make sure he's at a safe distance from our guests. I have some . . . objectives to complete," Prat states. The "work" that I claimed by Prat consists of keeping the CIA at bay, and as two officers keep watch over Roger in the meantime.

"I've been meaning to speak with William, but he seemed to be unavailable whenever I went to his house," Inspector Cohan states to Roger.

"Well, we all know now. I think?" Roger says with a smile to Cohan.

Roger returns to his office. "You think? What do you expect to do?" Cohan questions Roger.

"Evidently, that's up to me now," Roger says with confidence.

One officer (Jim) stands outside the doorway, and the other (Dan) stands watch inside. Cohan shakes his head, sighs, and takes his leave. Jim closes the door, and Dan locks it from the inside. Roger stops in front of his desk, slowly opens the folder's secrets; his eyes scroll downwards to the paper, reading it . . .

Chapter 13

Pt. 2

The Genesis of Purpose

with Animus, a Foreboding Presence

Facing a God, Creation Unfolded

(After what's happened: Descent increases by +10 from any destruction caused, and Ascent increases by +5 from William's strong fortitude.)

Emily and David try collecting themselves. Emily bows her head, expelling tears of heartache. David moves over to hold her. "He's OK, I know it. Don't worry . . . we'll reach him and leave this abominable palace." He uses his hands to hold her face up as the tears cascade.

"What do we do, then? We don't exactly know if he died in there," Emily says.

"Since a giant barricade covers our only way closest to him, we'll have to find another way around. No way are we leaving him, even if death did occur," David says fussily.

Their minds dwell around the very thought of William's assumed death. A question they won't be able to answer until later. The building shakes randomly. Maintaining their balance isn't too hard. The quaking effect stops shortly after. "That can't be a good sign. We need to hurry," Emily speaks in obvious context. Continuing forward, obstacles seize any efforts at every corner. Quakes come about again, and they both fall over, and so do the guards farther in. The shaking stops again. Getting up, Emily asks David about their current weapon situation. "How much do you have?"

David responds by showing her that he has only minimal ammunition . . . and one gun. "William's right—you don't have much to show." David looks at her with annoyance from her comment. "Cause of one gun? Hey, this is no time to joke."

Emily laughs. "Well, I guess someone does need to keep you on your toes," she says while moving forward with a grin. "You only have one too!" Pride rises in her, and she turns to reveal an abundance of stashed daggers within her clothing. A surprised reaction overcomes David; his eyes open wide in slight awe. "Woman, we need to talk."

Emily turns back around and charges against the collapsed watchmen.

David follows behind, but the guards notice their movements nearly instantly. Two of the four stands up and raise their guns, and she hastily throws two knives at them. One penetrates the forehead and the other blade hits the center of the chest, piercing the heart, causing instant death. She jumps in the air over them, lands behind in a kneeling posture, pulls out two more, and stabs a couple more in the head. "You know what, I'll hold off the talk." David becomes confounded, as well as replying to her outstanding and agile movements. Emily smiles back and then retrieves her blades. Both continue on through the complex. Around the corner, a guard runs into David and stumbles back. David attacks quickly by picking him up and slamming against a wall. David's target fell unconscious to the ground. Three more unwanted incomers arrive. Again the quaking occurs; this time it's worse than before.

That section the guards came from crumble, and they drop through. Chunks of marble plummet on top of the group and dust shoots upward. A crack follows to where Emily and David are positioned. The floor caves in—breaking away, falling beneath. David quickly grabs the edge and Emily grabs David's left ankle. Uneasy from the incident, he looks down and sees her. "These tremors are annoying!" David exclaims.

"Just get me up. Hanging above a chasm isn't the ideal situation!" Emily says, overcoming uneasiness from the current view and subjection.

David pulls himself up with all his might with her. Eventually, she grabs onto a ledge. David helps her up the rest of the way. They stare into the destruction below that was created from those quakes. Questions just pile up. No other way but back.

Below their feet is a deathly and doomed situation. An intact section of the floor is still left, but they'll have to cross carefully. Their backs are placed flat against the wall, and they begin to cross over.

Half way through, the cavernous hole that's before them still waits for their demise . . . any mistake could be their last. "Last time I had to be this careful was when I had to break up with my former girlfriend. Not a pretty site either. She was quite a mess, just like this predicament. If you were to fall into that pussy, it'd keep you down, claws and everything. I told myself not to get caught in the trap, or for a second time. Here we are again! Black, endless, scary . . ." David then clenches his teeth, exposes them and looks at Emily while making a low growl.

Her head turns slowly to the right with a raised eyebrow, baffled by his random statement/forewarning advice. In a way, she tries to compare significantly in some fashion to his words. "I don't know what to say . . . uh, that was indifferently profound, I guess? What does this have to do with our current dilemma?"

David isn't alarmed for her dispassionate response—unaffected in any other aspect by it anyways. "This just reminded me of its effect— quite blasé, honestly," He says to conclude. He nudges her, causing a loss of balance. Speedily recovering, she gives him a stern stare, and then targets his groin. He bends over slightly from the hit and regains his posture. "We are having a meaningful conversation when we're done here, young lady! Your mom is going to be very upset." Emily lightly nods her head and chuckles.

"No trepidation on my part. She already is," Emily says.

William lies still—eyes closed, a black setting surrounding him. Bright lights awaken him suddenly, but bearable to the eyes. Comforting sounds: wildlife emits noises and streams rush . . . the sweet smells of flowers hit the nasal passages. Vision prolongs its blurred occurrence. A human shape arranges in front of him silently and slowly kneels over him. William reaches out, but the figure moves away. His strength is low, and trying to move around is difficult. After a bit, enough energy is gathered unhurriedly. His vision becomes normal again: amazingly, a witness to a beautiful sight, like out of a portrait. Surrounded by nature's beauty, William walks over to a small stream that flows softly. Kneeling, touching softly . . . So much authenticity, he lifts his hand and watches the water droplets return to the stream. Standing back up, birds fly by. Stunned from spectacular views, an understanding of where "this" is must conduct. It's similar to a dream. Though its realism captures awe in William. Every bit of land is strewn with tall grasses and flowers; bugs fly around, landing on flowers or munching on them. Animals of the earth also scurry around. William feels no fear, no foreboding alertness to be seen or heard anywhere within this realm.

Peace overcomes him fully; the essences of body and mind aren't filled with discomfort or worries. Only tranquility is present. William walks on a path he's currently positioned on. Still in awe of this striking sight, laughter emits from inside, and he's laughing like he hasn't in years—a reprieve like no other. Mercifully providing a consistent comforting impression from this very moment by overcoming, it completely vanquishes all worldly troubles. Not one spot of darkness controls any parts of this landscape. William walks up a hill, step after step, and the view becomes increasingly extravagant . . .

Finally reaches maximum height and stands on the precipice, staring into vastness of the land and the horizon's long distance. He places his right hand on a tree, prevailing before the infinite.

Taking in the moment . . . before moving on, a noise conducts from behind. Where is it coming from? Nothing was to be found nor heard again . . . After turning back around, the same noise happens once more. Reluctant to move, someone is heard coming abroad his back side. A slight turn of his head, seeing through peripherals, a womanly figure appears. They end up staring straight into each other's eyes somewhat . . . William readies himself just in case an altercation emerges. Reaching for his gun, but he feels his right thigh in place of his weapon, holster, and pants. A quick look down to know that not only she is naked, but he is as well. Clothed before, but his whole body stripped of any type of clothing/covering. William unnervingly looks back at her.

William is approached. Her face is unclear: a white, blurry film covers its entirety, and yet not too bright that it's blinding to the eye. She places her hands on his face, and William becomes paralyzed by the physical contact. She releases placement, moves both arms and hands back down to her side. "What did you do?" William asks.

"I just needed to clarify if you were real. Are you the one who brings pandemonium?" She says.

William hesitates to reply but finds what little courage to. "To answer your question with another question: who are you?" William asks as she then points to the tree that's next to them. William's mind is boggled by the gesture she's performing, because her pointing at the tree is supposed to mean something to him? Examining it, William notices fruit hanging from multiple branches. He shifts his view to her . . . then back to the tree once more. "Am I to take it?" he asks.

But she quickly places her left hand on his shoulder to push him back slightly. "The serpent, do not follow its example," she says as an explanation to her action.

Confused still, he starts to examine each gesture and word.

Realization churns with intensity, William starts to recollect on a familiar scripture and figures out that this is the Garden of Eden. William nods his head left and right. "No, this can't be . . . Are you . . ." Bodily tremors ripple as he checks if this claim is real. Skin is warm and soft, but he retracts his hand quickly from committing any possible sin upon her.

"That man you trail—he's predominately known throughout history: gathering people to strengthen perpetual armies. Coercion is the game. Let's not forget all out war grows every second till formed into an ultimate catastrophe."

William tries to collect himself before freaking out. "You're serious? He's—" Eve answers in an instance.

"The infernal one walked this very earth again, strutting back and forth, ideas flourishing endlessly. One came to interest, but wanted to bargain one last time. Crafty as always, the bargain was complete. Don't ask how it persuaded God. I don't know myself, but it was a wish for me to come into existence again. I've only been used to precede the servant's plan—nothing else. It's the juxtaposition for this infernal one's arrival. Eternal darkness comes, your world will burn; seas will churn, and high above will rain fire. But you only face the servant." She sighs. "That's enough negativity for now."

Still in awe, William places his hand on her face again, cries a little with a hint of hysteria from an overloaded experience. Eve wraps her arms around him, embracing him tightly. Foremost, an experience of this caliber is excessively moving for him; emotions escalate greatly, releasing them through tears.

"What must I do? I mean, can we be saved?" William asks.

To regain hope, Eve tells him, "Yes." Animals approach them up at the precipice, surrounding them in a 360-degree radius, silent, watching with concentration. "You'll meet a man, you'll somewhat know him—fidgety and extremely smart. He'll aid you to no end. You three will prevail over complete disorder that is being sowed. Whom you chase relentlessly—experiments created whilst performed under unethical and immoral motives and reasons. Many have suffered, as you already know. I've not much help to give . . . Knowing of my presence, as you do now, I only expect you to keep it to yourself.

Use this hope to bring the world back to its initial normality, if that's what you want to call it."

William contemplates this momentarily and then speaks up. "If you don't mind me asking . . . What does he use you for?"

"I do not wish to answer that," Eve says.

William looks at her. Eve's silence convinces him enough. He shifts his eyes from her.

Eve moves her hand and points to the exit; the hordes of animals open a pathway leading to it. William gives himself one last glimpse of what "heaven" might be. He walks back down and out, and finishes his enterprise. What a place to experience firsthand; it reveals what most dream of. William turns around and looks up. As Eve watches William, she releases strands of light that soon travels down. Hovering above . . . it swirls downward and around consistently. Revitalized and invigorated, he can now visualize and feel a light that fills his heart. He looks at Eve again. She turns away to disappear over the hills horizon seconds later. William smiles unflinchingly with this whole scene that's placed before him. The door of reality lies in front of him, but possessing an ability to leave such a graceful sight is harder. Then again, an end must be formulated. No backing out now; He didn't think he ever could, to begin with. A new path has directed him now. What would be the outcome if he didn't choose this route? One would guess. The door opens, and William proceeds.

An arduous task to not look back, William regains control of all emotions. He takes a deep breath. The door closes behind him, and reality returns. Motionless and tranquil, consolidation of all choices; all his clothes are still off him. "This is awkward," He says to himself. The building shakes again. Almost losing balance, but it doesn't faze him much. Clouded judgment arises from Eve's truth, but William continues his venture. As he's running down the hallway, enemies spot him, and before they could fire, the ceiling collapses above them and crushes all under. An echoing voice expands in his mind saying,

"Go!" Assuming who said it, but shakes it off. Unexpectedly comes to a stairway that only enables a descent is the ultimatum.

At the bottom of the stairway, William turns through a doorway. He spots Emily and David and yells out their names. Again, the building shakes another time. Part of the room collapses and causes an obstruction in opposition to the entire exit, all remainders of other pathways. Looking for alternate ways to leave, an only option is to go back upstairs to see if there is another way through the section. Back up top, looking in every room. No luck. Many garrisons come from nowhere, but they don't see William yet. One door left . . . It was the one he came out of earlier. No choice, he opens it, but it reveals nothing. A doorway to absolutely nothing that presents a void where a room is supposed to be and what was inside . . . Instead, a tall tree resembling Hyperion's height is in front of the door way; the extravagant view creates quite an unsettling notion. An uncomfortable thought quickly pops in mind: to jump . . . Each step backward produces a greater sense of nervousness. Only one way out—one last step—he and takes a deep breath . . .

Additional companies arrive out of nowhere spontaneously and identify him. Suddenly, walls on both sides of the group begin to crush them left and right. William witnesses the impacted marble against flesh, bones cracking and blood spattering. Unstable obliteration is reaching him. He hastily runs and then jumps through the air into the tree. Branch after branch snaps, causing William's plummet. Smack! Snap! Whip! Branch after branch, he reacts quickly and grabs on one before plummeting further. It snaps, and he continues to fall . . . A strong grasp utilized, he stops himself before hitting below (only forty feet above the ground, to be exact) and holds on. Looking down, two guards stop below him seconds after his fall. Many branches and leaves have fallen. Also, those weird machines, which were ridden on earlier, are next to them. William slowly makes his way downward without trying to create the slightest of sounds.

One guard looks around, William seizes movement. Soon returning to the initial stance, and William drops to one of those hovering machines, which are already on; the scouts quickly turn. William pushes on a pedal and drives off. He gives them the middle finger in succession. One gives chase. Swerving and dodging through green and brown settings—thick as its visage is while beholding many obstructions. A hasty escape is a priority. Thoughts swirl in William's head consisting of how Emily and David are doing. "I hope they're all right? Can they get out? Or have they? I have abandoned them." The guard who's chasing from behind starts to close in. Not long: phenomenally, a supernatural force takes over the guard's spot.

William's foe explodes, and "MoS" takes over. Unknown to him, the main enemy is behind him. To self: "You shall burn with this planet! You will be delivered pain eternally, my prized and desired subject! If I must take down my own catalyst to this world's demise, you'll be trampled upon its termination at once!" His voice turns into a demonic tone and he says, "Crushed under its force, your time is nigh!"

William still doesn't know of the evil presence behind him. Not sure why an opening in the forest isn't appearing, he makes a quick turn in a different direction.

Catching a slight glimpse of something from his back side, only to finally realize he's being chased by "MoS." Wings of fire burst from its back and completely changes into a nightmarish form. William's eyes open wide. The figure jumps from the vehicle, and it crashes into some trees and explodes. The beast arises above and rains fire down upon William, but with quick reflexes William allows avoidance of the assaults. Trees collapse, earthly ground explodes, debris fly everywhere. William switches paths continuously to avoid annihilation. Thoughts race through his mind, adrenaline rushes, his spirit increases from the chase. "Why am I happy?! Am I really getting a high off this?! What is wrong with me?!" he says to himself through a moment of hysteria. The demon drops in front of William's path and launches a huge fireball from its hands. William pulls the controls towards himself, and the vehicle thrusts upward above the fiery blast that shoots past his previous placement. A huge inferno nova appears below. William rides high above the trees like the eagle does above mountains. A burst of excitement overcomes him, and he laughs loudly. A pillar of fire forms upward; the pursuant emerges from it. This specific moment makes William become increasingly amused, leaving all fear behind. A trail of fire is created from incredible speed as the demon soars toward William.

William pushes the breaks hurriedly, and the wind forcefully impacts his backside. "MoS" is currently behind him now and performs a U-turn, then trails again. William returns to the forest to try to lose this adversary, even though that's going to be a tricky task. Spreading both wings widely, "MoS" then travels downward as it vaporizes anything in its course. The entrance comes into view at last. William makes haste. Reaching an entry point, it plateaus to a high-rising hill that continues upward. Everything is quiet . . . looking in every direction, too suspicious in the midst of it all. A ring of fire suddenly fortifies every direction, abruptly disables all vehicle functions. William is flung off as the machine by the abrupt halt and hits the ground rolling. Surpassing the vent, he rises to his feet and readies for combat, but how can someone really fight an actual deity? Hope can either kill or save a man. I like to believe it saves, but maybe it's just overconfidence William wields?

Appearing like a badass through the wall of conflagration, drawing nearer. Surprisingly, William's breathing is steady. Unwavering in moments pre-battle—a sturdy stance is created. Powering up for another attack, William readies himself for impact. Firing, blazing, molten . . . Wondering why he isn't encumbered with pain, William opens his eyes and sees an illuminating spectral barrier fortified around him. A spirit forms from that barrier, but instantaneously attacks the deity. Both surge upward. Standing in shock and very curious about what happened, only to think to himself, "It had to be that power Eve put in me." A giant, hundred-foot rock wall form all around Island 404, blocking any escape. Sweat profusely drips from the surrounding heat; he tries to grasp the situation now that every ounce of adrenaline has decreased. Looks at each hand, turning it; he looks up and nods his head. Looks down again . . . and realizes he's still naked. "Oh, yeah, I still don't have any clothes on. Gosh, I'm so indecent. Well, like it matters right now."

Chapter 13

(Finale)

Rhythm of the Earth

12:30 p.m.

While William doesn't notice Emily and David's presence up on the hill's precipice; the sounds of multiple guns firing in that direction are conspicuous. The loud commotion catches his full attention, giving possible means to travel towards it cautiously. As William moves uphill explosions occur, bullets ricochet off surfaces, and cries of pain amplify. Close to the top, William slowly peaks upward and a couple bullets impacts close to his head. William withdraws quickly and drops to the ground. Getting back on his feet, William notices two people being fired upon. "Unbelievable!" he exclaims in astonishment.

(Special +2) William sneakily runs behind a car that's positioned to the left.)

In the distance, David sees a naked man, not knowing its William, and wonders if it is. David shakes his head to continue focusing on the battle at hand. William stations himself on a turret that's attached to the vehicle but knocks out the man controlling it, first. Emily and David duck behind cover again as soon as the firing commences. Shards burst off a fallen tree they hide behind, and steel penetrates nearly everything when contact is made and blood spouts from bodies. As the firing stops, the atmosphere becomes calm—only minor breezes of wind are heard. All enemies lie in blood. A couple seconds later, William speaks loudly, saying, *mimics gun sounds* He-he-he."

Emily and David look at each other in disbelief from the childish noises; each stand from behind their defensive area. "William?

He's . . . Where the fuck did you come from?! My man!!! You're alive!!!" David speaks aloud with excitement.

"What? No welcoming committee?" William replies with no consideration to the emotional scarring all have been induced under.

Emily glares with relief as she trudges, but the relief soon turns into a rightfully placed rage and picks up pace. "I'm going to fucking kill you!" Emily says while moving ever so quicker at William with the intent to do a great deal of justification.

"Uh-oh . . ." William says as he grows fretful from her action.

She climbs the car and goes to grab him. He slips inside and out the side door. She jumps down and continues her raging trail. "Why are you naked? That gives me an idea." William's face drops with fear. He covers his crotch from harm, which he thinks she'll deliver too.

David runs to Emily and positions himself in front of her. "Let's not worry about this now! I radioed ahead. They have our location, thanks in part to the chip they installed into him." David explains to William as he turns to face him.

"Please tell me there is someone behind me or someone else we're speaking of? What chip? What's next . . . a leash? No trust these days. (Jester: +2)." William says in a glib tone to cope with the revelation from being upset with the knowledge of mistrust by others. "On the contrary" Emily says with displeasure against William. David ends the conflict temporarily by saying, "There could be more arriving here, so let's get ready at least. And knock off the quarrels with each other, OK? For now . . ."

William observes from afar where the friendly spirit and demon are currently located. The island quakes again.

"Not again," David exerts with fear.

Island 404 begins to rise upward, surrounding waters sink under from its increased levitation, and a vortex swirls underneath. Rising into the air higher and higher—an immaculate view from the hill can see any part of the island's edges, also the city afar. Both deities are raised above everything, staying in the land's boundaries.

"What are they?" Emily says as she becomes enthralled by their godly performance.

David is just as mesmerized by the action. William watches closely. Two mighty powers clash non-stop, expelling their abilities, spreading wide. The island pauses at about a thousand feet (give or take fifty feet more or less). Fire and light dominates through the skies providing immense power—an incomprehensible might, a godly presentation to mortal eyes as a beautiful, destructive sight. An explosion occurs beyond downhill from within the building . . . more resistance speedily apprehends. Emily and David take notice and get ready. "William, wake up! More come our way!" David yells. William snaps out of his trance and takes refuge as advised.

Many guards come rushing uphill; William takes a mount on the same turret. As they reach the precipice, the carnage persists aggressively. Bodies are blown off vehicles, redirected in different directions, to then explode elsewhere from crashing against anything; earth flies from speedy metal hitting the ground. Enemy personnel close in with unstoppable integrity. Three large vehicles come forth now. William's ammunition is depleted; devising a quick plan is a must.

(Special +2) William places one of the hovering vehicles aimed at the bottom of the hill, turns it on and lets it go.)

Flying down at high speeds, it hits the middle-positioned vehicle, incapacitating the machine. As its remainders ricochets pass by, the two remaining enemies begin to fire; rockets are launched.

The extraction team David informed from earlier draws near. From above, they witness an epic duel between anomalies that hover above and perceive William, Emily, and David. The extraction team descends. Both cars reach up top and begin to fire their turrets and reload rockets to fire yet again. The helicopter takes a twenty-five foot drop. Viciously, the extraction team was slain, even before any help was allowed.

"Shit! We need to help them now!" Emily says in a worried state.

David and Emily give cover fire for William on either side of the helicopter. The metal storm causes the enemy to stay inside a safe haven. William goes through the other side of the helicopter. As he enters it, he can see a rocket launcher. He picks it up and opens the other side door . . . Exposed skin embraces the breeze; his genitals hang freely in the void. (Jester +10) Many are confused by the unpleasant view. William unleashes without hesitance, blowing away the two cars: forcing them to fly in opposite directions from exploding. A few more run through the blaze and smoke, unleashing blind shots. William gets hit a couple times: one in the right shoulder, under his left pectoral, and the right thigh, in front. David and Emily witness the event. David runs in to rescue William, and Emily brings a deadly resolution. She kills off two, but a third comes around the side and shoots at David; he gets hit in the left arm twice, right calf and his neck is grazed.

Emily appears randomly and pulls out two daggers; then she gracefully attacks, cutting the guard's tendons in both legs and arms consecutively: stabs and slices the legs, abdomen, chest, neck, and face. She spins around to his back and cuts his head off.

"Ugh . . . Don't worry, buddy. We're getting out of here," David says to bring reassurance to William. Emily joins them shortly. "How is he? You OK?" Emily says as she worries for both friends. She scans throughout for any medical supplies but finds none, so she rips her shirt into strands and wraps his wounds to halt additional blood loss. She does the same for David.

William's bullet inflictions are opposing aid . . . It helps with creating pressure at least; places another portion of her shirt on his chest wound by wrapping around the area as well. William lies on the floor with immense pain—his face expresses agony. "Watch him," Emily says as David looks at her in an obtuse fashion. "I'm getting us out of here. Hopefully, nothing was damaged to the point this won't work," Emily tells David again as she takes control of the cockpit and makes an attempt for their escape. More guards come with deathly intentions. David deploys a machine gun that hangs by him inside and then reloads the rocket launcher hastily. "Damn, they're relentless!" He exclaims. David utilizes the machine gun first. Hands grip tightly as the machine of death unloads; a respectable majority is annihilated.

A random grenade is thrown and explodes near the cockpit's external perimeter. The windows shatter and speedy fragments of metal and glass hit Emily's face and neck. Her jaw is blown nearly off; it hangs with missing parts.

In the right hand, David lets loose a rocket that slows the coming horde while maintaining a high hit count. Air force pilots approach Island 404 and notice an aircraft below; the signal comes directly from it and William. One pilot radio's to the vessel below. David crawls over to Emily. His eyes view her state of carnage. The only thoughts cascading in his mind are only fear and sadness for her. As he helps himself up, he examines her. Slowly moving her head . . . Her pulse is active but slow. "Hold on. Oh God. Fuck!" She remains unconscious. David uses what he can to cover her injury, as he can only use whatever cloth is on him. Allies above call. a quick response by David; one of them lands. The helicopter exposes . . . a plethora approach to oppose, but the massive machine obliterates them with ease.

The aerial machine lands and multiple soldiers disperse to rush inside the other aircraft; they perceive the three lying with injuries. All three are transported on the other helicopter. After the rescue, other aircraft maneuver around continually to secure their locality.

Out the right window: William watches as the immortal beings challenge each other continuously. The island starts caving in; the earth underneath drops to the ocean below. During the altercation,

William's "guardian" placed a barrier to deflect any of the demon's assaults from nearing. A couple blasts of fire near are deflected by the barrier. "MoS" charges forward. The benevolent spirit impacts from above and grabs the demon as it's occupied by its deathly intentions to kill William. As they plummet into the crumbling land, it implodes; a nova releases, spreading for miles. A white radiant blast flows through the air . . . and the light shoots skyward. "Incoming!" one of the trooper's say aloud. It radiates, traveling, but miraculously, no harm is being done to them or any lives outside of it.

"The music plays in harmony: each rhythm, each beat pulsates through time, and so it creates balance." David looks down and listens to William. "We've witnessed disharmony as in death, and the unity as in life. We compose sour notes to stir chaos or a peaceful melody to bring hope. I've touched a face close to God. I've been controlled, and nearly fought one." A moment's pause . . . "I'm tired." William falls unconscious from severe blood loss. (Ascent Dialogue +3)

"William . . ." David says.

"Hey! Hey! Stay with us!" David says as he becomes saddened and worried. Emily lies still and unconscious from the traumatic experience. "You're not dying on my watch—definitely not getting off this easy. He stopped breathing!" David says as he then performs CPR. Air force jets are prolific in all positions in making sure of William, David and Emily's safety. The extraction team lands on Malibu's beach shortly (as told to). The U.S. Army is waiting at the beach they're nearing. At the landing site, sand is whipped up from the helicopter's propellers; all in proximity protect their faces from letting it affect them. The helicopter lands and the flight commander open the door quickly and yell for help by telling the medics about the injured party. A couple ambulances are already present, fortunately. Medics attend to all three, carefully pick them up, place the three inside, and drive to the hospital.

Ambulance #1: "What happened?" An EMT wonders how Emily's face was torn to shreds.

Ambulance #2: "You wouldn't be able to comprehend it beyond my injuries. Don't worry about it," David says.

Ambulance #3: William lies unconscious while all aids are given to sustain life.

William, on a stretcher, shakes slightly from the uneven ground as the vehicle treads over uneven terrain. Medics check on him, performing what they can muster and also use a monitor to ensure his life continues. He bleeds consistently; life slowly leaks from within—all sins stay intact. The ambulances reach their initial destination at 2:47 PM. Upon stopping, medics open the back doors and unload William, rushing him into an emergency room where aid will take place. David and Emily are transported to be taken care of as well. "We need to hurry people!" says one of the couple of doctors who are externally collaborating with other aiding medical professionals. Both entrance doors are opened, and everyone rushes into the hospital.

A couple days pass. At 5:03 p.m., post-surgery, David is wide awake. Dr. Torrence comes into the room to inspect David's state. "How are they?" David asks.

"William is in better condition now. From the one wound in his chest, we thought he wasn't going to live, and Emily is going to be prolonged. Nearly her whole jaw is being reconfigured. She'll have mostly prosthetic pieces. There was immense carnage. I couldn't even fathom what could have eviscerated her throat either, and the top part of her esophagus. I was told it was a crazy shootout. To its fortuitousness, the vocal cords were shredded. She's lucky nothing hit the carotid. To add: an abundance of blood was lost from William and Emily; they both needed a transfusion. Unfortunately, his blood type is AB-negative. It was difficult to come by. Hey, we're taking great care of them," Dr. Torrence says.

David can only wait in suspense. He asks to change his clothes and to sit out in the waiting room. David is released first, his injuries being the least fatal. Bandages fortify his flesh trauma. Putting on his clothes is not such a daunting task, especially having Dr. Torrence helping him concurrently. All finished. With one crutch, David travels out of his room. Slow steps, pain still resonates, but it's bearable for the time being. Arriving at the waiting area, he immediately finds a seat. "Oh, yeah . . ." David says in relief while sitting.

6:25 p.m.

An hour and twenty-two minutes later, Dr. Torrence tells David that William is allowed to be seen, and he'll be in room 3, which is just down the hall from the waiting room.

Adam and Roger, together with other government officials, enter; and before setting it back on the table next to him, he turns around and notices the group's intrusion. "Here comes the circus," David says. David tries to leave quickly . . .

The receptionist asks, "What's going on? Can I help you?" One agent comes closer to her, showing her his badge and explains that it's government business. The manager is summoned by the receptionist right after.

As they draw near, someone calls out to him. "David, David, David," Adam says as he then places his hand on David's shoulder to force him back down in his seat; and Roger sits on the left of David. Adam tries to get a grasp on the whole situation with questioning. Instead, he takes another deep breath first and then says, "A floating island." David nods in response.

"I have to say that was pretty rad," Roger tells David, who smiles at the comment.

Adam speaks again in disbelief, saying, "Two unknown beings flying through the air fighting and a floating island?" David nods his head again.

"I wish I was there. I mean, you had whoosh, smack, bang, big explosions, and hot metal flying everywhere I bet, right?" Roger says intrigued.

David nods his head in excitement. "If only you were there my friend," he assures Roger.

Adam's patience grows thin, but now he exerts aggravation one more time. "Floating island, two unknown beings flying around fighting and then exploding, creating no other casualties, but could've had potential to . . ." David looks at Adam and nods his head slowly. "Damn you, Roger!" Adam says as he arises and tries grabbing Roger, but some of the military figures intervene between their debacles. They sit him back down, place their hands upon his shoulders and make sure he knows he cannot move from the seat. Roger sneaks in a high-five with David then crosses his arms afterward with a smirk. To antagonize him further, Roger gives a weird, disrespectful facial expression. Adam squint both eyes at Roger, and then averts them with displeasure. The manager, Elizabeth, confronts the military figures, but Commander Lycanne takes her aside and explains, with a little fibbing.

Moments later, a woman dressed casually and wearing glasses saunters by the group. David spots her by chance and watches her movement down the hall. The woman walks into William's room. Time discontinues abruptly for a couple seconds. Time after the event, everything returns to normal again. Nobody takes any acknowledgment from it. David's curiosity flourishes and arises slowly. He uses his crutch and consecutively moves to William's room. David eventually arrives with whatever speed he can modulate. At the doorway, he enters but sees no one in the bed. Behind the curtain to his left, a slight noise permits. Moving around, he sees William standing in front of the window on the other side of the room and is observant with seeing all bandages strewn on the floor around William. Each step is slow . . . Now behind and goes to touch him on the shoulder. Williams turns to see David, and says, "Did you see a woman enter your room just a few seconds ago?"

"No," William says.

David looks at William's shoulder and chest; no scar or any marks present. "What happened to your wounds? Even with surgery you'd have scars still. Time to heal is necessary!" David says with curiosity and confusion.

(Williams chooses whether to react or stay silent.)

(Ascent action +2) "A miracle . . . I was told I'll be here for a while, though. They implied I need to be "evaluated and tamed." They are baffled by the weighty answer, but David still isn't convinced enough to believe William's words. William shifts his head to the window and views the vast horizon. "I'm sorry. I know you're both mad at me. My indecency, along with my carelessness, is implausible." David interrupts his apology, saying, "More than that . . . There are many more reasons why your actions were unethical in so many ways."

"Well, that is true. What really bothers me is how this all started. Yes, it's ironic of me saying this. What I mean is that it's amazing that it only takes one move to shift the universe on a different path . . . a whole new understanding. Misconstruing my ideals, turning them against everyone, letting my anger get the best of me—mislead my soul to despair. Lying is void. I feel . . . strangely rejuvenated. As odd as it sounds . . . yeah, that's odd. One man's paradise is another man's living hell. Presuming we just witnessed something of the marvelous. Was it a mistake? Setting in motion a ruinous ploy—I know I won't be forgiven. I am, however, more than ready for them to render judgment against me." (Ascent increases +10)

Finding a spot to give respect for expressing accepting thoughts, David says, "Now you're ready? We thought we lost you. I won't make this any more depressing than it should be. Anyways, you won't believe—well, you will. There's quite a committee waiting for us three out in the waiting room, as a forewarning. It's what you wanted, right?" William knows his coming punishment well enough and tries to enjoy the little things before the hammer falls. "It's beautiful, isn't it?" David wonders what he's talking about. "It's actually amazing.

You mess up one note and it all fails . . . We didn't. We played the piece just right." David looks at him with slight content from the statement.

"You better put your bandages back on. They're going to wonder how you don't have a single scratch, or stitches. On another note, I still don't understand you—you're weird. I'm not going to lie." William laughs subtly and continues putting his bandages on as David helps him concomitantly. "I'm still perplexed on the idea of your oddly, hastened healing," David says with ceaseless doubt.

"I could keep telling you. There's no need to cause a bother anymore," William says in return.

"Emily . . . she had major facial damage . . . the jaw mostly. I also heard her vocal chords were damaged in a way that they're somewhat unable to fully revert it to its absolute normality. She's lucky. Dr. Torrence came to me a second time after he let me leave my room and said they might have a different method of remedying the issue. She'll live despite the fact, thankfully. I just needed to let you know before I go."

William feels accountable for their injured conditions. "That's awful." He says in a guilty manner. "I'll have to see her. Oh boy, I'm in trouble . . ." William says.

He departs to visit Emily, but David stops him. "Her exact words would be: 'I'm going to kill you.' We aren't allowed to see her just yet. She'll be fine, don't worry," David says.

"Too true, it is," William says while laughing a little.

"How long you think?" William asks.

   "No idea. They'll let us know. Get your rest. Let's see if they'll let you be for a time," David replies. Afterward, he exits.
William, to self, "A reign of terror has ceased. So I guess we can just sit back and enjoy life. You think . . . Who knows . . ."

Two CIA agents proceed to William's room. "You, where is he?" one of the agents asks.

"He was recently discharged, and you want to pester him?" David defensively says.

"He is coming with us. An explanation is well needed," the agent demands.

"No, he is not!" David says as he puts his hand on the agent's chest. "Time for recovery is required. Under such prolonged stress will only hurt him and the healing process. What you two can do is leave. You'll receive your explanation when the time comes." The left-positioned agent pulls a .9mm pistol on David. "Kill me as you may, but I've seen horrors that shouldn't even exist. A gun has no effect," David bravely says.

Amid the yelling, three soldiers cautiously appear from behind the agents in the distance, but fortunately for David, the event was perceived. "So this is what you're doing. Put the weapon down! Agent Wallace, stand down!" Commander Lycanne says. David sternly stares as Wallace lowers his firearm and places it back into his holster. Commander Lycanne and his comrades stand down too as the tense atmosphere lifts. "Come with us," Lycanne says to the others. David and the two agents follow the servicemen back to the waiting room. Other people are curious as to why so many government officials are in the waiting room. David sits back down, but this time he's across from everyone. The two government officials are brought outside the hospital.

Down the steps, each emissary acts quickly, removes their guns from their holsters, turns around to face the soldiers, and shoots two of the three. Lieutenant Kingsly shoots quickly and delivers killing blows against both men. One soldier is killed by a shot through the chest. The Commander only has a wounded arm.

"Are you hurt?" Lycanne asks Kingsly.
"No," Kingsly responds.

Lycanne checks Lieutenant Volsky. No signs of life. Lycanne looks up at Kingsly, implying the obvious answer through silence. Everyone inside the hospital rushes to the doors. David slowly, but surely makes his way to the front doors. Adam and Roger exit with their guns drawn. People move aside so the medical personal can make way to the men who were shot.

"Never-ending, isn't it?" David says rhetorically.

Medical staff transports the soldiers to the OR, but Lieutenant Kingsly waits outside. The police soon come to the hospital. William comes out of his room to see what's going on. David sees him and meets up. William meets him halfway. "Those two CIA officials went rogue, but they were shot dead. One soldier had been killed, regrettably." David tells William.

"Let's go back to my room and talk about something else . . . or do something else," William says.

Upon entering, Roger comes in right behind them. "Hey. How are you guys?" Roger asks.

No answer from the two. "I see. Hopefully, this'll just stop and we can breathe."

David sits on a chair, and William lies down on the bed. Roger just stares at them awkwardly. Williams tilts his head at Roger and says, "It's not that enticing."

David agrees and says, "Likewise."

Roger isn't buying it, so he asks, "Could you please tell me from beginning to end?" He plops on the ground and waits for a bed time story like a child. David and William look at each other, and then back at Roger. Roger slowly pulls out a candy bar, opens it, and takes a bite. William and David start smiling, progressively snicker, and then burst out laughing.

"In all seriousness, may I please have this chip removed from my ass? I don't know when this happened. My lesson was learned," William says.

"Okay. I don't know either," Roger says.

"I was just kidding. Sorry. It was a stupid statement to symbolize for your behavior," David said.

"Symbolize, huh? I'm actually disappointed. You could've done better." He lifts his left hand, makes a fist and sticks his middle finger up. "How's that for symbolism?" William says.

David smirks from the gesture.

"It's so good to see you guys. We're just one big family," Roger says jokingly.

"A family of assholes, that's what it is," David says.

"But you love those assholes. That's why you stick with them, you dick. Why else would you be here?" William says with glibness.

They all share a laugh from the unannounced conversation. Their chatter continues for some time, but it does alleviate some of the tension. And life goes on . . .

Emily

Expect the unexpected, besides the obvious.

We return to the precinct, following a psychiatrist who we know as Laura. Laura enters her office enraged, slamming the door, and transfers to a chair that resides at her desk. Angrily searching through the desk, she slams every drawer as if she's trying to find a specific something. She pulls out a potent bottle of whiskey, accompanied with a small glass. Hesitation overcomes her. She takes a deep breath, and looks at the desk's surface: multiple papers cover it completely. "Why do I do this to myself? Why did you leave this behind?" she says to herself. Fifteen minutes later, the phone rings. "Hello?" The person on the other end tells her about Emily's present condition and whereabouts. Laura tells the informant to bring her into the office. She stares at the bottle but hesitates again. People outside of the office catch attention from the reappearance of David, Emily, and William with their other company.

A small amount of whiskey is poured. She forwards it to her mouth . . . A moment of reprised strength causes her to yield the glass from making contact with her mouth, and she ends up pouring it back in and deposits the bottle and glass in the middle drawer. Laura recollects her composure to quickly retain professionalism. Emily soon opens the door and enters. "It's been a while," Laura says. Emily settles across the room from Laura, staring with disgust. "You guys really worry me, especially you," Laura says.

Emily crosses her arms with an attempt to force herself to speak. "Why'd you call me here? Besides, wanting a needed pity party?" Emily angrily says.

Laura smiles at the thought. "You're on the side of order to uphold the law, not cause unrest with opposition. You guys always seem to go beyond rationality. You know no bounds... deny limits. My motives are laid out, and mainly you're aware," Laura says.

Emily grows impatient every second and returns fire. "Bounds, limits . . . What would you understand of the notions? Look, I'm not here for a lecture. You called me, and I came. What is it you need?"

Laura arises, transitions, and positions before Emily. As she stands over her, looking down, Laura feels utter sadness in her heart. Emily notices specific concerns. "I just thought I lost you. If you hadn't given me that information on your threes predicament, I would've been at a complete loss, literally."

Emily tries to hold off on her true feelings. "Not just you, me, David's family, and William's family. Don't forget others are here. None of this had to happen," Emily says as she tries to control her emotions, but they outweigh her logical stance and she moves upward to hug Laura tightly. "I'm sorry, Mother. I'm so sorry." Their bond exceed over any means as a parent and as a daughter—no limits.

Laura steps back and props each hand on Emily's shoulders. "Please, don't traumatize me like that again. I didn't know what to do. If you died, I wouldn't be able to live with myself. Your face disfigured, your voice is . . . Why do you follow him with such confidence? You three are inseparable, but your actions are terrifying."

Laura sits herself on the couch. Emily looks at her mother and sits next to her. Emily wipes the tears from her face; blows into a tissue. Emily stares forward. Laura waits patiently. As of this moment, Emily also feels strangely rejuvenated as she ponders what to exert about William. It might misconstrue her thoughts. "He's . . . he's very alluring. I don't' know, there's just something mysterious about him. It's like he's trying to find something. I have no suggestions, or if that's even it in fact? He possesses that aura where you reflect a complexity of feelings, and furthermore, forces dismay in others; it poses just as life threatening and violent. I don't know what pushes him to the extreme. Maybe he's already reached madness or surpassed it into a never-ending spiral of insanity. If so, he's 'hiding it' quite well. Not now of course, obviously. Never forces you to do anything, never will lie to you, and, most importantly, never loses confidence."

Laura tries to understand, but is finding nothing but difficulties. "So, ideally, you'd follow someone into hell instead of listening to reason?" she questions.

Emily comes up with a "reasonable" response yet mostly inappropriate. "Not just anybody, Mother. It's like good sex. You know, at first you're in and its level of pleasure rises every second. When you reach the apex, it's fucking ecstasy! When you slow down, the pleasure levels out evenly throughout the body and you're content with it all, paradoxically speaking with comparing that to our adventure."

Laura is surprised by the remark made in regard to her question. Emily just shrugs her shoulders.

"I don't know what to say. Is that what you really think or feel the whole time with him?" she wonders. Emily lowers her head, and she rolls her eyes up at her mother. "You're kidding?!" Emily nods her head in a 'No' gesture. Astonished at her crudeness, Laura then says, "I assumed you two were. You're cautious, right? The quiet ones are the freaks in bed."

Emily reacts in shock to the question. "No, we actually didn't. He's quite passionate, though. I just wanted to witness your reaction," she responds.

Laura laughs with annoyance. "What am I going to do with you?" She says.

Wiping the rest of her tears from her face, Emily stands up from the couch and claps her hands a single time. "I think it's time for me to go." She walks to the door to depart. She grabs the door handle but turns around to finish their conversation. "Do you really want to know why I care at all?" Laura looks up at her with readiness. "I believe in him. Yes, I don't always agree with his actions, but I know he means . . ." Emily's eyes scroll to the left then back at Laura "Well, kept me and David in good shape." Laura gives her a discontenting look. "Okay . . . Alive . . . so far . . . William can be honorable. Lately, he hasn't been logical. Much credit for what was accomplished at least. Retrospectively, he's strange, but surreal." Laura is still, to some extent, perplexed by Emily's speech; words of her own are choked on over its ambiguity.

(Each action and word performed by William has prepared her to believe or assume who he is. Everything that has happened led to convey this culmination.)

Acknowledging everything William's done, Emily decides to give an oddly progressive reaction with a hint of an adventurous, yet spirited inspirational answer. She gives a better reason in conclusion. "Sometimes I wonder what dwells in his mind. Could it just be a big explosive collaboration of conjured images, scenes, obscured thoughts and chaos? Or is it just a stagnate enigma trying to form any sort of personality to revitalize what's left, to regain? That's a notion neither I nor anyone else will ever know. I know it seems like I'm making him out to be this huge character, but he's human like everyone else. I really don't know what sets him off. In a way, he transitioned from sanity to madness and vice-versa. Maybe he could be controlling the changes consciously, or not? I don't blame him totally for his actions, but what had happened did scar us in different ways . . . to elaborate, our feelings were concentrated. William's was an intense emotional shift; mine was a profound recognition of life, and David's faith in his best friend was nearly demolished. To understand what each of us went through as a whole would melt your brain. It's better to stay at a safe distance, if I can, try to regain my sense of reality. I never want to go through such a war-sought path like that again . . . no—never again."

Laura comforts Emily in her loving arms. Emily tries to hold back her tears, but the moment is too strong to even succeed. Releasing her grasp, Laura brushes Emily's hair back to expose a beautiful face . . . They look at each other with sincere love. That instance holds a mutual bond between them deep inside. Emily exits and closes the door. Laura lingers in confusion, trying to reason with her own conflicting logic and emotions. She can only speak hysterically to sum it up and briefly massages her face to relieve some stress. "What can I say? I need to go against everything within my conscience? Is it that I'm just too reluctant to except this whole debacle of events as a whole? My daughter almost dies—mind controlling psychopaths—demons?! Ugh . . . sanity: error 404, not found, people." Laura removes herself from the chair and walks out as well. But before she actually leaves the room, she then says, "Or is it still there?" She shrugs her shoulders with uncertainty and exits.

Reliving a nightmare begets confrontation to completely
annihilate your very fear(s).

"The darkness can withhold many uncertainties. Anyone can falter
from the Titans that crush the very light of hope, or you can crush
their very soul of existence in your consciousness. I've lived with
doubt, befriended despair, and obliterated my very fears. It was
gruesome . . . All intricate details are forever imprinted in my mind,
and I don't foresee any issues for the coming future. 'Nightmares
made flesh' no doubt, and to assure you, I have a stronger capacity
from the pain to protect me. With much conviction, I implore you
to exact your vengeance against the legions of evil that haunt your
mental aptitude, your reality. Maintain full integrity, and foremost,
your own power."

(DLC for: Conspiracy Endeavor)

Trials / Pt. 1/3

A Test of the Declaration from a Divine Promise

Greek Legacy

07/26/2028, 01:02 p.m.

A couple of weeks later, following a mended status subsequent to William and David entering the station, William sits down on a chair next to the chief's office as David wanders off elsewhere. His whole physique has fully healed from the egregious events that transpired weeks prior, his physical afflictions miraculously fully healed, and a surviving compromised mental state to create its je ne sais quoi. Still clinging to what sanity is left, fate can be met gracefully. William drifts off in his mind, not realizing Adam's standing next to him from his doorway to the office. A clearing of the throat, William shakes his head from an involuntary trance and notices the Chief standing close by. William removes himself from the chair and enters the office first. The door is closed behind them by Adam and transitions to sit at his desk. William is gestured to sit in the chair in front of Adam's desk. A silence emits throughout the room. William twiddles his fingers from the awkwardness. Adam takes a single breath then exhales. "I'm glad you're all right. And by your retained existence, it was successful. What are your plans now? Are you going to stick with the SWAT force, or will you go your way? I can assume this was an extreme radical upon your knowledge of the extraordinary." William looks up and glares at Adam momentarily then says, "More than that . . . with assurance. I'd rather just call it an excessive education for my life. Anything's possible. I'm staying."

"Don't let this victory blind you. Forget assuming it'll always be this way. What had happened, I have no idea of or what could have been the outcome if you had not intervened, but you have been warned with this continued life of yours. Don't ruin this second chance. Don't get arrogant either. I can't say what you've done was entirely stupid, because you're still animated. You brought the others back alive in succession. I just hope you've learned from this. We have, indubitably," Adam hastily replies with seriousness in his voice.

William looks down in shame. "I have. Irrationality won't get the best of me in the same way again. But can I really make that promise? How contrived . . ." (Ascent dialogue +2).

"Not at all . . . and it's not difficult of a choice. My mind escapes me. Annulled notions to grace upon what's occurred recently. I believe I need time to resuscitate. Lucky for you, I have connections within the government. I have a friend who's upon one of the highest positions in the military. He was able to pull some hefty strings so you don't get encountered by our secret friends from secret places, if you know what I mean. Shit, what time is it?" Adam says looking at the time. William is rushed out of the office abruptly, oddly, and sent on his way. Before leaving, by orders, he is told to take some time off again (I mean a lot of time) for his troubles . . . In doing so, he did as he was told by his superior. (William's mark left Adam with an unexpected feeling of respect . . . and with immense suspicion.)

07/28/2028, 4:21 p.m.

Two days in: Relaxing and absorbing the joy from having time off, William sits relaxed on a bench at the park. Children play, the wind blows subtly, cars drive by, and people moving to and from every direction make the moment excessively fantastic. Every aspect creates a peaceful feeling.

A muscular figure appears fifty yards behind. Unaware of the person, William leaves the bench and walks through the park. This man: standing tall, well built, possesses blonde hair, mysterious, wearing black glasses, jeans, and a white shirt (which has a lion on the back) follows behind with anticipation to seize William, it seems. William still doesn't realize the stalker. The field's end is afoot; William stops and looks both ways before crossing the road. Subterfuge is upheld. A nearby tree bordering the edge of the park is employed to keep the inconspicuous motive, and pretends to make a phone call. The man removes his sunglasses to clean them off and looks up to see if William is still near. Eyes of a predator: a light golden color with vertical pupils. Sunglasses return to conceal the visage; he places the cell phone in his back pocket and walks slowly. William is much farther down the street as of now, being as is, it makes the unfamiliar figure walk a little faster. A couple blocks down, William is coming closer to his house. Three people jog by the man pursuing William. A quick look around to see if anyone is catching suspicion at all, alert to no end. The sun's still suspended high in the sky, clear of any storms. Nothing seems to be bothering William at this point as all devastations seems to be done for good. He can live on, knowing a coming evil was stopped from forming. A few more blocks down, but one more to go before William reaches his house. Pursuer closes in. Several feet away . . . William reaches for his front door, opens it, and enters. The man peers at the house. Casually strolls by and disappears into the distance.

Tomorrow, it reaches around 4:30 p.m. A knock comes at the door. William goes to see who it is. His hand reaches the knob, twists, and opens the door. The only apparent view portrays a cloudy sky, people walking around, and cars driving by. William's perception averts to his right pocket, and before grabbing his phone, looks past it to see a package sitting below—an average-sized box: six by five inches, to be exact. William bends over to examine it, but taking it inside first is a better option; so he quickly returns inside with curiosity and preparedness to inspect the content(s). The box is set on the table, resting with all its mystery. A knife is retrieved from the kitchen to unravel its secret. The top is cut apart . . . Inside: plenty of bubble wrapping. Reaches in and pulls out something heavily wrapped in a hazy plastic. The plastic's unwrapping will bring clarity.

William holds a large white tooth. Slight confusion on why someone would send such a random gift such as this; he's not ungrateful, but he's perplexed. The rest of the box is scrutinized, but nothing else resides inside. The tooth's set down on the wooden surface, and moves it around to see if it presents anything else. It's just a large tooth. Suddenly, small noises emit behind him and William slowly turns to see a single man standing fifteen feet adjacent from him in his own house. William's unknown visitor raises a hand to gesture like one who's going to speak. "Give me a moment." The body deforms downward as pixels and reveals a past ally: Cithaeron! Relieved at the sight of a friend, and a tête-à-tête between them starts right away. "I thought I'd never see you again. Where've you been?" William says happily.

"I've been updating myself on your progress and following you, honestly," Cithaeron says.

His remark makes Williams eyebrows rise with shock. "I assume you know how it ended?" Nodding his head up and down indicates William's question has been answered. Cithaeron acts suspicious with his reluctance for formalities and has William wondering what could be the problem.

"Well, seeing that you're not here for pleasantries, I assume this parcel is from you, just a shot in the dark?" The silence is a definite yes. Cithaeron relocates to the tooth . . . He stands on his hind legs and utilizes his front legs, which are placed on top, giving support for an upright setting on the table. William is signaled to come closer.

"My message is odd. Your very mind will be surprised. Mysteriously, reality bending, but it will be interesting nonetheless, totally action worthy. I'm not sure if your 'friend' is responsible for its entirety . . . I can only presume such a terrible event to unfold. It already had during A.D. 81."

William starts to question how any of this is going to unfold before them. Maybe it's just a fib. Cithaeron explains how they're going to approach such an enemy, but he hasn't explained who the 'enemy' is. So he explains . . . "You know how in tales or legends that speak of how knights would save the princess and/or gain the spoils after an engagement by fighting certain threats? Well, there's going to be no one to save, or will there be treasure to gain, only our opposition. No knights either. It's also mixed with Greek ties."

"A dragon: an oversized lizard with wings and spits fire. Oh, and can kill nearly anything? I've been through so little as it is," William speaks out. (Jester dialogue +2)

William is interrupted quickly by Cithaeron's response by trying to persuade him. "I understand completely, though it's not totally what you think. It's a ploy to create an army—just like the one you and the others fought. This one is taking another form. To elaborate: The clash will be fierce, chaotic, and painful in all aspects. This was concealed knowledge I knew before we met. It was the first idea used by your nemesis; there is a tie somewhere. Back then he was a mortal and was captured after Boudicca's rebellion. Execution took place for him. Not sure if that's completely true. He's not who you think. This seems different, trust me. Yes, he was born from the fires of hell, metaphorically turn real. Yes, he's bent on complete control of this world. Yes, he'll fight to no ends to defeat you. Why not use a brute power to take control along with its possessed caliber, indefinitely. Onto the other part now, and I don't mean to offend: it was from a prophecy—more like fate, really. Your ancestor vowed to get vengeance for his enslavement. His testament was strong indeed. Can you live up to his wish? I implore you to take heed of this warning."

William's still bent on declining this grand attempt proposed by Cithaeron. Alas, he doesn't really have a choice. An outcome could be catastrophic if he doesn't comply most likely.

Cithaeron shares another piece of important info by telling a story of how it began.

To make it clearer, life was in a state of normality, but darkness always finds a way in or out. Eudagio was a part of the Coliseum's entertainment. No, he wasn't the announcer—he was one of the slaves that fought. One of their own people was enslaved for amusement: one of Rome's army's captains. Those reasons even I believe to be too brutal. The history behind it all was . . . unforgivable. (Cithaeron personally thinks back on the event of Eudagio's family's demise, being framed, and the subjection to the arena.) The masses were very pleased with all his performances, but one of them stood out from the others (cliché enough). "A prestigious figure, not of a man!" his predecessor shouted. The crowd died down quickly like warriors falling in battle. Silence . . . Suddenly, a man . . . or abomination, walked to the middle of the arena where your ancestor stood and took stance before all. The outfit was of abominable form: armor well-made, believing Hades himself created it; black armor covered him from head to toe, gold trim on the helmet, and posed an evil, demonic grin on it. The gauntlets were like the claws of Cerberus, horns ruptured out of both shoulders, roaring faces on the side, and eyes that followed your every move. That torso piece was magnificently beautiful: gauntlets and greaves were a compliment nonetheless. His herculean existence just felt glorious to all who witnessed. Each wielded weapon was massive: two axes that were made from the crying souls of the dead with the essence of their blood, along with its other materials that were derived from a multitude of other weapons, which took many lives before, nothing like anyone had ever seen. There was a suspenseful moment where they had an exchange, but luckily one of the lord's servants, who sat in the first row, was a savant at reading lips. Exclude that— their exchange was loud anyways. Everyone heard what they said. "Worthy of war: a force that strikes fear in all. Is war your desire, or is it glory?"

"It's really war against me. A man put against his will for petty amusement; a multitude against a single innocence," Eudagio proclaims.

It went quiet after that.

Shortly after, a person in the stands started to shout, "Polemo! Aima! Thanatos!" One by one, more and more started to shout it concurrently . . . and soon, the whole stadium. The Archon shouted, calling him Xediplonetai trela- "Unfolding madness." It looked up at him, but no one really knew what its facial expression was through that black mask.

The match commenced after their whole introduction. Visibly, it was fierce—kind of unfair, different. Everyone was wondering. No, I can't say that because they were too enveloped with the fight, but I can convey it was very satisfying to His Lordship. How your ancestor could maneuver around those oncoming attacks was astounding. All he had was the hide on his back and a battered steel sword given to him by his father. A little farther in time, his opponent started to use strange attacks of necromancy, I guess you could say. The undead started to burst from the ground and focused malevolent intentions at Eudagio. They didn't stand a chance; each blow he dealt was massive. Everyone fell, plunging downward back to hell. After the first debacle, they continued their initial fight. Swings from the axe's blunt side were both deadly and terrifying. You could literally hear the souls crying out from eternal torture. A couple clean hits befell Eudagio and he fell to the ground.

In a guttural tone: "Mallon tromero! As proothisoume ti dynami sas."

(Translation: "Rather formidable! Let's further your power.")

Both axes become propped downward into the ground and he begins to chant. "Adi, fylakas psychon, Theos tou kato kosmou. Ferte enan iso agona metaxy mas. Sas parakalo kyrie, afise aftn tin psychi na spataliso na einai i yposchesi mou se sena. Proteino toso evgenika gia tin anaktimeni zoi mou."

(Translation: Hades, keeper of souls, God of the underworld, bring forth an equal fight between us. I beg you, master; let this soul I squander be my promise unto you I so graciously propose for my regained life.)

Surprisingly, honor was shown, but everyone knew it was all a rouse, strangely. A swirling black mass forms under them. Black tentacles slowly protrude from the abyss and it attaches themselves to Eudagio's arms and lifts him ten feet. Retaining his fear from being exposed while forcefully levitating, discomfort passes through his arms as well. Also, it proves to be resilient. Black tentacles slowly retract, revealing gauntlets forming around his forearms and hands.

Each tentacle reached the end of his fingers, and he drops to the ground. Landing on his feet, knees slightly bent. To look at both his arms and hands after: they represent dragon limbs, a never- seen phenomenon. Everyone stood in awe from the sight. Laughter came from below as the black vortex dissipates. A deep, godly voice says, "Opos sas einai na einai to vraveio mou gia ti niki tou, kanei tin axia tou revmatos dinetai. An apofasiisete na parameinoun zontanoi, neoapoktitheisa exousia sas den einai choris orous . . ."

(Translation: As you are to be my prize for his victory, make worth of greater power given. If you decide to remain alive, your newfound power is not without condition . . .)

This new ability came exceptionally easier than expected—knowledge only known to a God flows through his mind like visions. Naturally, Eudagio accepts his fate with this new potential acquired. Survival is the only option. Additionally, it rectifies his faith immediately. Eudagio moves his arms and hands around, enabling a better feel for the gauntlets. Abruptly, Eudagio's opposition charges at him with great force: Shing! Shing! Shing! Shing! Deflecting attacks left and right with great integrity, Eudagio's next move is to go on the offensive. Each of their strikes causes quakes. The stadium shakes. Everyone in the audience shudders from its effect but cheers on simultaneously. Both contestants flee backward in opposite directions, but ready for an attack concurrently right after. As they collide, the ground splits wide. Eudagio is grabbed by his opponent and pulled under. A gaping hole is present as a form of aftermath. All eyes stare with disbelief.

The stadium above was left in silence from the prior event. The Archon rubs his eyes thinking it's all an illusion (just to keep the realism of shock with the crowd), but it's all real . . . "This is new," the Archon says. Both fighters plummet below . . . a rocky plateau soon approaches. A sudden force slows both down, allowing Eudagio to land on his feet gracefully enough, and Hades' servant lands several feet afar from him. They are shaken up, but they regain their composure. Unsure where he is, a voice shouts, "Welcome to your eternity! Walk among the titans. Your demise will come swiftly!" Eudagio looks around to see where it came from, and a powerful fist sucker-punch Eudagio, flies back several feet and rolls along the floor. Anger rises from inside. Rage assists him to his feet, and fire swirls around each arm. His entire body is gradually enveloped in an inferno. Anger turns to confusion, then to fear through the process. Hade's servant waits patiently from afar.

Eudagio goes through a transformation, to his surprise. Excruciating pain stretches through skin, each muscle fiber, and bone: a price for power. The flames calm; a shadow beneath his new form has appeared. Slowly landing, a dragon appears in substitute for the transformation from his former figure; standing on two legs, large expansive wings, white scales glittering from the light, claws like diamonds. His entire body is covered with illustrious armor of white, ivory and gold: an impenetrable fortress. Eyes open: a bright green color with black vertical pupils. A power named as Wyrm of the autonomous void forge. In short: Apogeio tis theotitas.

(Translation: Apogee of divinity.) For short: A'od.

Wrathful eyes pierce through the enemy's empty vessel with great intentions to annihilate . . . quickly lunges forward, and they continue their fight. Through these godforsaken lands, they endlessly brawled; Titans roam throughout certain areas of Tartarus. The only objective of A'od and Hades' servant is to destroy one another within its inevitable desolation, clearly.

Crashing through mountains, crumbling and shifting the terrain, every Titan, abandoned and forgotten, don't even bat an eyelash toward the battle between the two. Their souls seem lost, empty, and nullified of any emotion. Fumbling in the dark: no care, no love, no life . . . Unlimited power displayed among an unwelcoming hell is only making it seem less likely to be an eternal prison for Eudagio, because his integrity to survive is insurmountable. No room for mistakes or second guessing. Eudagio swiftly moves toward Hades' servant, and they fly off into the distance. Hades' servant's flight was from a massive leap. Suspended hundreds of feet, black wings burst from the opponent's back. Flying into each other: physical strikes conduct with godly powers that expend consistently. The middle of

Tartarus nears (close in proximity as it was from the beginning), and Eudagio attempts to strike fiercely . . . smashing the Abyssal Warrior into the ground as it caves in from the impact. Eudagio now lands on the ground, staring sternly; ready with continuity to defeat a vile foe.

The Abyssal Warrior unexpectedly creates a black barrier around the two. Rising from the ground, head down, weapons broken, armor lies in pieces, and fragments break off as he rises as blood falls from open wounds. Words subtly come forth . . . "Ouranos: aionia eirini. Kolasi: aionia dystychia."

(Translation: "Heaven: eternal peace. Hell: eternal misery.")

Disappearing into the blackened ground . . . suspense . . . A giant claw comes from beneath; another does. A demonic form takes place before Eudagio. This is not going to end well. Grabbing him with one hand, but Eudagio tries to counter. He fails. As a secondary: Eudagio's breaths of fire shooting around causes constriction to loosen, dropping him. A new plan: flying high up, hot on his trail not too far below, ready to expel grotesque powers once more. Black fire closes in; faces of demons cover the black conflagration with gaping mouths and hungry motives. Eudagio tries to break free from the dark field around them. He then forcefully exerts a blaze to stop all impending attacks, but nothing happens; trying to hit physically wasn't exactly working. The expelled flames split as Eudagio bursts through, and the abomination strives to swallow him. With another attempt, he reacts quickly, flies straight down and forces his way through the body with a mighty punch. Evil takes a massive hit; screams are heard from vast pain as Eudagio tears through the plagued souls who power and form this entity. The formless entity freaks out and bounces off the walls, making cracks along the vertical tunnel.

This massive body comes closer. With a quick decision to fully descend, there's realization that freedom is non-viable; Eudagio finally reaches the ground. No other options . . . Looks upward and chooses to embrace for an imminent collision. The body of malice fills the whole barricaded area. Upon impact, a loud, destructive explosion occurs. Boom!!! Assuming nothing would be left after such an action . . . While all haziness leisurely dissipates, Eudagio is left on the ground, back to normal form, unconscious, but still in one piece. One gauntlet must have shattered or flown off somewhere, and no evidence to be found of it anywhere. Whatever that thing he fought was is destroyed, hopefully. He breaths in deeply and exhales, his eyes slowly open, and vision is slightly blurry; but no pain is present. In the far distance, he sees a man on one of the Titan's hands. His opponent was forced afar after the clash. The other Titans come together and surround the titan who's holding Hades' servant. Hades soon emerges. Still in the Titan's hand, the servant's placed on the ground, to be forced down by each of them, securing the servant's detainment. Fear increases inside; attempts to escape were denied. No words or actions could allow release from an undeniable fate.

Hades makes his judgment by saying, "Chasate ti defter efkairia sas kai tora, pairnei ti thesis as sti niki. Akoma kai oi Titanes, pou den echo elencho, symfonoun me tin timoria sas. Sou leipei. Apodidete mono gia afto-kerdos choris times . . . choris pnevma. O peirasmos me itan poly efkolo gia esas kai oi energeies sas odigisan stin ptosi sas. It is time to pay what's due."

(Translation: "You wasted your second chance and now, he takes your place in victory. Even the Titans, who I have no control over, agree with your punishment. You lack will. You only perform for self-gain with no values . . . no spirit. Tempting me was too easy for you, and your actions led to your downfall.")

Hades' servant averts over at Eudagio with acceptance in his eyes, but with a hint of anger.

Thanatos materializes right before Hades takes his leave, with intentions to take the servant's soul. "His soul is very prominent. I could take him off your hands. You know, make your job easier." Hades turns and grabs Thanatos by the neck. "Do not pester me! We were under oath and this one failed on his part. I am simply taking what is rightfully mine as guaranteed." Thanatos transforms into a black mist and reappears to a normal state. Even the figure of death becomes relentless and continues to beg. "How many times have you undergone such an act with others? Was it four hundred and seventy-six times? That's quite a lot and many failures too." Hades pulls out two-bladed claws and pierces Thanatos with them through the torso. Through and through, the claws lengthen by separating into multiple links that wrap and penetrate brutally; Thanatos grabs the chains, pulling closer . . . Now merely inches away. "One day I will reign in your place, and I will see to it you are mine forever . . . I hope you recognize the notion, God or no God, that's a promise."

Thanatos evaporates into the air. Hades travels back to his own realm. Hades' servant starts to talk, but it's incoherent between the ranges of him and Eudagio. Hades takes his prize. Every Titan returns to their bleak states. Eudagio lies on the ground from a well-deserved triumph. Thunderous sounds, bright lights, godly presences blind him instantly. All godly figures stand before him but Hades, gazing with satisfaction. Blinding white lights appear again, and Eudagio is returned to the Colosseum's ground. Complete eyesight restored; the gauntlet that was left is still equipped on his arm, and he lies with a naked body. Eudagio's reappearance surprises every worker in the Colosseum who's fixing all the damages. They call out for one of the guards to retrieve the Archon. Every worker walks over to see if he's alive. Crowding around him, one asks, "Is he dead?" Another says, "No, he's still breathing. Amazing, he comes from the depths of Tartarus and remains alive. I was here when it happened, a wondrous display." The other people look at the man with bewilderment.

Chapter 14

Trials

(Starting Line) Pt. 1

Helios' Chariot

Cithaeron concludes his story. "That's as much as I can tell you from all the fragments I've heard or remembered within my lifetime there. It's almost identical to your encounters, but this one seems more 'family friendly.'

"It doesn't sound like we're going to be collecting a family photo on a vacation," William says rebuking the statement and in a jokingly manner. (Jester +1)

"Close, but it's an attraction nowadays—a wondrous site where man vs. man occurred through viciously brutal and bloody arena battles," Cithaeron says. Continually not approving with said words, William collects himself and accepts the proposed plan. "Good! At first light, we leave at 5:30 a.m. tomorrow to Rome, Italy," Cithaeron excitedly exerts.

William travels to the kitchen and makes dinner. "You want anything to eat?" William asks.

Cithaeron sits in the living room, and then starts playing with a ball he found. "No, I don't eat. They removed all functions for eating. Most organs were removed. The right half of my brain has had some modifications. Not to forget to note: the hypothalamus which resided in it, to tell you you're hungry, has also been absent long ago. So I have no urge in taking pleasure of gorging myself anymore. Though, canisters, which are placed in my underbelly, give nutrients to all parts that need nourishment. Replacement is every two months. I have the concoction plan I stole after my resurrection. The only organic divisions I have left are my lungs, heart, most of the right half of the brain (other half is a computing processor), one leg, one paw, one eye, half my face, only certain portions of my torso, some segments of muscle, and my untouched crotch."

The prepared meal is set on the table. William views his right side and smiles at the little kitty playing with his toy. "You are adorable." (Jester +1)

Cithaeron continues to amuse himself. "Don't start . . . I just happen to find it amusing. To be fair: I am a feline in all accordance."

William's smile lessens. "How does it feel? The mechanical parts I mean," He wonders.

"I don't feel any different besides what I've told you," Cithaeron replies.

"I feel bad. It's quite the common pleasure most love, but I hear what you're saying," William says sympathetically.

"Don't let my fate ruin your meal," Cithaeron says. Cithaeron continues to play with the ball, and William carries on eating.

A decision to question Cithaeron again about permanent changes with replacing organic with robotic. "Does it bother you?" William asks.

Cithaeron displays sadness but responds to the question. "Yes, these new additions that were forcefully made replaced parts of my soul and are beneficial. Sometimes, I wish I could be my whole self. To have my whole soul returned . . . If I sustain a positive mindset, I'll be OK. Well, having someone to talk or be around with helps. You know . . . a friend." William appreciates the thought process creating words of optimism. But to be called a friend was really surprising. A couple hours after their exchange, both go to bed.

For once, William sleeps peacefully and dreams of wonderful moments from his life, years previous; collective thoughts, metaphors, and symbolism collide into the magnificence.

07/30/2028, 4:30 a.m.

Alarm sounds. William opens both eyes in a struggle and takes a decent stretch. "I don't want to get up." he says. Now to the bathroom: he relieves himself, washes both hands, brushes teeth, and dresses himself. William exits his room and waits outside the doorway. Cithaeron stands a couple feet away with William's bags all prepped and ready to go. William looks down and sees them, much to the unexpected. "Thanks for doing that. What about your ticket and required 'info'?"

Cithaeron points to his head and says, "Seeing how mentally advanced I am, I can say arrangements were made long ago." All that's needed is grabbed. Next stop: airport. About nine minutes in their drive, halting before a stop light, another car pulls up to the right side and waits alongside them. The adjacent driver averts attention at William's car and becomes unsettled to see a lion in the front seat. Cithaeron turns and winks. Green light, William drives on. Cars behind the other citizen honk at the man who's still idle at the stop light.

William takes notice of the event. "It's extremely uncommon for a lion to be sitting in a car—the front seat of all places."

"I'm the least of their worries compared to what had or what is happening. We're fine," Cithaeron replies. William's stern look persuades Cithaeron. "All right, I'll change."

They arrive at the airport, exits, grab their bags, and walk over to a bus stop. Their bus arrives on schedule. William and Cithaeron climb aboard. Quietness lingers for the entirety of the bus ride. When they arrive at the airport's front doors, exit the bus, check in, and enter into their terminals. No trouble passing through security and such. All that can be done for now is to sit at their terminal and wait for the plane's arrival. Many people wait, workers walk around helping others or cleaning any sections of the airport. "Who or what is this apogee of divinity? I can't believe I had a relative that was a part of this," William says.

Cithaeron expels the details. "He played a small role, but nothing was discredited. A'od was the first dragon. The main purpose behind it was to either demolish or heal the lands. A similar part in comparison to the four horsemen, though it's typical, but fearful nonetheless. Hephaestus had a forge specifically meant for the deities' creation. Zeus himself demanded he make it. Its existence was from the inner fire of the blacksmith—his essence, partially. The armor was made first, and the idea, second. Something to throw the world in dismay: a monstrous beast to man . . . a tool for the gods. It was the first dragon to ever become reality and obviously where dragons arise. They allowed it so people would fear what could be."

"Unexpected for the most part, but couldn't they've just done it themselves?" William says observantly.

"Unexpected is a good word. They're Gods—they can do whatever they want," Cithaeron frankly replies.

William nods his head in compliance. "I mean that's an outstanding revelation. The more I hear about these divine interventions, mythical creatures, battles . . . it seems I'm questioning to myself in a paradoxical fashion now. There's no damage to my initial faith—"

Cithaeron unveils arcane knowledge. "Man is unstable. They fade in time like the beliefs in Gods through the ages. Each and every one had a trial, path . . . A test, you could say. Some are trivial while others are significant in comparison to others. Believe it or not, everything you do or will do sums up your character whilst building your own life concurrently. Even Gods know fear. But let's just say humanity has lost all respect from outside sources. Unfortunately, even within their kind, there's no abandonment, only a far reach. Don't think on it too hard. The process hasn't encumbered you, surprisingly, though. We aren't who fear but who are the feared."

William leans back and looks upward. "I don't see how most couldn't question if they knew about this." An agreement, accompanied with silence fell upon the duo; weight beyond any amount inside stressed consciousness. William continues to ponder, and a thought eventually comes to mind. "Do you know of anyone else or of my family who had experienced this intense caliber of events?" William asks. Cithaeron contemplates how to answer the question. "Nothing comes to mind. For all I know, that could be it."

Their plane arrives half an hour later. Over the intercom, everyone relevant to the flight is called to board. The massive vessel is entered with many; it's nearly completely filled. William's seat is A13 single seat. Cithaeron's is C13 aisle seat. There's some wondering why the seats are separated so far from each other, but William just keeps to himself. When everyone's aboard, an explanation of all the rules by the stewardess occurs, and then takeoff commences next. During their travels, all is going well. William contemplates something he assumes going to take place out of his own paranoia, but we'll see. *Bing!* Seatbelt indicator conveys that everyone can take them off now. Passengers talk softly, some are sleeping, and kids walk the aisles out of boredom. Three stewardesses come around with beverages and snacks. Cithaeron goes to the back where two bathrooms are located. William watches him the entire time until disappearing into the next section. Cithaeron abruptly comes rushing back after just walking off. "Good morning ladies and gentlemen. This is your captain speaking. Sorry for the late formalities. We are on a direct route to Rome, Italy (a one-way trip with no stops in between). Partial clouds—mostly a nice sunny view ahead for us in due time, and we hope you have a pleasant ride. Thank you."

A man walks out of the one of two stalls; nervousness can be seen from his body language and the sweat on his forehead. His eyes tell all. Cithaeron watches him while the man returns to his seat. Cithaeron arises and moves toward the back. In the bathroom, he scrutinizes inside for any complicit placements, or oddities. Now searching in the cabinet under the sink he finds a bomb, well placed, activated, but small in size. Its settings are for one hour. Immediately, once more, walking quickly back to his seat, William sees his return and with a glare which implies difficulties. Cithaeron makes the gesture with his mouth saying, "Boom!" William rolls his eyes and rests his back quickly in the seat facing forward, annoyed. William's heart beats faster, adrenaline increases, but he maintains complete composure externally. Cithaeron walks to the front where the man's primary seat is and approaches to confront him. Cithaeron proceeds to the gentleman sitting next to the nervous individual and asks if he could talk to him. The gentleman agrees and gets up to move briefly, and Cithaeron sits in his place. Nervousness floods throughout, but courage is found . . . "There are numerous people in here. Do you really need to continue such a heinous act? I advise you rethink your plot and disarm it."

The distraught man shakes his head. "It wants his soul personally. Your presence is known as well." A scared, trembling gaze lays upon Cithaeron as tears fall from the eyes. "I'd give him ten times that many souls just to see my family as he promised to me."

Cithaeron tries reasoning. "Is everyone here really worth destroying? The innocence harbored inside for your own gain? Whatever promised, whoever this person or thing is will not be retaining that promise."
"You don't know what I went through! That man in the other room was the result of their deaths. He still lives; they don't. I'll do whatever it takes to have them again . . . I assume you know? They were being watched by an anti-terrorism group, and by their leader Oman Shero. He said they would be protected, but they were massacred by their own people a couple of days after Oman's demise. They were murdered," the terrorist proclaims.

Cithaeron feels much sorrow for the man's loss. This terrible act cannot continue. "You'll be a part of the destruction and die with everyone else," Cithaeron replies quickly.

"No, I have a parachute close to the hatch and seconds before it's going to go off, I'll have escaped."

"That simple? The man you oppose for a promise saved many others from brutal experiments that very figure you serve has committed, who's 'going to bring your family back.' Who you despise has suffered losses, even from trying to save many," Cithaeron says as a last resort to persuade.

"No," was the response.

Eyes transform into the predator of the wild; a hand grabs the perspiring face, and claws form, sticking to the man's face. "Many men had followed the path you're choosing. You are no better than what you judge if murder is your criterion. Make amends. Help what could alleviate your misery," Cithaeron speaks indomitably. A passenger views the happening through the space between the seats Cithaeron and the terrorist sit in. Cithaeron slowly turns his head to look at the passenger and transitions his eyes to the normal setting. The witness returns to a normal sitting position in fright and curiosity. "What's your name? Are you accompanied by anyone else?" Cithaeron asks, staring sternly. The man trembles before Cithaeron but soon responds. "Brian. Yes. He's sitting in another cabin. His name is Ishro." Cithaeron nods his head in response. "OK, Brian. Let's go. Shall we fix this mess?" Cithaeron says.

William sits in suspense and waits for Cithaeron to return with more info. The two return to the bathroom in the back. Cithaeron nods at William as he walks by. Steven, the man who planted the explosive, revisits the bathroom to diffuse it. Cithaeron sits a couple rows from the bathroom to keep surveillance on Steven. Some tools are revealed, which were used on the construction of the explosive. a pair of cutters and screwdrivers are used first. He takes the plate off the front to reveal color coded wires that lead to the fuse and timer and other electronics. Sweat drips; suspense grows. William is losing patience. Cithaeron signals him to come over. A little explosion occurs in the bathroom. They quickly move to observe what happened, and everyone else nearest turns around to understand what's happening as well. Brian lies on the ground with a scorched face and a piece of metal had severed his neck. William gets on his knees and tries to stop the bleeding. Cithaeron looks into Brian's eyes, and Brian looks back with tears as he lies on the floor dying. Death soon takes its hold. A couple stewardesses rush over to see what had ensued. Cithaeron approaches the two ladies and makes sure they remain calm and aware of what's happening.

William clearly notices the device was rigged and that it has defenses against any diffusing; its timer now reads five minutes. "We obviously can't touch it or we'll be in the same situation as him. What are these capsules on here? It looks as if one had exploded.

(Special action- Inform the captain, or will devising a self-made plan be?)

What should we do? Tell the captain?" William asks.

"Maybe, but we also do not want to scare everyone. We'll have to be discreet with this. Not everyone onboard knows of this yet," Cithaeron replies.

(Ascent +4) Both make headway to the front . . . a stewardess approaches the two, but they stop William and Cithaeron from trekking any further, telling them to return to their seats. Cithaeron tells her what's going on and convinces plentifully. The door to the captain's deck is opened by the stewardess. (The bomb's timer is decreasing. In reality, a minute is left. Due to it being rigged, nothing can be done. Opening the hatch and disposing the bomb would only endanger others. No other areas that would allow the threat to be taken out were existent.)

"What's going on? Copilot Langsten blurts as William enters. William barges in, and the two surprised pilots tell him to leave immediately.

(Ascent dialogue: +4) William is unmoving. "You two are going to listen to me . . . There's an issue which is serious. Don't alarm everyone. Just tell them we're going to be hitting some turbulence soon."

"What do you mean?" Captain Walter asks.

William: "There is . . . a bomb. We're not sure if there's any more. Please be calm, and for everyone's sake onboard. I and my friend are going to intervene with this issue."

A decision to be calm about the situation was made (thirty seconds remain). The message is conveyed. Both can feel their hearts in their throats from the severity of the current dilemma. A distraction is produced.

"Attention folks, this is your captain speaking. We're going to be moving through increased winds. Turbulence will occur. Just make sure you stay in your seats and stay buckled up. Thank you." The seatbelt indicator lights up.

William approves of them doing as he asked and leaves the room. "Let's get ready." He says while he and Cithaeron walk to the back again. William's hit hard in the face by another person and falls. Cithaeron proceeds to detain the man. 3 . . . 2 . . . 1 . . . beep, beep, beep. Boom! Boom! Two explosions occur in back and decimate the tail end of the plane. Fire blazes where holes are present; air swirls and screeches through. The wind ferociously blows, but all passengers are buckled in and alive at least.

Cithaeron is grabbed and thrown into another section. The pilots are frightened but maintain their integrity. Multiple lights shine brightly, indicating the damaged areas of the plane. "The horizontal stabilizers are damaged, and the left elevator isn't responding," Captain Walter sternly says. Copilot Langsten makes a call over the intercom to ground team. Cithaeron arises and rushes toward Ishro. The suspect starts yelling at everyone. Cithaeron roars at the man and charges. Ishro readies himself. Ishro is equipped with strange gauntlets and attains a strong stance. Cithaeron nears and attacks with his claws. Ishro blocks each attack and punches twice: once to the gut then the face as blue pulses emit with each strike, knocking Cithaeron to the ground with ease. Ishro changes direction and moves to the cockpit. William's suddenly woken up from gun shots. Some slight issues recovering from the blow to the head are apparent, but he sees Cithaeron moving. Everyone's screaming or yelling in terror.

Ishro shoves a stewardess over. Cithaeron comes from the other side and clobbers Ishro with a fire extinguisher. Cithaeron then checks both aviators. Walter uses his remaining strength keeping it upright. Walter dies from the wound in his neck and blood loss seconds later. They are both dead. "Make sure everyone is seated and buckled, even you two," he commands the stewardesses. One of the stewardesses made the announcement over the intercom to all passengers. Cithaeron quickly enters the flight deck. "Help me out" he says to William. He and William try to move Walter and Langsten as respectful and quickly as they can. Both now sit in the cockpit; control is now in their hands.

Cithaeron explains to William what to do. The right engine suddenly explodes and makes the plane sway. Gradually, he levels out, and Cithaeron calls for help to convey which directions is best for landing and explains that both pilots are dead. A base closest gives the directions; however, it's not what they need. "We convey the problem and you won't be able to make it any farther without compromise. And I mean: everybody on board . . . Do you know how to operate an aircraft?"

"Yes. Air force: flight commander, fifteen year service," Cithaeron replies with a lie.

"That's a relief. Unfortunately, you're surrounded by a body of water in all directions for miles; it is your best bet. Sorry the news couldn't be more beneficial than this. We'll radio help for everyone's extraction. We'll have your exact coordinates the entire time. Luck is to you. Another thing: you ready to do your part again, Commander? The mission's yours," Communications from the control tower replies. Silence surrounds them for a bit, but Cithaeron complies with the orders given. Landing will not be as soft as some intend; hopefully, everyone survives it.

Cithaeron grasps the reigns, gently redirecting in a downward glide; suspended 32,000 feet and only. Down is their only option. Descending with this massive giant of the skies (31,999 feet, 31,998 feet, 31,997 feet . . .), closer and closer the water will come . . . The half way marker nears; everything seems the same for now. While lowering the altitude, an explosion occurs in the left engine and causes the aircraft to sway again. Both engines have exploded and damaged the slats. Still plummeting downward . . . pulling harder and harder—everyone is still panicking. These incursions aren't making it easy in any way. Only 14,000 feet left. He tries to make the landing adequate at least, seeing that 3 ends are decimated: 10,000 feet . . . 9,000 . . . 8,000 . . . 7,000 . . . 6,000 . . . 5,000 . . . 4,000 . . . 3,000 . . . 2,000 . . . Controlling is continually difficult. The 1000 foot marker appears. Each passing second is more difficult. He glides it downward so there isn't total instability. Now 500 feet . . . and control is maintained, miraculously. 100 feet . . . 50 feet . . . (10, 9, 8, 7, 6, 5, 4, 3, 2, 1) Crash! Water flies in every direction. All passengers are rattled around. Almost everyone else is in their seats, alive and safely buckled. Ishro is still lying on the floor.

All are shaken from the impact (jerked and yanked), and some elderly took it the worse (from the stress and impact). One of the stewardesses stands up to release the hatch. Two gigantic life rafts shoot out from both sides with two connecting slides in addition. This'll allow a safe exodus for the passengers. One by one a person slides down, entering on the rafts below. William and Cithaeron wait last to make sure everyone's out first and safely.

"Thank you," William says to Cithaeron after everyone has exited.

Cithaeron pats him on the shoulder. "I lead by example," Cithaeron says. William smiles from his moral statement. "We should retrieve the pilots," William says. Cithaeron helps William retrieve the bodies. "History repeats, huh?" Cithaeron says. William understands the idea. The upper sections of their bodies are concealed so the bullet wounds aren't shown to others. Placing each pilot in a seat, Cithaeron takes the gauntlets off Ishro's hands and crushes them. Both of Ishro's hands are then tied, picked up, and placed unconsciously on the slide and pushed down. Cithaeron and William both carry a body, and they soon go down the slide that leads to a raft. Cithaeron throws the destroyed gauntlets into the ocean as they descend. People gasp and are saddened by the two bodies. Trivial waves brush up against who reside in rafts. At least they have sun shine and minimal cloud coverage. With everyone safe, fear dies down. Voices spread through the finite domain; only patience to be rescued prevails.

"He'd have my head if only this was known," William says.

"Then its fine that I brought you, right? He'll never know," Cithaeron says. William gives Cithaeron a displeasing look. "Hey, don't shoot the messenger. This was the easy part." William thinks of a retort. "Messengers don't typically have extravagant events tagged to messages," William says in discontent. On the other side, the second rafts move closer and meets up with everyone else. Using oars to paddle around the wreckage, the stewardess who's on Williams and Cithaeron's raft throws a rope to connect the second raft. As each connects, they pull closer.

"Can I have your attention, everyone? While in our descent, we were contacted by ground control, and they're giving us naval support. Thank you. We wouldn't be here if it weren't for you," Stewardess Janice says. "We should be picked up at any time."

Small murmurs joint . . . One passenger turns to say thank you to Cithaeron. Many soon mimic the gesture. Gratitude was given for Cithaeron's brave attempt to help all survive this frightening crash.

Cithaeron takes note of his actions that were gratefully acknowledged. Within his mind: "Odigisame to arma tou Iliou ypo akraio tromo kathos lampei, afinontas kafstika monopatia. San ton ourano gemato me ti lamperi tou kolasi. O ilios lampei apo to aktinovolo arma tou apo chryso, lefko kai asimi. Fotia aloga kalpazoun me megali andreia, kai oi fones tous taxidepsan sta edafi. Alla o Poseidonas simera einai eleimon. Ta kymata liknizoun tis zoes mas. Echete exasfalisei ena meros stin epikrateia sas. Me tin akatanoiti dynami stin katochi, Thee to nero, kalosorizoume tis iremes palirroies tou thanatou."

(Translation: We rode Helios's chariot under extreme terror as it shone, leaving scorched trails. Like the sky filled with his shining hell. The sun gleamed off his radiant chariot of gold, white, and silver. Fire-born horses galloped with great prowess, and their voices traveled across the lands. But Poseidon is merciful today. Waves cradle our very lives. You've secured a place on your territory. With the incomprehensible power in possession, water God, we mortal's welcome quiet tides.)

Chapter 15

Trials

(Halfway Mark) Pt. 2

Hermes' Tenacity

5:02 p.m.

Their rescue was much needed after such a terrifying moment, especially what everyone was dealt. Cithaeron (along with William) asks to be dropped off at the nearest coast of Portugal; every person aboard from the plane is taken to the nearest hospital. On board medics, thankfully, take amazing care of each passenger; they are able to contact their families and/or friends to notify them of their situation at a later time. Commander Nosephta and a couple of officers acquired all info and make a record of what happened. Admiral Kingston has called ahead for locomotive transport for everyone. So now, William and Cithaeron can go to their initial destination. William and Cithaeron sneak off when the opportunity came. Nearly an hour later, a carriage comes along, and both receive a ride to their destination.

Shaken up from the incident, sheer luck or divine intervention had played a part. Huh . . . your guess is as good as mine.

"You understand fate?" William asks Cithaeron.

"The meaning is obvious, but discerning the true idea is too complex, next to being stuck in the midst of it," Cithaeron claims.

"I'm scared and a little angry," William says while sitting back. He turns his head left and looks straight at Cithaeron.

Eyes meet. "Embrace the quality; outweigh the first, the scared part. It'll push you. No remorse. A guardian I stand before you, likelihood for bondage. Here are my words concerning you . . . fearsome perception by significant superiors: the prospect of wrath," Cithaeron says, turning his head forward after.

William sits quietly. Eyes averted downward, eyebrows scrunch, looks up again and relaxes his face, reflects upon spoken words. Several minutes later, before the city, on the edge, a little village resides. Their ride comes to a stop. William and Cithaeron exit from the vehicle. The driver speaks no English, so Cithaeron nods as a gesture for "thank you." The driver does as well, in return. The scenery displays a quaint sector of proportional size and tranquility. A naturally fashioned atmosphere of peace brings calmness to the body, mind and soul.

William's stomach growl indicates that hunger is afoot. They soon find a little business that supplies food, a ten-by-twenty hut that harbors two people. A sign displays all names of who reside here. Precenda (mother), Grucaar (son), and their elderly German shepherd named Cencille. Precenda gives them a list of what they make. William chooses one of the biggest meals', of course. Fifteen minutes later, his meals finished. A plate that contains rice, chicken, bread, celery, carrots, and lettuce; he immediately ate like who hasn't eaten in days. Cithaeron and Precenda look at William. She smiles. "It's good to know another appreciates my cooking."

"He could ingest a meal that a whale intakes if he wanted to he-he," Cithaeron says. After finishing, Cithaeron asks Precenda for directions to any civilization beyond here. She says that it's about 45 minutes down the road by vehicle, or an hour and a half on foot.

One of the younger kids approach William: a young girl who's no older than seven, pulls on his arm, innocence in all accordance. "That's Srivinta. How are you?" Precenda says.

"I'm good. Can he play with us, please?" Srivinta gains approval from Precenda.

"Don't worry about us. We'll be fine here. I won't leave you," Cithaeron calmly says.

William departs and runs with the young girl as she clings to his arm, pulling consistently with excitement. Villagers of all sizes and ages are working, playing, or doing something productive. A small hut behind the chicken coup seems to be their chosen location. The straw door opens by her little hand; twelve barrels are evenly placed inside, and hay lies all around on the sides. She runs to a barrel at a farther end and hides in it. It's quiet for a moment. William opens the container that Srivinta is currently in. He lifts the lid, but no one's inside . . . Baffled by the disappearance, he tips it to observe if the bottom has a hole or a movable compartment, but he perceives clear indication that there is. A tunnel system must be in use. Little voices laugh. Moving to another barrel . . . he opens the adjacent barrel's lid . . . No one . . . A different kid pops up from one barrel at the southern end. Surprised, William quickly moves. Nothing exists inside, same result . . . Assuming a pattern is used, a thought comes to mind.

(William thinks of an intuitive idea on how to beat this game or knock them over.)

(Special +3) William devises a cunning idea to find them and steps back for a bit. When the thought turns decisive, he chooses the middle barrel because the ends are already used. Reaching for the sixth, he opens it . . . One down! Srivinta is found. William goes to the south end again. Opening the eleventh, he retrieves two more this time! Another kid pops up. William walks to the front, but the same kid pops up from one barrel behind. William waits in the center. Unknowing to the fourth child, William stands right in front of the next spot the child, unassuming, will sprout from. He slowly opening the lid . . . and the last one is found. "He's good. Let's go again!" Srivinta says.

(William thinks of agreeing or ending the game.)

(Cooperative dialogue +1) "Sure. This was fun. We can go again," William says happily.

"How come your people decided to keep this standard of living?" Cithaeron asks Precenda.

"Our ways were preserved since two hundred years ago, by our leader, Frezeen. He was upright and kept the peace among our community with endless benevolence. During the end of his leading role, his mother passed from an illness, but before that . . . his father was slain. Nobody still knows why or how Trisdon, his father, was murdered. The original family built this colony a couple miles from Mt. Cithaeron with just his wife, brother, and son. I'll spare you the gloomy remainders. Such tragedy and sadness, but we uphold what graciousness that was left after the passing of such a great family."

Randomly not too far in the village, there's a small farm where the chickens run loose and cause an alarming uproar.

Five farmers try to acquire the multiple chickens that came from one of the smaller coups behind the farm. Difficult to accomplish, the incidence catches everyone else's attention. Cithaeron arises from his chair. Another explosion transpires in the distance, additionally blowing a small household to smithereens. Precenda and Cithaeron fear for William and Srivinta's lives and for the other children's. Loud shouts can be heard near or around the explosion's site. Cithaeron runs toward the chaos to see if there's anyone in need of help. William tells the kids to stay inside. Exiting to the outside to give additional help . . . he is suddenly tackled from the left side. William quickly shakes it off, then looks up and sees a figure shrouded in white garments. Cithaeron realizes it's too late to save anyone from the blast as nothing was left in the aftermath, and only fiery remnants delay their leave.

Frightened people are appalled by the scene. William rises and pursues. Cithaeron turns to see William's not present and then looks in other directions to find him. Upon the outer parts, Cithaeron glimpses William running; catches interest and follows to discern what the situation's about. A grand chase happens through fields of tall grass. William is persistent; the other is deviant. This cloaked figure is faster than William thought, but it won't decline his spirit. A blast of wind projects from a covered hand clobbering William intensely, knocking him over; he slides across the ground twenty feet back. Cithaeron meets up, but instead decides to change back to his normal form.

Running valiantly to aid William, they make eye contact as he passes; quickly Cithaeron runs, transforming. In doing so, an advantage is applied. The unidentified figure turns to see William isn't behind him. Grass starts to shift. Something or someone is closing in . . . Forced air projects everywhere: swirling vortexes and chaotic gusts. Suspense . . . Cithaeron reveals his self from the tall grass and lunges for their target. They clash! And their battle is intense . . . large paws with sharp claws wrap around this figure's torso, unintentionally spins once but tries to break free from the attack. Attempting to dig every fang in its face, but is shot far up above and casts a raging vortex to finish Cithaeron. But to regain full composure in midair does not bode well for their enemy. He darts down like lightning bolt; William's eyes expresses awe from the sight of godly power. Mortal eyes watch Cithaeron's abilities come to life. In absolute awe: a crashing, thunderous sound arises; and the earth trembles from the wicked impact.

Villagers watch fearfully from a safe proximity; all eyes are attracted to the show. William waits for a sign. The smoke is thick. Cithaeron emerges from its haze with a scroll in his mouth. William meets up with him. Cithaeron lifts his head to give the scroll to William. Cithaeron changes back to "human form." Luckily, none of the remaining villagers were hurt, killed, nor could any see the shape-shifting happen at least. The smoke thinned; the entity lies still.

"I don't think he'll be getting up," Cithaeron confidently says. William opens the scroll to reveal a note saying, "Messenger: Sas enimerono oti tha nikisete to liontari Nemeas pou eiche nikisei o Iraklis, alla fainetai oti yparchei ena archetype. I anasa pou sou dinetai einai ena theiko doro. I ekplirosi mias mono archis einai i moni sas ergasia."

William asks Cithaeron to translate it.

(Translation: Messenger: I hereby inform you that you are to vanquish the Nemean lion Hercules had defeated, but it seems there's an archetype. The breath given back to you is a divine gift. Fulfilling a single principle is your only task.)

"All right, I can't hold this in anymore. What the fuck is going on! And who's the one that created the message?! This appears too coincidental. It's bad enough we had such a monumental incident earlier." (Critical dialogue +1)

"You freak out now?! You're aware of what we're facing, and this isn't going to be peaceful. I warned you beforehand." Cithaeron says. William gestures that he's aware. "Is that a doppelganger of Hermes? And it's a demented copy. It can't be him. An 'appealing' gift in this fashion doesn't sound like . . ."

The body lying on the ground starts rising. It reaches fifteen feet up and explodes into numerous turtles, scattering over the area and causing them to barrage William and Cithaeron, knocking them over. Their opponent sprints away. Cithaeron's rage builds . . . "Get on and hold tightly." William listens to him. Sitting on his back, he leans forward, and two handles and a waste belt appear from his upper back. William utilizes each handle and is fastened securely. Unaware of the extreme speed Cithaeron possess, William holds on with all available strength for security reasons.

Wind rushes around them with the ferocity of a maelstrom. William is having difficulties keeping his eyes open from the opposing winds. Within the field, but coming to an end, a valley comes into sight ahead. The doppelganger enters and zooms along its walls. William and Cithaeron reach it as well. Cithaeron jumps from wall to wall, enabling them to gain ground behind their target. To see them trailing not too far back, small tornadoes are thrown. Cithaeron leaps high above the valley over the projected winds. Running above, the doppelganger observes them and soars upward. Now he turns to face the duo and it lunges forward. Cithaeron mimics the lunging action. "Hold on tight!" he says to William with all seriousness. Gaining ground . . . a group collision occurs. Shrouded Doppelganger grabs them and flies up high. William continues holding on with all his might. It lets them go. Pauses . . . and moves both even farther away with a cyclone. As it's facing them, it flies backward, and turns back around, now facing away, to resume fleeing.

Cithaeron prays silently, and their descent slows down. A thin barrier covers William's entire body. Stopping in midair . . . Calm before the storm . . . Lightning falls from the skies as a gyre forms. Electric bolts also surround them. William flinches—assuming they're going to be struck. Electricity swirls around with no compromise to their lives or health. Cithaeron opens his eyes and says, "Mercy to none." William lays his body's upper half against Cithaeron's back. Cithaeron speedily bolts straight for the escapee; lightning follows behind and flows throughout the sky. Roaring through the void, Shrouded Doppelganger takes notice of the impending danger. William is surreptitiously shocked, amazed by the event that is happening, and still maintains his grip on Cithaeron's back. Shrouded Doppelganger turns around and creates huge air blades to cut through them, but lightning smites all in succession, each one down. Cithaeron is ready to finish this whole altercation. Cithaeron's maw is open wide and aims for the doppelgangers throat. Crunch!!! The ground is the clear objective for the next move . . . it fights continuously, but Cithaeron clutches both arms tightly with his paws. Though, squirming to release itself, no decline within Cithaeron's integrity will occur. The barrier formed around William to protect him from the speedy pursuit still persists. The soon-to-be immense collision nears . . . Slammed into the earth. Lightning strikes with immeasurable intensity and forcefully slides the false god along the ground. William's eyes are still closed.

The protective barrier shuts down. A godly battle ends. Cithaeron's jaw remains closed on their foe's neck, though it shows no movement or life. William gradually opens his eyes. Complete carnage is visible. The sky above calms; the forcefully made electric occurrence subsides. William gets off of Cithaeron's back, but stumbles a little from being astonished. Looking back shows scars from the mighty powers. Spots of fire, rubble . . . Breathing is slightly heavier from the after-effects. Eternally grateful for being protected and continuing to be alive after what just happened. William walks around to the front and observes the body is limp and lifeless, apparently. "He . . . it's . . . he . . . whatever . . . I assume . . . dead?" William asks.

The doppelganger hastily eye's opens its eyes.

While pretending to be dead, it was powering up for another escape. It creates a force field and pushes the two away, making Cithaeron release his hold from the surprising action. William is shoved back several feet. Teeth gashed its neck after its forceful release, though it shows no signs of injury or weakness. Running off again . . . Cithaeron becomes annoyed . . . Ejecting both handles indicates William's second ride. William sighs at the implication, joins Cithaeron with this continued chase. Not for long, a cave in the side of a massive hill features in the distance; their target disappears inside. Running faster to catch up, they soon enter the cave, but it's completely dark. William pulls out his phone to use its flashlight app to light their way, but Cithaeron can see better in the dark than William anyways. "I'll light the way," Cithaeron says before illuminating the cavernous pathway. (Radiant flame: The entirety of his body casts a beautiful white light. Flames shoot from his mouth that causes embers to stick to the walls in a gentle fashion every few feet.)

William puts his phone away. "Impressive." William says in amazement. A careful tread through the tunnel is rational. Who knows what tricks are next? "Do many obtain rides with you?" William asks.

"Before I became this, Zeus has," Cithaeron says.

"What the hell did they do?" William questions curiously.

"Joy riding, breaking sound barriers," Cithaeron says in a low voice. William stares at him with a berated, baffled look. William then averts his reaction. "You remember that freakish event two years, five days, three hours, fourteen minutes, and twenty-three seconds back?"

William mutes himself briefly. An awkward silence transpires. "April 5, the 6.0 earth quake, category 5 tornado, and widespread lightning storm: a historical marker in humanity's natural disasters."

William knows exactly what he's speaking of. "Everybody thought it was the apocalypse. My parents lost their house . . . and so did many others. Some died."

Cithaeron's ears lower and he shifts both eyes to the right in a discomfited manner. "Sorry to hear," Cithaeron says sympathetically. William shakes his head left and right from the ridiculous revelation. A light begins to shine at the end.

"You think it's still here, or did it move on?" William asks softly.

"Definitely wouldn't have stayed here: too small and too tight of an area to maneuver in. Stalactites and stalagmites cover copiously inside of the mountain tunnels," Cithaeron replies.

Cautious evermore . . . The end is nearing. Sudden illumination brightens. Walking through, they end up in a coliseum. Stunned from an immaculate view, their moment of arrival in a completely different atmosphere is stunning. Desolate ruins: echoed mirth's, cries of pain. Ruins lay silent, wind blows through archways: abandoned concept, harbored structure of death. Cithaeron walks forward a couple feet from William.

"This must have been a portal to this location, but where did it go?" Cithaeron says.

"Seem familiar?" William says as a presentiment about Cithaeron's unending prowess and knowledge. "You've been quite confident, unflinching the entire time we've been here. You weren't a project entirely created from our friend in the past. Were you, your name, those miraculous moments, your divine abilities?"

(William's keen sense is noticed.) Cithaeron's back still faces William . . . "Very astute of you, but you see, this war is bigger than anyone could possibly think. It hasn't reached mid-way nor has it ended, nor will it ever come to an end . . . I wouldn't even call it a war. I'd call it penance for glory. The records were never meant to be updated, only forgotten. You think they're the only ones who have witnessed the end coming? Though I can assure you that what you've accomplished days back was only the start . . . There is a beginning. The Gods collide like a big bang. Your feats sustain only the harmoniousness between them. You control your very own movements every second. Your worth is greater than you think. I'm not trying to make you out to be greater than anyone else—just human, but with a big heart. There's more than you believe. Trust me," Cithaeron finally explains the reasoning behind his purpose. "We are among Mt. Cithaeron; the arena is on the epicenter of this rocky mass. I am the God of this mountain. The resurrection of the Nemean lion, which roamed on my elevated ranges, became my newfound curse since this figure you fought came into light. It took five years for them to capture me and two seconds for me to fight the reanimated beast: skinless and bloody, a ravenous appetite for my death. I ate the beast to halt its terror from spreading across my lands and out ever again. The flesh was most unappetizing, the organs were despoiled, and its bones I crushed and scattered among a furious fire."

William is having a hard time swallowing such an ordeal just said now.

(Thinking of weather to deny such proposed knowledge or accept it.)

"I would have never presumed or spouted, nor shown arrogance to anyone. It is a heavy notion—I don't know if I'm exactly what a higher power would need. How does an individual convey yet know how to handle such a grand capacity this poses? Significant in form, but to realize your actual purpose beyond freewill is frightening. I've let many die from my choices. I've killed many, but I live to suffer the thought of my . . . If what you say is true, then I will accept this position indubitably and unquestioningly." (Ascent +2)

Cithaeron understands William's reluctance with needing and understanding, but he's also feeling empathetic. Inevitability is a part of life which everyone deals with, even if it goes against one's integrity: mentally or physically, or both.

Memories start to flash through William's mind: reminiscences of his ancestor dwell in this arena; brutal battles never end and they certainly aren't civil; flashes of blood, dismembered limbs, deathly screams, and the crowd roaring for more. The Archon sits in approval of such barbaric acts of violence and chaotic entertainment. As the Archon claps, William awakens from his trance on one knee. As he looks upward, spectral figures in the stands cheer, but no noise is produced. All around, ghostly figures of people pause and watch from above. Back down, he detects the enemy standing on the other side of the arena.

"I was going to ask something about my ancestor. I guess I'll wait," William says.

Cithaeron is ready to aggress at any moment. The Archon emerges; the whole crowd cheers loudly. Giving an approval to kill, Shrouded Doppelganger holds its left hand out and flicks each appendage outward one at a time. A pillar rises from below in random areas near them as each appendage is flicked upward, like a puppeteer; then a pedestal rose to reside at the epicenter after the fist was clenched. On the middle pedestal lies the one gauntlet his ancestor wielded; Cithaeron recognizes it immediately.

Quickly releasing the clench, all pillars separate to each corner, but they spawn white beams that travel to the gauntlet to protect it until a victor arises; the main pedestal shoots upwards out of harm's reach too. William and Cithaeron take note of the situation. Cithaeron institutes the duel by charging forward. Vanishing before being struck, Shrouded Doppelganger materializes behind William; he taps William on the shoulder, and William turns. Shrouded Doppelganger lifts William up with a furious gale that surrounds his whole body. Unable to move, he continues to crush him, and his breath is fading from suffocation. Approaching behind is Cithaeron; his roars create sound waves that push them both into a near wall. One of the pillars crumbles from the opposition's clash; the pedestal descends a little.

The doppelganger stands fully upright and produces bulwarks of wind and launches them at Cithaeron. Cithaeron is pushed back with ease, but unbeknownst to the doppelganger, William joins in.

(William gains Fury Haste [passive ability, triggered from high damage.]: a short burst of fury only to last ten seconds, but at the benefit of gaining higher physicality, damage reduction, and attack speed at a 50 percent increase.) Transitioning, it sweep-kicks its legs and grabs it by the neck midair, then in a one-handed chokehold. It fights back, but its punches aren't fazing William. He twists its body 180 degrees and slams it into the ground face-first. Cithaeron jumps up, and William rolls out of the way. Landing right on top of the doppelganger, Cithaeron widens his maw and shoves the doppelganger's head in his mouth then throws it at another pillar, shattering from the collision; only four pillars remain. The main pedestal descends again.

Swiftly, Cithaeron transforms his body in a strange way—grabs William and combines each other. A synthesis was performed; now the two can combine their prowess to defeat this annoyance once and for all. The collaboration represents a fierce warrior: part machine, part lion, part human, and part deity. William wears the skin of the Nemean. Robotic parts have minimal exposure, and his head represents pride and strength. "I can only do this once. We're going to use it here. The Nemean lion that was defeated by the demigod Hercules, son of Zeus, of such, the beast I eradicated afterward, became my new curse. An den boro, gia na nikiso ton antipalo mou, afiste ton christi na syndyastei mazi mou, kai esti kai oi dyo tha prepei na paroun ton elencho."

(Translation: If I cannot, to defeat my opponent, let my user combine with me, and so both will have to take control.)

"What was that last part?" William asks.

Cithaeron doesn't answer and becomes dejected. The doppelganger throws air blades at William from afar. William dashes forward, dodging the attacks—flipping over, spinning around, and ducking under for avoidance. Closer, the doppelganger springs up to avoid confrontation. Floating above, William distinguishes its movements. Though, he thinks of a personal plan. William jolts to his right, dodging more incoming threats in the process, grabs a pillar using all his strength to pull it out of the ground, and then moves to his left to acquire another. Digging five claws deeply into the metal of each pillar, William leaps upward to strike boldly. William dodges all wind-based hostilities while wielding the two pillars. Quicker than it could think, an intense smash befell the doppelganger. Falling like a meteor to earth, William makes another assault. Coming in fast, slams the polls on top, sending the opposed deep underground in a never-ending pit. The Archon smiles over the outcome to be.

Chapter 16

Trials

(Finish Line) Pt.3/Finale

Wind-Walker's Fall / Ancestral Blood

Light gradually appears during descent. Behold the view of Tartarus, a forlorn site in all accordance. William points his body downward to gain additional speed, jets toward the doppelganger (who's currently unconscious). With both pillars in firm grasp, William angrily plows harshly into the doppelganger, causing it to promptly crash down further. Before William and the doppelganger hits the ground, he launches each pillar one at a time, shattering upon impact on top of the enemy, who then plows into a lower foundation. William finally lands, and debris and dust rises and spreads.

(Cithaeron takes notice of William's offensive integrity.) "Keep that anger intact. You're performing elegantly," Cithaeron says to himself deep inside his consciousness.

Dust settles and clears. Looking at his surroundings—nothing seems familiar. Up above in the arena, lightning bolts strikes all remaining pillars above, destroying them. The main pedestal drops below, arriving where Cithaeron, William, and Shrouded Doppelganger are presently located. William tries to understand the current whereabouts but is still ignorant of the current environment. Unfortunately, that pedestal moves and stably secures on the precipice of a tall, skinny rock formation; a bridge leads to it. Cithaeron locks on to the true prize with his technologically advanced optics and tells William of its location. William attempts to retrieve his ancestor's gauntlet, but the doppelganger arises and swiftly travels in front of William and stands still. Cithaeron's eyes glow red with fury. It points to a spot before the bridge. William is skeptical of this gesture, but their foe insists. "Accept," Cithaeron says.

Shrouded Doppelganger approaches the bridge. Stone built gray structure, unknown creator. Waiting for William . . . (Its length extends fifty miles, width is fifteen feet. The support beams extend downward through the perpetual darkness beneath, old and ready to crumble). William stands parallel to his opposition. Shrouded Doppelganger raises its right hand and begins a countdown. Tension rises with each second (2, 1. they race to the finish). Faster and faster, they ran with unattainable speeds than any mere human could. The wind in their faces from greater momentum, their fastness, their speed at this moment, creates winds of up to a category 3 tornado.

Half way through now: lesser integral pieces begin to break away behind them. The ground starts trembling, making the bridge quiver as well. Two-thirds past, their prize is so close. A giant hand comes from underneath, breaking the bridge into pieces where that section was hit. Both fly upward. Coming near a mountain side, William clings on the side. Shrouded Doppelganger initiates down to where the gauntlet is. William jumps for the same area. Before landing, a Titan rises upward, and as William descends, the doppelganger tries to open the case protecting the item of interest. Cronus extends his reach and grabs the doppelganger, crushing it into dust. William is closer to the pedestal, but Cronus strikes William. Smacked brutally downward, he loses control of his fall and harshly hits the ground near the pedestal. William tries his hardest to get back on his feet.

His feet stumble as he runs with such determination. Drops on one knee, averts attention upward, reaches and retrieves. Cithaeron separates himself from William, and they both topple over on their backs; their symbiotic combination has been exhausted. William gazes in awe and silence, equipped and unaware of a certain power. Cithaeron smiles while breathing heavily and says, "Well done! So glad it's in your hands. I have an idea what you'll do now. You were impressive. I salute your heroism. Akoma kai os symvolo tis yperifaneias kai tis dynamis, richno mia afthonia ntropis ston eafto mou kai syneiditopoio poios einai kalyteros i poios echei kyriarchisei pano mou."

(Translation: "Even as the symbol of pride and strength, I cast an abundance of shame on myself and realize who is better, or who has prevailed over me.")

"I'm better than no one. In fact, no one in the entire universe is above another. You can only rise above your own self when the belief in yourself is existent. The only way to be at our best would be if we form a unity, consistently bringing civility among each other; foremost, understand one another. That's exactly what we achieved here. To contradict my words and to not: you could be preeminent of another, but that's usually through skill you've obtained, but then again, anyone can do want they what if one puts their mind to it. Don't be so hard on yourself. We're a team." William replies (Ascent dialogue +3). Cithaeron agrees silently to honorably spoken words.

More Titans appear; surrounding them are Mnemosyne, Tethys, Theia, Phoebe, Rhea, Themis, Oceanus, Hyperion, Coeus, Crius, Lapetus, Selene, Eos, Lelantos, Leto, Asteria, Atlas, Prometheus, Epimetheus, Menoetius, Metis, Astraeus, Pallas, Perses. Cronus lays down his right hand.

"Katastrepste ton bastardo pou katastrefei to chaos," he says.

(Translation: "Destroy the bastard who wreaks havoc.")

William nods his head. "You understood that too?" asks Cithaeron.

"I believe I somewhat have," William replies. They walk on Cronus's hand, which transports them to who knows where. William and Cithaeron commerce within the duration; Cithaeron speaks first. "I didn't know you understood Greek language. Does that mean you comprehended what I said earlier?"

(Blunt dialogue +2) "It was mostly an assumption. The tone had a specific sound. To be honest: not totally—but I had to say something. There's no time to worry these days either. I just needed to reassure you. You're a symbol of pride and power—use it to your advantage. Strike fear into any who oppose you. Your eyes can pierce through souls. A great warning to any it'll pose. Truthfully, the Greek language seems to be understandable in small increments since our collaboration and from equipping this gauntlet, presumably," William replies under duress from the current condition.

(Cithaeron will remember that.) He respects the fact William is understanding and brave. It increases their friendship from his continued support. The colossal beings take long strides, traveling to their destination; each step comes with echoes spreading far throughout Tartarus. (Kind dialogue +1) "Sorry for the way I spoke. I'm just flustered from our venture and, above all, from our symbiotic moment." (Cithaeron took notice of that.) Transportation stops . . . Lowered, a couple steps lead to a circular floor.

All present Titans surround them like a barricade. William feels pain in his right arm. The gauntlet starts meshing into a singular body; whitened veins appear up the right arm, spreading to his neck, face, torso, and the rest of his body. He gets down on both knees, subtly moaning from increasing agony. Cithaeron takes note and says, "It's happening . . ." William's skin changes to a snow-white tone, and wings start to suddenly emerge from his back. A black wall appears at the opposite end. Cithaeron stands watch, and William is still crouched over on the ground from uninterrupted discomfort. A stalwart figure in colorless armor appears through that blackened wall. This doesn't bode well. Two axes extend from the warrior's arms—a tight grip to ensue battle, and hearing metal tighten around each handle produces an eerie sound. An adrenaline rush occurs in Cithaeron from knowledge of coming chaos.

Madness can be instantly noticed even through the darkened helmet as it flows through this diabolical presence. Upon a dark existence, a threshold created that would even pull the sanest person into an ocean of emptiness and hopelessness. The warrior impales, dually, the ground with both axes and sits on the floor, after. William's body finishes its transformation. He grows to be seven feet tall, dark orange/bronze and chrome scales completely cover the body. Equipped with vicious claws, but his right arm has no presence of the gauntlet either; it has meshed to match his new formation. A curious

aura surrounds him. Armor appears steadily on his body: covered in
gold and white head to toe.

"It's always worth it when you're allowed to fight your nemesis,
especially close to two thousand years later. Demonstrate your ire!
Illustrate your despair!" the Abyssal Knight speaks.

Each ax is lifted, and the Abyssal Knight launches itself in the air.
Coming down to strike, William speedily casts himself to the side.
Cithaeron begins an attack, but a black aura surrounds all areas that
halt him from proceeding. A demonic voice from somewhere says,
"This is not your fight. We must see his potency."

Cithaeron backs down, watching with extreme focus. "If you must . . ."
Cithaeron says with disapproval.

The Abyssal Warrior goes on the offense again. William deflects
the attacks—strike after strike; he deflects and counters each one
so far. William's opponent now conjures up dark figures to forward
an attack. As a counter, William breathes fire on them, but some
run through unscathed and persist on attacking. The nearest ones
are grabbed and whipped upward; it jumps up, spins around, and
knocks them down with a massive tail swing. William's opponent
moves away from the incoming lackeys. Jumping at William . . . In
arms reach, William clasps each ax to halt the coming attacks, spins
the Knight around above ground, lifts upwards and slams the enemy
into the ground. William steps back, and the warrior returns to its
feet. He lifts his hands to conjure up spectral swords. The battling
continues . . . William's gauntlets expend long blades from them; he
uses them to defend himself. They move with a smooth flow, and
the show is like a rendition of a well-choreographed dance, but with
fighting in addition. The Abyssal Warrior lands a couple of good
blows to William's side, making him stumble backward.

The Abyssal Warrior withdraws both spectral swords, goes to retrieve
both axes, now. Dragging them along the ground . . . He lifts them
and creates black waves with punishing force from each swing
against William, making him slide back when struck. Nearly off the

edge, the right heel of his foot hangs off the side as debris break off, falling endlessly. William lowers his head then bolts forward. Before a reaction, William collides with intensity and knocks his opponent off the arena.

A couple of seconds later, the Abyssal Warrior soars into the air high above. "I want to witness the fear in your eyes before you die," He says before striking the side of the mountain. Huge chunks cascade and cause a landslide or plummet through air. William directs upward—in succession, dodges multiple incoming stones. Boulders drop without any care with tremendous weight: Swoosh! Swoosh! Swoosh! Swoosh! William comes closer, but the warrior jumps off the side he was clanged to, plunging to another foundation below their initial one.

William tackles one of the boulders, trying to stop it from falling by flapping his wings to stay airborne. More are coming! Quickly moving, seeing where his opponent is heading, he maneuvers upward, inhales deeply, tosses the boulder upward, and as soon as it is angled just right after falling downward, William blasts the boulder with raging fire, and it launches with ferocity. Landing on the plateau, the Abyssal Warrior turns to see that same boulder which was forcefully pushed coming his way and prepares by conjuring up an attack to decimate it. Bam!!! Multiple pieces break away as his axes slash through it with ease, but William appears right after he breaks the boulder, ramming into him. Both slide along the ground. William starts to punch at a consistent rate. Pow! Bam! Pow! Bam! Each hit fazes the warrior. An end comes to the multiple strikes and forces William away with a powerful shove. By using his wings to forcefully push him from going back any farther; also, several powerful wing flutters create strong gusts. William's foe progresses while compromised through the wind tunnel, using his axes to dig in the ground to give him leeway for movement, but sooner manages to close in for the offensive.

A telekinetic force is used to launch one ax at William, his wings stop flapping—he grabs the incoming ax and directs it back, and it hits the Abyssal Warrior's head and makes the figure topple over flat on its back. Cithaeron watches high above in suspense while keeping ceaseless faith in William. The helmet splits in half . . . Inside it reveals—Dante. William's brother! Dante slowly forces himself up; he appears to be not injured. William becomes increasingly saddened by this revelation and plods toward him. Dante casts his one ax, hitting William in the abdomen making him bend over from the impact. The blow cracks his fortification. Dante throws the other one, and it bashes William's face directly, causing him to spin 180 degrees to the right. William falls to his knees and hands; Dante approaches William. William turns and looks through a cracked helmet and sees that Dante's face is decayed. "How does it feel to be dragged into a position that's not wanted? Cast down to be eternally enslaved next to giants long depraved?"

(William thinks of how to act: be compassionate or shout out displeasure from this revelation.)

"I . . . I did. Your affiliation was without warning—an allied stance with such decadence. I knew vengeance wasn't going to bring resolve or bring you back. My revenge was learned through the roughest manners, but its vengeance that retaliates on you." William's helmet breaks away and rattles to the ground.

Dante partially accepts his words but insists on adding to William's distress. "I've waited long years in the dark following these hopeless figures who blindly walk endlessly. For all eternity, I'll never even see my family or friends again!"

William is still on his hands and knees. (Empathetic dialogue/Ascent +10): "I mourned your death with much sorrow; more came with it every day. I let that man who killed you live because I knew he wasn't significantly worth stealing a life. All I could do was weep . . . every day . . . Every second was torture that you're not with me, Mom, Dad, and Sarah. We all felt a piece was missing; our family is incomplete. I'm sorry . . . I'm sorry that I couldn't save you from that tragedy, sending it into obscurity. Blame was cast on me by me every day for reasons known that could have helped you stray from a brazen life style. I'd prefer remembering the days we played and laughed than revel in your death. Just as much in the living world, we suffered just as much with your departure."

William breaks down in tears. Dante stands tall, witnessing total shame. "I do, though. It hurts every second, William. We fight over past times—well, I did most of the provoking." Dante says as he walks past William. Dante turns to face William but continues to move backward at the edge . . . his feet rest on the boundary where an endless pit extends beyond. Dante continues . . . "I know they're dead, but if you truly want to be at peace, let me finally rest so I can be with them. Let me know what true peace feels like, and I'll be on familiar terms with you acknowledging my forgiveness because I forgave you already." Dante tilts backwards . . .

(William thinks quickly whether to save Dante or let him fall into that deep, dark abyss.)

(Special +2) William's eyes open wide; he rushes to Dante before he fluxes into nothingness. William seizes Dante's left ankle. "We can leave this desolate place. Come back with me. We can start over. Better yet, a family to reunite and become whole again!"

Dante's eyes unveil vexation and undeniable sorrow, but he had chosen not to exist and let William live knowing forgiveness has been given. A bond hangs between a hold, albeit if William abides by his brother's wish, tranquility will be achieved. If he pulls him up, they can be reunited.

(Special +5/Ascent +5) William decides to pull him up instead and Cithaeron's in relief from William's action.

"They're alive?" Dante asks. A chain shoots from the void, pulling Dante down into the abyss. William's eyes open wide from the incident. To follow is a must—diving in as well, giving chase to save his brother. Other chains fly in William's direction; some are dodged, but some also cut through his flesh and the incisions make him scream. Each hit from the chained blades breaks away chunks of armor. More come en route for William and slice and impale him as well. Roaring loudly, he keeps his eyes focused on Dante. Unfortunately, he descends quicker; the sight of him lessens. Moments anon, he vanishes into prominent darkness. Unexpectedly, an ethereal plain comes into sight as a dark-green aura. Arcane ruins upon the landscape strewn about, and where ancient skeletons have lain still for an eternity. A couple of chains grab the split helmet Dante wore from above and yank them below soon after.

Abruptly stopping a couple of feet above, a voice can be heard all in the region of them. William tries discerning where it came from. There's no apparent evidence of who's talking. The chains and blades release their hold. William and Dante drop to the ground. William's wounds have vanished. He searches for any indication, null of any explanation for the remarkable healing. Dante's armor slowly rises off his body and transfers to a corner of the ruined palace. In the shadows, it formats like an armor covering a body. The armor begins to walk forward . . . White eyes stare, a formless face slightly shows its teeth. The helmet covers the figure's head one piece at a time, slowly. The crack welds miraculously. "Too bad you're not him . . . Eudagio. We'd have a great rematch. But your brother, lying naked and weak, will die just like the fool he is. You had to resurrect the potency once arcane hands held before me and defeated me with. Residing in eternal agony is not the life I wanted! My wife flogged! My daughter raped! My will ignored. A terrible price for vengeance . . ."

As a side note: Earlier, during his transformation, William gained the ability to fully understand and speak Greek. "Tha se kleiso apo tin orgi mou. Analamvanete na gnorizete ton pono kathos o thymos sas synkrouetai me tous fovous sas pou sas trone apo mesa? Den eiste pia ton zontanon, aplos i ensarkosi enos kakou paradeigmatos: ena tromero stin pragmatikotita." William replies.

(Translation: "I'll make you shudder from my wrath. Do you undertake to know the pain as your anger collides with your fears eating you from inside? You're not of the living anymore, just the embodiment of a bad example: a terrible one, in fact.")

The battle commences . . . William extends his blades from each gauntlet. As the starting offensive: blasts a vast blaze that covers his whole perimeter; the flames stay strong. William waits patiently for retaliation. A giant black skull jolts forward at William, breaking away to reveal the Abyssal Knight flying toward him. He embraces William and they crash into a wall near a different side.

Bam! Bam! Bam! Bam! Bam!

William is punched with such strength, plowing him into the same wall, farther through. One last punch makes William break through enough and cause a rockslide to barrage down on him. Abyssal Knight takes a few steps back with pride thinking victory has arrived. That's not the case . . . Now the fiend approaches Dante. He grips Dante's throat firmly and lifts him off the ground. "You'll be easier to deal with," the Abyssal Knight says with great malice. A'od slowly breaks his wings free from the rubble as quietly as possible. A'od observes the Abyssal Knight's motive. Slowly, he inhales deeply and then rapidly unleashes a tremendous fire burst, which also simultaneously launches rocks (which are currently piled on himself) to propel against his new opponent.

Dante is thrown to the right and the Abyssal Knight is bombarded with fire-covered stones. Bam! Pow! Smash! Consistently hit in succession, William sits up, uses his back legs, and lunges forward, barrel rolling as the wind whips from his speedy attack; he makes contact with a wicked head butt, causing the Abyssal Knight to roll along the floor. William collects a pillar, which supported the structure long ago, lying on the ground and launches it with tremendous strength hitting the warrior which moves him back even beyond. Recovering from a large-scale attack, they begin physical combat. Dodging, ducking, blocking, deflecting, reversals, and contacted hits at a rapid rate occur. William initiates a tail swing, but instead was grabbed, swung around and thrown.

William recovers . . . he stomps the ground and causes an earthquake. Up above, anybody can feel the quaking of the ground. The Titans above could care less about their battle anyways. The knight flips in the air and lands on top of a still-standing pillar. William takes flight at his enemy. He clutches the knight and they both plummet to the ground subsequent to the initial action. Smash! Another idea comes to mind. Flying upward, William holds on tightly. Ascending continuously . . . returning to the upper regions, every Titan sees them arise from lower a region, and William projects the knight at one of them. Prometheus sees him near—grabs the knight, crushing him in an instant. But something else happens . . . A black anomaly climbs up the inside of the titan's right arm and ends up blasting out of the left eye of Prometheus, making blood spray widely. Other Titans take notice; they come to aid. The warrior jumps to the others, bashing them by jumping off each one separately. Attempts to swat him down take action, but each effort fails. William returns to Cithaeron.

Jumping off the last Titan, the Black Knight navigates to where William went. The barrier drops... Before reaching the foundation, Cithaeron roars; widespread bolts shoot out; and lightning crashes from the collisions. Lightning surrounds the knight, holding him in place. Lightning crashes down, relentlessly attacking. Zap! Zap! Kerzap! Zap! Electric shackles form around his ankles and wrists, spreading his posture wide.

"Oi theoi sas voithoun?" the Abyssal Knight says.

(Translation: "The Gods aid you?")

The Titans walk to the Abyssal Knight and stand behind him. He turns to see them. "An afti einai i moira mou, tha protimousa na parameino sti lithi."

(Translation: "If this is to be my fate, I'd rather have remained in oblivion.")

Each titan sets one hand on another's—hovering above him. He looks up at William and Cithaeron, eyes revealing a long-sought release from an involuntary prison. The Titan's push downward together, crushing him as the rocky structure crumbles under their pressure. Loud sounds saturate throughout Tartarus. Dust floats over the entire area; rubble will now lie still among everlasting darkness. After it clears, they slowly raise their hands and walk off into the distance . . . still lost and depraved as ever. Cithaeron looks down with absolute satisfaction. William returns back down to that ethereal palace where Dante is. Light shoots upward past William as he descends. A beautiful, calming site makes him feel serene in comparison. Spirits fly past with the anticipation of finally achieving a peaceful rest. William reaches the bottom and searches for Dante. Frantic he has come to be. The current form William is in changes back to normal. "Ah!" William shouts, as his body is restored to normal. He grunts from ample aches resulting from the reverse transformation. On the ground, William then spots Dante and utilizes all his strength to get up and rush to his side.

Dropping to a kneeling position, William places Dante in his arms. "William, don't fret. That panoply unleashes your feelings in an intense style. On the positive side, I can rest now, and the conflicts between us or anyone are over."

"No. I made a promise to you. Don't leave us again, please," William quickly responds.

Dante finds comfort with the thought. "You don't need to promise me anything—you've always been an excellent figure. I never meant to be mad at you. I was blind. It's obvious I made a difficult plight for myself, naïve to the end. Don't blame yourself anymore. Don't cry for me. Let the good memories of our past be your happiness and as a motivation to move forward. I always will love you, Mom, Dad, and Sarah. Death will allow my sought comfort. Look at them. It's so beautiful." As Dante refers to the unshackled spirits rising to the heavens above, the final words are expelled from his mouth. William can only cry. Rising to a standing position with his brother in both arms, light starts to emit from Dante's body, and he dissolves progressively. William holds on tightly until the body fully disappears. Solitary; the quietness is deafening. Clenching both fists . . . Randomly, an unknowingly bright figure appears in front of William. The spirit reaches out and raises William's lowered head.

His eyes open to see a spectral figure. William's hands are lifted; the soft touch relaxes his emotions. The spectral figure retrieves the gauntlet slowly. In conclusion, it transports William back to a familiar moment in time.

Interlude

"Beginnings / A Trial Passed"

After William's teleportation, the spectral figure revels at the site of the gauntlet for a couple seconds before disappearing. A divine palace is its destination; it reappears, bowing down on both knees and holding the gauntlet. Several characters walk up to this entity, but it only looks up enough to see their lower stature. The spirit raises the gauntlet up, implying it to be relinquished; and one of the beings takes possession of it. "I yposchesi tirithike. Poso entyposiako. Enas thnitos me aperioristi dynami kai pathos opos kanenas allos. Dynami aftou tou megethous den borei na erthei se epafi me anidea myala i kleista matia akoma. Se eftheto chrono, tha doume pragmatikes dynatotites."

(Translation: "The promise was kept. How impressive. A mortal with limitless fortitude and a fervor like no other. Power of this magnitude cannot contact ignorant minds or closed eyes just yet. In due time, we'll see true potential.")

Epilogue

Adding an Element

09/13/2028, 4:56 p.m.

William awakes from a restful state, sits up and observes his setting. Sweat covers his face, and he decides to get out of bed and walk to the window. He opens the window to cool down; the fresh air is inviting.

Emily enters his room but doesn't realize his presence behind the curtain across the room. A noise is heard behind the drape. She walks toward it, and around the curtain, he's standing in front of a window that's a little distant from her. Every bandage was also on the floor. She walks slowly . . . Now behind him, she goes to touch him on the shoulder. He turns to see her, and she says, "Did you see a woman enter your room just now?"

William replies, "No. I'm so glad to see you." He hugs her tightly.

Emily finds comfort in his action, and she holds him snugly as well.

She steps back and looks at his shoulder, noticing his chest and left arm: absent scars, or any other marks that were present; and the cloth sling for his injured arm is also absent. "What happened to your wounds? Even with surgery, you'd have scars still." Emily says in a surprised tone.

"A miracle, I guess," William answers.

Baffled by his response, Emily still isn't convinced enough to believe him, much to her encounter as well as David's. "I shouldn't be surprised, especially what we experienced," Emily says.

"Sorry. I wanted to see you beforehand. Sorry won't cut it," William says as he lifts his right hand, sighs, and softly feels her facial prosthetic. Emily's eye shifts to his hand: she places her left hand on top, closes both eyes, and controls his hand adjacent from her injuries, to the other side, moving it in a caressing fashion. "It's really sexy, actually. Your voice, I mean," William says.

Emily opens her eyes then looks at him with a smile. "Don't worry about me. I'm OK now. Soreness radiates seldom, eating has come easier, but the synthetics will acclimate better in time. I'll come to terms soon." William feels utter guilt for all his actions, in view of the fact he allowed such ire bringing suffering to others. William lowers his hand back down to his side.

He shifts his gaze to the window and views the landscapes' vast distance. "I know you're mad at me. That's an understatement. An apology is implausible. Death isn't foreign, but it has shown me how fragile life is. That moment where we stood in proximity of each other, the door separating us—that wasn't me. Not wholly. Thanks in part to those chemicals which were pumped in me with unceasing intent and my possessor making me continue my deathly ploy. I feel ashamed."

Emily interrupts his apology by saying, "More than that. There are many explanations why your actions were unethical in numerous ways. Vacancy will not come to be in my heart, William. I was thinking of you more than about myself ever since you left."

William acknowledges what she said. "I can be pretty elusive. Asides from joking, you have me there. What really bothers me is how this all started. Yes, it's ironic of me saying this, but what I mean is, it's amazing that it only takes one move to shift the universe on a different path, a whole new experience. Misconstruing my ideals and turning them against everyone, letting my emotions get the best of me, misleading my soul to despair. I'm not going to lie: the sensation was strangely rejuvenating. Odd as that is, but . . . Yeah, it's odd. One man's paradise is another man's living hell. I presume we just witnessed something of the marvelous, or was it a mistake? I set in motion a destructive stratagem. It won't be a forgive-and-forget scenario that'll sit so easily with many . . . or all. Who knows? But rendering judgment against me is appropriate now."

Emily finds enough room to respect him for expressing his personal thoughts. "It should have never happened. We thought we lost you... Your empirical evidence is known. I can say likewise for us too, in other aspects. Anyways, you won't believe—well, you will now."

William fills in the blanks by saying, "There's quite a committee waiting for us three out in the waiting room."

"Yes, how'd you know?" Emily says with suspicion of his knowledge. "Just wondering: are you going to look past what I said a moment ago?"

William knows his coming punishment well enough and tries to enjoy the little things before hells' hammer falls. "It's beautiful, isn't it?" Emily wonders what he's talking about. "It's amazing actually. You mess up one note and it all fails. We didn't," William says.

Overfilled happiness bestows him for said claim by Emily. "You better put your bandages and sling back on, because they're going to wonder how you have no wounds or stitches even after surgery if you don't. On another note: I still don't understand you. You're weird. I'm not going to be dishonest," she says. William laughs subtly, continues to put his bandages on, and she also helps him reapply them all. Afterward, Emily leaves the room first.

"I'm allowed to go? I was told I'd be here for more than a couple weeks . . . what I remember."

"It's been ten, actually... *moans in pain* I was here for 8, mostly healing and therapy. David came by to see how we were doing. He said you were sleeping every time he came," Emily informs him.

A spark of happiness overcomes William. "David's OK?!" William asks.

Emily nods positively. "He sustained minimal compared to us. I was with him out in the lobby."

Overwhelmed with joy, William then turns to look out the window from a peculiar sense and familiarity. Cithaeron and Eve sit outside on a bench; Cithaeron waves. William's mouth is ajar with his revelation. He then ponders on a recent event.

"Ready?" Emily asks.

"Yeah . . . ten weeks you said?" William asks with uneasiness.

"You don't remember anything with your doctors, psychiatrist or physical therapist?" Emily asks. "That's improbable"
"Sure I do. I'm just . . . flustered. I also remember David coming to see me." William states in return.

"Were leaving, right? Let's get this done," Emily says.

William exits the room to foregather in the waiting room. Emily waits. "Ahem."

William stops, turns, and sees Emily holding up her hand. A smirk forms on his face. Moving to her, he grabs her hand and walks on. "Right, I love you too," William says. (Romance increases to a new level.) Emily looks at him and smiles wholeheartedly. Upon her presence, William's eyes are filled with satisfaction and fullness.

"Mortal Words / Cause Breeds Certainty"

"Well, what does a beautiful woman like you going to do now?" Cithaeron asks.

Eve shortly ponders on the thought . . . "Maybe live together with humanity for a time. Maybe I could just go back to my wonderful façade of a paradise. All that was possible is done for now, I guess."

Cithaeron smiles at her thoughts. "You know, that's not a bad idea. At times, you must break repetition and live a little, right?"

Eve laughs with agreement. "That's true. But let's be optimistic it stays repetitively peaceful for now. This world has witnessed—had been dealt too much suffering. It'll be nice to see tranquility amid all."

Cithaeron stands to his feet. "I agree. Since you want to mingle in mortal reality, why don't you and I . . . as it is said, go out sometime?"

Eve looks at him with astonishment and stands up too. "Aren't you of the opposite species? How's that even going to work?"

Eve's questioning insults Cithaeron's. "I can maintain this form! Plus, much more comes with it. This is only a minor setback," Cithaeron says, and then winks at her after and concurrently nudging her in the shoulder.

Eve sighs. "You're going to have to do better than that. It wouldn't work out as well as you think." Cithaeron looks down in defeat and chuckles. A foreboding, looming and guilty thought comes to Eve. Cithaeron takes notice of her disposition and distinguishes what's flowing through her head. "It's still unknown," he declares.

"Guilt sure does take a toll. I lied so he could go on knowing what was done was justified. I couldn't confuse him with knowledge of this posing as a war between the heavens and everlasting hell that roams these lands. He had to be told something. To elaborate: not only God, but all God's. Our enemy will come in droves: relentless, savage, no remorse," Eve states.

Finishing midway through her speech, Eve stops and extends her hands out. Light emits around her body, head to toe. Light slowly fades to reveal a tall woman dressed Goddess-like.

"I see . . . what is it really?" Cithaeron says astonishingly while questioning quickly.

"Trials, appeasement, proof. An agreement to save each and every one was made. Alas, it completely relies on one man. He will hate us most likely, he-he. We're relying on him alone. A perpetual darkness hovers over humanity. One light relentlessly pierces the entirety, though. You were successful, right? That was step one. Next is Odin's trial, but first: William must go through his own trial next. Appeasement occurs afterwards, and then proof must be made for the others as the premise," Vor heavily states.

"That's a hefty agenda to accomplish. Seems never-ending . . . Was keeping the important information from him needed?" Cithaeron obviously states, to then ask her with concernment.

"It wasn't arrantly a charade. It was just an explanation about what did exist presently, not the future, or about me. When you give a man enough hope, faith is restored. But it was needed to end the suffering many were dealt. Thus, it was accomplished," Vor says in her defense.

"You know there will be a reoccurrence. Whatever it is never dies..." Cithaeron claims as retaliation for her assertions.

"Trade was never commenced," Vor says.

Cithaeron is perplexed, Vor elaborates.

"What I really meant to say to him was that a trade between God and Lucifer was allowed. I was that which was traded—to come abroad a landscape emulating Eden, a lie to give expectation for a prolonged battle to finish all confliction. Let's backtrack. The only reason for being captured was due to 'mischievous ploys' in Valhalla. My captor said I was fitting. Ignorant as I was, I misunderstood my quest beforehand, which was given to me at an early time to carry out. Their judgment, after my quest's completion, during the exchange caused me to be banished due to false treasonous claims. That's why I'm here now. Thankfully, breaking this imprisonment, and grateful for such a freedom from it. Returning will not be pleasant. The plan was already known about the Antichrist creating a scheme to progress complete domination. It was obvious . . . God enticed the happening by being 'ignorant'. Abbadon's powers were stripped—he fooled Lucifer and the Antichrist; and in return, nothing was gained after the fifth trumpet blew. The sound was emulated. Becoming nearly mortal—Abbadon had some contingencies in addition. It wasn't betrayal, only intelligence by design. By then, I bet it was a revelation to the Antichrist about Abbadon. Maybe . . . but simultaneously, he was given Eve, even though her and Adam are long gone. Making this plan greater, days before Ragnarok's eventful moment and Odin's death, Odin conjured the idea during my banishment, and God added a piece to it which was my façade as impersonating Eve. Both went along with it: thus created the deal, my capture, and the absolution of the abominable stronghold was welcoming. Events ripple through the realms of the Gods; each one has equal knowledge of the happenings every time. The plan was known, so why not sabotage and make it a double loss for the enemy. A lot of pride sure was damaged," She explains in detail.

"You're sneaky motherfuckers . . . Brilliant! I bow to its elegance. Anyways, you think it's palpable?" Cithaeron says.

"Yes. I believe in due time, in some way, my lie will be unearthed by our friend. I'm not sure if the Antichrist had, or not," Vor says.

To the curiosity of Cithaeron, he asks, "Why were you really banished? Be honest."

Vor removes a curious item from her a satchel. "I stole this," she says.

Fenrir's soul resides in a clear two-by-two glass cube; unbound rage swirls inside. Cithaeron reacts astonishingly.

"I and three others were 'accused of stealing' it, but my banishment came first. "No evidence" was found on my part, although to see someone exiled was to demonstrate a lesson to whoever became treasonous. I was used in the ploy they created—that was my 'consequence' instead. The others, however, I have no indication. You'd think something with this grand potential, and be put to death or banished to the void realm. That was my mission and something I'm not fond of. Sadly, I couldn't stop Odin's death. He told me it'd be easier if liabilities were lessened. Then again, recap on what I told you," She confesses.

"The soul was wanted. You were exchanged in its place. The evil that roams this planet wanted to bring back an entity that was responsible for Odin's death, something that wielded great power that could help dominate the world in succession," Cithaeron says.

Vor nods her head in agreement. "William's involvement wasn't forced. It was unexpected and hapless for him. The idea of a 'mortal savior' wasn't intended completely, but the divine plan's vicissitude of accomplishment was met. Let's hope his part wasn't only a mistake. I guess we immortals are in need of assistance from mortals. Loki controlled Fenrir somehow, but he disappeared sometime after Ragnarok ended. As it were to be the eternal winter, a decision was made to end it and see who survived . . . as in what humans were left. Only seventy-two people in the entire world survived. A second chance was given. Not just for them but for us too. For Hel, she was bound in eternal shame and imprisonment," She says in conclusion.

They continue to converse among each other with notions that nearly conceive future events to happen, and will turn reality if William continues or not. If negligible, it'll only get worse. Not to forget: being successful in his own effort which transpired as a mortal.

At the post-battle site of Island 404 . . .

Among ruins drowned in water, an erected hand through the remains. Fingers twitch. Hand clenches. Whatever being that had strength pulls it underneath, disappearing below. Bubbles rise to the surface, and all aquatic life scatters from danger. An opening forms. All remnants of the abominable fortress cave in. A deep hole: the formation of the abyss.

0100100101101110 011101000110100001100101 01100100011000
0101110010011010110110010101110011011101000 0111000001100
0010111001001110100 0110111101100110 0110110101111001 0110
110101101001011011100110010001001001 011010000110000101
11011001100101 011000011011011000110000101110010011010010
111010001111001 0110001011011100110010000 0110000101101110
0110000101101110 0111010101101110011001000110010101110010
0111001101110100011000010110111001100100011010010110111 0
01100111 0110111101100110 01100011011011110110111001110011
011001010111000010111010101100101011011100110001101100101.

01000001 0110011001101100011000010110110101101001011011 10
01100111 011000100111001001100001011110100110100101100101
01110010 011100110110100101110100011100110111010101110000
0110111101101110 0110000101101100011011000110100001101001
0110011101101000 0110000101100010011011110111101110011001 01
0110100101101110 011101000110100001101000011010010111001 10110010
0011000010111001001101011011100101011011100110010101100100
0111001001100101011000010110110001101101 0110000101110011
01100001 0111001101111001011011010110101100010011011110110 1100
0111010001101111 0110110101111001 011101000110010101110011
01110100011010010110110101100101011011100110100.

9 781664 128569